CROSSING DARKNESS

ALEXANDER C. JUDEN

5points press

E-book ISBN: 979-8-9867905-3-4

Print ISBN: 979-8-9867905-4-1

Hardcover ISBN: 979-8-9867905-7-2

JudenBooks@gmail.com

CONTENTS

North East France, Belgium and Germany
after the signing of the Treaty of Versailles
June 1919
Königsberg
EAST
PRUSSIA
NETHERLANDS
GERMANY
POLAND
Hanover
Berlin
demilitarized
zone
Leipzig
Brussels
BELGIUM
Liège
British
Koblenz
American
Mainz
French
CZECHOSLOVAKIA
occupied
zone
Paris
FRANCE
Freiburg
am Breisgau
AUSTRIA
Basel
SWITZERLAND

1

A Job of the Heart

The ceiling above me looked familiar. It took me a moment to realize I was in the same hospital room in Neuilly-sur-Seine that had been my home since Sarah Willoughby had died in my arms. Sarah. Beautiful, intelligent, fanatical Sarah. The perfect girl for me. Gone now. I'd fallen in love in just a few days, or perhaps it was just mindless obsession. But one felt so close to the other that it made no difference to my heart. I knew the actual time we had spent together could be measured in just hours. It didn't matter. The heart wants what it wants, and mine was now broken, for Sarah was gone. I was broken. I had a bullet hole in my chest and one in my side. The pain these wounds caused paled when compared to the grief I felt at Sarah's death. I missed her, or perhaps I missed the idea of her. I didn't know which, but I felt paralyzed by her loss.

I could still smell her perfume.

I closed my eyes.

Wait.

I really could smell her perfume. I opened my eyes and turned my head slightly. Patricia Armistan was sitting in the chair next to the bed. Patricia was Sarah's best friend. She was also the lover of my buddy, William Mitchell, a former Navy corpsman, who was nowhere to be seen. I supposed the young women had shared the same perfume. I wondered what had brought her to my side without William. Patricia and I were not friends, but I didn't have the energy to dwell on the reasons for her presence at my bedside.

Patricia sat quietly reading. She was the picture of a demure, well-bred young woman. The chair was closer to the bed than when Mitchell had visited a few days before. She glowed with health and an otherworldly beauty and looked so much like Sarah that they could have been sisters instead of sisters-in-law. My heart ached at the thought. Mitchell was infatuated with her. As I watched her read quietly, gracefully turning each page with her delicate hands, I reminded myself that she was also a murderer.

People were not monolithic blocks carved of one stone. We were all many things. Patricia was beautiful, intelligent, loving, calculating, and merciless. Sarah had been the same, but she was gone now. As I said, they could have been sisters.

Just a few weeks before, Patricia had shot her husband in the face and fooled us all. We'd been convinced that Gavin Kingsbury had been accidentally killed in the cross fire during a gunfight with Bolsheviks in Garches on the outskirts of Paris. He hadn't. She'd seen the opportunity to free herself from him and from her father's yoke, and she had coldly blown a hole in his handsome head. Hell, I'd given her the gun. Oddly, I didn't despise her for it. I respected her. Part of me even liked her. She reminded me of a bobcat I'd once seen as I was riding in central Texas: small, graceful, adaptable, beautiful to watch, yet deadly.

I took a shuddering breath, and Patricia looked up and closed her book when she saw I was awake.

"John, it's good to see you recovering," she said with a small, sad smile. I believed her. I thought she liked me, though she believed she disgusted me. Only I knew that she had murdered Gavin. Mitchell did not, and I'd promised her I wouldn't tell him. I'd promised for him, not for her.

"I am so sorry about Sarah." Patricia's eyes filled with tears. Despite myself, I felt mine begin to water.

"She loved James and didn't have it in her to let his death go," I rasped.

Patricia poured me a glass of water from the pitcher on the tray next to my bed. When she handed me the glass, the tears were running down her cheeks. I took a sip and handed back the glass. She sat again and leaned toward me.

"She loved you, John," Patricia said with certainty.

"Yes, but it wasn't enough," I answered. My anguish was too close to the surface. Too raw. I looked down so that she wouldn't see the tears on my cheeks.

She reached out and squeezed my hand, and I squeezed back.

"I thought it would be," she told me. "It should have been."

"What now for you?" I asked to change the subject and regain control.

"Are you sure you want to know, John?"

"I think I already do, but I want to hear you say it, and then I want to tell you not to involve Mitchell," I answered.

"You are very clever. You make it easy to forget that with your simple, no-nonsense manner and battered, crooked looks."

"Don't involve Will."

She watched me for a moment. "Fine, you want to hear me say it. Good. In saying it to you, it will become true and inevitable. And it needs to be real. I'm going to kill my father. I have no choice. I am free now, but if I go back, he'll find some way to trap me again."

"Patricia," I said, shaking my head, "don't go back. Stay here with Will. Grow old here. You have the money."

"I blame my father for all this," she said, waving a hand at the ward and the windows that let the sunlight stream into the room.

"Oh, I do too," I said ominously. I could see the familiar look of calculation enter her eyes. Before she could speak, I said, "Stop. You don't have to manipulate me. You don't have to use your wiles to get me to do your bidding. Promise me you'll leave William out of it, and I'll find a way to remove your father from your life."

I had reached this decision without consciously thinking about it. Armistan had conspired with Gavin to restart the war. Gavin did it for revolution. Harry Armistan did it for money. With all my heart, I wanted to see Armistan dead for what he had done. It was a frightening decision, and by saying it out loud, I was committing to it just as Patricia had. Would I really kill Armistan? Yes, I would, if it came to that. I wasn't surprised by the realization.

She leaned back and gave a small laugh.

"You would have been a good big brother," she said affectionately.

"I was the youngest," I said. "And I'll be doing it for me, not for you."

"But it will feel like you're doing it for me, John."

"Then you can hold that happy glow next to your heart, but keep Will out of it."

She looked at me with genuine warmth, and I reminded myself not to believe whatever she chose to show me.

"All right," she promised. "I can wait. I like Paris, and I love spending time with William."

"You may have to wait awhile," I told her. "I have some work to do for the French once I recover."

"What kind of work?" she asked.

"Good question. The head of the Paris police visited me earlier and told me that the US government was loaning me to the French. He was the same policeman I'd told that I work for

Colonel House and the American legation. Apparently, House is reminding me that lies come with a cost. The cost for me will be working for the French."

"Well, with the war over, that should be pretty straightforward," she said hopefully.

"You would think so except that Raux seems particularly impressed with my ability to kill Bolsheviks."

"That means it's my turn to warn you off, John. Please keep William out of whatever you get into. I don't want him killed, and trouble and death cling to you like bad cologne." I must have looked hurt because she continued, "I'm sorry, but you must know it's true."

And I did.

"I'll try, Patricia. I won't bring him into anything, but if he thinks I need help, there'll be no stopping him. He can be stubborn."

"I know," she answered. "Just don't invite him."

"Understood."

"Now I must go meet William for lunch. I am sure he will be back later to visit you."

She rose from the chair and pecked me on the cheek.

"Get well, Mr. Griffin. You have work to do," she said.

<hr>

Once alone, I had plenty of time to think. I really did blame Armistan for Sarah's death. He had manipulated Gavin and, indirectly, Horace Merchant, Gavin's fellow conspirator and lover. He'd abused Patricia, and his money had paved the path that Sarah had walked to her death. I'd find a way to repay him for the grief and chaos he had sponsored. There would likely be no formal way to do so. The American government wouldn't pursue Harry Armistan based on anything that I said. He had completely insulated himself from any blame for the attacks on

Clemenceau. He was now the duped father-in-law, who was just thankful his little girl had survived. Of course, no one knew he had prostituted her for the purpose of restarting the war.

I would have to be very careful when I returned to the States to settle the score with Armistan. He was a rich, powerful man, who likely had many friends. However, he was also the failed investor in an arms industry that wasn't going to skyrocket, at least not in the near future. Perhaps Armistan would be vulnerable through his business partners. Something else for me to think about. I would have to navigate a world I knew little about. I was looking forward to it, which made me chuckle. Through Armistan, I had found Sarah. And in losing her, I had found new purpose. Harry Armistan had unintentionally given me another job. A job of the heart. God help him.

2

―――――

The Perfect Tool

Over the following days, some of my strength returned, but the wounds continued to pain me. Miss Clarke,[1] the ward nurse responsible for my care, would walk me along the corridors daily to build my stamina, but despite her kindness, I dreaded our walks.

One afternoon, I received a welcome visitor.

Madeline Moore, a pretty, flaxen-haired Midwesterner with a light dusting of freckles across her nose, breezed into my room with a smile. Madeline had come to France with the YMCA to do her part to support the war effort. With the end of the war, she and her friend, Rachel Eisen, had moved to Paris and immersed themselves in the Parisian artist community. It was through them that Mitchell and I had found Patricia and made friends of some of the musicians and performers in Montparnasse. Our particular friends were Eugene Bullard,[2] a black expatriate drummer and French war hero, and Kiki Prin,[3] a dancer, singer, and performer in the cabarets. Mitchell had been entranced by Kiki until Patricia Kingsbury had stolen him away. Madeline and I had a mutual attraction, but my link to Sarah had prevented anything coming of it.

"Hey, beautiful," I said with a smile as she stepped into the room. I tried to sit up a little straighter and look a little less pathetic.

"Hey, yourself." She smiled as she came to the beside to adjust the pillows behind my back.

"It's good to see you, Maddy. Thanks for coming. I guess Neuilly isn't one of your usual haunts."

"Oh, I love the country, John. It's a joy to cross the river, wade through the horse manure, and convince protective dragons to let me see you."

"Miss Clarke is not a dragon," I said defensively.

"I know," she said, "but she is very protective of you." She pulled the chair Patricia had used even closer to the bedside and sat.

"Yeah, well, she's seen the French police taking an interest in me, and I don't think she likes that. I know I don't."

Madeline raised an eyebrow. She was a clever girl and understood that, if she asked why the French authorities had an interest in me, we would tumble down a rabbit hole where we would find Bolsheviks, Clemenceau, and Sarah Willoughby. She didn't want to take me there.

"I'm glad she's here to guard you then," she assured me. "Do you know when you'll be up and around?"

"I've been strolling the hospital halls already, and I expect to be out in a few days, I guess."

"Good," she said decisively. "Eugene's been worried, Rachel's upset, and Kiki's..." She thought for a moment. "Well, I think she's worked up about something. I'm just not sure what. Anyway, it would be good for you to get your lazy bones out of bed and come to see us."

"Thank you." Without thinking, I reached out and snared

her hand, giving it a squeeze. "It's good to see you, and I'm glad to hear that everyone misses me."

"Oh, I never said they missed you!" She laughed. "Eugene's worried about the club, Rachel's upset with our landlady, and Kiki's, well, Kiki. We need you around so we can think about someone besides ourselves."

I laughed with her and awkwardly released her hand. My imagination insisted that she had been reluctant to let go.

We talked about Joey Zelli's club, which Eugene managed and where he played drums in the band. Madeline described Kiki's plans for her cabaret act, which seemed scandalous to my Victorian upbringing. She noted that Rachel had started to make noise about going back to the States. I found it soothing to discuss the mundane.

I recalled my visit to the Polo Grounds for the baseball game in New York City, just after I'd taken the job for Harry Armistan. It seemed like a million years ago now, but it was in late April,[4] a few short months ago. I'd been disgusted by the simple everyday worries of the civilians around me when so many good men had died in the war. Yet now the simple subjects we spoke of were a balm for my troubled mind. I realized that, while I had lost friends in the war, I had not lost anyone that I loved so passionately and deeply as I had Sarah. I now thoroughly understood loss.

Madeline sensed the change in my mood.

"You're tired. I should go." She stood and gave me a quick kiss on the cheek. "Get well, John Griffin," she demanded.

Madeline was right. I was tired. I needed to rest and recover from the bullet wounds and the broken heart. I needed to do both quickly because the French expected me to work for them once I was released from the hospital.

Specifically, a few days earlier, Préfet Raux, the chief of the Paris police had visited my hospital bed and told me I would be required to do a job for him. He knew I'd killed several people in Paris, and he knew that my friends, Eugene Bullard and Kiki Prin, were involved. He'd threatened to investigate both. I couldn't let that happen. If he really did start to examine the various gun battles I'd been involved in, he would likely find enough evidence to toss Gene in jail. And Kiki was hardly a model of demure behavior. If he wanted to, he could lock her up on indecency charges just for her cabaret shows. I wouldn't put Gene or Kiki at risk of such attention. I didn't have so many friends that I could abandon these two. If working for the French was the only way to protect my friends, I would do it.

———

Dr. Ryan, my attending physician, had predicted the timing of my release to be three or so weeks from when I was admitted. My wounds remained uninfected, and three weeks to the day after arriving at Military Hospital No. 1, Dr. Ryan released me. He was clear that I needed to be careful with any activities but stressed that I would need to exercise to build up my stamina. He was impressed that the bullet wounds had drained well and closed without festering.

Dressed in a suit Mitchell had brought for me, I walked gingerly down the echoing corridors of the hospital that had mostly emptied of its war wounded. Miss Clarke had insisted on escorting me to the front of the hospital, and she clutched my arm as if she was certain each step would bring disaster. She pushed the front door open for me, and I stepped out into the cool spring morning. Late June in Paris, and there was a slight chill in the air. I thanked Miss Clarke and wished her well. She hesitated and then stretched up to kiss my cheek.

"Be careful, John."

"I will, Miss Clarke. I heard Dr. Ryan. I'll obey," I answered.

"That's not what I meant. I meant be careful doing whatever you're involved with. I saw the French policeman and William and the pretty young ladies who visited. You're headed for more trouble. I can see it."

"Okay, Miss Clarke. You have a keen eye. I'll take care where I can."

"You do that," she insisted. "And John, my name is Alma."

"Alma, of course, and thank you."

A military motorcar was parked in the gravel courtyard in front of the hospital, and a smiling Walt Disney[5] waved from behind the wheel. It was time to head back to the trenches.

I climbed into the car next to Disney.

"Walt, did you steal a car from the Army?" I asked to forestall any questions.

"No. I chauffeur Army bigwigs around now. Hell, I even drive the general's kid around too, if you can believe it."

"Christ, you've got to be joking."

"Nope, but it's not hard duty."

"How are things going otherwise?" I asked.

"Fine. Good. Since you've been in the hospital, things have sure quieted down."

"That's a good thing, right?"

"Well, I was too young to sign up to fight, and then when I finally got overseas with the Red Cross, the war was over. So, to tell you the truth, John, having you here has been the most excitement I've had in my entire life. Scary as hell, but exciting. I guess quiet is good, but I wanted to do my part. Being around you let me do at least a little."

I examined him as he drove. He was a young man just about bursting with life and enthusiasm. He couldn't have been more than twenty years old. Just a few years younger than me, but a lifetime of horror separated us.

"You've done your part, Walt. It could have been you killed just as easy as it was Shed. So don't feel like you didn't do your part. You have. No one will tell you, but you helped stop the war resuming, and for that, you should be proud."

Disney had been our driver when we destroyed some of the weapons that the Bolsheviks intended to use to attack the various Allied and German leaders. Shed Bean, a veteran and new friend to us all, had been killed in the attack.

Disney was quiet for a moment, but I knew it couldn't last.

"Sure, John. And thanks. But keep me in mind if you need a driver, a forger, or just an extra pair of hands. As I said, they've got me driving around General Pershing's kid, and that's not my idea of exciting."

"Honestly?" I asked. "You said 'the general,' but General Pershing's kid? That's who you're driving around. Now that's funny. And of course I'll keep you in mind. But I sure hope I'm out of the Bolshevik hunting business. And if I need a forger, things are really bad. I didn't know you excelled at crime, Walt."

"I'm not much of a forger, but I did change my birth date on my passport application, so I have some experience," he said proudly.

Disney's admission made me smile.

"Walt, you are officially added to my stable of criminal contacts. And to think I just thought you were a talented driver."

He flashed me a smile as he expertly maneuvered us through the Parisian morning traffic.

Disney drove me straight to the Hôtel Vendôme and not the run-down pensione hotel that I'd been staying at before being wounded.

"Mrs. Kingsbury asked that I bring you here. You've got a room," Disney explained.

I climbed carefully from the automobile and turned back to Disney. "Thanks for the ride. I appreciate it."

"Sure. And don't forget to call if you need me."

I prayed that was a call I would never have to make.

I presented myself to the concierge, who welcomed me like I was Patricia Kingsbury's long-lost brother. He insisted the bellman escort me to my room. Once we got there, I found that it was a suite. The bellman started opening the bureau doors to show me the clothes that Patricia had supplied for me, but I quickly dismissed him with a few francs.

When he was gone, I sat down on the end of the enormous bed, exhausted. Just a few short weeks ago Sarah had been alive and in my arms in this very hotel. Shed, Gavin, Horace, and Sarah all killed because of me or by me. I found myself staring sightlessly at my hands. A murderer's hands. The promise I had made Patricia wouldn't be hard to keep. Harry Armistan was an abomination. It would be a joy to choke the life from him, but I couldn't pursue him until I was clear of Préfet Raux and Colonel House. I would try to see House tomorrow. I was too wrung out to see him today.

I kicked off my shoes and fell back onto the bed. Despite my fatigue, my thoughts jumped around in my head with no anchor. From Sarah to Will and Patricia. To Bullard and Kiki. To Armistan and Reynolds and back to Sarah. Always Sarah. I would force rest to come. I closed my eyes and let the images flash as they would. I focused on my breathing and on the throbbing pain in my chest and hip. I focused on the pain in my heart. I thought about the pain until it lost meaning and the images evaporated. And I slept.

When I heard a light knock on the suite door, it was dark outside and I could just make out the luminous hands on my Army-issued wristwatch: 2100 hours. Nine in the evening.

I rolled off the bed carefully and ran my hands through my hair.

Leaving my shoes where I'd left them, I shuffled through the suite. Mitchell stood in the doorway, leaning against the frame as I pulled the door open. He looked relaxed.

"Evening, John. Feel like some dinner? Patricia and I were going to eat in the dining room here, and she suggested I invite you."

"I don't want to horn in on your romantic dinner, Doc," I said.

"Oh, don't worry about that," he assured me with a huge grin. "We've had plenty of those while you were out snooping and getting shot up." He blanched at the last, realizing that he might be reminding me of Sarah's death. I chuckled to let him know his small joke was fine. Everything around me reminded me of Sarah and her death, and his lame quip wouldn't send me into a tailspin.

I pulled on my shoes, splashed some water on my face, and considered a shave but dismissed the thought. I had no need to spruce up for Patricia Armistan.

When we arrived at the restaurant, Patricia was already seated at a table, near some french doors overlooking the street. Sitting next to her and speaking earnestly was Morgan Reynolds, her father's fixer and, ostensibly, hers as well.

I had no use for Reynolds. He was a liar and very likely still in Harry Armistan's pocket. Unfortunately, I needed all the intelligence that I could get on Armistan, which meant I would have to be civil to Reynolds.

"Sorry, John, I didn't know he'd be here. He still sniffs around Patricia now and then, but he won't stay long with me nearby."

"No problem, Will. I hold no grudge against Mr. Reynolds."

Mitchell looked at me with surprise, trying to decide whether I was being honest. Before he could decide, we had reached the table.

"Morgan, it's good to see you again," I lied with a smile.

Reynolds had glanced up sharply from his conversation with

Patricia. He was obviously suspicious of me and clearly afraid of Mitchell. He was afraid of Mitchell for good reason. In an alley outside a Parisian café, Doc had tortured him for information about Patricia's whereabouts. He disliked me because, in addition to my friendship with Mitchell, I slapped him around like a woman in that very same alley.

He stood and took my offered hand. "Yes, good to see you healing," he lied back. He glanced at Mitchell and turned to Patricia. "I must be going, but you should think about my suggestion, Trish."

"I will, Morgan, and thank you for coming," she answered.

Once Reynolds was gone and we were seated around the table, Mitchell couldn't help but ask what Reynolds had suggested.

"With Gavin dead and his money—really, my money—soon to be under my control, Morgan was trying to convince me to go back to New York. I suspect he thinks if he can get me to return to Daddy, my father will give me to him like I'm some sort of cheap carnival prize. That will never happen," she said fervently.

Mitchell laughed and shook his head, which surprised me. "What?" he asked me. My astonishment must have shown on my face. "Patricia would eat Reynolds alive if her dad tried to arrange a marriage to him. No point in getting angry about something that ain't ever gonna happen."

Apparently, Patricia had not told Mitchell about her appalling relationship with her father, but she smiled at his comment and his confidence in her.

"You two should get married," I said without thought. Spontaneously. I guess Sarah's loss had reminded me that I would always be alone, and I didn't want to see that for the two of them. Their faces told me that I should mind my own business.

"Or we could order." I frantically waved at the waiter, who promptly arrived. "Drinks?" I suggested.

I could see them glancing surreptitiously at each other, each trying to judge the other's reaction to my unfortunate suggestion.

"Oh, for Christ's sake," I said, exasperated, turning to the waiter. "*Martinis, pour nous trois, vite.*[6] Stop sneaking each other looks. You can talk about my asinine suggestion later when I'm not there for you to make uncomfortable. What have you heard about the treaty since I've been in the hospital?" I gracelessly changed the subject.

"It's been agreed." Mitchell happily seized the new topic. "The Allies gave the Germans an ultimatum. Threatened to restart the fight if the Germans didn't accept the deal with no changes. The formal signing is later this month."

"Well, hell! Clemenceau gets what he wants."[7]

"Perhaps," answered Patricia. "But the Bolshevik plot failed. The war has not restarted, and my father will be despondent thinking about the profits generated by automobile manufacturers and dish soap concerns instead of his armament companies."

I smiled at the thought. Her father would also be in hot water with his business partners.

"So the Bolshevik plot has been foiled, thanks to you, John. Have you given any more thought to what Préfet Raux may want with you?" Mitchell asked.

I felt a sharp pain under my heart at Mitchell's inadvertent reminder that I'd delayed Sarah's efforts to kill Clemenceau too. I didn't kill her, but I did distract her, which was sufficient for the French marksmen to take care of the rest. I pulled my thoughts back to his question.

"I'm the perfect tool for a man who wants to crush any remaining Bolshevik activity in France. I'm American, which means I will be viewed as naive. Any revolutionaries won't see me as part of the French government, because I won't be. I can speak French well enough. I have the right skills, given that I have a history of prolific killing of Reds. Of course, when talking to me, Raux always insists that the folks I killed were German nationalists resisting Germany's defeat in the war. But he and Clemenceau both know it was a Bolshevik plot, and I think that scares them."

"You think they want you to help them hunt down any remaining Reds?" Patricia asked.

"I think that would be too much. There are Reds under every rock in France. I'll bet he's got something a little more specific in mind. In any case, I plan on going to Colonel House to see if I can get out of it."

"I wouldn't hold your breath, Griff," Mitchell said pessimistically.

After Mitchell's unhelpful advice, we ordered and ate. By the end of dinner, I was ready to hit the rack and did.

3

———

The Inevitability of Service

Early the next morning, I forced myself from bed. I ignored the pain of my mostly healed but still tender wounds and took a walk. I used the time to organize my thoughts in preparation for seeing Colonel House. At 0830, I walked over to the Hôtel de Crillon and presented myself to the Army corporal at the entrance. I'd been there once before, with Préfet Raux when he was testing the truth of my story of being an American agent.

That visit had been easy. Raux was known and expected. On this visit, I was unknown and unexpected.

"I was told to come see Colonel House," I explained to the soldier. A bit of a stretch, but to my way of thinking, Préfet Raux had told me to see the colonel.

"Name?" the corporal demanded.

I gave him my name, and he flipped through papers on a clipboard.

"I don't find you," he declared.

"I'd suggest you bring that up with Colonel House. I've been working under his direction with the French police on the recent attacks. He directed me to see him this morning."

He looked over at a civilian deeper in the grand entry hall, who sat scribbling at a desk.

"Go see Mr. Simmons there," he said, pointing with his chin. "If he gives you a pass, you can see the colonel. If not, you're out on the street."

"Thank you." I crossed the hall slowly, and by the time I reached Simmons's desk, the corporal was engaged with another supplicant.

"Mr. Simmons?" I asked as I arrived. On his desk was a stack of preprinted passes.

Simmons raised his head, and as he nodded, I said, "The corporal told me that you would provide me a pass to see Colonel House."

Simmons looked over at the corporal, who was still busy with another visitor.

"Fine. Name?"

"John Griffin."

Simmons pulled a permit from the stack and filled in my name and room number 201. He also wrote my time of entry as 0845.

"Upstairs?" I asked.

"Yeah. Third floor," he said, handing me the permit and pointing to the stairs. "I wouldn't bother with the elevators," he added. "Too slow."

As I climbed the stairs, I studied my permit, which was pompously titled AMERICAN COMMISSION TO NEGOTIATE PEACE VISITOR'S PASS. After the first turn, I paused to catch my breath, and I looked around from the staircase. I hadn't had the chance to study the hotel on my first visit. It was beautiful in a gold-leaf-and-marble kind of way. Expensive. God only knew how much the commission was costing. Given Clemenceau's manipulations, the damn peace wasn't going to be worth the money we spent on it.

I found room 201 without any problem. A distinguished-looking man with thinning blond hair and an easy smile sat behind a heavy wood desk guarding the door behind him.

"I'm here to see Colonel House," I said.

"Mr. Griffin?" he asked.

"Yeah."

"I'm Stanton Simms," he said. He stood and offered his hand. "It's a pleasure to meet you. I've heard a lot about you."

"I'll bet," I said glumly, thinking about House telling folks he had an agent working for the French.

"Sorry, but I'll need to look at your pass," he said, holding out his hand.

I gave it to him.

He took a quick look and handed it back. "Wait here."

He tapped lightly on the door behind him, entering without any invitation that I could hear. Unfortunately, he shut the door behind him.

A few seconds later, he reappeared and ushered me into the office. As he left, he pulled the door closed.

House stood from behind his desk, and he came around it to shake my hand. He wore a broad smile, which surprised me.

"Mr. Griffin, it's a pleasure to see you up and around. Your heroics on behalf of the United States have been nothing short of Homeric," he gushed.

"Colonel, thank you for seeing me," I answered, uncomfortable with his compliments.

"Of course, of course. You, sir, are like a fine bird dog," he said, his small hands fluttering before him. "You never lose the scent, and you never give up. Tracking the final conspirator was genius."

"Thank you, sir." Like Préfet Raux, he found my interference with Sarah's plan to be clever and courageous.

"I don't know how you figured out those plots," he continued, "but you certainly have a keen mind and a nose for finding conspiracies. In fact, Préfet Raux has specifically asked that you assist him with a task he needs accomplished. I, of course, assured him that you were just the man and would be eager to help once you had recovered sufficiently from your wounds. And here you are! Outstanding timing."

"Yes, sir. I am here to speak with you about the French and their expectations."

"Certainly."

A knock on the door interrupted the colonel. The assistant reappeared and said, "It's time for you to leave for your appointment, Colonel. The car is waiting." He held the colonel's hat.

"Thank you, Stanton. Please call and let them know that Mr. Griffin will be joining me."

Stanton looked at me with a raised eyebrow. I was sure he was trying to tell me something, but I didn't know what.

"Follow me, John. I trust I may call you John?" House asked.

Without waiting for an answer, House collected his hat and hurried out of his office. Despite his diminutive stature, I was forced to lengthen my stride to keep up.

He sped through his secretary's anteroom and into the hallway directly to the elevator.

"Where are we going, sir?" I asked as we endured the wait for the elevator to arrive.

"It's just a short drive. I have a surprise for you," he promised, and he would say no more.

We bundled into a motorcar waiting immediately in front of the building entrance. Once in, the car turned out of the Place de la Concorde onto the Champs-Élysées. I found myself wishing that Disney was our driver. A short time later, we turned in to a typical well-to-do Parisian square.

"Welcome to Place des États-Unis and the temporary White House, John," Colonel House said with a self-satisfied grin.

The driver hurried around the bonnet to open the door for the colonel. I was left to operate my door without any help.

I looked at the colonel and back at the building that now housed the president of the United States. Two American soldiers armed with Springfield rifles stood stiffly outside the entrance.

"When we first came in December, the Murat family placed their beautiful home at the disposal of the president. The family are relations of George Washington, you know. An excellent choice by the French. An unsubtle reminder of France's historic ties to the United States. Of course, the president was loath to acknowledge these links. He wanted to remain impartial in the negotiations. He stayed at the palace but was unmoved by any historic ties. This annoyed the French. Given his approach, when the president returned from the United States in March, they saw no point in putting him back in the palace. Instead, he was placed here." House clearly did not agree with the decision to remain aloof of historical connections.

The building certainly looked splendid enough. It was difficult to imagine that the French had installed Wilson in an even grander residence when he'd first come to Paris. In any event, the French made an excellent choice in lodging the president away from his staff. By ensconcing Wilson in this aptly named square, they had isolated him from his support at the Hôtel de Crillon. Communication would be delayed and more difficult, even with telephone lines in place. He had been disadvantaged in the treaty negotiations, and he and House had allowed it to happen.

A soldier ushered us through the ornate entry. An imposing older woman backed by yet another armed soldier conducted one more identity check before she opened a door to a large study.

"Please go through, gentlemen."

I followed House into the room, and behind a heavy wooden desk covered with work papers sat the president of the United States, Woodrow Wilson.

"Mr. President," House said eagerly, "this is the fellow I told you about. John Griffin, formerly of the Second Division and hero to the French." He presented me to the president as if I were a Christmas puppy.

Of course, I had seen photographs of the president in newspapers, but I never thought I'd have cause to meet him. I wished I still had none. Despite my reluctance and House's introduction, I was impressed that I was standing before the president of the United States.

The president rose from his chair. He was a tall, thin man, who reminded me of a stork, with long limbs and stooping posture. He looked old and tired with sunken cheeks. Yet behind rimless spectacles, his eyes gleamed with interest. Although he looked unused to smiling, he smiled as he came around his desk to offer me his hand.

"Mr. Griffin, the colonel has told me about your efforts on our behalf. I am proud to meet you, my boy. Through your work for the colonel, we kept our allies safe." Despite a very slight Southern drawl, he spoke with a measured pace I associated with the exclusive northeastern colleges, which I supposed was logical, given his connection to Princeton. I didn't know how to respond to his comment, so I didn't.

He took my arm and gestured to a set of cushioned chairs. The door to his office opened, and the female gatekeeper carried in a coffee tray.

We sat, and as she filled our cups, the president said, "It may surprise you to know that I am disappointed in the terms of the peace treaty."

He looked at me for confirmation.

"It does, Mr. President," I said to satisfy him.

"Indeed. But certain concessions were made while I was back in the United States of which I was unaware. With the attack on the French prime minister, any renegotiation of those terms is now an impossibility." The president cast a dark look toward House, who looked down and refused to meet the president's eye.

"Our task now," the president stated, "is to engage the American people in the importance of the peace, as it is. To take up the mantle of leadership bestowed upon us as a result of this terrible war. We must get the Senate to ratify this treaty, unchanged."

"Yes, sir," I said, given that he seemed to expect some response.

"For this treaty is a readjustment of those great injustices that underlie the whole structure of European and Asiatic society," he continued, warming to his subject. "It addresses all the questions that have eaten into the confidence of men toward their governments." He spoke with the passion of a Methodist minister on Easter Sunday.

"Indeed, Mr. President," Colonel House interjected obsequiously.

Wilson glanced at House, and I thought I caught the hint of a sneer on his face.

"You, Mr. Griffin, when you went to France, you and boys like you, were going forth to prove the might of justice and right, and as a result, all the world believes in America as it believes in no other nation organized in the modern world. You did that and at a horrible cost. We must see this treaty ratified, not only for you and those like you, who came home, but for those dear ghosts that still deploy upon the fields of France."[1]

While I was sure that I had not gone to France to prove the strength of justice and right, I didn't want to tell the president that. He seemed like such a sincere, idealistic old fellow that it would have been impolite. Also, any peace was better than no peace.

"I firmly agree that the peace treaty is essential, Mr. President," I declared patriotically.

He studied me closely, perhaps sensing the larger disagreement in my tone.

"Yes, well, our beloved country needs to work in concert with all the other great fighting nations of the world to assure that this is truly the last war. That includes France, perhaps our greatest partner in this crusade."

With a sinking feeling, I felt compelled to nod my head.

"Colonel House assures me that you have the trust of the French. He has agreed to second you to their police. There remain enemies opposed to peace and stability, Mr. Griffin. It is these forces that we must defeat. My opponents happen to be in the Senate," he said with obvious distaste. "Yours, sir, are here. I know you have already given much, Mr. Griffin, but I trust that, as your president, I may ask this last task of you."

I was caught, trapped by my own lies to the French. I simply didn't have it in me to refuse the president.

At that moment, a tap on the door announced the entry of a square-faced, matronly, middle-aged woman, who walked directly to the president's side.

Colonel House and I stood, and the president started to rise to greet her, but she placed a possessive hand on his shoulder, restraining him.

"Edith, this is John Griffin, the young man the colonel told us about," the president said, introducing us. "He's the one who saved Georges.[2] Mr. Griffin, my wife, Edith Wilson." I was surprised House had mentioned me to the First Lady as well.

Edith Wilson studied me briefly, her mouth a grim line not so different from the president's. Then she smiled, and with her smile, she seemed both younger and less forbidding.

"Thank you so much, Mr. Griffin. We've been told of your exploits. Is it true you worked in secrecy under the direction of Colonel House to safeguard Monsieur Clemenceau? Truly, fantastic. Why even the president and I knew nothing of your heroic efforts."

"Colonel House has supported me in my endeavors, ma'am," I assured her vaguely.

She turned to Colonel House. "Colonel, you must be commended on your initiative and discretion," she said with what I thought might be sarcasm. "It seems that making decisions independently of the president has become a habit." It *was* sarcasm.

From the corner of my eye, I could see Colonel House redden.

"I must protest, Mrs. Wilson," House blustered. "I have only done what the president has directed me to do. Yes, I have acted quietly in this instance, but it was necessary."

"As it was with the liberties you took with the treaty negotiations?" the president asked acidly.

I was a stranger to these people, and they were squabbling in front of me like they were just another unhappy, fractured family walking up the steps to church. They were the most powerful people in America for Christ's sake. I was disappointed and embarrassed by the exchange.

House stood, and I followed.

"I am and have always been at your service, Mr. President," he said.

"Of course, Edward," Mrs. Wilson said, answering in the president's place. She wore a smile, which seemed sincere. "In this instance, your service is greatly appreciated. And Mr. Griffin, thank you so much for what you have done for the United States."

The president nodded his agreement and stood as well.

"Yes, thank you, Mr. Griffin. Do what you can for the French, and we'll see you well rewarded," he promised.

I didn't know what the president was promising, and I wasn't going to ask. I just wanted to escape the room.

"And Mr. Griffin," Mrs. Wilson interjected, "should we need your help when you finish your task here, how can we find you when you return home?"

"I will remain in touch with him," House volunteered.

"Oh, we wouldn't want to bother you, Edward," Mrs. Wilson stated.

I had no interest in continuing to assist the Wilsons or House, but to end the debate and escape the room, I quickly said, "I can be reached through the Pennsylvania Hotel in New York City, ma'am."

The president offered his hand, which I took. Together, House and I fled.

We didn't speak in the motorcar during our return to Hôtel de Crillon. Once back in House's office, he tossed off his suit coat and called for coffee.

"My apologies, Mr. Griffin. The First Lady does not care for me. I was not a supporter of the president's hasty marriage to her after his first wife, Ellen, died. I'm afraid Mrs. Wilson hasn't forgiven me for that. Also, the president feels I overstepped in the treaty negotiations. He believes I gave too much away to our allies."

"Did you, sir?" I couldn't resist asking.

"No, but it doesn't matter. These negotiations were devilishly difficult," House said with some heat. "The president went home in February, and he left me in charge. We have literally redrawn nearly the entire map of the world. To reach agreement on the key issue, it was my judgment that we had to surrender others. The president has always been most committed to the last point of his Fourteen Points. Keep in mind that I helped draft the damn things. I know what is important. I got the final point in the treaty for heaven's sake. The treaty will create a general association of nations formed for the purpose of affording mutual guarantees of political independence and territorial integrity to all nations.[3] This is exactly what the president wanted, but he resents the dilution on the other points and blames me."

For the first time in my association with House, I felt sorry for him. He was a man doing the best he could in a bad situation. Having met Clemenceau, I could imagine how difficult any negotiation with him would be.

"I'll talk to Préfet Raux and do what I can," I said. "I hope it will help you with the president, Colonel."

"Thank you, Mr. Griffin. I doubt the First Lady will let anything you or I do change the president's opinion of me, but this is now about America and peace. The French are our allies, and they say they need you. I do not always trust them, but I believe them on this. Assisting them will support the treaty and peace, and Griffin, the continuation of peace is no sure thing. It sits on a knife's edge, and a nudge could send the world tumbling back to war. Help the French. Convince them we are with them because we need this peace to last. Hell, the whole world needs it. You'll have our resources. I've made sure of it. I've advised Captain Gordon,[4] who is on the staff here, of your mission. You can trust him, and he'll give you every possible assistance. Stanton Simms, my assistant, can help. He may not have the pull Gordon does, but he isn't afraid to wield my name like a headsman's axe when the need arises. He knows everybody at the Crillon and speaks French like a native."

"Understood, sir," I said as the gloom of the inevitability of service to Raux and the French settled over me.

"Griffin, the president and I will likely be returning to the

States immediately after the treaty is signed, which could be within the week. If you need anything beyond what Gordon can do, don't hesitate to contact me. You'll have to send a cable. Let Simms know. I'll do what I can. And God bless America. She needs you!"

4

―――――

Two Enemies

R ather than delay the inevitable, I decided to see Préfet Raux immediately. While I didn't know the exact location of the headquarters of the Paris police, I did know that it was near Notre Dame Cathedral on the Île de la Cité, a small island in the center of Paris. Since my meetings with Colonel House and the president had been brief, the morning was still young. I decided to walk through the Tuileries Garden, past the Louvre, and along the river to Notre Dame. I was surprised to come across a crater in the garden itself. Although Paris had not been the scene of direct fighting, by the grace of God and the US Marine Corps, it had clearly seen the destructive power of modern war.

Although the city was alive with autocars, buses, and carts, Paris remained a city of the weary, the displaced, and the ruined. In short, it was a city recovering from war. Many shops remained closed. Young mothers and small children stood begging on street corners, and limbless men populated the ends of bridges and Metro entrances.

This Paris of the morning was very different from the Paris of the night I had seen while hunting for Gavin Kingsbury. No bands playing wild jazz music or former soldiers and young women dancing the foxtrot or tango with abandon. It was also different from the luxurious Paris I saw during my brief days with Sarah.

I stopped to lean against the wall overlooking the Seine. The visit with Colonel House and President and Mrs. Wilson had exhausted me. Their byplay seemed to cheapen the sacrifice of the past four years, and I already felt physically ill from losing Sarah.

I took a deep breath. If I was going to successfully navigate the coming meeting with Préfet Raux, I needed to be sharp. In control.

I took a second breath and pushed off the wall. Stop thinking and move. Now was not the time for imagination or memories. I hoped to hell this walk along the Seine would count as exercise in Doc Ryan's prescription book. I know it did in mine.

I pressed on to the Île de la Cité. Although I thought I'd made good time, what should have been a thirty-minute walk turned into forty-five minutes with the many stops I took.

But I was in no hurry. Raux had no reason to be expecting me.

I crossed Pont Neuf on the west side of the island and walked south and east along the perimeter of the Île de la Cité. As I approached Pont Saint-Michel, I could see the Saint-Michel fountain across the river. I came across a small *boulangerie*[1] and was captured by the smell of freshly baked bread. I ducked inside and bought a baguette from a young woman dressed in black. I asked directions, and I was assured that the Préfecture of Police was just a few blocks away.

I followed the young widow's instructions, eating the crusty and still warm French bread as I walked. A few minutes later I came to the Cité Metro stop and found the Police Préfecture across the square. I hesitated but pushed myself forward. I would not solve the Raux problem by avoiding him. I put the remaining half of the baguette on a park bench, confident either a pigeon or a hungry man would find it, and walked into the building.

The Préfecture was much as I expected. Policemen bustled about. I made my way to what I assumed was the equivalent of the desk sergeant. He wore a luxuriant mustache and was missing his left arm at the shoulder.

"*Le Préfet Raux, s'il vous plaît.*"[2]

"*Qui êste-vous?*"[3] he demanded briskly.

"John Griffin, *l'Américain*," I told him, arrogantly thinking all French policemen would know that an American named Griffin had saved their prime minister. I was wrong. He didn't react, and I didn't press him. He seemed in no hurry to allow me to see Préfet Raux. Fine. I had tried. I considered my obligation fulfilled. I would walk away. I looked at my watch and then asked, "*Votre nom?*"[4]

"*Sub-Brigadier Vissac,*" he answered proudly. Yes, a desk sergeant.

Armed with the sergeant's name and the time, I would have a defense if Raux accused me of avoiding him. I needed to deflect his ire with this visit to prevent any police problems for Kiki or Eugene.

"*D'accord,*" I told him. "*Dites au Préfet Raux que je l'ai demandé.*"[5]

"*Attendez là-bas.*"[6] He pointed at a bench along the wall.

I patted my pockets and found a business card from the Hôtel de Vendôme that I had picked up at the hotel's front desk. I reached across the desk, took the sergeant's pen, and scribbled my name on the back of the card.

"*Pour le Préfet Raux,*"[7] I said, dropping the card in front of the sergeant.

I left without another word.

While I hoped Raux would forget about me, I was sure that

he would find me when he was ready. I walked into the sunlight to find a taxicab. The pain in my chest told me there was no way in hell I was going to walk back to the Vendôme.

ONCE BACK AT THE HOTEL AND ALONE IN MY ROOM, I HAD TIME TO think. Of course, there wasn't much that I wanted to think about. Every mental thread led me back to Sarah, and when I thought about Sarah, the dormant ache under my heart would come alive. I wanted a drink. I wanted several drinks, but I remembered how I had fallen into a bottle when I returned to the States after leaving the British Army. I didn't want to end up a drunk again.

I lost track of time trapped in my self-pity, but the ringing of the room telephone jarred me from my increasingly morbid thoughts.

"Monsieur Griffin, vous avez des visiteurs dans le hall. Voulez-vous que je vous les envoie?"[8]

"Qui sont-ils?"[9] I asked.

"Le Préfet Raux et une jeune femme."[10]

Well, shit! That was quick.

"Je descends."[11]

A woman. This couldn't be good. I straightened my tie, pulled on my jacket, grabbed my hat, and went to face the music.

As the elevator doors opened, I saw Raux immediately. The lobby was not large, and he was impossible to miss. He had stationed himself so that he could watch both the Art Nouveau elevator doors and the exit from the stairwell. I was certain he positioned himself to prevent me from sneaking out of the hotel.

His expressionless shark's eyes watched me as I stepped out of the elevator. Standing next to him was the young woman the concierge had promised. Tall and thin by prewar standards, she was dressed in a plain but well-made dress with a more obvious waist and longer hem than the shorter, sleeker dresses Madeline, Rachel, and Kiki wore. She was certainly not one of the new modern girls that Paris seemed full of and whose company I so enjoyed. She was, however, remarkably attractive. Her mahogany hair was coiled under her hat, and she wore no jewelry other than a wedding band. She held her head high as she watched me cross the patterned granite floor to meet them. Neither Raux nor the girl smiled any greeting. I surmised this was to be my introduction to whatever plans the French had for me.

"Monsieur Griffin." Préfet Raux[12] extended his hand. "Thank you for contacting me at the Préfecture."

I shook the inspector's hand and turned to his companion.

"Madame Masson, allow me to introduce Monsieur John Griffin, formerly of the United States Marine Corps and currently an operative of Colonel House and the president of the United States."

She met my eyes without surprise at this description.

"Madame Masson, a pleasure," I said.

She extended her hand as Raux had.

"The pleasure is mine," she said as I shook her hand. "Préfet Raux has told me of your exploits on behalf of France." Her golden eyes studied me. Her voice was deep and melodious, and I could detect no accent to her English. I considered correcting her misconception that I had done anything at all on behalf of France but recognized that I would be wasting my time.

"You speak English with an American accent. Where did you learn it?" I asked. I was genuinely curious how she spoke such flawless Americanized English.

"My father was in the diplomatic corps. I spent several years in the United States."

I nodded.

"Come," Raux said, "we will speak in the restaurant." He led us to the elevator and pushed the button for the restaurant. We stood awkwardly in the slow-moving car, but I was behind Madame Masson and had the opportunity to admire her neck and jawline. When the door opened, Raux went directly to the maître d' and showed him some sort of identification.

"*Fermez le restaurant. Immédiatement. Sécurité de l'État. Et apportez du café,*"[13] he instructed gruffly. He then picked a table away from the entrance and overlooking the street.

Raux commandeered the seat nearest the window without making any effort to seat Madame Masson. She was close behind the Préfet, and I was left with no choice but to seat her next to Raux. I ended up facing the Préfet with Madame Masson on my right and the restaurant entrance at my back. I was certain Raux had orchestrated the seating to make me uncomfortable, as if I were some sort of Western gunfighter, nervous with the door at my back. Surprised, I found myself admiring his thoroughness in pursuing every advantage. I couldn't help but smile.

"Why are you happy, monsieur?" he demanded. His English wasn't as good as Madame Masson's.

"I like you, Préfet Raux. You are a careful, calculating man. You have deliberately placed me with my back to the entrance. You did this to make me uncomfortable and disadvantaged. Madame Masson played her part well. The two of you are like gifted ballroom dancers. So I enjoyed the demonstration of your skill," I said. "You must have known each other for a while to accomplish even this small thing so well." I looked from one to the other, waiting for confirmation.

Madame Masson remained expressionless. Her chin tilted up slightly, putting her graceful neck on display. I wondered if this was calculated as well. She struck me as someone who was serious and had no time for anyone who was not. I was certain that we would not be friends.

"We have known each other since early in the war," Raux said simply. "We met through her late husband."

"Of course."

The waiter arrived and poured coffee for the three of us. I hoped fruitlessly for some pastries as well, but Préfet Raux did not seem to believe in fueling his briefings with anything other than caffeine.

"This discussion is confidential. You must not share what we say here with others. I would very much regret acting against you should you ignore these instructions. Do you understand?" he demanded.

"Perfectly," I promised.

"As part of my duties as Préfet of Police for Paris, I work in concert with the Deuxième Bureau," he said bluntly.

I was unfamiliar with the French police's bureaucratic structure, and he must have read the ignorance on my face.

"The Deuxième Bureau is France's military intelligence," he stated.

"I see," I said, not understanding the connection but confident he would explain it.

"In addition to policing, I am also responsible for certain aspects of counterintelligence work and intelligence gathering. We have found, working in tandem with the Deuxième Bureau, we can prevent espionage as well as crime. I am proud to say that the Paris police are the most modern in the world. We have been forced to modernize. In the years before the war, bands of criminals, *Apaches*, ran rampant through the city. We had strikes, assassinations. Anarchists were very active. It was a busy time."

He was leading up to something, but I couldn't tell what.

"In response, we established the mobile police, *les Brigades du Tigre*, named for the prime minister, of course. *Les Brigades* react very quickly to crimes. With the telephone and the automobile, they can be on site while the gun smoke is still in the air." He smiled at his description, glancing at Madame Masson, who did not deign to react. Not put off in the slightest, he continued. "These men are very competent. And, as I say, they are very quick to the scenes of the crimes. In fact, it was *les Brigades du Tigre* that responded recently to certain criminal events in Montparnasse, on rue de Babylone and in Garches."

That was what he was leading to. He paused to gauge my reaction.

I nodded, keeping my face impassive. When he'd visited me in the hospital, he had hinted that he knew I was involved in both events.

"It was *les Brigades* who questioned the survivors at the Montparnasse explosion. There were no survivors in Garches."

"That's a shame," I said.

"Yes. The survivors *les Brigades* questioned were all Bolsheviks. The dead that we were able to identify were Bolsheviks as well."

So the explosion and fire had rendered Shed Bean's body unrecognizable. Poor Shed. Machine-gunned down in a Parisian foyer by a Red. What a damn waste.

"Yet despite this Bolshevik activity in France, we must not lose focus on Germany. German militarism. In a few short years, German industry will outstrip our own. The German population already is greater. Despite the treaty, it is a certainty that they will remain hostile and aggressive. The attempts on the prime minister are evidence of this."

I couldn't refrain from shaking my head at that statement. The French had insisted that Clemenceau's attackers were German soldiers. In the street, with their dead bodies around us, I had told Clemenceau that the assassination attempt was by Bolsheviks trying to restart the war. He didn't want to see dead Bolsheviks masquerading as Germans. He only wanted to see dead Germans. He had ignored me. He perpetuated the lie that Germans and not Bolsheviks had made the attempt on his life, despite my insistence otherwise. In addition, Colonel House had directed me to stop arguing that it was a Bolshevik plot. He realized that with the attack on Clemenceau, the French would demand a resumption of the war if the Germans didn't sign the treaty without any of Germany's suggested changes. House felt compelled to support the French. "Bowing to political reality," he had called it.

"It is true," Raux stressed. "And you, Monsieur Griffin, have confronted both of these threats here in Paris."

I started to protest, and Raux waved me off.

"Please, monsieur. You killed Germans on rue Franklin. The prime minister saw you. And we examined the bodies in Garches. My doctors took from them large bullets. What pistol is it that you carry, monsieur? One of Mr. Browning's ingenious inventions, yes? The bullet is over ten millimeters. We found such bullets in several of the dead. I do not fault you. In fact, it is because of your abilities that we are speaking."

I could feel Madame Masson studying me, but I kept my attention on Raux.

He tapped his finger against his coffee spoon, thinking. Whether he was gathering his thoughts or giving me time to object, I didn't know. Given that they'd found .45 slugs in the bodies in Garches, I decided silence was the safest response.

"France has two enemies," he continued dramatically. "The historic and unchanging enemy: Germany. And the new and unpredictable enemy: Bolsheviks. These both must be defeated, and we fear that they are working together."

"What do you want from me, Monsieur le Préfet?" I gave up on silence.

"It is clear from your activities here in Paris that the United States is opposed to Bolshevism. You will work with us, specifically with Madame Masson, and pursue a broader plot. We believe the Germans are manipulating the Bolsheviks and hope to use the threat of a Bolshevik revolution in Germany to mislead our allies, particularly the United States, into softening enforcement of the treaty terms. Madame Masson is..." Raux raised his chin toward the ceiling in thought. "An operative. For

France. She is a member of the Deuxième Bureau." He looked from me to Madame Masson and gave her a slight nod.

"I have been monitoring German agents in Paris for years now," Madame Masson said.

"Not doing a particularly good job, are you, madame?" I said rudely. I would find no way of avoiding working with the French. I had trapped myself with my lie, which House had perpetuated and Raux chose to believe. This fact made me surly and impolite. Poor Madame Masson would have to bear the brunt of my petulance.

My honesty earned a stern look from Raux.

Masson was unflustered. "Your criticism is fair. As you might imagine, Monsieur Griffin, I have focused on the German threat more than the Bolshevik one. It was more immediate. I agree that I failed entirely to detect the plot targeting the prime minister," she said without any apparent animosity.

"Don't feel badly, madame. I feel confident that you couldn't have detected a *German* plot even if you'd been sitting in Berlin at the table where the German spymasters plan their nefarious deeds," I said sincerely, stressing the *German* part of the plot.

She bobbed her head, accepting my assurance and either missing or choosing to ignore the sarcasm of my words. I wondered if she knew the attackers had been Bolsheviks. It occurred to me that, for the French, it didn't matter. They saw in the plot the hand of Germany. Bolsheviks manipulated by the Germans. That thought gave me pause. Maybe they were right. I had no proof that the Bolsheviks hadn't been aided and directed by the Germans. I only knew what Gavin, Horace, and Sarah had told me. Yes, they told me what they believed, but they might not have known the hand of Germany was on their puppet strings along with Harry Armistan's. Perhaps I should shut up and keep an open mind. I was new to this, and Madame Masson and Préfet Raux were not.

"The Germans remain very active," she assured me. "Even

with the treaty agreed, they seek to undermine the security of France. If that means supporting the Bolsheviks here, they will do so."

Unconsciously I rubbed the mostly healed wound in my chest, which itched incessantly. I stopped when I noticed Madame Masson watching my hand.

"What about in Germany? Do you think Germans support the idea of a Bolshevik revolution?" I asked, mostly to distract her from watching me as I pawed myself like a monkey.

"No," she declared with certainty.

"So you don't fear a Bolshevik revolution in Germany, but you fear the Germans will work for a Bolshevik revolution here, in France?" I asked.

"*Exactement!*" Préfet Raux exclaimed.

The serious Madame Masson glanced at Raux before continuing. I sensed she was both impatient with his interruption and disagreed with his statement. I was curious how she would respond.

"The opportunity for a Bolshevik revolution in Germany is gone," she said. "With the German military firmly siding with the government and the elimination of the Bavarian Soviet Republic in May, we believe there is no real chance of such a revolution in Germany. This does not mean that the German government and military will not use the threat of Bolshevism as a tool against France. It also does not mean that Germany genuinely wants a Bolshevik France. They want France weak and discredited with her allies, the British, and particularly the Americans. They are treading a fine line of pushing Bolshevik conspiracies in France while insisting that Bolshevism is a real threat in Germany. The first destabilizes Paris, and resisting the latter would require weapons and resources the Treaty of Versailles denies them. In short, the Germans are using the Red threat as an excuse to lobby for maintaining a strong military.

Your country and the British, so fearful of the Bolshevik threat, tend to believe their claims."

She paused, allowing me to absorb the information.

I sipped my coffee, considering her words.

"We want you to travel to Germany, to Berlin and the Rhineland," she continued. "We want you to see for yourself the reality on the ground. We want you to report back to Colonel House, who will report to your president."

"What if I find evidence the Reds may succeed in creating a revolution in Germany?"

"You will see that there is no evidence of such a revolution," Madame Masson assured me.

It was time to make the arguments against including me.

"I'm sorry, but your plan for me is flawed for at least two reasons," I began. "Colonel House is not as influential as you may hope. He is not currently on the best of terms with the president. Anything I tell him, even if he believed me, would likely fall on deaf ears when he tells the president." I felt no guilt about airing America's dirty laundry after being forced to sit through the unpleasantness of President and Mrs. Wilson's interaction with Colonel House, particularly if I could avoid the French mission.

"We will take that risk," Préfet Raux answered.

"Also, I don't speak German, I've never been to Germany, and I couldn't tell a German Bolshevik from a German Freikorps soldier." I knew I wasn't convincing, but I didn't think I'd persuade my marble-eyed audience in any event.

"I speak German fluently," answered Madame Masson. "And I can recognize both, I assure you. I will accompany you."

"That's a terrible idea," I exclaimed.

Madame Masson raised a graceful eyebrow at my objection.

"I'm not a spy," I continued. "I'm not trained. I'll put you at risk. Hell, I'll put me at risk. This is a silly plan."

With a slight smile on his face, Préfet Raux looked to Madame Masson to answer.

She smiled as well, and I found her smile disturbing. It made her even more attractive. I didn't like that.

"You are correct. You are not trained. This is good. The Germans suspect all things French. They look to Americans to soften any peace. We have crafted a story that fits your skills and your lack of espionage experience. You will be an American marine officer who has been directed by low-level functionaries in your department of state to examine the current condition of Germany: military, economic, political. They will not suspect you like they would a Frenchman or even Englishman conducting the same review. You will be a minor, unimportant player on a complex stage. You will not worry them," she answered confidently.

This was a disaster.

"The Germans will have American and French sources, just as you do with them," I declared with certainty. "They will know this story is false."

"No, the Germans won't. Colonel House has arranged this with your State Department and your army. You really will be working for the United States," Préfet Raux assured me. "You will be working for us as well. Allies. You will have the papers, et cetera, to support your bona fides."

House. That cunning son of a bitch! He knew this was all arranged. I could hear him saying to me *Help the French. You'll have our resources as well. I've made sure of it*. He knew all along. His plotting didn't change anything, but it made me feel used. House's final *God bless America* echoed it my head.

I had no good arguments left.

"Look, you're a married woman," I said to Madame Masson, "who would be traveling with a man who is not her husband. It's not proper. Surely you have people better suited for this than I am."

"You are perfect," Madame Masson assured me with the glint of humor in her eyes.

I shook my head. "It is not proper."

"We do what we must," Madame Masson said firmly.

"It is already settled. You will travel as husband and wife," Raux stated. "She has papers indicating that she is American. She has traveled extensively in your country and lived there. You said yourself she sounds like an American. She will be convincing as your American wife, and no one will pay much attention to an unimportant low-ranking officer or his wife. And you will be promoted. You will be a major in your marines. Madame Masson will direct you to the appropriate locations where you will see what France faces. And remember, everything we have discussed is confidential."

"I never wanted to be an officer, and I don't want to be one now," I said, hoping I kept the sullen anger I felt out of my voice.

"The paperwork is being completed as we speak. Your job is a simple one: assess the threat of a Bolshevik revolution in Germany and report your findings back to Colonel House. You must be a midlevel officer for this task. We will have uniforms made as well," Raux informed me. "You will be a marine major. You will impress the Germans but not too much. It is settled. *Compris?*"[14]

I was trapped. There was no benefit in pushing my objections to the point where Raux threatened my friends again. And if it helped prevent a future war, perhaps I would be doing something Sarah would want done.

"Yes, I understand."

"Congratulations on your promotion," Raux said.

"I am not fully recovered. I need a few more weeks," I said, ignoring his insincere felicitations. "And if you want us to pretend we are married," I said, turning to Madame Masson, "I probably ought to know your Christian name."

"Marie," she answered, this time smiling with a sweetness

and warmth that nearly convinced me she was looking forward to masquerading as my wife. Jesus Christ! No wonder she was a spy for France. She was a better actress than Mary Pickford.

"Marie," I repeated with a nod.

Grudgingly, Raux agreed to give me a few weeks more of recovery time. He said he would send a tailor to the hotel for my uniform measurements. Once time was up, I was to report at ten a.m. to an address in the ninth arrondissement: 10 rue Choron. I was to be packed, new uniforms and all, and ready to depart. They left shortly after with their mission accomplished. All I'd accomplished was to empty the coffee carafe.

I sat alone at the table, trying to comprehend my predicament. A few short weeks ago, I had been in love with a future that, if not clear, was at least brightening. Now I was a mercenary for the French. A mercenary was just what Patricia had called me at our first meeting. I had thought I was better than that. I was trying to rescue her after all. Now I didn't have that excuse. I was protecting my friends. Perhaps that was noble enough. I certainly wasn't a very good mercenary. I hadn't even thought to ask about the pay. The maître d' cautiously approached, and I assured him he could reopen the restaurant. Despite Raux's warning of secrecy, I needed to discuss the affair with Mitchell. He wouldn't be able to get me out of my German adventure, but he'd help me make some sense of the situation.

5

———————

Leather Bags

I left the restaurant and went directly to Patricia's suite. Mitchell had moved out of his room and into Patricia's while I was in the hospital. No point in paying for two rooms when they were only using one.

Mitchell answered my knock on the door.

"You look worse than you did in the hospital," he said. He smiled to take some of the sting out of his greeting.

I laughed. "Funny, I feel worse too."

"Come in. Trish is still asleep, but we can talk in the sitting room," he said, leading me into the suite.

"Late night?" I asked.

"Hell, it seems like every night is a late night. I'm not sure I have the stamina for this," he said jokingly.

"Well, speaking of stamina, I've got just a few weeks to improve mine," I answered. "In less than a month, I go to work for Raux. In Germany."

"Shit! I thought they wanted you to hunt Bolsheviks in Paris not Germany."

"Yeah, me too, but they don't want me to hunt Bolsheviks at

45

all. At least not directly. The French are cleverer than that. Raux certainly is. But Will, I've got to warn you: everything I'm going to tell you is secret. Raux made no bones about punishing me or anyone else I might tell of their plans for me."

"Then you'd better tell us both at the same time so I can pretend you only told William," Patricia said, standing in the bedroom doorway, wrapped in a thin robe.

She looked sleep tousled, but I couldn't prevent the lurch in my heart when I first saw her. She looked so much like Sarah. I pulled my eyes away from her as she curled herself gracefully against Will's side.

"The French see a German plot in everything. This doesn't mean they're wrong, but everywhere they look, they see Prussian militarism and threats to France. This is why Clemenceau refused to believe me when I told him his attackers were Bolsheviks. For him and for Raux, it doesn't matter. They are convinced the Germans are using the Bolsheviks as pawns to undermine France's security."

"What does that have to do with you though?" Patricia asked.

"They want to use my relationship with Colonel House to influence President Wilson, and through him, the Americans in Congress."

"Well, that sounds like a pretty stupid plan," Mitchell said, joking.

"Not really. They think I have House's ear. They think House has the president's ear, and they think the president can move American foreign policy. It is logical from their point of view, but they haven't seen House and the president up close like I have."

"What!" both Patricia and Mitchell exclaimed.

"Let me start from the beginning," I said, making calming motions with my hands. I explained my day up to that point, stressing the strained relationship between Colonel House and the Wilsons and Raux's misconception of that relationship. I mentioned in passing the need to work with a French agent. I also told them that House fully supported my working for the French.

"Tell us about the French spy," Patricia said.

That prompted me to cock my head at her, silently questioning her motives.

"Come on, Jack," Mitchell added. "You say more when you don't say anything. She's got to be interesting, or you would have said more about her. Omission is a classic Griffin sign of interest."

"Fine, but I don't know what you two are talking about," I said, ignoring the look they exchanged. "She's my age, I think, maybe a little older. Twenty-six, twenty-seven or so. Carries herself like she's older. She was married, but she's a widow now. She doesn't speak unless she has something relevant to say. She likes Raux well enough, but he might get on her nerves. She dresses conservatively, but that makes sense if she's trying not to stand out. She speaks excellent English and, apparently, German. She's smart, or at least sounds smart. I really don't know much more than that. We are supposed to travel together to Germany, with me masquerading as a Marine major and her as my wife." I realized as I said the last part that they would seize on it.

"Hah!" they exclaimed in unison.

"I didn't plan the damn mission," I said with some heat. "The French did."

"It'll be good for you, John," Patricia said sincerely. "This will divert you from thinking too much, and time and work are the best antidotes for a broken heart. And you should call Colonel House to let him know you are on the job and doing as he asked. The help he offered might come in handy."

"Tricia's right, Griff," Mitchell confirmed. "And this job really is just what the doctor ordered."

I didn't want to be cured. I wanted to wallow in my sorrow, goddamn it!

"I need to shape up over the next few weeks. I know the French think this is just a simple fact-finding mission, but I'm still weak as a kitten. I don't want to get killed because of it."

"I have the solution for that too," Mitchell assured me confidently.

THE NEXT MORNING, I TELEPHONED HOUSE AT THE CRILLON. HE wasn't available, and I spoke with Simms.

"Mr. Simms, let Colonel House know that, against my better judgment, I'll be going to Berlin in a few weeks for our damned French allies."

Simms laughed. "I'll let him know when you're going, and I'll tell him you're raring to go."

It was my turn to laugh. "Yeah, you tell him that. But you stay handy till I get back. It wouldn't surprise me if I need all the help you or Gordon can give me."

"I'll be here, and I know Gordon has been briefed. You can rely on me, Mr. Griffin, and good luck. I don't envy you that trip."

I rang off and hoped that I didn't need Gordon or Simms. Unfortunately, I was sure that my hope was in vain.

That afternoon, Mitchell arranged for us to meet Eugene Bullard for lunch. Eugene had been a boxer, among other things, before the war, and Mitchell wanted to team with Bullard to get me in "fighting" shape, as he called it.

"The best thing for you: exercise to exhaustion, eat right, and sleep. You'll be fit as a fiddle before you know it," Mitchell declared.

The weather was fair, and we had taken a table outside a café Eugene had recommended. Eugene had not yet arrived when the waiter appeared, and I tried to order a beer.

"No!" Mitchell intervened. "No beer, no alcohol at all. You're in training now!"

He ordered a beer for himself and a carafe of water for me.

"What the hell are you talking about?" I demanded as the waiter disappeared.

"You didn't drink beer in basic training, did you? Hell no! Milk and water, Griffin, milk and water. And castor oil. That's all you'll be drinking for the next few weeks," Mitchell said with glee. "Good thing you were in the hospital for a few weeks where you couldn't drink at all. Shouldn't be as bad weaning yourself off your evil habits," he said seriously as he lit a cigarette. "And no coffee," he added, almost as an afterthought.

"You're kidding. Really. No drinks, no coffee?"

"You could smoke, 'cause it's good for you," he said cruelly, "but I know the doc told you not to. That makes no sense to me. It's clearly good for your lungs, but I suppose you'll follow the doctor's advice on that one."

I saw Gene Bullard crossing the street toward the café. He was arriving just in time to save me from Mitchell's zeal.

"Gene, get over here," I called. "You've got to help me."

Bullard pulled up a chair and sat, waiting for my explanation.

"Eugene," Mitchell began before I could speak. "John is about to go on a mission, very secret, by the way. For the French. We need him to be fit, but you can see how pathetic he looks now. We need to strengthen him up. I was laying down the rules for what he can drink, and I hadn't gotten to what he can eat yet, but you, as a former boxer, will be able to help me. He's being hardheaded and won't take good advice."

"First tell me about this mission," Bullard instructed.

"Gene, the most important thing to know is that the mission is secret," I said, giving Mitchell a stern glance that bounced off him. "You should also know that Préfet Raux, the man running it, will toss all of us into a very dark hole if he learns we're talking about it."

"This is France, John. Chances are good everybody he doesn't want to know already knows," Bullard assured me. "So tell me about it."

And I did. I explained the French plan and their desire to use me as a conduit to the American president, which impressed Bullard. I also told him about the French spy.

"You met Wilson?" he asked.

"And his wife," I answered. "I wasn't all that taken with either one of them."

"But the French would be. The fact that you met with them is persuasive, and believe me, the French know you met them," said Bullard.

"Too true. Raux believes I can influence the president," I said.

"And this French spy, is she pretty?" Bullard asked with a gleam in his eye.

"She is, but that's not the point."

"*Au contraire*, Monsieur Griffin. That is the most important point. Everything Mitchell has said, I agree with," he said, smiling.

"But you haven't even heard what he's said. It's crazy stuff. No alcohol. Milk and water only. It sounds like the brig."

"I don't need to know what he's said. I know you. Trouble will find you. There's a bunch of folks out there, somewhere, that you'll end up killing. And we want it that way. We don't want it the other way around. So you need to be fit, John. Between Mitchell and me, we'll get you healthy, which will keep you alive. How long do we have?" he asked Mitchell.

"Damn it, Gene! You can't be serious," I scoffed.

"A few weeks," Mitchell supplied.

"Barely enough time," Bullard judged. "Mitchell's right. No alcohol. For you, Prohibition has come to France, my friend. I'm sorry, but it will make it easier to get Mitchell and the girls back to their hotels with at least one sober chaperone."

Both men shared a laugh.

"Steaks. You need to eat steaks. Just like the old Jack London story,"[1] Mitchell added.

"About the boxer," Bullard volunteered.

"Exactly," Mitchell confirmed. "You need meat to get strong, Griffin. And eggs," he added.

Bullard ordered a beer from the passing waiter.

"Now you're just being cruel," I told him.

"Can you get us some castor oil, Gene?" Mitchell asked, indifferent to my complaints. Mitchell's evil streak threatened to make my life so miserable that I would welcome reporting to rue Choron.

"Sure. No problem. What about training? Have you talked about that? I have some firm ideas about physical training. I've trained with some of the best. Hell, I can help train you in the afternoons," Bullard generously offered.

"Excellent!" Mitchell was ecstatic that he had found an ally in Bullard.

"I think you gentlemen are taking this much too seriously," I said. "I just need some rest, and I'll be fine. How's Henry?"[2] I asked, hoping to change the subject. Henry Johnson was a US Army veteran who'd helped us fight the Bolsheviks in Garches. He was a war hero to the French, winning the Croix de Guerre, but for the American Army, he was just another colored. Good to work as a stevedore or a ditch-digger but not so good as a combat soldier. I had found that I liked him. Together with Gene, Henry Johnson had forced me to reconsider my views of blacks. If I ever got back to the States, I planned to judge men on what they did and not what they looked like, but I knew it would be easy to fall back into my old ignorant way of thinking in my lily-white world there.

"He's gone home," Bullard said as his beer arrived and

Mitchell ordered another. "I'd hoped he'd stay, but his health really isn't good."

"It's a shame. He'd tell you both that to recover from wounds, I just need some rest."

"That's nonsense, Griffin," Mitchell declared sharply. "The way the French have set this up, I can't go with you. But if I can't go, I can make sure you're prepared. Gene, we start tomorrow. Tell me where, and I'll have Griffin there ready to train."

"Let me find a place. I'll set it up and let you know. Let's meet at two o'clock. We'll make a real fighting hall. It might cost a few francs to set it up the way I want, but I think I'll be able to make some money out of this." Bullard was positively bubbling as he considered the possibilities.

"Here." Mitchell held out a handful of francs to Bullard. "I'll be your first investor. If you need more, let me know, and I'll steal it from Griffin. We don't have much time."

Bullard quaffed the remainder of his beer. "Work to do," he said, setting down his empty glass. "*Á demain, messieurs.*"[3] Bullard took the money and hurried off. He clearly couldn't wait to get started on the gymnasium.

I felt a certain amount of trepidation at being trained, even if just for a short time, by a former professional boxer, friend or not. While my wounds were closed, they still pained me, and I was stiff and slow.

"What's to keep me from drinking when you're not around, Doc?" I challenged.

"Your good conscience. I'm doing this for your own good."

I drank my water and then folded my arms across my chest. I was annoyed with Mitchell and Bullard both. I knew they had my best interests at heart, but the coming weeks promised misery, followed by the misery of grubbing after signs of Bolshevism in Germany.

"I don't expect you out at night either," Mitchell declared as he lit another cigarette. "Rest, red meat, and training. We don't have much time, and time is precious."

THE NEXT DAY MITCHELL AND BULLARD'S THREATS BECAME reality. After forcing me to eat a hearty breakfast of scrambled eggs and toast, chased with hot chocolate, Mitchell walked me down along the river. "Gentle exercise this morning to prepare for this afternoon," Mitchell said happily.

With his passion to train me, I was seeing more of Mitchell than I had before Sarah's death. Our relationship had returned to what it had been during the war. I was still a wreck emotionally and physically, and I very much needed his company and his friendship. If his attention to my fitness was the price, I was willing to pay it. It occurred to me that his focus might be the result of boredom. Even for Mitchell, drinking, dancing, parties, and Patricia might not be enough for weeks on end. I wondered if his relationship with Patricia would last. Perhaps his boredom was a sign that he was tiring of her. I hoped so. She was a murderer, and while she might love William Mitchell, I was convinced she was too cold-blooded to remain with him.

My hopes that he might be bored with Patricia were dashed when he arranged for us to meet her for lunch. Once there, Mitchell ordered a rare entrecôte steak for me without even a glance. As we ate, the two of them drank champagne and laughed as they discussed my future. Despite their apparent joint joy at my predicament, I enjoyed lunch, even without champagne. As it ended, Mitchell told me he would collect me shortly for the walk to Eugene's gymnasium.

"Dress in comfortable clothes that you don't mind getting dirty," he said as we parted after lunch.

After meeting with Raux's tailor, who was very efficient in

taking my measurements, I left the hotel with Mitchell to face my first test at Eugene's gymnasium. The weather cooperated as Mitchell led me north away from our hotel.

"Gene found a place in Pigalle. Not the best neighborhood, but he thinks it will work," Mitchell promised.

I didn't have any doubt that Bullard would find a place where he could train me.

Mitchell timed our walk well. We turned down rue Mansart just before two o'clock, and Mitchell knocked on the door of number 15 on the hour.[4]

Gene answered. He was beaming. "This is gonna be great. I don't have all the equipment yet, but I have enough to get started, and more is coming by the end of the week. Come in, come in!"

We entered and found a large open room with a rug rolled out on the stone floor and a large leather punching bag leaning against one wall.

"Can you jump rope, John?" Bullard asked.

"Of course I can jump rope, but why would I want to?"

Gene walked to a low table and picked up a jump rope. "For your lungs," he said, and then, despite his game leg, he put on a display of rope jumping that would not have been out of place in a circus. Fast, crossovers, backward, forward.

"This will be your warm-up. Every day. Ten minutes. Well, working up to ten minutes. Get started," he ordered.

"Eugene, I've got to warn you. I inhaled gas at some point. I can't promise my wind will be very good."

"Well, I can promise you it will be better when I'm done with you," he said without sympathy.

I wasn't sure why he thought I would need to work up to ten minutes until I started jumping. After about two minutes, I tried to take a break, and both Mitchell and Bullard shouted at me to keep jumping. As I jumped, they were discussing the layout and equipment of the "athletic club," as they were calling it. After a few more minutes, I stopped. I was winded, and the impact of landing after each jump was painful, especially in my chest. My lungs labored trying to bring in enough air.

"As I said, you'll work up to ten minutes. Now a little shadowboxing," Bullard declared. He showed me a series of three punch combinations he wanted me to mirror. "Repeat these until I tell you to stop. The form matters, Griffin."

He proceeded to show me exactly how he wanted me to move. I found the repetition and focus on form exhausting. It didn't help that I was breathing like a bellows.

I peeled off my now soaking shirt, leaving me in my equally soaked undershirt.

"Let's toss the medicine ball now," Bullard said happily.

Bullard's imagination was endless. Push-ups, sit-ups, which were impossibly painful, ducking and dodging his slow punches. Crawling, jumping, stretching. We finished with "light" sparring, as Gene called it. It was all I feared it would be, and Mitchell was glowing with happiness as I finished.

"Not bad for the first day," Bullard advised me as I pulled on my shirt. "You might want more comfortable clothes though."

"And shoes," I groused.

"We'll speed up the sparring as we go. We need to work on stretching more as well. You need it."

"I might want to go back to the damn hospital," I retorted, which brought a laugh from both men.

Escorted by Mitchell, I stumbled back to the hotel, took a bath, and fell into bed.

<hr>

AFTER THE WORKOUT THE NEXT DAY, BULLARD DECREED THAT I needed a day of rest. I wasn't going to argue. I was happy to find myself with a free afternoon and equally happy to have no painful exercise for at least one day. But as it got later in the afternoon, I was restless and went for a walk. Paris was preparing for the Bastille Day parade, which would be the first since the war ended. Judging by the activity in the city, the Parisians and Clemenceau's government were taking the event seriously.

My feet took me south of the Seine. When I finally focused on where I was, I found myself across the street from Café de Flore, where I had appealed to Gavin to give up his mad scheme and to take Sarah home to England. I went in for a cup of coffee. As I entered, I saw the older Spanish woman Gavin had been speaking with when I had originally found him at the café all those weeks ago.

I felt an urge to speak with her. To find out what she knew of Gavin. To understand him a little better.

She glanced up from her coffee as I approached her table, and her eyes widened in recognition.

"*Puis-je me joindre à vous pour un instant?*"[5] I asked.

"Please do. You knew Gavin. The last time I saw him you were speaking with him. At the table in the back. I saw you," she explained in slightly accented English.

"Yes, ma'am. My name is John Griffin. I knew Gavin through his wife and father-in-law."

She nodded. "I am Eugenia Errázuriz."[6] She did not offer her hand.

I pulled out a chair and asked her if I could order her anything. She shook her head.

"You frightened Gavin," she told me. "Why did you frighten him?" She was intelligent and had no reason to be civil.

"Madame Errázuriz, I have some painful news. Gavin passed away a few weeks ago."

"Yes. I know. Did you kill him?"

"No, ma'am." I studied her for a moment. "Did you know that he was a Bolshevik?"

"I do not care about his politics. I do not care about politics. I love art. He loves... loved art. The day I saw you, we were speaking about art with our friend Pablo. Gavin wanted to collect, but he wanted to do so in a way that would benefit the artist. He wanted to sponsor artists, as I do. Pablo was encouraging him."

"He had just married a very wealthy young woman, and while I suppose he could have afforded to sponsor an artist or two, he was instead trying to sponsor a Bolshevik revolution and a continuation of the war," I said unkindly.

She looked at me coldly. "You are the type of man that caused all the pain the world has suffered these past four years. Please take yourself elsewhere."

And I did.

***

MY DAYS QUICKLY RAN TOGETHER AS MITCHELL AND BULLARD established a pattern that differed only in the exercises Bullard demanded of me. I spent two hours a day at the gym. Gene added bars of various heights, and by the end of the first week, he had hung the heavy punching bag and added a speed bag and a "double-end" bag to the rue Mansart hall. After each workout, he would have me sit in a cold hydrotherapy bath, which he also added. As the training progressed, the dread of my hours at the athletic club with Bullard lessened a bit.

It was then that he introduced me to Georges Carpentier.[7] Georges was a renowned French boxer who had fought for and won various world boxing titles. Carpentier had known Gene as a pilot during the war, and Gene had invited him to the club to get his opinion about future improvements to the gym.

"He's not just a great boxer," Eugene explained in introducing Georges. "He is a world champion savateur."

"I mean no offense, Georges," I responded. "But what the hell is a savateur?"

"It is an old ruffian's art that uses kicking and other methods. But not your Anglo-Saxon fisticuffs. No punching. Combined with boxing, it can be devastating," Georges answered with conviction. "I will teach you. May I train here a few days per week, Jacques?" Carpentier asked Gene. I recalled that Bullard's French friends called him "Jacques."

"Of course, Georges."

***

With Carpentier training at the athletic hall with me, I found myself pressed to work harder. My fitness improved as did my martial prowess with hands and feet, which delighted Mitchell.

"You kick like a little girl." He would laugh, and I would invite him to experience my kicks firsthand in the "ring" that Bullard had created as a centerpiece of the hall. Mitchell would only laugh and wave me off. In truth, I wasn't sure I could lay a glove or a foot on Mitchell, and I certainly couldn't on Georges Carpentier. When I sparred with the elusive Frenchman, my punches would miss his bobbing head, and I learned quickly the wisdom in doing my best to avoid his thunderous punches, which he certainly pulled. Even with Carpentier's consideration, he still rang my bell time and again when I stupidly stepped into his punches. These instances also entertained Mitchell, who would provide sage advice like "don't do that," or "you're gonna get hurt if you don't keep your hands up." Helpful.

Despite Mitchell's abuse, I was stronger than I'd had any hope of being just a few weeks before. The grueling training would soon end. But there was no light at the end of the tunnel, only a trip to Germany, spying for the French.

                                   6
                               ———————

Pandora's Box

With the improvement of my health and stamina, I went
back out into the Parisian night. Mitchell relaxed his
injunction on alcohol, but I found that I drank less.

The first night I went out, Patricia insisted we go to the
opera. I was sure she wanted to distract me and provide some
cultural education for William. Unfortunately, the opera she
chose was *Madama Butterfly*. It was by Puccini she told us. She
did not tell us it was a tragedy, but I should have guessed this. It
was an opera after all. From the start, I loathed the American
Navy lieutenant, Pinkerton, and feared for the geisha, Kiku-san
—rightly, as it turns out. Lies, betrayal, blind loyalty, love, and
suicide. All too close to home for me.

As we left the Palais Garnier, I thanked Patricia and told
them both that I needed a little air after the crowd of the opera
house. I stood on the opera steps as they climbed into a motor
taxi with concerned looks on their faces.

"Join us at the Majestic, Griff," Mitchell called to me as he
shut the motorcar door.

I nodded and waved. The English peace delegation

continued to hold wild parties at the Hotel Majestic. Delegates and their wives, daughters, secretaries, and prostitutes, along with generals and the generals' and delegates' minions, all dancing and drinking until the sky turned pink. I would not go that night.

That was the night I discovered that, when drunk, I only thought of the dead. I walked until I found an undistinguished, uncrowded bar. I sat alone at a table and proceeded to drink like it was my job. The purpose in getting blotto was to forget, but that failed. Instead, I remembered. Sarah, Merchant, Gavin, even poor Yvette, the revolutionary I'd never met until I shot her dead in the street in front of Clemenceau's home. From the cottage in Surrey and the streets of Paris to the mud of Flanders and the shattered trees of the Argonne forest, so many dead for no good purpose. The peace was flawed, and I feared it couldn't last. I didn't remember the trip back to the Vendôme.

After that first night, I kept to the company of the American girls and, at times, Kiki. Fewer and less frequent drinks kept me sober as Madeline and Rachel enjoyed the new modern freedom of the Parisian nightlife. I accompanied them to Kiki's cabaret, Eugene's club, or to Le Dôme. They were attractive, witty, energetic women, who did all they could to keep me from moping. They'd pull me up to dance. They'd ask my opinion as they introduced me to partygoers, including artists and writers, whose names I couldn't recall. I was sure I was poor company for them, but they continued to allow me to join them night after night.

When I went out with Madeline and Rachel, Patricia and Will did not go. The girls did not like Patricia.

The nights out with the two American girls were a welcome distraction from my thoughts. They drew men like flies, and I was their shepherd of sorts. They used me as a buffer against men they weren't interested in and as a foil for their jokes for the men they were. My formal role was that of big brother, but I could feel an attraction to Madeline always there. We'd catch each other's eyes, share a small smile, and then the whirlwind of the Parisian night would swirl us apart.

I felt disloyal to Sarah for my attraction, and I raised my guilty conscience with Mitchell as we walked to the athletic club one afternoon.

"So let me understand the problem precisely," he said in his most pedantic tone. "You believe Madeline is attracted to you, and you feel badly that you are attracted to Madeline. Correct?"

"Not precisely," I said, unwilling to entirely agree with him. "I don't know if Madeline is attracted to me. But I feel like I am betraying Sarah somehow just by being attracted to Madeline."

Mitchell stopped walking and turned to face me. "You're an imbecile!"

"That's your medical opinion, is it?"

"It's not a medical opinion. It's a goddamn fact. We've all carefully avoided the topic of Sarah because you've been so damn weepy about her," Mitchell began.

I could feel myself getting angry.

"We've walked on eggshells because we knew you were hurting. But let's be clear, Griffin; she didn't choose you. You gave her a choice. You tried to save her. You gave her a choice," he repeated to make sure that I heard him. "And she made her choice. She chose a dead James Willoughby. Not you!" he said brutally. "I'm sorry, but she didn't choose you."

He stopped speaking, waiting for my explosion on the Paris sidewalk. Indifferent pedestrians streamed by us as I stood without moving, struggling with Mitchell's statement. I couldn't speak. I heard his words. I heard their truth, but I couldn't accept it. I loved her. She loved me. She said so. Why *didn't* she choose me over death?

"And I'm sorry she didn't choose you," he said sadly. "I liked her. She made you happy, but you were competing against a dead man. And she had already moved to a place where only revenge and death waited. And she moved there before you ever knocked on her cottage door. There was nothing you could have done to change that."

Mitchell was right. I was unpleasant company, and I was choosing to believe in a lie. A lie that Sarah and I could have been happy together. We would never have been happy together. She was not happy, and I was not going to make her happy. You can't make someone happy. They have to do that themselves. I had to get over it. I wasn't sure I knew how, but I did know that I had to stop parading my misery for all to see. It was embarrassing.

I pushed my hands into my pockets, turned, and continued the walk toward Gene's club.

"You're right. She didn't choose me. And she wasn't ever going to," I said.

He walked alongside me without speaking, but I knew that couldn't last.

"Go out with Madeline tonight. Have a good time. It doesn't have to be forever. Hell, I remember a guy, not too long ago, who couldn't see past sunrise the next day. Be that guy again."

"Sure, I'll try that," I said.

Mitchell laughed, hearing the uncertainty in my voice.

"Come on, Griffin. It's not that hard. Just stop thinking so goddamn much. It's not like you're very good at it anyway."

That night, I followed Mitchell's advice. I met Madeline at Le Dôme. It was a fine evening, and we sat on the terrace. As we waited for Rachel and Kiki to appear, Madeline drank French seventy-fives and I sipped a beer. As I would start to feel guilty, I would recognize it and then forcibly banish the thought with meaningless conversation about the weather, the treaty, or other patrons. I was surprised at how often the feeling came. Guilt and remorse had become a habit. I had a lot of work to do to break the habit.

I laughed and shook my head.

"Are you okay, John?" Madeline asked with concern.

Despite Mitchell's injunction about thinking, I thought about Madeline's question.

"Yes and no, Madeline, yes and no." I decided to try honesty to see what would happen. I had nothing to lose. In a few days, I would be steaming north on a train bound for Germany.

"You and I haven't talked about it, but I'm sure you've talked about Sarah Willoughby and her death with some of the others."

She nodded and looked painfully uncomfortable.

"It's okay. I'm not gonna cry," I said with a smile as I thought about crying. "And I know you don't want to be out on the town with some sad excuse for a man with tears on his cheeks."

My reassurance didn't seem to help, but I pushed ahead.

"Look, I fell for Sarah. Hard. And her death hit me hard. Harder than any of the other deaths during the war, and there were plenty. And now I feel guilty. Every time I feel the slightest pleasure, I feel like I shouldn't. My heart keeps telling me that, with her gone, there should be no joy in the world. And just so you know, I know that's bullshit. Doc Mitchell made sure to tell me that. So I have to keep reminding myself that it's okay to have fun. I wanted you to know I'm trying. I'm getting better. And I know it's okay to sit outside with a pretty girl at a Parisian café in the summertime."

"Just a pretty girl?" she said with a raised eyebrow.

"Well, stunning or gorgeous seems excessive."

She smacked me on the shoulder with her fist. Hard.

"Okay fine!" I laughed. "You're easily stunning. And bordering on gorgeous. But you are also warm and intelligent and wickedly funny. Which makes you just about perfect," I said with more honesty than I intended.

"Why, John Griffin," she said, beaming, "if I didn't know better, I'd say you're flirting with me. And it's about damn time."

"All right, maybe not intelligent," I said, earning another shot to the arm. "Madeline, I can't say I won't fade out now and then, but I really do enjoy spending time with you."

She leaned across the small table, grabbed my chin with her punching hand, and gave me a soft, lingering kiss.

"What the hell is going on?" Rachel Eisen demanded as she arrived at our table.

"You're late, and I was curious, so I decided to kiss John."

I shrugged and nodded at Madeline's admission. "Pretty daring of her, really," I said.

"So Mr. Misty-eyes is gone?" Rachel asked.

"Look, I'm sorry. I apologized to Madeline, and I should apologize to you too. I've been terrible company, and the two of you, and Kiki, have been putting up with me, and I appreciate it. It means a lot to me."

"Do I get a kiss as well?" she asked.

"Of course," I answered, hearing a low growl from Madeline as I leaned in and gave Rachel a chaste peck on the lips.

"Jeez, it's like kissing my brother."

"That's exactly what Madeline said." I grinned, and both girls laughed.

"Kiki's on her way. Tonight we go to Zelli's and dance till we have blisters on our feet," Rachel commanded.

"My God, I hope Walt's there," I groaned.

As we finished our second round of drinks, Kiki arrived bearing gifts.

"I know, Johnny. I know you have been down," she said with a sad smile, "and I have a friend who has given me some medicine for you. It will bring you up and make you smile again."

"Kiki, I have just told the ladies that I know I haven't been great company, but I'm working on being better. I'm sure I don't need any medicine."

"And Madeline kissed him," Rachel added unnecessarily.

Her comment added a gleam to Kiki's already shining eyes.

"Excellent," Kiki responded. "My cocaine will also help your recovery, and I think you should kiss Madeline more." She giggled at her play on Madeline's last name.

I rolled my eyes, but I could feel Madeline watching me. So I met her gaze and said, "I'd like that, but I'm not sure about this cocaine thing. Isn't that illegal?"

"Perhaps, but legal, not legal, *non pertinent.*[1]" Kiki shrugged. "You need a lift to your mood for you to recover, and this will help."

"I thought drugs like cocaine were part of a German plot during the war to undermine France's fighting spirit," I said, trying to avoid the drug.

"*Absurdité,*" she answered. "With this in your veins, you would fight like a lion, and you will want to do more than fight. You will want to make love, most energetically." She glanced at Madeline and then gave me her best Cheshire cat smile.

"This is an awful idea," I said, looking at Madeline and then Rachel for support.

"Oh, don't be such a stick-in-the-mud, Griffin," Rachel said. "It's fine that you recognize how morose you've been, but for tonight at least, this will give you a kick in the pants. A good shove down the path to recovery." Turning to Kiki, she stated formally, "We will be happy to join you in your spiral into decadence."

Kiki clapped her hands. She opened her handbag and took out a small glass vial. She then removed her crucifix necklace, which had been nestled between her breasts. She handed the necklace to Rachel as she unscrewed the tiny cap to the vial. She took the crucifix back from Rachel, and I could see that the end of the necklace was fashioned as a miniature spoon.

"Now watch carefully, John." She dipped the spoon into the vial and brought out a tiny mound of white powder. She then delicately leaned down, closing one nostril with her thumb as she held the vial, and sniffed the powder off the spoon. She leaned back, lowering the now empty spoon and sniffed again, her eyes watering. She smiled at me.

She handed the vial and her necklace around the table, first to Rachel and then to Madeline, who raised an eyebrow at me just before bending down to the spoon.

"And now the evening truly begins," Kiki proclaimed with glee.

Not a single café patron's head turned at their actions.

Madeline handed me the vial and the necklace.

I was certain I was making a mistake as I mimicked Kiki's actions. To say I felt silly feeding my right nostril with a tiny spoon would be an understatement, but God help me, I did it. I had been a miserable shadow of myself since the events at the apartment off rue Franklin. I owed the girls at least the attempt to have fun. As I sniffed the drug off the spoon, I felt a burn up the right side of my sinuses. My eyes watered as well. I shook my head and felt my heart kick over.

"I have a syringe, but that is too quick for tonight. This will last longer as we laugh and dance," Kiki declared as she packed up the vial and dropped her necklace back over her head, but not before giving the tiny spoon a dainty lick.

"You're never getting me to use a syringe, Kiki," I said as I felt a sense of euphoria building under my heart.

"*Bien,*" she answered. "As I said, this way will last longer, and we have many grams for tonight."

Kiki was absolutely correct in her pronouncement that the party really began with her opening of the vial. It was a small glass Pandora's box. We drank, laughed, and inhaled more of the little spoons of powder.

We moved from Le Dôme to Zelli's club where Gene was

playing drums that night. We danced and drank some more. Even though we had skipped dinner, we never considered eating. Kiki seemed to have an endless supply of the powder.

The drug made me talkative and aggressive. It certainly elevated my mood, and it gave me no option but to engage with the girls, particularly Madeline. I did find that after twenty or so minutes, the rush associated with taking a spoon of cocaine would wane, but, inevitably, Kiki, with singular timing, fished the little vial from her bag, and the cycle would begin again.

As the partying crowd swirled around us, my link with Madeline became more obvious. We both knew that when we left the club, we would leave together. And we did. One last goodbye spoonful with Rachel and Kiki. With hugs, giggles, and kisses, Madeline and I left arm in arm for the short walk to the Vendôme.

Despite being drunk, I was nervous. I felt like a boy on his first date. I supposed it was my first date since Sarah. The cocaine didn't help since it made my heart thud like a jackhammer.

"Are you sure about this, John?" Madeline asked, sensing my nerves.

"Hell, Madeline, I'm not sure about much of anything with all of Kiki's cocaine inside me. But I am sure about this."

I pulled her to me and kissed her. She smelled good: a hint of perfume, cigarettes, and wine, and something uniquely female. She wrapped her arms around me and kissed me back. I leaned her back against an apartment building entryway. We accidentally pressed the electric doorbell, and we could hear it buzzing inside. We broke apart laughing and stumbled down the street as lights flickered on in the building.

When we got to my room at the Vendôme, we didn't talk. We fumbled with each other's clothes, chuckling, kissing, exploring. There was a bleary-eyed madness to it all that created gaps in my memory, but I do remember we didn't sleep much. As the sun came up, I tried to doze with Madeline curled against me. Every time I closed my eyes, images would flicker against my eyelids and jumbled thoughts would bounce around in my head. I pulled Madeline tight against me as if she could purge the cocaine and death hangover from my blood.

———

Madeline left after a late room service brunch. We made plans to see each other that evening. I found myself looking forward to it, but I was also worried that I'd started something I wasn't ready for. I was not looking forward to the session at Gene's athletic club. As usual, I met Mitchell in the lobby, and we walked to the club.

"Good night?" he asked innocently.

"Yes, Doc, it was a good night."

He nodded knowingly.

"But it was a hell of a night too. Kiki showed up with cocaine, and I'm feeling kinda fragile right now," I elaborated.

"Hell, Griff, Kiki got you to inject cocaine?" he said with alarm. "That stuff is dangerous. Smoking opium is much better for the spirit, but you have to be careful to manage your use or you become an addict. Cocaine just creates endless desire for more. As your doctor, I suggest you stop using it."

"Thanks for the advice, Dr. Mitchell, but I've only used it last night, and we didn't inject it. We sniffed it off a little spoon at the end of Kiki's crucifix."

"I remember that crucifix," Mitchell said fondly.

"I'll bet you do. I think I might need to skip training today," I said, changing the subject to one more immediate and important. "I'm feeling poorly."

"Oh no you don't! You're training. You never know when a crazy German Bolshevik might come for you. You fight when there's a fight, not when you're ready for a fight."

When we got to the gymnasium, Gene met me with a grin.

"Oh, my pale friend." He chortled. "I watched you and the young ladies last night. I'm surprised you're even here. Kiki had the three of you filled to the stuffings with cocaine. Was it worth it?" he asked.

I gave him a murderous glare, which left him unbothered. He handed me the jump rope.

"Time to start your penance. Only a few days left until you leave," he told me.

I should have died in those two hours. Gene and Mitchell would not let me slow down or slack off. The only blessing was Carpentier was not there for me to spar. It was a miracle I didn't black out or vomit or both. Gene and Will enjoyed themselves immensely.

The few days that followed before my departure saw me spending the afternoons with Mitchell, Bullard, and Carpentier and my evenings with Madeline. The night out with Kiki, Madeline, and Rachel had been so intense and excessive that I had no intention of repeating it. I would meet all three women for drinks early in the evening, and then I would steal Madeline away before the party migrated to Zelli's club or another venue where things could get out of control. Kiki kept her necklace around her neck and her vial in her purse. She would smirk at me as I dragged Madeline away. She completely understood that I was avoiding any repeat of that cocaine-fueled night, and she also knew exactly how hard it was to flee. I suspected she was just patiently waiting for a repeat, but it was not to come.

On the day before my departure, I was having breakfast alone at the hotel when Préfet Raux came into the dining room. The maître d' recognized him from his previous visit, and he started to flutter around Raux, hoping to prevent him from closing the restaurant. Raux shooed him away and came directly to my table uninvited.

"I will not stay long. I know you leave tomorrow."

"I do."

"I came only to say that you must be careful."

"That is not particularly helpful advice."

He gave a small smile. "I am sure your task in Germany has many layers, Monsieur Griffin. You and I, we have only discussed the top layer."

"Then tell me about the others."

"I cannot. I am not sure they exist, but I fear that they do. You must discover the layers beneath for yourself and for France. It is these that are likely the most important. Be careful," he said again.

"It sounds like you think my *simple* mission will be dangerous." I remembered his claim at the Vendôme that the job was simple.

He shrugged. "Perhaps that is because it is," he said ominously.

He stood and offered me his hand, which I took.

"*Bonne chance,*"[2] he said, and he was gone.

<hr>

THE MORNING OF MY REPORTING DATE, MADELINE SAT IN MY BED at the Vendôme and watched me pack. My new uniforms had arrived the day before, an unwelcome reminder of my task. I had opened the suitcase in which they'd come and examined them to assure myself I wouldn't look like a fraud. The uniforms were beautifully cut, and the French had placed all the insignia correctly, from the anchor and globe on the collar to the ribbons over the left pocket. I'd examined the Second Division sleeve insignia on the left shoulder: an Indian head inside a white star on a red square field. They even got my battalion right. I was both reassured and disturbed by the French attention to detail. They knew what they were doing, and I did not.

As Raux had promised, I was indeed promoted to the rank of

major for this trip. I repacked all but one uniform, which I wore. I had my Colt pushed in the holster hanging from the polished Sam Browne belt. I guessed the French would want me to be conspicuous as Madame Masson and I traveled.

I separated out the German MP-18 machine pistols and the broomhandle Mauser pistol that I'd taken from the dead Bolsheviks during the hunt for Gavin. I wrapped them in a hotel bathrobe identical to the one Madeline was wearing. I'd tell Mitchell to move them to his room for safekeeping. There was no way I was going to bring them to Germany. I just hoped I had no cause to collect more weapons.

Madeline watched me silently. No tears. No emotion. Just acceptance.

I thought of my mother watching my father pack for deployment. The one time I really remembered he was going to some godforsaken place we were invading... Nicaragua, Haiti, I wasn't sure. But he was packing again. Leaving again, and my mother quietly watched just like Madeline was.

"You would make a great Army wife, Madeline." I made the compliment without thinking about the words. Really, *wife*. Wives were created one way: marriage. Now Madeline would think I was thinking about marriage, or now she would be. What a moron.

"Oh yeah, why's that?" she asked lightly.

"You look like my mom when she watched my dad put on his uniform and pack to leave. He left a lot it seemed like. As he got ready, she'd sit quietly just like you are. She never made it hard."

"So while she watched your dad get ready to march away, your mom would sit on their bed, wearing nothing but a bathrobe? I'll bet that made it pretty hard," she said with a smirk.

I barked out a laugh. "I guess it would have. And does. I take it back. You are way too sly to be a good Army wife."

I finished buckling my new suitcase filled with my new clothes delivered by Préfet Raux's people.

"Maddy, I don't know how long I'll be gone or how long all this will take." I picked the suitcase up and put it on the floor by the door. I turned back to her. "You mean a lot to me. But don't wait. I don't know if I'll be back."

I wasn't trying to give her the brush-off. I was trying to tell her that I cared about her, but I didn't know what the future would bring. I wanted her to be free to choose her own future without worrying about waiting for me.

She frowned. "You're an idiot, Griffin. I'm a big girl. I'll do what I want. I'll be fine. Just take care of yourself. Try not to get shot, okay?"

I moved to the bed and sat next to her. I leaned over and kissed her, cupping her face in my hand. I found myself thinking about her body under the robe.

I stood. "You take care of yourself too, Madeline. I hope I see you soon."

She smiled. "See you soon, John."

I picked up my suitcase and left the hotel room, gently closing the door behind me while still thinking about the girl wrapped in the bathrobe.

I *was* an idiot.

7

———————

Part of the Job

I took a taxicab to the address on rue Choron. The building, unremarkable by Parisian standards, had two heavy wood doors, each with horizontal polished brass rails set at waist height. There was no outside latch. An electric buzzer was fixed on the wall to the right of the doors with one button. I looked at my watch: 0955. I took a deep breath, slowly released it, and pressed the buzzer.

As I waited, passersby glanced at my uniform, my shadowed face under the marine officer cover, and looked away. They were tired of uniforms and war. Likely particularly tired of Americans in uniform.

The door opened. I couldn't see into the shadows, but I stepped in anyway.

As the door closed, I turned to find my greeter. Madame Masson. She wore an off-white, light traveling dress or what I assumed was a traveling dress. Not too modern but certainly not dated. As when I first met her, her hair was pinned up beneath a hat.

"Major Griffin. John," she said, correcting herself. "Welcome. Follow me please." She shut the door and immediately led me deeper into the building, which had an old, damp feel. We entered a small room with a gritty stone floor and spartan furnishings, only a desk with two wooden chairs and no window. Leaning against the desk was a heavyset man with a mustache, a square jaw, and a pipe clenched between his teeth. His hair was slicked back with oil.

"Commandant Ladoux,[1] please meet Major John Griffin of the United States Marine Corps," Marie said. I shook hands with Ladoux. "Commandant Ladoux is the head of the Central Intelligence Section, French counterintelligence. He will be overseeing this mission."

"My pleasure," Ladoux said and moved straight to business. "It is good you are in uniform. It is important for the Germans to see you as an official representative of the United States. They will try to convince you that Bolshevism is a risk, and we want you to hear these claims. But then use your eyes to see the truth. Bolshevism is an excuse for them to avoid the disarmament requirements of the treaty."

I nodded, as if in agreement, and said, "That's it? That's the mission? Go to Germany and listen to false claims of an impending Bolshevik revolution?"

I glanced at Masson, and she looked right back with no expression.

"Yes," Ladoux answered. "It is not complicated, but we are aware of your work for Colonel House and his for the president. We need someone they trust to see the truth about Germany."

I shrugged. "It sounds easy enough." I was thinking of the president's lack of trust in House and the unidentified danger Raux warned me of.

"It should be if you are careful and listen to Madame Masson."

"I can do that," I said.

"These are your papers. Your commission, promotion documents, American travel documents appropriate for a low-level officer on government business." He handed me a small stack of papers. "Préfet Raux has created an account in your name at Morgan, Harjes & Co. It is associated with the American bank, J.P. Morgan & Co. The amount promised you has already been deposited there. This is your banking information." He gave me a small bank book. He also handed me an unsealed envelope. "Cash," he explained. "Papiermarks and francs."

I didn't recall any promise of payment, but I wasn't going to argue. I'd find out what was in the account eventually.

"Madame Masson's documents?" I asked.

"In her care," Ladoux answered.

I turned to her. "While I'm sure you are used to carrying your own documents, it would not be normal for the wife of an American marine officer to do so." I couldn't resist demanding her papers. I felt the need to exercise what little control I had.

She opened her purse and passed me an oft-folded, well-used American passport. I didn't bother unfolding it. Her face was impassive. She was not bothered in the least by my pathetic effort to assert my dominance.

"This is your current itinerary," Ladoux said, handing me a folio. "Madame Masson will determine the hotels at each location. Only the Adlon in Berlin is reserved. We wanted you to have some flexibility."

I opened the folder and examined the schedule. Each city we were to visit was listed with arrival and departure information and a local contact. Only Berlin and Paris had hotels included.

"This has us staying in Paris tonight. I thought we were going right away."

"For you and Madame Masson, it is important that you

spend the day getting to know each other. Since you will be traveling as husband and wife, you need some interaction between you for your relationship to be"—he searched for the right word—"believable. You will be staying at Le Meurice on the rue de Rivoli tonight."

I glanced at the woman. I didn't like this development. I wanted to get started and get done.

"I will be going to Berlin tonight, quietly," Ladoux added. "France has no representative in Berlin, so I will go to help as needed. I will be incognito." He seemed to be amused by the use of the word. "America has a representative in Berlin. You will see him, of course, but he does not know any of the details of the mission. He only knows that a marine major is arriving in Berlin to assess the military situation."

"It seems simple enough," I said, flipping through the bank book.

"Do not be deceived. The Germans know of your mission. They may not know you report to Colonel House, but they know an American officer is coming to assess the risks of revolution. Your visit is official, after all. They will do what they can to convince you of the danger from the Bolsheviks. For that reason, it is possible that the itinerary will change as we learn additional information about their plans, Major," Ladoux said.

At his use of the rank, I had to suppress the urge to look around the room to see who he was addressing. I was the major. I needed to remember that.

I looked again at the list, my stomach tightening. We would leave Paris for Brussels, and after a brief stop in Berlin, we would go to Prussia. Königsberg, Prussia, for Christ's sake. I wasn't even sure where that was. We'd take the train to Berlin, fly to Königsberg and then back to Berlin. Then Leipzig, Munich, and back to France by train.

"Why Königsberg?" I asked.

Madame Masson gave a polite smile, as if she had expected the question.

"It is only four hundred and sixty kilometers, three hundred miles, from Minsk, Russia. We think it important to judge the mood of the officials there. We suspect that, despite the nearness of Russia, the Germans have no fear of Bolshevism, but you will see that for yourself," she answered.

"You sure you haven't already decided what we will find, madame?"

"I know what we will find, and you should call me Marie."

WE LEFT THE GRUBBY BUILDING IN AN AUTOCAB, WHICH TOOK US to the Le Meurice. It was a beautiful hotel. One I would have expected to find Patricia patronizing. Perhaps I'd recommend it to her when I returned from Germany. If I returned from Germany.

We checked into the hotel. Madame Masson had one large travel trunk and a smaller travel bag. Lighter packing than I expected. I noted that our room had only one bed. I was unsurprised, but this promised to be a sleepless trip if I was going to have to curl up on the hotel room floor everywhere we stopped.

We left our bags packed since we would be leaving in the morning. Then, at Madame Masson's insistence, we went touring. A hired motorcar arranged by the hotel concierge crisscrossed Paris to show us the sights.

After a long day, we stopped for afternoon refreshments. The café was one I didn't know, but then the whole neighborhood was new to me. We were near the Basilica of Sacré-Cœur, which we had just visited. The weather was fine, and we sat at a small round table outside.

I had to admit Marie Masson was easy company. During the

hours touring with her, I had seen more of Paris than during the weeks I'd spent hunting for Gavin Kingsbury. Even my time with Sarah had been confined to short walks around the Hôtel de Vendôme and the hotel itself. But then I'd been infatuated with Sarah and couldn't have cared less about touring Paris. With thoughts of Sarah, my interest in Paris, the French mission, and Marie Masson evaporated. She could sense the change. She was a spy, and sensing such things was probably critical to her survival.

"What is wrong?" she asked when she noticed my distraction.

"Despite being my wife, it is not your business." I smiled, hoping to ease the sting of the words. "Tell me about yourself. Tell me things a husband should know about his wife," I demanded, forcing a change in the conversation.

She watched me for a moment, considering whether to let her question go unanswered. She shrugged.

"I am from New York City. My parents have passed away, but my mother was German, from Cologne. That is why I speak German. I am an only child. I attended Vassar College in Poughkeepsie, New York, for one year before volunteering with the Red Cross in 1917. I met you while you were recovering from wounds in Paris. We married shortly after the armistice. My maiden name is Morton." Her delivery was well rehearsed and believable.

"Very convincing," I told her. "Now tell me about Marie Masson."

"You do not need to know Marie Masson."

"Perhaps not, but I wish to."

It was clear that she did not want to talk about her past any more than I wanted to talk about mine.

"You do not need to know me. In fact, it will be unhelpful to our task. I am your adoring wife. We are newly married. Focus on those facts. Those are what you need to believe. The story of

Marie Masson will not help you. As you have said to me, it is not your business."

I didn't like her answer. I didn't like that she threw my words back at me, and I didn't like my part in this French masquerade. I could not make her help me to know her better, but her insistence on staying in character depressed me. I was determined to force her from her role.

I reached across the table and seized her hand, pulling it to me and kissing the back.

"Well, my dearest, I am a lucky man to have my lovely wife with me. We will have to make the most of this trip."

I released her hand, and she drew it back. Without any hesitation, she smiled a newlywed's promise of glorious nights ahead.

"Yes. Yes, we will."

She was a much better actor than I was. I could only think of Gavin and Patricia on their doomed honeymoon, but I resolved to play the newlywed game well. We would not be found out because of any lack of ardor on my part, but when we returned to the hotel, I found I needed time alone. She likely expected me to follow her to our room, but instead, I went to the hotel bar. I had an hour or so before the car was to take us to dinner. Time for a drink or three.

Dinner was at a well-regarded restaurant, La Tour d'Argent,[2] which was across the Seine from Notre Dame on the Quai de la Tournelle. We had pressed duck, which was the house specialty. We were told that each duck, being unique, was numbered. The meal was delicious and very French with subtle sauces and excellent wine. Despite the artificial conversation with my fake wife, I enjoyed myself.

"Remind me that when we get to the room, I have a gift for you," she told me as she picked at the raspberry tart she'd ordered for dessert. She had matched me glass for glass in finishing the second bottle of Chateau Margaux. The wine was produced in 1914, the last prewar vintage, which seemed appropriate for the evening. Marie's cheeks were flushed, and her eyes reflected back the golden light from the candles that lit the restaurant.

"I will."

We left the restaurant arm in arm and walked along the Seine to meet the car in front of the Saint-Michel Fountain. It felt natural to have her close. We didn't speak on the ride back to the hotel.

When we entered our hotel room, she turned and kissed me. It was a lover's kiss. Like the kisses I'd shared with Sarah and Madeline. But we weren't lovers, and we had no business kissing like that. It didn't feel right to kiss her. It was a good kiss but unwelcome.

I took her by the arms and gently moved her away from me.

"There's no need for that."

She turned in to the room and began to remove her clothing without any hint of modesty.

"There is a need," she answered. "To convince others that we are newly married, we must be lovers. It is a sacrifice you and I must make. It will not be so horrible," she promised.

No, it would not be, but I was not going to have sex with her for the sake of this mission. I thought about my resolution at dinner to display a newlywed's passion, but I hadn't considered this. I hadn't considered that she would expect us to be lovers, but now that she explained her reasoning, I wasn't surprised. Raux and Ladoux had known that Marie would seek to have sex with me. As my wife, the role required it. Sex was part of the job, and she was just doing her job.

"You promised me a gift," I said to stop her from disrobing. My effort failed. She had gotten down to her chemise and bloomers. Undeterred, she peeled off her remaining clothing and turned to her suitcase. Her long, lean body reflected the light coming in from the street below. I could see the lines of the muscles in her legs as she bent to search through her luggage. As she turned back to me, I could just make out faint stretch marks across her abdomen, which was otherwise flat and smooth. I was surprised to realize that as young as she was, she had carried a child. I applauded myself for my perception in a vain effort to distract myself from her nakedness. Her clinical requirement of sex was confusing to me, but I could not deny that she was desirable.

Entirely indifferent to her own nudity, she handed me a leather harness. I forced my attention from her to the object in my hand. I wanted to study her, but I knew that if I did, I would have no resolve to resist at all.

"A holster?" I asked.

"Yes, a shoulder holster, made for an American 1911 Colt .45 automatic. With it, your pistol will fit under your coat."

She reached behind her head and unpinned her hair, which cascaded down across her shoulders and breasts. She stepped toward me and began to unbutton my tunic. I let her undress me, paralyzed by disbelief and desire in equal parts. As she pulled my undershirt over my head, I realized that if I didn't stop her, we would indeed have sex, and the thought of having sex to further the machinations of Clemenceau appalled me. It would betray Sarah and disgust me. I would not do it. On the outside, Marie was beautiful and painfully inviting, but she was also manipulative, unemotional, and detached. For her, this was a necessary task to be completed to further the mission. The depression that haunted me earlier in the evening came back to overwhelm me.

I scooped her up and carried her to the bed. I laid her down, and she caressed my face, thinking this the start of our lovemaking. Instead, I pulled the bedclothes around her, trapping her arms and legs.

"We're not going to fuck," I said bluntly. "We're not."

She didn't struggle; she just looked at me.

"Are you sure? I think you want to."

I didn't answer and instead held her trapped beneath me.

"Fine, this can wait, but you must remain attentive to me," she said. "You must seem like a man in love or, at least, lust."

"Easy enough to do," I assured her, and it would be.

8

———————

Forlorn Hope

The next morning, we gathered our bags and climbed into a car that waited at the curb outside the hotel.

The driver took us to the Gare du Nord station, and I hired a porter to see to our bags. We would take the train to Brussels where we would spend the night, and from there we would travel on to Berlin the next morning.

The station wasn't crowded, and we followed the porter to our first-class car without difficulty. The train already had its steam up, giving the look of leaving on time.

After the porter loaded our bags, I handed Madame Masson into the train and tipped him with a few of the francs Ladoux had given me.

The trip to Brussels was about two hundred miles, five or so hours, and the train was scheduled to arrive in the afternoon. We walked down the passageway to our compartment. It was empty. Madame Masson sat by the window and looked out, watching the platform.

Marie. I needed to think of her as Marie. After last night, it would be absurd to think of her as Madame Masson. I sat and

83

pulled out her papers. She did not bother to turn from the window. Marie Morton was the name on the passport. The French were clever to retain her maiden name. If we'd married just after the armistice, she wouldn't have had time to get a new passport. It looked real enough to me. I refolded the paper and tucked it away in my tunic.

The train left on time. No one joined us in the compartment.

I needed to reach some understanding with Marie. I would not be a dupe for the French. If I didn't see evidence of the Germans manipulating the Bolsheviks, I would not lie to House in my report to him. But it wouldn't surprise me if the Germans were in contact with the Russians. They'd be fools not to be. In fact, it wouldn't surprise me if the French were exactly right in their belief that the Germans were conspiring with the Bolsheviks to weaken France. But the real question I needed to answer for House was whether a Bolshevik revolution was a real possibility in Germany, and I couldn't answer that until I went there.

"Marie."

She looked away from the window. The outskirts of Paris rolled silently by behind her.

"I have agreed to participate in this trip to find the truth about Bolshevism in Germany. I will not fabricate stories of Germany using a fake Red threat to avoid the treaty terms if I see a real risk of revolution there. I will report the truth as I see it to House and the president."

She stared at me, her head cocked slightly to the side as if asking me why I was speaking. In the morning light streaming through the train window, the glow of her eyes was captivating.

"I was under the impression that you had been ordered to participate, John."

She made my name sound like an insult. She was trying to reach an understanding as well.

"I will keep an open mind and report what I see and not what you want me to report."

"Of course. We would expect nothing else," she said. "But I will take you where you will see what you need to in order to form an intelligent assessment."

"You want America to be afraid of Germany more than of Bolshevism. I know this. I was there when Reds tried to kill Clemenceau. I'd tracked them. There was no German involvement. You French see Germany's hand behind everything even when it is not there."

"John." Now the tone she used was one suited for a stubborn child. "You are new to espionage. To international manipulation. I am not. France is not. I know you believe the attempt on the prime minister was a Bolshevik scheme. My job is not to convince you otherwise. My job is to show you Germany and the Germans as they are. Not as you want them to be."

"I hope to see them as they are and not as you want them to be, Marie." I tried to get the same inflection with her name as she had with mine and failed. Not surprising.

A blue-uniformed conductor pulled open the door to our compartment.

Marie moved from her seat across from me and sat down next to me. In that simple motion, she transformed from a distant French agent into a loving American military wife. She sat close, but she wasn't touching me. She gave the impression of sheltering in my shadow.

"Billets, s'il vous plaît."[1]

I handed him our tickets.

The conductor's eyes flickered to her and back to me. I could tell he found Marie attractive. He was also in no doubt that she was my wife. She continued to wear her wedding band, and her left hand rested atop her right as she leaned toward me.

He punched the tickets, and with one last look at Marie, he left the compartment.

I looked down at her. She smiled, her tawny irises twinkling with amusement. She knew what she had done, and she knew I had seen it. She had demonstrated her expertise more effectively than any words could have done.

"You see, John?"

"I see that you are very good at what you do, Marie. I just want to make sure that you do not *manipulate* me," I said.

"I will not need to. You'll see that too," she told me.

THE TRAIN CONTINUED NORTH, AND SHORTLY WE STARTED TO SEE the signs of the war. The German offensive of 1918 had nearly reached Paris, but I knew the devastation that we saw from our window did not compare with what we would see farther north. Marie stayed seated next to me, again looking out the window. I could not imagine what she must be feeling as the countryside rolled by.

It did not surprise me that the French saw the Germans as the ultimate enemy. Since Sedan[2] in 1870, if not before, the German bogey man had dominated their national imagination. And after the past four years, it was easy to see why the French viewed the Germans with such loathing and fear, although I wasn't sure they would admit to the fear. And of course, the French had forgotten they were the ones who declared war on Prussia in 1870, never mind that Bismarck had duped them into it. Those wonderful Gauls also had forgotten that their series of treaties and agreements lent a hand to the coming of the recent war. But then so had the English.

But in my heart, I didn't really blame the French. I blamed the Germans. They were a bigger, more populous country and warlike besides. The French efforts both before and after the war were the desperate gambits of an overmatched boxer. Yes,

France had the upper hand now, but it couldn't last. And the French knew it.

The last hour and a half before arriving in Brussels was depressing. At points, the countryside looked like a moonscape, devoid of any structure or trees and pocked in a way no earthly landscape should be.

Marie sat next to me the entire trip. Without speaking, she still managed to force my attention out the window. She wanted to remind me of the devastation the Germans had caused. She didn't know I had lived in that alien ground. But then she only knew of my service with the marines. She didn't know that, with the English, I had existed in the trenches and craters beyond the windows. I knew the devastation firsthand. I also knew that countless artillery shells were fired by Germans, French, and British alike. Once aloft, they struck without regard for flag. The gas poisoned where the wind blew. The white bones sticking from the soil knew no nationality. But she wasn't aware that I knew these truths.

———

WE ARRIVED IN BRUSSELS IN THE EARLY AFTERNOON. ON MARIE'S instruction, I directed a taxi to take us to the Résidence Le Quinze, a hotel on the main square and just a short distance from the train station. From our window, we could see the multispired town hall a few steps down the Grand Place from our hotel. Gothic guild halls lined the square. In another time, I might have thought the square beautiful, but now I thought it gaudy. I wondered at the fact that Brussels had survived nearly unscathed, but then I recalled the German atrocities of the first weeks of the war. Perhaps Brussels still stood, unshelled and apparently whole, but I was certain the Belgians didn't feel unharmed.

Hell, earlier this year, before I'd met Armistan but after I'd been released from the hospital and the Marine Corps, I recalled reading an article in the *New York Times* about a Senate hearing investigating claims of German atrocities in Belgium. The Senate first heard from some Boche bureaucrat claiming their armies had done nothing worse than the United States did to the southern states during Sherman's march to the sea or when trying to pacify the Philippines. All crap, of course. Then the senators questioned an officer in the US Military Intelligence Service who'd been in Belgium in 1914. This fellow had firsthand knowledge of what the Germans had done, and he described it. At the end of his testimony, a senator asked if he had anything more to add, and he said something I'll never forget. He said, "It is not a case of anything more. It is a case of trying to forget."[3] The hatred of Germany in this part of the world would run deep.

At Marie's suggestion, we took a walk. She linked her arm through mine, and we walked through the Grand Place. I still wore the uniform. The khaki tunic and Sam Browne belt were enough to alert the people we passed that I was not German. Smiling men stopped us to shake my hand.

"*Anglais?*" they would ask.

"*Américain,*" I would answer, and they would pump my hand harder. They would turn to those around them and inform them that I was an American.

Women still dressed in the somber colors of mourning would seize my free hand and say softly, "*Merci,*" then move on. Their wide-eyed children studied me cautiously, as if I were a dangerous circus animal. Even those who did not stop us would smile and nod or tip their caps.

We tried to explore the narrow, cobbled streets around the square, but it was difficult with the many interruptions.

"Let's get a coffee," I suggested, hoping to escape the attention.

Marie agreed, and we ducked into a small café.

A thin man dressed in suspenders under an apron welcomed us. He was clearly the owner, and he tried to sit us by the front window. I insisted on a small table near the back.

Once seated, I looked to Marie. "Coffee?"

"*Café, s'il vous plaît,*"[4] she said to the proprietor.

"*Et une bière,*"[5] I added.

"We have English beers," he said, proud of both his English and the fact that he had English beers.

"Really, what kind?" I asked.

"Worthington's Stout, Bass Pale Ale," he answered enthusiastically.

"A Bass."

"Are you English?" he inquired. The other customers in the café leaned in to hear the conversation.

"American," I answered.

"My husband is an American marine," Marie said proudly. "He fought at Bois de Belleau."[6]

I gave her a glare, which had no effect.

The owner's eyes widened.

"We know of the famous American marines here!"

I could just imagine General Pershing's snarl at the fact that even in this Belgian café far from Paris, the owner had heard of the marines. For the newspaper reporters, Pershing had a strict policy against naming units involved in any battles. But a reporter had accompanied the marine attack on Belleau Wood. He wrote a glowing dispatch of the fight before the battle even started, which he gave to a friend. The report mentioned the marines by name. Unfortunately for the reporter, but fortunately for the fame of the Marine Corps, the reporter had been seriously wounded. In sympathy for his injuries, the censors passed his fabricated version of the battle. It even made it into the *New York Times*. I'd found the clipping at my parents' house at the same time I found Harry Armistan's letter to me. It made me happy that Pershing's effort at controlling the press had failed so spectacularly that even here in Belgium they knew of the marines. I didn't much care for General Pershing.

The patron rushed off to get our drinks.

"Marie, I know what you are doing, and it really isn't necessary," I said.

She tilted her head toward me, waiting for me to explain.

"I don't need the entire population of Brussels backslapping me and asking me to kiss their damn babies, as if I'm some kind of savior." I was leaning across the small table toward her, and I could feel myself getting angry, which I knew would undermine my argument.

"John, you are their savior, or at least the only representative nearby. They know that without America, there would have been no armistice in November. They know the Germans would still be sitting in this café. It is important that you understand the depth of their gratitude."

"The depth of their gratitude isn't what I'm here to determine, and you know it."

"They fear the Germans. That is what you need to see. For four years, the Germans reigned as conquerors across Belgium, and these people don't want it to happen again, but they fear it might." She believed what she was saying, and her passion made her even more attractive. "Seeing you, a big, fearsome American, with your ribbons, your pistol, and your beautiful wife, gives them hope that it won't happen again. They believe in Woodrow Wilson, and they believe in America."

"My beautiful wife?" I raised an eyebrow.

"I say what they see."

"And what I see," I said under my breath as the owner delivered our drinks.

I could tell from the small smile that crossed her lips she had heard me.

We stayed in the café and talked until the sun set. I didn't want to be accosted anymore, and Marie knew that she had made her point. The owner refused payment for our drinks, but I left some money on the table anyway. That's what saviors do I supposed.

As we left, Marie again put her arm through mine, and we strolled down the cobbled lanes. I grudgingly admitted to myself that it was just as well that Brussels had been spared the awful destruction that Ypres and other French and Belgian cities had endured. It was a charming city, too ancient and beautiful to be crushed by German, French, and British artillery.

I was very aware of Marie's arm through mine and her warmth pressed against my side.

"Let's have dinner at the hotel," I suggested.

"All right," Marie agreed. "In the cellar underneath, yes?"

"Yes, in the cave," I said, joking.

Tucked just to the side of the steps to our hotel was the entrance to a cellar restaurant. We walked down the short flight of stairs into a long room with a low arched brick ceiling. Benches and tables lined the walls, and a single row of tables ran the length of the restaurant back to the kitchen.

Although there was little to be had, I asked for some privacy, and the maître d' seated us in the far corner against one wall in an area not yet surrounded by other diners.

Without consulting Marie, I ordered a bottle of champagne. I decided it was in keeping with our roles.

Marie insisted that we share some snails. I knew she believed sharing to be consistent with our masquerade. Unfortunately, her choice in appetizer reminded me of the dinner at L'Escargot de Montorgueil with William and Patricia just a few short weeks before but a lifetime ago. Sarah had been alive then, and all things were possible.

"You have become more gloomy," Marie stated, sensing my mood change.

"More gloomy?"

"Yes, you were already annoyed by the locals, but something has happened to make you more dispirited."

Yes, *dispirited* was a good word for how I felt.

"You are astute, Marie."

"What is it?" she asked.

"Not something for discussion," I answered.

For dinner, Marie ordered a fish, whose name I did not know, and I ordered, at Marie's suggestion, a Belgian beef dish stewed in beer. It was sweeter than I expected. I pretended to enjoy it for Marie's sake and was annoyed with myself for doing so. I supposed that is what a new husband would do. We finished the bottle of champagne, and I ordered another. With the proper lubrication, I hoped she would drop the mask of my doting wife. It was a forlorn hope. She giggled appropriately and reached across the table to touch my arm as we spoke, but she was always Marie Griffin, the wife, never Marie Masson, the French spy.

When we retired to the room, she shucked off all her clothes again and curled up in the bed, indifferent to my discomfort. I didn't touch her, but I could feel her warmth next to me. Her body beside me made sleep difficult, but I wouldn't have slept at all if we'd had sex.

9

―――――

Razor Wits

Our train for Berlin left early the next morning. I dressed in one of the new civilian suits Raux's contacts had made for me, and I pulled on the new shoulder holster. It fit like a charm and was certainly more comfortable and practical than pushing the pistol behind my belt. I put on my suit coat and practiced drawing the Colt from under it. Marie watched me with some amusement, but I ignored her.

After we had a coffee and pastry at the hotel, we left to catch the train. The station was not crowded. Not many folks were eager to make the sixteen-hour trip from Brussels to Berlin. Again, our tickets were in first class, and the porter led us to our sleeping compartment, which was empty of any other travelers. The train was scheduled to arrive in Berlin around midnight, and I would welcome the narrow bed. As the train rolled out of the station, we sat by the compartment windows, facing each other, looking out at the countryside and thinking our own thoughts.

The train took us through Liège, where it stopped to take on passengers. The city showed some signs of shelling, and the train passed by one of the huge forts that had delayed the German advance in the opening days of the war. Other than the shell-pocked landscape around it, the villages and land beyond Liège showed few signs of war. Shortly before lunch, we passed into Germany, but it was not apparent. The Belgians administered this part of Germany under the new treaty, and we were unaware that we had entered Germany until the train stopped in a town called Eschweiler to allow the German border police to board the train. Although they were efficient in their review of the passengers, they were careful to check everyone, which took time. Our American papers drew a long, measured look before they moved on. Their diligence caused us to miss the lunch hours of the dining car. It was almost as if the train staff planned the hours to conflict with the border crossing.

As we steamed into Germany, I felt compelled to ask again about the agenda for the trip.

"Why Königsberg and then Berlin, Marie? Why not just Berlin?" I asked.

"Königsberg is the heart of Prussia, which is the heart of Germany. You must see it. Although separated from the rest of Germany by your president's corridor to the sea,[1] the trip there will be valuable. You need to see the Prussians' attitude toward the war and the peace. Germany gets its warlike spirit from Prussia after all. It is there that the fires of militarism continue to burn the hottest."

"Fair enough, but how do you expect me to see these things?"

"We will tell the truth. You are an American tasked with reviewing the German authorities' and peoples' view of the Treaty of Versailles and the war. You will learn all you need to know from these conversations. The truth about Germany will reveal itself."

I was not so sure that the Germans wouldn't just tell me

what they thought I wanted to hear, but Marie was convinced they would not. One way or another, I would have to form an opinion to share with Colonel House, and he would likely pass it on to the president. I was unhappy with Marie's answer, but I wasn't going to learn anything she didn't want me to know.

"Given its proximity to Russia, don't you expect to see evidence of Bolshevism in Königsberg?"

Marie laughed. "There will be no Reds in Königsberg. It is Prussia."

With nothing to do but watch the countryside roll by, I tried again to draw out some of her true past. Marie Masson's not Marie Morton's. Instead, she obstinately answered using stories of her made-up American family and made-up memories. She described her life after her fictional parents died, how she had to live by her wits, navigating grasping relatives and lecherous men. I wondered how much of the stories she told were true and just modified to fit the fictional Marie Morton. Eventually, despite the possibility that I was learning small kernels of truth, I gave up.

Tired of staring out the windows at Germany's green fields, I invited her to the dining car for an early dinner. She agreed, and once seated in the public car, I decided I needed to continue acting the newlywed.

"You look lovely despite traveling all day, my dear," I said softly, but not so softly that the nearby diners could not hear me. Most seemed to be French speaking, but there were some German speakers in the car as well.

"Thank you, John. I do look forward to our night in Berlin. Please tell me we don't have to leave for Königsberg until the following day."

"Of course. We can leave the following day," I assured her, knowing that she controlled our schedule.

As we spoke, I noticed three men enter the car from the far end by the galley. They took a table near where they entered. I couldn't make out their faces, but one had a limp and there was something familiar about him. They shifted as they sat, and I got a glimpse of the man. Bertrand. He was an associate of Morgan Reynolds. I'd tangled with Bertrand in a bar fight the night we'd first found Patricia Armistan. He had been deep in conversation with Reynolds when I'd first seen him. Finding him here, on the same train with me on the way to Berlin, could not be a coincidence.

He saw me watching him and nodded a cynical greeting. His two companions turned to see the object of his attention. I didn't recognize either man, but they looked like hard men. Men who had seen war.

Marie turned to follow my stare. She looked back to me with an eyebrow raised in question.

"An old acquaintance, I'm afraid," I told her. "This probably isn't good news for our little trip."

"And why is that?" she asked.

I could think of no reason for Bertrand to be on this train other than Reynolds had paid him to be. And Reynolds wouldn't have ordered him here for a happy chat. He'd sent him to deliver a message, which would either be painful or fatal.

"He works for a man who, despite my recent efforts, hates me. I think he is here for me."

"For you?"

"Yes, we had a bit of a fight a few weeks ago." I left out the fact that I'd done my best to shatter his knee and blind him. Other than the limp, he looked none the worse for wear.

"What can he want from you?"

"He is either here to send a message of the most painful kind, or he is here to kill me," I answered pessimistically.

"Nonsense. He may be here for an innocent reason," she decided. "You should ask him."

I smiled. "You are exactly right, Marie. I should ask him."

I started to stand, and she reached out a restraining hand. She apparently didn't like the look on my face.

"Perhaps after we eat," she suggested.

I looked again at their table, but Bertrand had turned away. If they were still there after dinner, I would confront them. Better to do so in a public dining car than in an empty train corridor. I appreciated the weight of the Colt under my left arm.

"Of course, Marie."

Our meal was unremarkable for both its quality and the conversation. Marie was wrapped in her own thoughts, perhaps worried about the outcome of her mission if I were killed. I was thinking about how to isolate Bertrand and each of the men with him. By the time we finished, Bertrand was gone. One of his fellows remained at their table, but as our table was cleared of our coffees, he too disappeared toward the sleeping cars.

"So much for asking," I said to Marie.

"It might be better to wait or ignore him."

"I doubt it, but I have no choice now," I said, looking at the corridor where he'd gone.

We made our way back to our compartment unmolested. I pulled the curtains and lowered one of the beds for Marie without asking. I didn't bother with one for me. I knew I wouldn't sleep with Bertrand on board.

I felt the train slowing and pulled aside the curtains to see we were entering a station. I saw a sign for Hanover slide by as we rolled to a stop. My geography of Germany was spotty, but I thought that put us about four hours from Berlin, which sounded about right given our planned arrival time. I watched the passengers hurry off and on the train, but I didn't see Bertrand or his men.

Marie undressed to lie down on the train bunk.

"Come, John, lie down for a bit. We will be in Berlin in a few hours," she invited.

She was on her back on the small bed, with one leg pulled

up, her feet and ankles exposed. It was tempting, but that was the point.

"No, thanks," I said bluntly.

She rolled away from me.

I tossed one of the train blankets over her.

I found that sitting in the compartment waiting for Bertrand to appear was impossible.

"I'm going to stretch my legs. I'll be back in a bit," I said to Marie's back.

"Be careful," I heard her say as I pulled the compartment door shut.

I needed to find their compartment without being discovered. If I could catch them individually, I might be able to get rid of them one at a time.

Our car was in the middle of the train behind the dining car. I worked my way to the back of the train, peeking in compartments where the curtains weren't drawn. I swayed and bumped my way down the corridor as the train picked up speed as we left Hanover behind us. For those compartments with curtains pulled closed, I made a mental note to check again, if needed.

I worked my way through one car and was moving over the coupler to the next when I came upon the first man. I had just rehooked the chain between cars and was reaching for the door when he opened it for me. As he stepped through, I recognized him, and I saw the flash of recognition in his eyes. Without thought, I grabbed him with both hands, one hand on his tie and the other his lapel, and spun him, hard, out the door, across the gangway, over the chain and guardrail, and off the train. He was gone in an instant.

His hat had fallen off. I tossed it off the train after him.

My heart should have been thundering, but it happened so fast that only now did my body start to react. I took a deep breath and stepped through the still-open door. Thank God there had only been one of them.

It occurred to me then that I shouldn't have left Marie alone. She was a woman and vulnerable. I should have told her to lock the door when I left. Now my heart was beating fast. I turned and lurched back up the train, bouncing off the corridor walls and windows, nearly running as the train rocked down the tracks.

I slowed as I came to our cabin and pulled the Colt from under my jacket. The curtains were drawn across the compartment windows as I had left them.

I cracked the door open. The room was dark. Marie must have turned off the electric light after I left.

"Entre. Ferme la porte."[2]

The second man was in our compartment.

"Vite!"[3] he demanded.

I followed his instructions, stepping into the dim compartment, hiding the gun behind my leg.

Despite the shadows, I could see him standing against the window with Marie pulled tightly against him. His right arm held a knife to her throat. Her hands were tugging futilely at his arms.

"I suppose I should have locked the door, John," she said softly.

Her hair was disheveled. It looked like she had fought him, but he had her now. He was pulling her off-balance. She shifted her feet to counter the train's motion, and he was forced to widen his stance to keep from falling as he held her.

"Put the gun you think you are hiding on the bed," he said in heavily accented English. He was French. It figured. To emphasize his command, he pushed the knife against Marie's throat. I couldn't tell if he'd drawn blood, but I heard her take a sharp breath.

I could see Marie watching me.

I put the pistol on the bed.

"Lie down on the floor."

Marie's right hand left his arm and dipped inside her chemise. When it came back out, I could see something. Her assailant could not. He was focused on me. Her jaw was set in determination, and I was sure she was about to do something. I needed to be ready.

"Why?" I asked.

I could see him grin. He understood that I was asking why he was planning to kill me.

"*Pour l'argent.*"[4]

Marie shifted her hips as if with the train's motion, and her right hand flashed out and down toward his groin and then up again. She dropped whatever was in her right hand and grabbed his knife hand with both of hers, doing her best to pull the knife away from her neck.

"*Salope!*"[5] he grunted.

I jumped forward and pushed the knife away from Marie. She ducked under me and spun toward the compartment door.

I pinned his knife hand to the window and had my forearm across his neck, cutting off his air. For such a tough-looking guy, he hardly struggled at all. In just a few seconds, he went completely slack and collapsed to the floor when I released him.

"What the hell?"

Marie locked the compartment door and turned on the electric light.

A pool of blood surrounded the death-deflated body.

"We must clean this up. His body needs to disappear," Marie declared. "We do not want his death connected to us."

"How?" I asked.

"The big blood vessel in his leg. I cut it." She was unbothered. In fact, she seemed indifferent to killing the man. She bent down and picked up the straight razor she had dropped after cutting him. She carefully wiped it on his shirt, folded it closed, and replaced it inside her clothing.

Jesus Christ! Her war must have been just as savage as mine.

I questioned whether this was the first man she had ever killed or killed with a razor. I was certain it was not—on both counts. Her attitude was not so different from when she tried to have sex with me. No real emotion or emotional engagement in the act. She was detached. I wondered what the war had done to her to make her like this. I felt sorry for her. My old nemesis raised its goddamn head. I needed to help her. To save her. Rescuing the damsel in distress. The reason I took Armistan's job in the first place and the reason I pursued Sarah.

Goddamnit!

I thought of Madeline. She didn't need saving. She was just smart, funny, and attractive. But I wouldn't chase after her. What the hell was the matter with me?

I went in search of tools to clean up the mess in our compartment. I discovered a small utility closet at the end of the car with a mop and bucket and extra bedclothes and some towels. When I returned to the room, I found that Marie had spent her time searching the dead man's pockets. His belongings were piled on the bunk next to my pistol, which I quickly reholstered. I should have recovered it before leaving Marie alone again, but I was shocked at her efficient dispatching of the poor sod on the floor.

In his pockets she found some money but not enough to buy our murders, a pack of cigarettes, and a card with the name of Pierre Bauer for the Confédération Generale du Travail, a French labor union. He also had a scrap of paper with my handwritten name and train compartment number on it. His knife was also on the bunk.

"Bauer, sounds German," I said.

"Likely Alsatian," she clarified.

"So he was a German citizen until recently," I noted,

referring to the requirement of the Treaty of Versailles that Germany return Alsace to France.

"Yes, but it was France not too long ago."

"A union card. Does that make him a Bolshevik?" I asked.

"No. Certainly there are some Reds in the unions, but by no means all."

"I'll bet," I said with more sarcasm than was necessary. "A Bolshevik union man in Germany trying to kill us. Why does this seem like it doesn't support Préfet Raux's theory that the Bolshevik threat in Germany is just a fairy tale?"

"You should not overreact to one piece of paper. Also, you said yourself that you thought he was here for you, because of your old associate. It is more likely he and his friends were hired to kill you than as part of a Bolshevik plot. It seems personal. Meant for you," she said.

"Perhaps," I answered. "But I try to keep an open mind where murderous Bolsheviks are concerned."

"There is no proof he is a Bolshevik," she said, trying one more time to convince me. I picked up the union card and waved it in front of her face. She frowned and started cleaning the floor with some of the towels.

I took the open knife from the bed, unlocked it, and folded it shut. It was a "palm" knife, named after the palm-shaped locking mechanism on its back. Palm knives had been issued to French soldiers during the war. It was a *poilu*[6] knife, useful for all manner of things including silent killing during trench raids. I ran my thumb across the carvings on the wooden handle. I almost felt sorry for the poor French bastard, whose body lay cooling on the floor. He had no idea what he had stepped into when he came through the compartment door.

I put the union card and the note with my name on it in my pocket.

"You shouldn't keep those," Marie said. "If the police find his body, identify him, and find you with his union card, you will be implicated."

"Nope," I said with a smile. "I'll just blame you."

It took nearly an hour to clean the compartment. I wrapped the corpse of our unwelcome guest in some bedclothes and dragged it to the back of our train car and onto the gangway, where I rolled it off the train. I had trusted my luck to not be seen in the darkness, and as far as I knew, I wasn't.

10

Dada Revolution

Our train pulled into Berlin at half past midnight. I kept an eye out for Bertrand, but I was convinced that he had gotten off the train in Hanover. He had left his assassins to kill us and was likely on the first train back to Paris.

Even though I had stubbornly insisted to Marie that Bertrand's man was a Bolshevik, I was certain that he was acting for Reynolds and not as part of any Bolshevik-German scheme. I needed to warn Mitchell. If Reynolds had sent those men after me, he could do the same to Mitchell in Paris.

The weather was clear but cool. We found a taxi, and Marie directed it to the Hotel Adlon, where a reservation awaited us. I told Marie that I needed to send Mitchell a warning. She seemed reassured that if I was alerting Mitchell, I didn't really believe the men were Bolsheviks. When we got to the hotel, she helped me communicate with the concierge to arrange a telegram to the Vendôme in the morning.

As with the night in Brussels, Marie climbed into bed with me, but she made no overtures, for which I was both thankful and disappointed.

THE NEXT MORNING, AFTER I SENT A WARNING TO MITCHELL, I visited the American mission in Berlin. Marie insisted I needed to wear my uniform to impress upon my countryman the importance of my assignment. She would not be coming since it would be odd for the wife of an officer to accompany him on official business. I realized wearing the uniform was a bad idea because of the looks I got from the hotel staff. But I worked for the French now, and my orders came from Marie.

There was no actual American embassy in Berlin and hadn't been since 1917. President Wilson was in no hurry to reward the Germans with an embassy. It seemed he believed the Germans were on probation for having the temerity to start a war. I supposed he thought the best way to establish a viable democracy in the middle of Europe, as a Bolshevik revolution raged around it, was to ignore the Germans once they signed the peace treaty. Marie had mentioned that even the food aid the United States had sent was not clearly identified to the German people as coming from America. She explained that many Germans thought the food had actually come from Russia. I wasn't sure if I believed this story, but it wouldn't have surprised me. In any event, it didn't look like there would be official US representation in Germany, other than occupying soldiers, for a while.

Instead of an embassy, Marie had given me the address of the poor sap who'd been designated to observe Germany's uncertain steps toward a hoped-for democratic future. Charles Dyar,[1] a young and nonessential functionary of the State Department, had this unenviable role. He had no office and instead operated the US mission from his flat, which was located at Albrechtstrasse 14. Using Marie as a translator with the hotel staff, I got directions to his apartment, which was a five-minute taxi ride or a ten-minute walk north across the Spree River. The concierge insisted I take the hotel car, but I refused. It was a nice day, if cloudy, and I wanted the exercise.

Walking in Berlin while wearing an American uniform was decidedly different from strolling through Brussels. I still got the stares, but no thanks, no pats on the back, no offered hands. The looks were affronted at best, hostile at worst. My presence offended these people. Whether older men or young women pushing prams, they universally did not appreciate my Marine khakis.

By the time I crossed the river, I had picked up a shadow. He was well dressed, wearing an expensive suit with a Homburg-style hat on his head and an unnecessary scarf around his neck. He kept his shoes well shined.

I decided to let him pass me. I was nearing my destination and didn't want him to follow me there.

I turned, put my back to a building wall and waited. When I turned, he stopped. He wasn't more than fifteen feet from me. He was about my age, and his face was scarred. Not like mine though. A long scar on the left side of his head from his hairline through his eyebrow to just below his eye. A single clean pink line. It could have been a Prussian dueling scar except for its location. More likely, it was the result of the vagaries of flying shrapnel that happened to flay him open in just the way a saber slash might. I envied him the symmetry of the wound. It wasn't a puckered stain on his face; rather, it added a gravity to his aspect. He looked at me with such intensity I was certain he was about to attack me. Automatically my hand crept up to the holster hanging from my Sam Browne belt. He resumed walking toward me with his empty hands at his sides.

"You are a fool," he said harshly. His German accent was slight.

"Excuse me?"

"You are a fool. Only a fool would wear a British uniform on the streets of Berlin."

People turned and watched us as they passed. Fortunately, none stopped. Given his attitude, I was starting to worry that the entire population of Berlin might attack me.

"It's an American uniform," I told him.

"Idiot!"

I decided that I didn't like this German. But then I didn't really like any Germans.

"Come with me." He grabbed my arm and hustled me down Albrechtstrasse directly to a red brick apartment house: number 14.

"Come in, quickly!" my escort demanded. We entered the building's foyer. Once in, he immediately began to climb the stairs. I followed him, if only because this was my destination in any event.

At the first landing, he knocked and opened the door without waiting for an answer.

"Charles," he called out as he strode across the sitting room into what looked to be a dining room.

I shut the door behind me.

A young man barely older than I appeared in a second doorway. He was in shirtsleeves and not dressed for visitors. He was cleaning his spectacles on an untucked corner of his shirt.

"Hello, Hans. I see you brought a guest." He didn't seem perturbed by Hans's unannounced entrance or surprised at my presence. He had a mischievous sparkle in his eyes. I already liked him better than Hans.

"Mr. Dyar?" I asked.

"Yes. You must be Griffin. I was warned you were coming." He finished cleaning his glasses and put them on. "Why in God's name are you in uniform?" The words came out in a rush.

"I was under the impression that General Bliss[2] ordered all American officers to wear uniforms when in Germany," I said pompously. At least that was how it sounded to my ears.

"Bliss is an imbecile. And he's in Paris, not here. That

ridiculous order nearly got Captain Gheradi[3] killed. He came here in January. He wore his uniform and narrowly avoided being both the first American to come here and the first American assassinated here. The more radical Germans assassinate those wearing allied uniforms."

"Really?" I asked, less worried than I should have been.

"A uniformed French sergeant major was murdered outside the French Embassy here just last week.[4] No one with a lick of sense wears a uniform," Dyar said. "The order has been countermanded by Bliss himself." I thought about Mitchell's warning that no war is truly won until the enemy's capital is taken and their armies destroyed. It was a sad state of affairs when the winners were afraid to show their colors to the losers.

"I guess I got bad information. I was told specifically to wear my uniform to impress the locals." I thought of Raux. Could it be that the French wanted me dead?

"You will surely impress the Berliners. You will impress upon them the need to kick you to death," Hans volunteered. The comment didn't make me like him any better.

I decided I needed to start again with both men and offered my hand to Dyar. "John Griffin, Mr. Dyar."

"A pleasure. Please call me Charles. George Gordon sent me a cable warning me you were coming. This is my friend, Hans Richter. He is a local artist of some note. Despite the scar he got fighting for the Fatherland, he's not fond of the old monarchists or the militarists."

"Well, we can certainly agree on that," I said, turning to Richter and offering my hand to him as well.

"Perhaps you are not a complete fool?" Richter told me. He made it a question, whether on purpose or because his English was imperfect, I didn't know, but I laughed anyway.

"Don't make that judgment yet, Mr. Richter. There are plenty of people who think I am." I looked at his scarred head. "I hope we didn't give that to you."

"Russians. It is fortunate for you that I was on my way to visit Charles. The people do not appreciate foreigners, especially foreigners in uniform who are a reminder of defeat, which they do not believe. They believe in betrayal."

"And do you believe it was betrayal and not defeat?" Now was as good a time as any to gather information about German attitudes.

"I do not. But what I believe does not matter. The people believe that the army fought well, with honor, and would have won. They do not believe Germany was defeated. They cannot accept that Germany lost because it changes our place in the world. Instead, they claim the socialist diplomats and Jewish merchants betrayed Germany for power, and the treaty was the price to obtain that power. But in our hearts, we know we lost, and it has changed us."

"What do the people think about Bolsheviks, Bolshevism, and revolution?" I asked.

"Why not a revolution? But that is what I think. We are a deeply conservative people. We will have enough trouble with democracy. Bolshevism is too much. Most are afraid of Bolshevism."

"That's what his mouth says, but you should see his art, and that of his friends. It's as crazy as any revolution," Dyar assured me. "What do you call it, Hans?"

Richter rolled his eyes. "I have told you several times, Charles. It is not art. It is anti-art. It is Dada. It is against all things that *art* supports. It is against conformity, against capitalism, against militarism and imperialism."

"How's it feel about baseball?" I couldn't resist. Richter was clearly passionate about his anti-art movement, but I didn't really care.

Dyar snickered.

Richter raised an eyebrow at me. "It does not care for baseball," he said with finality.

"You made that up," I objected. "I guarantee Dada doesn't know enough about baseball to make a judgment."

"Yes, but I am sure your American baseball is traditional. It is a sport to divert the common man. It is tribal, as all team sports are. It promotes distraction. I am right. But you are correct. I did just make that up." He smiled as he pulled a pipe from his coat pocket.

"I've got a friend you need to meet, Mr. Richter. He insists the war is not over." I was thinking of Mitchell and his views on world peace.

"I would like him. He is correct."

I turned to Dyar. "I was told to check in with you. My task is to assess the Bolshevik threat in Germany and Germany's commitment to the peace treaty."

"I thought that was my job," Dyar answered.

"It probably is. It's a long story, but I've been buffaloed into doing this as a special job directly for Colonel House." I didn't want to tell him about the French involvement, especially in front of Richter. "I'm happy to give you all the credit for whatever I find. I will mention you specifically when I meet with House. In fact, you can save me a lot of trouble by telling me what you know. My plan is to fly to Königsberg tomorrow and come back through Berlin on the way to Munich. My wife is traveling with me."

"Despite what the *New York Times* reported last year, [5] the Bolshevik revolution is real. The Bolsheviks may have taken money and even been sponsored by the German General Staff, but the revolution is real now, and the fighting here a few months ago proves it in my book. Did you say your wife is traveling with you?"

"Yes, we're recently married."

"Why on earth would you bring your wife here?" Dyar asked.

Richter was listening closely.

"She insisted, and I brought her here for the art, of course," I said.

We made plans to meet that evening for dinner. Dyar said that Hans and a few other Germans he knew would attend. He insisted I change out of the uniform before returning to the Adlon. He gave me a cloth cap, a shirt, and some trousers to wear. The clothes were too small, but the walk wasn't long. He also gave me a bag to pack the uniform in. I wore the uniform boots with the trousers over them, and I walked directly back to the hotel. I had some questions for Marie.

11

———

Frau Doctor

Marie was not at the hotel when I arrived. I changed into my civilian clothes and decided to walk the neighborhood to see if I could find her.

As I came out of the hotel and considered which direction to take, I saw the Brandenburg Gate to my left. It chilled me to see it in person. Dyar's flat had been east and north of the hotel. The gate was directly west. I forced myself to turn toward the gate. I walked down Unter den Linden, the broad boulevard running to and beyond the gate. Just looking at the damn columned edifice with the chariot mounted on top made my stomach knot. For me, it was a symbol of German imperialism, militarism, and thirst for power. Yet here it stood, undamaged and unchanged, despite four years of a war Germany lost. I walked quickly past the gate, crossing the wide thoroughfares busy with motorcars, horse-drawn wagons, and horse cabs and ventured into the park beyond. I thought it unlikely that I would find Marie strolling through nature. I started to turn back, but to my surprise, I saw her deeper in the park, walking along the path, arm in arm with a woman.

It had become a beautiful day, and they were walking toward me. If they didn't turn, they would pass me in just a few minutes. I stepped to the side so I could observe them without being seen. The other woman was older than Marie. She looked to be in her early thirties. She wore a dark hat and dress. The woman was speaking to Marie intently. I wished I could hear them. It was likely they weren't speaking English or French, but the tone of the words would have told me a lot.

I decided I would wait for them to pass. I leaned against a tree and waited. I would surprise Marie and have the opportunity to meet her mystery friend. The reaction of both women would be telling.

As they came abreast of the tree, their words reached me. They spoke German, and the older woman sounded as if she were teaching. Marie's head was bowed, and she nodded now and again.

"Marie, I'm glad I found you," I said, stepping out to reveal myself.

The women stopped at my call.

As I'd hoped, I surprised Marie, but she was unfazed by my appearance. The other woman simply studied me. She had dark hair, and other than the intensity of her gaze, she was unremarkable in every way.

"I looked at the hotel, and you were gone. I know you speak German, but you need to be careful, my dear," I said with worry in my voice.

I turned to the woman, waiting, and Marie was forced to introduce us.

"There is no need to worry about me." She gestured to me and said, "Dr. Elsbeth Schragmüller,[1] this is my husband, Major John Griffin."

Dr. Schragmüller held out her hand in an old-fashioned manner, inviting me to kiss it, so I brushed my lips over the top of her gloved fingers.

"Frau Doctor, it is a pleasure to meet you." I looked to Marie. "How do you know each other?"

Marie glanced at the older woman fondly.

"I studied with her before the war," Marie answered. She seemed affectionate toward the doctor, which surprised me. So far, I hadn't seen her as anything but aloof with anyone, but something about the good doctor thawed her normal frosty exterior.

"You remember I told you I studied here," Marie said, buttressing our newlywed image.

"She was an excellent student, and she is an even better woman." Dr. Schragmüller smiled at Marie. Her English was crisp with only a slight Germanic accent. "It is a shame the war cut short her studies, but perhaps someday soon she will be able to resume them." She looked at me to confirm that I would permit my new wife to study whatever she used to study.

"That will be up to Marie, of course," I said. "What did you teach Marie, Dr. Schragmüller?"

"Civics and geography, among other things. But she is a gifted artist, and art was at the heart of her studies and her abilities, but I am sure you know that."

"Of course. I am sorry to interrupt, but I need to speak to my wife for a few moments."

"Naturally. We were done catching up, weren't we, dear?"

Marie bobbed her head.

She looked at me to say her farewells, and I asked, "Perhaps we can have dinner one night? We leave for Königsberg tomorrow, but we return in a few days, and I am sure we can find an evening for dinner."

"Unfortunately, I leave tomorrow as well. I return to Freiburg."

"A lucky coincidence that you got to see Marie here then. Perhaps our trip will take us through Freiburg, and we could see you then."

"I would like that," she said, looking at Marie. "Marie knows how to contact me. Until then." She offered her hand again, and I kissed the air above it.

Dr. Schragmüller turned back into the park, walking briskly away from us.

I watched Marie while I waited for her teacher to pass out of earshot. She watched me back, her mask of indifference in place.

"So you are friends with a German doctor?"

"Yes. I had a life before the war you know, and she was a small but important part of it."

"How long did you study with her?"

"Just over a year, but we have stayed in touch despite the war. You said you needed to speak with me," she said, turning the conversation from her past.

"Does she know you work for the Deuxième Bureau?" I asked, ignoring her comment.

"Of course not! She knows I was a nurse for France, and I told her how we met while you were in the hospital."

"Does she know you are pretending to be an American?"

"No! And she does not need to know. She is my friend. My only friend. We speak of art. She is not political. I had the chance to see her, and I took it. Now what did you need to see me about?"

Marie was very protective of her friend and didn't want me to foul it up, but I couldn't let it go.

"What did you tell her about me? What will you tell her when this job is done and I'm gone?"

"As I said, I told her we fell in love during your recovery. It is not so hard to believe these days. When you are gone, I will tell her you died. That is not so hard to believe these days either. Why were you looking for me anyway?"

"Yeah, it's a funny thing. Préfet Raux and Major Ladoux both seemed to think it was a good idea for me to dress up as an American major. And you did too. So I wore the damned uniform." Her eyes had no trouble meeting mine. "As I walked to the American commissioner's apartment, the locals were giving me the eye, like they wanted to kill me. When I got to Dyar's flat, he wanted to know why I was in uniform. In January, American military observers in Berlin were threatened with assassination while in uniform."

"Those threats were not credible," Marie declared. "You came from the hotel to find me just to tell me this?"

"Really? Not credible. Despite a French soldier in uniform being killed just last week, and even though months ago the US Army rescinded the order requiring the wearing of uniforms while on duty in Berlin?"

"I am not privy to what the US military orders or does not order. I know what our mission calls for, and it called for you to wear the *damned* uniform," she snapped, throwing my profanity back at me. "As to the Frenchman, soldiers die in war, and this one is not over. That is what you are here to see."

"Does it call for me to die as well?"

"You are being ridiculous. You cannot be so flighty that the warnings of one lone bureaucrat here in Berlin convince you to give up already."

I was starting to get sore. "Oh, I'm not giving up, but I'm done wearing the uniform. And Marie, I'm getting close to being done trusting you."

"That is your prerogative, but you will continue the mission under my direction. Your own Colonel House requires it."

"I'll continue, but I'll use my judgment." I turned and started back toward the hotel. "We have dinner with Dyar tonight," I said over my shoulder. I didn't tell her that Richter would be there too.

12

––––––

Hell on Earth

When I returned to the hotel, I gathered the uniforms and sent them to Dyar's flat with a note telling him to send them to me at the Hôtel de Vendôme. I included money for postage with the note. I wanted to remove the uniforms from Marie's menu of manipulation. Fortunately, an English-speaking concierge was on duty and the delivery was easily arranged. I then went down to the hotel bar to wait. I didn't want to inhabit the same space as Marie when she returned from her walk to dress for dinner.

We took a horse cab to the restaurant to meet Dyar. The restaurant, Max und Moritz, was located at Oranien Strasse 162. Marie, who had been silent much of the afternoon, studied the sign bearing the name and shook her head. I didn't understand why, but after our quarrel in the park, I was unwilling to ask.

Dyar was waiting at the front of the establishment next to the maître d'. From what I could see, the place was a cross between a restaurant, a beer hall, and a club. For a moment, I felt homesick for Paris and my friends rollicking in the cafés and clubs until all hours.

"Ah, good, you're just in time. I sent the others to the table." He turned to Marie.

"Charles Dyar. Mrs. Griffin, it is a pleasure to meet you," he said.

"Others?" Marie asked.

"Yes, Charles knows some locals, who should be able to help me with my work," I told her. Her frown told me her view of this unscripted meeting. I was glad for the extra guests.

"I got your box. I'll take care of it," Dyar said, gesturing for the maître d' to take us to our table.

"Thanks. What's with the restaurant name?" I asked Dyar as I followed him.

"It's named after a children's picture book. Two useless boys who play pranks on widows and such. Filled with the brutal, slapstick humor Germans love."

"Odd name for a restaurant."

"It works for the Berliners. They are a bit different from the rest of the Germans. Cynical, worldly, and increasingly decadent."

I gave him a questioning look but said nothing. I was skeptical that any place could be as decadent as Paris.

The maître d' took us to a rectangular table against one wall paneled with bluish and green art nouveau tiles over bench seats. Richter and three others, two men and one woman, were at the table. The men stood as we approached. All three sets of eyes watched Marie. I couldn't blame them. She wore a clinging red silk dress for the occasion. It wasn't the shorter modern look, but she had our attention wearing it.

Despite our spat in the park, she played the devoted wife as we were introduced to the group.

Richter, after introducing himself to Marie, played host.

"I would like to present Otto Dix,[1] who is visiting from Dresden." Dix was an intense-looking, unsmiling man with an ugly pink scar along his neck. He was the picture of Teutonic ruggedness. "Like me, he is an artist, but he outshines us all with the unflinching honesty of his work." Richter's words were serious, but I could tell he was poking fun at Dix.

I shook Dix's hand. His eyes had already moved on to Marie. He took her hand in both of his and tried to smile. It looked to me like he failed, but Marie smiled back.

Richter introduced us to the final two.

"Karl Fuchs. He is not an artist. He works for the foreign ministry."

"Directly with me," Dyar interjected. "He's our primary contact with the German government."

"And this is Anita Berber,[2]" Richter continued. "She is a motion-picture actress and dancer of unique style." He smirked as he said the last, which told me something was up with the woman. "I thought you would enjoy meeting her."

Anita had a broad nose and strong jaw. Her eyes, which seemed very bright, were outlined with dark kohl. She wore a man's jacket over tightly tailored slacks. She leaned over to accept my hand, and I got a whiff of some sort of antiseptic, as if her perfume was used to clean wounds. She took Marie's hands in both of hers, almost in mockery of Dix. Unlike him, she kissed Marie's hand in an overtly erotic fashion and smiled at me.

"You can kiss my hand too, if you'll do it like that," I said unthinkingly.

Dyar and Richter guffawed, and Fuchs laughed out loud. Even Dix smiled.

Anita's smile became a lascivious leer, and she said in heavily accented English, "I like you Americans."

I raised my scarred eyebrow. "That may be the scariest thing I've heard since the war. I think I might need a drink. Marie?"

"Of course!" Richter shouted. He waved to the waiter, and I heard him say *bier* along with a bunch of other German words.

We sat with Anita claiming a seat between Marie and me. Dix

sat on the far side of Marie at the end of the table. Fuchs sat directly across from me, against the tiled wall, with Dyar next to him and Richter at the far end. Marie spoke with Dix and Richter in German as Anita leaned in. They were clearly delighted that she knew German, and all four of them began to jabber away. I heard the word *artist* several times. The three Germans seemed taken with Marie.

"I'm impressed with how well you all speak English," I told Fuchs.

"In school we are required to take a foreign language. Most choose English, but some choose French. Since I work for the foreign ministry, English and French are a requirement of my role. I have worked there since before the war and was unfit for military service. My heart," he finished with an entirely fake shrug of regret.

I chuckled.

"Well, there're a lot of dead fellows who might have wished they'd had heart trouble. I hope it doesn't cause you discomfort," I said.

"In 1914, I regretted my weak heart, but by 1918, I did not," he said sincerely. "It does not pain me. It does make exercise difficult."

"Selfishly, I'm glad you survived. Your speaking English is very convenient for me."

He laughed.

I liked Karl Fuchs. He had a sense of humor and didn't take himself too seriously. He was not what I expected of a German diplomat. I decided I needed his point of view about the challenges facing Germany. I knew he would be spouting the German government's angle on things, but that didn't mean it wasn't worth hearing.

"How are the German people settling into the postwar world?" Like a guilty schoolboy, I glanced over to make sure Marie wasn't listening. She was fully engaged with the two men and Anita. I was free to gather information without her interference.

"Not well," Fuchs said in answer to my question. "The truth is that the army could not have continued to fight. They were beaten. But that does not stop the nationalists and even the army itself from telling lies. They claim that the German people were betrayed by the politicians and the Jews, and the people believe them. The people cannot accept the loss. It is not within their ability to do this. They believe in the German military and *Deutsche Erhe*, German honor. The treaty is dishonorable, and most do not accept it."

"What does this mean for the future?" I asked.

"With time, I hope the war and the anger around the treaty will fade. But it is important that Germany is supported in the transition that is underway. Your country must remain committed to European diplomacy and give Germany an ear that neither England nor France will. Without that, I think the lies will fester and infect the country. I will work for the new republic, as many of us will, but we Germans have no history or experience with such government."

The beers and platters of appetizers arrived. Despite the starving children in many parts of Europe, there was no starving at that Berlin table that night.

"Do you know the work of Thomas Mann? He is famous, at least in Europe, for his book *Buddenbrooks*. It is a story of a wealthy German family over many generations," Fuchs said, continuing our conversation.

"I don't. Should I?" I was realizing my education was narrower than my ego believed.

"Yes. Just last year he published a new book. Hundreds of pages long. In English, it is called *Reflections of a Nonpolitical Man*. [3] In it, he represents very clearly the problem Germany now faces. But he does not support the transition. He explains and defends the attitudes that endanger the success of liberal democracy in Germany."

"How so?" I valued this conversation with Fuchs. Dyar listened as well. The other four continued their conversation in German, unbothered by our political one.

"Mann believes, and many with him, that to attempt to mold Germany into a middle-class democracy in the Western sense would be to eliminate what is best in Germans, making us dull and stupid. Many like him do not want to live in a Germany broken and beaten by the West, and so they refuse to accept the defeat and refuse to accept the trappings of the republic we have adopted in response to the defeat. They find it grotesque that we mimic Western democracies with our new republic. They do not want to submit to democracy."

"And you?" I asked.

"I am a patriot. I love my country, just like you love yours, I expect. I do not care whether we are a republic, a monarchy or, God forbid, a Bolshevik collective, but I do want a sovereign, powerful nation, unchained from the bonds of the Treaty of Versailles."

I thought about what Fuchs said. Did I love my country? I had done awful things on her behalf. I had become an awful thing. And the world was no better for it. In the end, I supposed I did love my country. I could no more shake that love than shake the bones from my body. It was like religion. Just by a different name. I resented it. And I still hated Germany. And myself. I had become what I was because I was stupid, lustful, and cowardly. Those traits put me in the trenches with the British and drove me out again. The rest just followed from my own defective nature like a freight car following a train engine. The drink, the self-loathing, and the Marine Corps.

I laughed. "Then I suppose you shouldn't have lost the war." I looked him directly in the eye.

Fuchs eyes narrowed, and then he laughed too. "Only a

German victory would have guaranteed the peace of Europe," he said sincerely. "You will see."

"Mr. Fuchs, given your perception and understanding of Germany's current political challenges, do you think it possible that your superiors would allow you to accompany me, at least to Königsberg? You would enable me to achieve an understanding of the country that I would otherwise never reach. And there would be a benefit to Germany in that you could be sure your point of view was being considered."

"I am sure they would allow me to do so. In fact, I think they will insist on it."

"And I'll come too," Dyar volunteered.

I glanced down the table and caught Marie watching me. She wore the same expression as the one she'd had just before she'd slashed the poor bastard on the train. Determined and focused—on me. I didn't like that look directed at me. Too bad. I needed a viewpoint beyond Marie's.

We had finished our drinks, and a second round arrived. The main course, which had been ordered without consulting me, arrived as well. Platters of big knots of meat that could only be pork knuckles were swimming in gravy and placed at each end of the table. Bowls of potatoes and sauerkraut landed beside them. I had truly arrived in Germany.

We ate the food and drank more beer. The Germans became louder, and everyone at the table lapsed into German. It didn't bother me. I didn't need the conversation. I found myself thinking about Sarah and then Madeline. Anita fished a pendant from beneath her blouse, and I realized that, like Kiki, she carried a pharmacy between her breasts. She opened the little top to the vial and nudged me with her shoulder, offering me the vial.

"Cocaine?" I asked.

"Of course. This is Berlin," she said.

I shook my head. A quick look of disappointment flashed

across her face, but she turned to Marie. Marie hesitated and then shook her head. Anita passed the vial and a little spoon to Dix and then Richter. Dyar and Fuchs also declined. I suppose the artists were just more inclined to test the boundaries of traditional behavior. For me, I knew propriety and civilization were a sham designed to trap me. But I was here to play a role, and so I would. Major Griffin, honorable and respected hero of the American Expeditionary Force, would not snuffle cocaine off a spoon. I knew Marie was playing her role as well. Also, I had no desire to try to duplicate the frenetic yet memorable evening I'd spent with Kiki and Madeline.

Without the cocaine rush overfocusing my senses to the point of limiting them, I enjoyed watching the two women, Richter, and Dix chatter away in German, joking and laughing. Dyar insisted on paying the bill, and the seven of us stumbled out into the street.

"It is still early. We shall go to the club where I perform," Anita declared. "We will drink *Sekt* and dance with the *Nuttes*,[4] looking for extra money and lesbians for company. Then we will go home and make love and start all over again."

The group laughed, thinking she was joking. I was sure she was not. Richter hailed a taxicab, and we crammed ourselves in. The only word I understood him to say to the driver was *Friedrichstadt*.

Once out of the taxi, Anita led us through a series of alleyways, passing every manner of prostitute imaginable. Young children wearing cosmetics pulled at our clothes, and old, clown-like trollops in their war paint called after us.

At one point we passed a blinded German veteran, missing both his arms and legs, propped against the wall along the sidewalk, selling matchbooks. His iron cross was pinned to his coat. He perched unnoticed as the riotous pedestrian traffic streamed past. Only a small dog stopped to lift its leg next to the soldier.[5] I caught Dix's eye, and he just shook his head. This was the new postwar, post-Kaiser Berlin. To me it felt like hell on earth. I wondered if the average German thought the same.

We arrived at a nondescript door with a sign above, which said WEISSE MAUS. I looked at Marie for a translation.

"White Mouse," she said. "We should go back to the hotel."

"We are here to learn. Don't be so *flighty*," I said nastily.

She narrowed her eyes at me and followed Anita into the club.

"The name is a joke," Richter told me. "Like the Chat Noir[6] in Paris. The white mouse here. Your wife might be right about returning to the hotel."

"We'll be fine," I said, brushing him off.

Once inside, we were offered domino masks, white or black, which covered our eyes. I tried to wave mine away.

"Take one," Anita insisted. "They make it easier to immerse yourself in the experience."

We each put on a mask to hide behind. We drank *Sekt*, the German version of champagne, and we also saw teenagers of both sexes engaging with their older male and female escorts. In addition to dancing, the entertainment included an hour-long performance with nudity and graphic sexually provocative dancing.

The uninhibited atmosphere of the club infected our group. I was not. They swilled *Sekt* and emptied Anita's vial. Except for the cocaine, even Marie participated. I was not beguiled. The place felt poisoned to me. Having lost the war, something had broken in Germany, or at least in Berlin. The restraints that defined civilized behavior and society had fallen away. I was mindful of my hypocrisy. I knew I no longer believed in civilization's boundaries. I knew they were artificial and crafted to hold the rich and poor alike in their roles. But with the traditional conventions totally broken or gone, it left only a corrupted reality that disgusted me more than the fabricated "peace" that Wilson, Lloyd George, and Clemenceau were peddling to the world. I felt sick, but even a flawed peace was better than war. I just wasn't fooled into thinking it was world changing, but the depravity of Berlin *was* world changing, and not for the better.

A gentleman I thought of as the "ringmaster" introduced the show. Laughing, Fuchs translated enough of his words for me to understand that the ringmaster denied any base sexual or pornographic intention. Instead, the exhibition was for the sake of "beauty." The crowd roared as he delivered his disclaimer. The acts were so far beyond anything I'd seen in Paris that it was like Kiki and her peers were doing Sunday school pageants. Each performance was more pornographic and unsettling than the last. Nudity, fornication, and more. I didn't want the images in my head. The crowd's reaction was more disgusting than the show. The audience was euphoric. They wanted more. For most of those watching, the entertainment had not gone far enough, but it had gone beyond the pale for me. I felt queasy and regretted my refusal to leave. I looked around our table and saw none of the disgust I felt. Even Dyar had become inured to what we were seeing.

"Jesus Christ," I said to myself. Marie was watching me with a very slight I-told-you-so smile.

We arrived back at the Adlon in the early-morning hours after having stopped at Anita's apartment house. She dragged Richter, Marie, and me up to her flat, insisting that she wanted to show us her monkey. Although I was tired and disgusted, her suggestion seemed so absurd that I couldn't resist. I didn't believe she had a monkey, but I wanted to make sure. Marie had been angling to go back to the hotel for the last two hours, but I refused. I was punishing her, and I wasn't sure why. For using me, for my decision to go into the White Mouse, for being tempting. I didn't know, and it didn't matter. I was angry. She was stuck because no dutiful, respectable wife would navigate early morning Berlin without her husband.

Anita's apartment was scattered with clothes, half-full drinks and overflowing ashtrays. To my disappointment, there was no monkey. She did have rose petals infused with a concoction of chloroform and ether. She insisted the combination was the perfect answer for relaxing after a cocaine binge. She demonstrated by swirling the liquid in a short glass and then inhaling the vapors. Then, with exaggerated care, she stirred the contents with a rose petal, which she had plucked from a vase on the mantel. She inhaled once more, and ate the petal, licking her fingers with satisfaction. She offered the glass to us, and we demurred. I think Anita had finally managed to shock Richter. As the drugs took effect, any lingering intelligence and awareness faded from her eyes. All that remained of her was her human body operating with a lizard brain. At that point, we excused ourselves, but she followed us down to the street calling after us. We managed to avoid her clutching hands, and the three of us scrambled into a motorcab.

I hated Berlin. It was nothing like I expected and still worse in every way.

<hr>

When we got back to the hotel, Marie had stripped off her clothes and fell face down onto the bed, exhausted. She made no effort to seduce me, which I appreciated. We needed to rise in just a few hours. I climbed into bed as well.

A nightmare woke me. Seeing the blinded, crippled veteran must have triggered the dream.

I am back in the English hospital after being blinded by the sniper. But I'm not just blind. Both my arms and legs are gone.

Evelyn, the object of my childish obsession at the start of the war, sits next to me. Her small hand rests on my shoulder above my missing left arm. She's crying, and, under her breath, she keeps saying again and again, "You'll be okay, Jack, you'll be okay." I can feel her small dog, which she'd put on the bed, urinating on me. I know the dog is hers just as I know I have no arms or legs.

The claws of an awful panic grip me. How will I live? I can't.

"Time for your feeding," a nurse says. Feeding? Babies feed. Animals feed. Men don't feed.

My heart was pounding so hard it woke me.

I got out of bed and dressed, watching my hands work as I did so. I had hands. I had legs. I could see. I was okay. My heart slowed.

I thought about the horribly wounded veteran on the sidewalk. Christ, I hoped we took better care of our wounded than the damned Germans did.

I sat in the armchair in the room, thinking and waiting for the sun to rise. It was safe to say that Berlin was more decadent than Paris by a long shot. Berlin was unhealthy in its excesses. What we encountered was not "good, clean fun." I didn't see how the broader German population would allow the perversions we saw to continue. I wasn't sure how long Anita could continue. Maybe Germany did need a Bolshevik revolution. Their new republic didn't seem like it worked. I thought about Fuchs' words and Thomas Mann. Germany was broken, and sitting there in the dark, I was certain Europe would see another war.

As the sun started to lighten the horizon, I packed my bag. There was a lot of room without the uniforms. My movements woke Marie. She stretched like a cat, which was distracting. I found her robe and tossed it to her without a word.

13

––––––––

Easy Prey

The trip to Königsberg was uncomfortable. The previous night, just before he fled and the rest of us trooped up to Anita's apartment, Dyar had told us to report to a field south of the city. Tempelhof, he called the place.

When we arrived at what looked like a barracks muster ground with a few hangars, Fuchs was already there asleep in a folding chair. Dyar arrived shortly after.

Fuchs stood, rubbing his face with his hands. Neither of the men nor Marie were feeling particularly spry given their excesses of the previous evening. Compared to them, I was fresh as a daisy.

"Welcome to the Tempelhof parade ground. It is now an aerodrome. Today we fly, which is the most efficient way to reach Königsberg. But I do not complain. I like to fly," Fuchs told us.

I knew from Ladoux's itinerary that the distance to East Prussia meant we would have to fly.

"A new model. A Junkers J.13," Fuchs said proudly. "Brand

new. Just tested. It will revolutionize travel in Germany. We should be able to reach Königsberg without stopping for fuel. It will be up to the pilot, of course."

After donning heavy oversized coats, the four of us bundled into the back, which was cramped and had the unwelcome addition of belted seats, reminding us of the very real possibility of a crash. I sat in the back seat hip-to-hip with Marie. Dyar sat in a single seat in front of Marie, and Fuchs sat in front of me by the door.

I thought of Bullard and Mitchell, both of whom would have been all too happy to fly in this contraption. I missed them. I missed Paris.

Once we were in with our lap belts fastened, the pilot started the engine. The sky was clear, and it looked like a good day for flying. Of course, I was no judge. The plane jerked forward as the pilot released the brake and started to taxi down the grass toward the end of the field. I saw a wind sock hanging limply. Nevertheless, the pilot was taxiing to what he thought was downwind to take advantage of the non-existent breeze, leading me to believe he needed every bit of help he could get to become airborne—even if just faith in the wind direction.

We should have taken the train.

At the end of the field, the plane stopped. The pitch of the engine changed, just like a motorcar revving its engine when not in gear. The brakes came off again, and we started to roll. I had butterflies in my stomach and my heart in my throat as we bounced down the grass field.

I looked at Marie crammed next to me. She glanced at me, unsmiling. At first I didn't understand her look, but then I realized that she had flown before. This was not new for her. She was indifferent to the experience.

The plane rotated off the ground and started to climb.

I laughed. I couldn't help it. It was unnatural, but I could see why Mitchell had learned, and Bullard and Nungesser enjoyed it.

"You've flown before?" I shouted the question in Marie's ear.

She pointed to her ear and shrugged. Maybe it was too loud for her to hear me, or, more likely, she just didn't feel like having a shouted conversation. She turned to look out the window.

I wondered when she would have flown. And why? When she worked for Raux, I supposed. Still, it seemed improbable.

As we left Berlin behind us, the cold began to penetrate despite the coats. We leveled off high above the small towns, farms, and forests below. The brown and green patchwork camouflage on the airplanes above no man's land made sense seeing the quilt-like land below.

After twenty minutes, the novelty of flying had disappeared, and I was numb from the cold and vibrations. Marie had curled her head into my shoulder and appeared to be asleep. It looked like Dyar and Fuchs slept as well. The night's excesses had caught up with them.

I felt sorry for the pilot, whose only protection from the elements was a small windscreen, but I then remembered he was German. Also, he needed to stay awake, and the bracing chill of the wind slapping him in the face would do the trick.

I didn't sleep. Instead, I considered Marie and the mission that Raux had given me. Raux wanted me to see Germany and the Germans. He might have achieved more than he wanted. I was convinced that democracy was not good for Germany, and I thought many Germans would ultimately be convinced too. Berlin was a cesspool of depravity that ordinary Germans would ultimately not tolerate. The new Weimar Republic that Germany had adopted with the armistice, and the unchecked impulses I saw in Berlin, had brought a decadence that could not last.

I was curious about what I would find in Königsberg. It was

the Prussian heart of Germany. I wondered if the rot of Berlin would be repeated in the east. I had asked Dyar about it, but he did not know. Königsberg sat just on the edge of the redrawn Germany, isolated, with the new country of Lithuania to its east and an independent Poland to the south. Neither country would be favorably disposed toward Russia or Bolshevism originating from Russia. Given its location, I did not think I would find much evidence of wantonness or Bolshevism in Königsberg.

After three and a half bone-numbing hours, the plane bounced down on a field northeast of the city proper. I had examined Königsberg as we flew over. Two rivers joined just east of a small island in the middle of town and then the larger river ran west, emptying into a bay. The river below the island was crowded with steamships tied to wharves and other ships navigating up and down the river. Despite the treaty separating East Prussia from the rest of Germany, Königsberg seemed to be thriving.

New buildings were under construction along the grass runway. It looked like the Germans were building an aerodrome. The plane taxied to a low structure where an automobile waited. As our pilot shut down the airplane engine, the driver stepped from the car and crossed to the airplane to open the door to the compartment. The four of us climbed from the plane, stiff and thankful to be out of the cold.

"Welcome to Königsberg," Fuchs said as he followed the driver to the waiting car. "We will visit the local administrators at the *Schloss* and then have a late luncheon. All is planned."

All is planned. Great. The Germans would put on their Bolshevik dog and pony show, while Marie would whisper in my ear that it all was fabricated.

The drive from the airfield to the town was illuminating. The city was so old it felt like we were driving into the Middle Ages. Gingerbread stucco buildings with exposed structural beams lined the cobbled streets. The more modern buildings were a dark red brick or gray stone, heavy and serious, as one would expect from Prussia. The people too seemed dark, in conservative clothing with no smiles or energy. No eye-catching modern fashions were apparent on the sidewalks. The Germans were going to have to put on a pretty convincing display to sway my first impression that this town wanted nothing to do with Bolshevism.

The automobile pulled up through a brick archway into a courtyard dominated by a tall, spired clock tower.

An eager young man with thinning hair met us as we stepped from the car.

"Johann Ditzel," he said earnestly, reaching for my hand. "It is a pleasure to meet you." His English was precise if heavily accented. "I will act as translator." I wasn't sure why he singled me out, but there must have been something about me that shouted "foreigner."

"My wife can translate," I said.

He laughed. "Oh, there will be no need to burden you, madame," he said to Marie. "We have pastries and coffee set aside for you while your husband conducts his business."

It was clear, at least to me, that Marie wanted to argue, but she was bustled off by a nearby German woman, who outweighed me by at least twenty pounds.

Ditzel led us to a conference room where three officials waited. Two were heavy-set burghers, with muttonchop whiskers belonging to the previous century. The third man was a narrow-faced rat-looking fellow with slicked back hair and a weak smile. One of the Herr Muttonchops greeted us with a barrage of German, gesturing to the other two men, and I looked to Ditzel to translate.

"Provincial President Grawert welcomes you and your mission. He introduces Oberburgermeister Rattman, head of the city of Königsberg government, and Herr Krautschat, of the German empire Interior Ministry."

"Empire?" I asked, trying not to chuckle over the unfortunately named Krautschat.

"Yes, we remain the Reich, but we are also a republic now," Ditzel said with certainty.

I wasn't there to argue. I shrugged, and the lead Muttonchops started talking, Ditzel started translating, and I stopped listening. An hour later, after all three men voiced various complaints about Lithuanian saboteurs, Polish anarchist infiltrators, and increased arrests of anti-government ne'er-do-wells, I had heard nothing that convinced me Prussian Germany was facing an imminent revolution by Reds from Russia or anywhere else.

As the one-sided discussion ended, I smiled, nodded my thanks to the three functionaries, and stood. I didn't know if the Germans planned for the meeting to be over, but it was over for me.

"Do you have any questions for these gentlemen?" Ditzel asked hopefully.

"Not at present. I need to think about what I have been told," I said. "If I have any questions, how should I convey them to these gentlemen?"

Ditzel translated to the three, and after a short discussion, he answered. "Through me, tonight or in the morning. I will be at your disposal."

Dyar left the room and walked down the hallway toward the courtyard. As I entered the hallway, Fuchs stopped me. He signaled Ditzel, who closed the door on the other three Germans, and joined us. Marie stood out in the courtyard where she must have been deposited after her coffee and cakes. She started toward the doorway to join us, but I shook my head.

"Herr Major," Fuchs said, "a moment." He looked at the closed door. "I know this meeting was not satisfying. These old men do not know what they see or what is happening in their own city or their own province. They expect to see what they saw when the Kaiser ruled. Now we warn them of Bolsheviks, and all they see are Poles, Russians, and anarchists. If you are willing, Herr Ditzel will take us on an *Exkursion* tonight. A little trip. But it will be late tonight. We will show you the activities of the Reds in Königsberg. Johann has diligently tracked them, and he has learned that they will be having a meeting in the *Lagerhof*, the warehouse district by the river. Herr Major, this is not a trip for a woman. There will be danger."

"What about Dyar?" I asked.

"As I said, it will be dangerous if we are discovered. It is up to you."

I doubted we would actually find any Reds, and I doubted they would be dangerous if we did. Bolsheviks in Germany were a Kraut fairy tale.

"Of course I will go with you. Mrs. Griffin will remain at the hotel, and we will leave Mr. Dyar unbothered this evening," I said. At least Marie and Charles would get a full night's sleep.

"We will meet you outside your hotel at ten thirty tonight."

<hr>

DESPITE THE UNSAVORY NATURE OF THE PREVIOUS NIGHT, IT served me well. Dyar and Marie called it quits early, both retiring immediately after our mediocre dinner at the hotel restaurant. I followed Marie up to the room. When she withdrew to the bathroom, I pulled the pistol from the bottom of my bag and slotted it into the shoulder holster she had given me. I shrugged on the holster and pulled my jacket over it. Good enough. Anyone would have to be looking for a pistol to see the bulge. I called through the door that I was going to the hotel bar and left.

With nearly two hours to kill, I did what any self-respecting former marine would do. I left the hotel and found a bar. The Palast-café. The name was deceiving. It was a bar not a café. It sat on the second floor of a building one street over from our hotel. It wasn't crowded, and I had a table to myself. When the waiter arrived, he babbled at me in German. I gambled that he was asking me what I wanted, and I answered with one of my very few German phrases: *"Ein Bier, bitte."* I was in luck. He brought me a large blonde beer with an inch of white foam on top.

I considered my mission for Raux. Tomorrow I would try to convince Marie that we should fly back to Berlin and meet with some of Fuchs's bosses, with Dyar in tow. They'd try to convince me there were Reds in the woodwork. I would nod and agree. Then I'd tell Marie that we should go back to Paris, skipping the rest of the itinerary. I would sing the song that Raux wanted. There was no reason to waste any more time.

I thought about the men on the train to Berlin and Bertrand. Reynolds must have sent them. He had wanted Mitchell and me dead because of Paris and to get us out of his way with Patricia. He was indifferent to the need to kill Marie to make it happen. It would be time for me to settle with both Reynolds and Armistan once I got the French off my back.

I ordered a second beer to lubricate my thinking as I planned for my return to Paris and then New York City. Mitchell could help me in Paris, but I would honor my promise to Patricia. I wouldn't bring Mitchell with me when I settled Armistan's hash in New York.

It occurred to me that I was getting ahead of myself. I had to survive the current mission for the French before I could face Armistan and Reynolds. I was thinking like a spectator, watching events from the outside. I was behaving as if the mission for Raux was not mine at all. It was a French mission after all. Unfortunately, I wasn't a bystander. I was a character essential to, responsible for, and impacted by the outcome. I could be killed on a French mission just as easily as one for myself. I needed to take this trip more seriously, or it would kill me. I needed to focus. My marine drill instructor at Parris Island had tried to beat into our thick recruit heads that we had to *finish*. "Don't half step," he'd say. "Don't take the pack off; you're not done marching." I was thinking like I was already done with Raux's mission, done marching.

Don't take the pack off, Griffin. I had to survive this task for the French.

As I sat at the scarred wooden table in an out-of-the-way German city, nursing my beer, I realized I was supposed to die on this mission. It was in no one's interest that I survive. The French wanted me dead. They would claim I was murdered by the Germans, who wanted to prevent me from revealing that the Bolshevik threat in Germany was a sham. The Germans would happily kill me and then claim it was the Bolshevik menace that killed me. No doubt they would share evidence with Dyar or others to show that they should not have to disarm to the level required by the treaty. Each side would tell the story to their advantage, but I would be dead. It was all in the story that each side told Dyar and, ultimately, House. They didn't need me to tell their stories. The thought gave me chills.

For the French, Marie was my beautiful escort to the gallows. Her role was to confound me and ultimately deliver me to slaughter, ideally at the hands of Germans.

I took a sip of my beer and studied the room around me. No one was paying me any attention. They apparently didn't plan on killing me at the Palast-café. They would likely try to kill me on this late-night field trip away from Dyar and Marie. The trip with Ditzel and Fuchs would support the German version of events—a Bolshevik threat to Germany. My dead body would verify this story. I was glad for the pistol under my coat and glad for the focus that the chill down my spine had given me.

I looked at my watch. Ten twenty. I threw some Papiermarks

on the table. Too much, I was sure. It wasn't my money. The bills were from the oily Ladoux's envelope of cash.

Both Fuchs and Ditzel were in front of the hotel, leaning against a motorcar, when I arrived.

"We will need to drive. The meeting place is down the Pregel," Ditzel told me.

"The Pregel?" I asked.

"The river. The new and the old Pregel join to the east of here. We will be going west to the storage houses along the river," he explained.

"You know that I won't understand anything anyone is saying. If we're sneaking around, a whispered translation from the two of you probably isn't the smartest idea." I was trying to focus on keeping myself alive by limiting stupid choices.

"We know. The circumstances will have to be explanation enough," Fuchs said. Great, that answer wasn't reassuring.

Fuchs ushered me into the passenger seat of the motorcar, which Ditzel drove, and he climbed in back. Ditzel was a good driver but not as smooth on the gears as Disney.

We turned south to the river and then west as promised. The city lights reflected off the water, which looked choppy to my eye. I was sure it was damn cold despite the time of year. After about a mile and a half, Ditzel cut off his headlights and coasted next to a long, four- or five-story brick building that ran parallel to the river for what seemed like another half mile. We were definitely in the warehouse district.

"There is a Bolshevik meeting inside." Ditzel nodded to the building. "We will watch from the back. Do not speak, and stay with us. If we remain unnoticed, we should be safe enough."

We entered the structure and walked down a hallway made from crates piled so high they disappeared into the shadows above. Gaps in the stacks led off into the dark, but the rumble of many voices in low conversation guided us deeper into the building. We stepped out into a large storage area lit with oil lamps placed on wooden barrels throughout the space. A stairway zigzagged to the levels above. About twenty or so men, wearing cloth caps and work clothes, milled around the base of the stairs. Two men stood on the first landing above the floor, speaking with their heads together. I realized they intended to use the landing as a makeshift podium.

A few of the nearer men glanced at us, their eyes taking in our tailored clothes, shined shoes, and the scar on my face. They did not look friendly. I was reminded of my uniformed morning walk through Berlin. We wore the wrong uniform now. We might as well have been three peacocks for all our similarity to the men in the warehouse. Fuchs and Ditzel were fools for thinking they could sneak into a meeting of Bolsheviks, and I was a fool for trusting them.

Fuchs was nearest me, and I took his elbow. He turned, and I shook my head. He smiled and made a calming motion.

He had not struck me as an idiot when I spoke with him in Berlin, but he struck me as one now.

I pushed ahead and grabbed Ditzel's shoulder.

More of the men were noticing us now, and their calls drew the attention of one of the men on the landing. He was young, just the right age to have fought in the war. He spoke to the older man. "Look what we have here," I imagined him saying. Both men stared at us.

Finally Ditzel and Fuchs were paying attention, but we also had the attention of everyone in the room.

"Entschuldigen Sie. Wir sind am falschen Ort," Fuchs said to the crowd. I hoped he was telling them we were lost. I started to back toward the break in the crates. Ditzel and then Fuchs followed. Two workers blocked the path to the exit. Ditzel's eyes widened. I was surprised that he really hadn't expected trouble.

"*Unser Fehler*," Fuchs called to the men on the landing. "*Wir gehen.*" I understood the second part. "We're going." You're damn right we're going. I turned to face the two men blocking our way. They both opened their coats to show that they had pistols tucked behind their belt buckles. I guessed they were the security for this little meeting.

"*Scheisse*," I heard Ditzel whisper. Even I knew what that meant. I kept walking toward the exit and the two men. Both put their hands on their pistols.

Well, hell!

"Socialism, friends!" I called out. "Eugene Debs sent me to study European socialism! Tell them!" I shouted at Ditzel. "Tell them I am a representative of American socialist leader Eugene Debs." Colonel House and now Eugene Debs. I hoped this claim didn't bite me on the ass like my lies to Clemenceau and the French had.

"*Was*? What?" Ditzel asked, clearly frightened and having difficulty separating his German from his English. It likely didn't help that, against their express direction, I had not just spoken English, I had shouted it.

"Fuchs, tell them I work for the American socialist presidential candidate, Eugene Debs. Tell them I am here to learn from our socialist brothers in Germany how to bring a real change to America and American capitalism. Tell them you are my translator and Johann is our local contact. And hurry up."

Both the security men had their pistols pointing at my chest. I was committed to the bluff.

Despite my questions about Fuchs's intelligence, he understood what I was trying to do before Ditzel. Ditzel was too frightened to think.

Fuchs began to speak to the men on the landing. He ignored the gunmen and the rest of the hostile crowd. I heard "Debs" and "socialism" several times. They answered faster than I could pick out any words. I hoped Fuchs was a good liar. Every time he said "Debs" and "America," I nodded enthusiastically.

Now to be clear, I didn't know much about Eugene Debs. I knew he was bald as an egg from a picture I'd once seen. I knew he was a longtime rabblerouser. Before I was born, I was pretty sure he'd been tossed in the clink because he caused a railroad strike. I knew he ran for president in 1912, a few years before I left for England. My father had laughed the day after the election when he learned that Debs, a socialist, had run second in Florida to Wilson, doing better there than Roosevelt. He'd said to me, "Exactly what you should expect from Florida, son, Democrats and socialists." A month-old copy of the *New York Times* had made the rounds of the hospital where I'd been convalescing at the end of 1918. I'd read that Debs had been sentenced to ten years in federal prison for sedition. He'd made the mistake of speaking out against Wilson's decision to enter the war and the draft that the decision required. Debs was just the type of fellow all the old men who'd caused the war would hate and all the young socialist fire-eaters, who fought it, would love... if they'd heard of him. I wondered if Gavin or Horace, both Bolsheviks, would have heard of Eugene Debs. If not, then it wasn't likely the Germans in the warehouse would have.

I only had seven bullets in the Colt to open the way out.

"*Halt die Klappe!*" the older man shouted at Fuchs. "You are American?" he asked me. His accent was strong, but I could understand him.

"Well, yes, yes I am."

"It is dangerous for you to be here. Dangerous for you and dangerous for us. What do you want?"

"I was sent by Mr. Debs's socialist organization in the United States of America to understand how Germany, and all of Europe really, are organizing to promote the coming of a workers' revolution."

"We do not promote revolution. We are just workers. Organizing to make life better. There are no socialists here."

I looked around the warehouse floor. He was a liar. They were all socialists, but this was Prussia. The German Freikorps troops had just slaughtered all the Bolsheviks they could find earlier in the year in Berlin. These men were wise not to trumpet their politics. Socialist or Bolshevik added up to the same thing for the reactionary Freikorps soldiers I was sure were patrolling in Königsberg.

"I understand. Would you mind if I watched your proceeding?" I asked. "I do not speak German, but just seeing how you organize your meetings would be helpful to me."

He didn't like the request. He spoke to the young man next to him, who immediately left.

He turned back to me. "Very well. You may stay, but do not interrupt."

I looked at Fuchs and Ditzel. Both men smiled with relief. They were showing me Bolsheviks just as they'd promised, and it didn't look like we'd be beaten or killed.

The next hour was mind-numbing. Perhaps by design. I wasn't really sure what was happening, but I was sure I wouldn't have cared about it if I had known. Various men spoke. The crowd agreed with some, argued with others. At times, it seemed like they were voting. Through it all, the participants shot us dark looks.

Thank God the meeting ended before midnight. We were among the first to leave. I thanked the older gentleman. Hell, I shook his hand. By then, the younger man had returned. I shook his hand too.

The three of us retreated through the stacked goods back outside. I was in a hurry to get the hell out of there. I got to the motorcar first and jumped in back. Ditzel let Fuchs drive. Fuchs was rougher handling the automobile than Ditzel, but I didn't care because we were moving.

He jerked the car around and drove back down the river toward town. The two Germans laughed with relief at our escape. I wasn't ready to laugh, but I couldn't help but smile. I was relieved too.

"I thought we would be killed," Fuchs said to me over his shoulder.

"You and me both," I answered, and I was serious. In the warehouse, I had been sure the *Exkursion* would be the death of me.

"Very quick thinking," Ditzel added. "You were very convincing, but who is this Debs?"

I did laugh at that.

We hadn't gone a hundred yards when two silhouettes illuminated by the city behind them stepped into the road in front of us. Fuchs let off the accelerator and coasted toward them. As the headlights reached them, I could see that they were armed.

"Don't stop!" I shouted, leaning forward over the bench seat. "Drive through them!"

Too late. Both men raised their weapons. Automatic gunfire lit the night.

Goddamn machine pistols!

On instinct, Fuchs cut the steering wheel away from the gunfire.

The windscreen exploded in front of Ditzel, and the car rocked from the impact of the bullets. I dropped behind the driver's seat. As the car came to a stop, I pushed the back door open and rolled out of the car. I stayed low, keeping the car between me and the bullets hammering into the engine and frame. I got Fuchs's door open and pulled him out. I turned back to get Ditzel. He was dead. He had taken the brunt of the machine gunfire. His head no longer resembled anything human.

But for the grace of God and my hurry to get the hell out of the area, I would have been sitting in the front seat.

I found the Colt in my hand, and I jacked back the slide. Fuchs tried to get up from where I'd tossed him, and I pushed him back down. I looked over the steaming engine.

The gunmen were gone.

Fuchs tried to stand.

"Stay down!"

"Johann?" he asked.

"Dead. He's dead."

<hr>

The car was ruined, and we had to leave Ditzel's body. While the walk back into town wasn't far, it took nearly an hour because of my caution. Fuchs just stumbled blindly after me. Ditzel's killing had overwhelmed him. By the time we reached the hotel, Fuchs had recovered enough to rouse the local authorities who, in turn, alerted the German military. I woke Marie and Dyar and explained to them what had happened and then answered a lot of translated questions from the German authorities, civilian and military alike.

"John," Fuchs said to me during a break in our questioning, "attacks like this are why Germany needs to remain strong. The treaty will make us weak and easy prey for the Bolsheviks."

Fuchs's comment ignored the fact that, since Ditzel's murder, uniformed German soldiers in their camouflaged coal scuttle helmets had invaded the town. Stormtroopers. Seeing them up close made my stomach knot. My memories of the war remained too fresh to see them without a visceral reaction. They stood on the street corners armed with the Bergmann machine pistols of the very type that had killed Ditzel. Fuchs explained that, given its proximity to the east, a garrison of several thousand soldiers remained stationed in Königsberg. The

Germans soldiers I saw didn't look like the treaty had affected them at all. When I was finally released from the questioning, I met Marie in the hotel restaurant for breakfast. I told her my impression of the attack knowing it was what she would want to hear.

"Yes. This is all show," she told me as we sat down. "The men you saw last night were not Bolsheviks. They were playactors."

"And I suppose Ditzel was playacting as well?" That shut her up. Although he was a squarehead, I'd liked Ditzel. He was an earnest, hardworking kid trying to make his country a better place, and he'd gotten killed for it.

I thought about my decision last night to play along with Marie and the French. Had I actually seen any Bolsheviks? Not really. I didn't know who the killers were. It was too much of a coincidence to think they were unrelated to the men in the factory. If they had been associated with the gathering workers, why didn't they just kill us in the warehouse? Why let us go?

I had no proof of anything except that Germany remained a dangerous, unsettled place, which helped Fuchs's argument about the treaty. Of course, the French didn't care if Germany was dangerous and unstable. They just wanted Germany weak, and Germany didn't look weak this morning.

"Let's go back to Paris," I told Marie. "There is nothing else for us to see in Germany."

"No," Marie said urgently. "You have the impression that Bolshevism is a real danger because of one event."

"No, Marie, I don't. The streets are filled with German soldiers with modern weapons. I don't know who Ditzel's killers were. They could be out patrolling the streets right now dressed as German soldiers. Hell, they might actually be German soldiers, who followed us to the warehouse. I had a beer at a bar last night. They might have followed me from there. I'm obviously a foreigner. They could be like the assassins who attacked the allied soldiers in Berlin. Nationalists who don't believe Germany lost the war. I will tell Colonel House and the president exactly what you and Raux want me to tell them. There is no danger of a Bolshevik revolution in Germany. We're not going to learn anything else here. With all the soldiers in the streets, even if the town was brimming with Bolsheviks, I wouldn't see them."

Marie sipped her coffee, trying to judge my sincerity. "We will go back to Berlin," she said, compromising. "We will contact Préfet Raux from there and confirm that we may return."

14

———

The Smallest Splinter

Although I thought I had been freed from questioning, the authorities in Königsberg kept us another day seeking the identity of the men in the warehouse and the purpose of our visit there. Herr Krautschat did the questioning.

"Explain to me your relationship with the American socialist criminal Eugene Debs," he'd demanded in our first meeting. Fuchs had translated the question for me. They'd refused to allow Marie to translate.

"Karl," I'd said, "please explain to Herr Krautschat that I invented the relationship so that we could escape the damn warehouse. Hell, why can't you just tell him what happened?"

"I have," Fuchs said calmly, trying to soothe my temper. "He wants to hear what happened in your words."

"All my words are through you. And if he's heard what you saw, then why the hell is he asking me about my relationship with Debs! I have no relationship with Debs!"

Krautschat lit a cigarette as I bridled at his question. He smiled through the smoke.

"He knows this, but it is his job to probe. He is like all policemen."

"I thought he was with the Interior Ministry," I said.

"He is with the Sicherheitspolitzei, the new Security Police. It really will be simpler if you just answer his questions."

My fabricated relationship with Debs threatened to become as much of a problem as my lies to Clemenceau had been.

"So do I need a lawyer?" I asked Fuchs.

He laughed. "John, this is Prussia. One may need a lawyer, but one does not get one. You will be fine. Remain calm and answer honestly."

"Everything I say is translated by you, Karl, so make sure I answer honestly. You know the truth as well as I."

Krautschat asked Fuchs a question. He rocked back in his seat, and he was clearly shocked by what was asked.

"He asks if you knew that your wife left the hotel just after ten thirty last night?"

I was surprised as well, but I saw no reason Krautschat would lie about Marie's midnight travels.

"No. *Nein.*" Short answers and a little German might shorten his questioning so that I could question Marie myself.

Krautschat waited for more. He was going to have a long wait.

He asked another question, which Fuchs translated.

"Where did she go?"

I looked at Fuchs as if to say "You've got to be kidding me," then I looked at Krautschat and said, "You've got to be kidding me. I didn't know she'd left the hotel. So I don't know where she went."

Krautschat spoke again.

"He says he will ask her then," Fuchs explained.

I shrugged, which was probably not the reaction they'd expected.

"Please do, and let me know what she tells you," I said.

Krautschat questioned me for two hours. He forced me to answer the same questions asked in different ways. I had no idea what Fuchs was actually saying in the translated answers, but eventually Krautschat dismissed me. I told Fuchs to let him know that we would be leaving for Berlin the following day. Krautschat didn't balk at my announcement.

I went looking for Marie to let her know that we were free to leave in the morning and to find out where she'd gone last night. I found her in our room.

———

SHE WAS STANDING BY THE WINDOW, STARING OUT AT THE SPIRES of the old town, dressed in a cream blouse and a high-waisted pleated skirt with pockets in front. She turned from the window, and I thought I saw regret in her eyes. She looked very beautiful.

"Are we free to leave?" she asked.

"Yes, at least so far." I walked to the window and stood next to her. "I learned something during my questioning that surprised me," I told her. "It might prompt some questions for you."

"Oh, what is that?"

"Herr Krautschat told me that you left the hotel last night. Just after I did."

She turned toward me and cupped my face in her left hand.

"It is a shame that we never made love," she said.

I frowned at her words. They confused me.

As I started to speak, her right hand flashed to her skirt pocket and flicked out to her side as her left hand fastened tight to my jaw.

Oh shit!

I jerked myself away from her, feeling her nails tear my cheek. The razor flashed under my chin. I honestly didn't know if she sliced my throat or not.

I backpedaled as she slashed again. I was pinned against the bed and pulled a pillow in front of me as a shield. I recognized the absurdity of using a pillow, but I had nothing else. She snapped the razor down, trying to slice the veins inside my arm holding the pillow. I snatched my arm back, and she used the distraction to whip the razor toward my neck. I knocked it past me, punched her. Hard. A straight jab to her jaw. Bullard and Carpentier would be embarrassed to know that the skills they'd drilled into me had been used to punch a woman. In my defense, she was a very dangerous woman.

The razor flew from her hand, and her eyes unfocused. I hit her again with a hook just where her lovely blouse tucked into her skirt. She sat down with a thump, gagging for breath. My mother would have been so proud. So much for not hitting girls, but these really were exceptional circumstances.

I found the razor, folded it shut, and put it in my pocket. I pulled one of the ridiculous tiebacks from the window curtains. Marie was struggling to stand, so I kicked her in the side. Not too hard but hard enough to get her attention. I threw her on her stomach and tied her hands behind her back. The knot wouldn't hold her long, but I just needed her restrained for a moment to figure out what the hell was going on.

I took her razor from my pocket and squatted down in front of her. I turned it over in my hands, flipped it open and shut it again. When I looked back at her, she was watching me. She was breathing better. Her jaw, where I'd punched her, was already swelling and starting to bruise. Oh well. I wasn't sure she was going to live through the next ten minutes, so a little bruising would be a minor inconvenience. She must have seen the thought cross my face.

"I'm sorry, John. I had my orders."

"Really. Orders. To kill me. From whom?"

"That's why I left the hotel last night. To receive new orders.

There was some worry that you might survive the attack at the warehouse. I was to be the solution in the event you did."

"The solution. As in my murderer," I said with certainty. I opened the razor.

"John, I had no choice." I had her complete attention.

"Marie, I'd like to say that I would never kill a woman, but that's just not true." I thought of poor Yvette, dressed in a German uniform coming around the end of the truck on the rue Franklin. I'd shot her twice in the chest. What had Horace Merchant told me about her? Ah, yes. He'd said "She just wanted to make the world a better place." Nearly exactly what I'd thought of Ditzel. And Sarah, who I'd distracted to her death. "I'm afraid you won't be the first woman I've killed. Or even the second."

I leaned toward her and laid the edge of the razor against her cheek. She held very still.

"Whose orders?"

"John, please. I had no choice." Her eyes were brimming with tears.

I shook my head.

"That won't work, Marie." She knew I meant the tears. Nevertheless, she started to sob.

I put the razor back in my pocket and picked her up. She struggled, and I banged her head off the doorframe of the bathroom. That stunned her enough for me to get her into the tub. She was on her back with her arms under her. I plugged the drain and turned both faucets on full.

I took out the razor again. She started to struggle and kick her legs, but her long, increasingly wet skirt made it difficult. I was sure she was trying to work her hands free. I stiff-armed my weight down onto her chest, trapping her still-bound arms, making it impossible for her to move them.

"Whose orders?" I asked again.

She started thrashing, and I pushed the straight razor against her neck.

"I'll make it look like suicide, Marie," I said over the noise of the running water.

She stopped moving and sagged back into the tub.

"Suicide by slicing your own neck would be unexpected, but I can be very convincing."

The tub continued to fill. I kept my weight on her and stared down into her eyes. Her gilded irises trapped me. She no longer looked panicked. She looked resigned.

"I have been an agent for Germany as well as France," she said. I wasn't sure I'd heard her right. I took the razor from her throat and turned off the water.

"What?" I asked.

"I am a German agent. A spy for Germany."

I rested my hand holding the razor on the edge of the tub. She could still see it, but it was a lot less threatening than when it was pressed to her neck. She was talking, which was what I wanted.

"I have no choice. They have my child. He is their hostage. They will kill him."

"You have a child?"

"Yes. He was born in 1912. His father was German. We met in the United States. Our fathers were diplomats in Washington. His for Germany and mine for France. The diplomatic community is a small one, and we went to school together. We became attached."

"That must have been awkward for your parents."

"Not at all. Our parents got along well. Diplomats, no matter the country, are not so different. They were happy for us. We were in love. We were married in Washington. Then we came back to Europe. Albert, my husband, had to complete his compulsory military service, so I lived in Berlin with his parents. We did not consider the possibility of war. He was killed in the first month fighting the Russians. Not far from here, in fact. I was shattered. His parents tried to convince me to stay in Berlin, but I took my son, Jean-Paul, and we left. By then, I wanted nothing to do with the war. My parents wanted me to move to the south of France with them, but I took Jean-Paul, and we went to Switzerland. But they found me and took my son."

"Who took him?"

"The Germans. They knew where I had gone. They had followed my moves, my life. They took him just after I moved to Basel and gave him to his grandparents. They knew I would do anything to protect my child."

I thought back to the night she'd tried to seduce me. She'd had stretch marks on her otherwise perfect belly. Marks from carrying a child. It made sense.

"I have had to do what they have demanded or they will kill my son," she continued.

"How did German intelligence know about you?"

"I'm not sure. Through Albert perhaps. He was in the infantry, but maybe he had spoken about me to his superiors. Or his father, who remained active in the Reich diplomatic corps, which has always been affiliated with German intelligence. When their son died, Albert's parents did not want me to leave Germany. They wanted to keep their grandson close. Keep him in Germany, but I could not stay. The passion for the war sickened me, and I thought I could escape. I was a fool."

"And Raux, how did you end up working for him?"

"The Germans wanted me working for the Deuxième Bureau. I was ordered to move back to Paris and to find a way to work for the French. I met Philippe Masson. A doctor. He was a good man, and he was well connected in France. He went to the proper schools. He knew the right people. He loved me."

I could imagine her seducing the poor bastard. He wouldn't have stood a chance.

"With the war, he didn't want to waste time," she continued.

"I didn't want to marry, but he insisted. And it was better for my position with the French. As his wife and a nurse, I was trusted. He was a reservist as most men were. He had already been called up, but he was stationed near Paris. I could travel to see him. By then, we knew the war would not be short. He died in 1915. Artillery struck his field hospital.

"It was through Philippe that I met Préfet Raux. After Philippe died, Préfet Raux was very enthusiastic to have me as a resource. I was the perfect candidate. I spoke English and German fluently. In his eyes, I was motivated to do anything necessary because of my husband's death. He was delighted when I volunteered."

"Raux has no idea you have a son?"

"No. No one in France knows."

I closed the razor and put it in my pocket. Then I pulled her up out of the water and set her on her feet.

"Don't do anything stupid, Marie. I don't want to hit you again." Her jaw looked painful. I was sure it hurt to talk. "Where is your son?"

"He is in Berlin."

I pushed her into the bedroom.

"What were your new orders?"

"If you survived the attack last night, I was to kill you. I would then reveal myself as a French spy secretly operating for the Bolsheviks. France would be embarrassed. As would America. My papers are American. Wilson and House would believe that Bolsheviks are everywhere in Germany and France, and they would resist the disarmament of Germany. Of course, I would be executed, but my son would live. I have been a good spy for Germany, but I would be sacrificed for the good of the Fatherland."

"But your son would be an orphan. And he'd grow up as a German without you to guide him. Better for him to die," I said brutally. I could not imagine raising a child as a German. They remained the enemy for me.

"You have no children. You don't know how much you can love your child. Or what you will do for them. I want my son to live, and I will do anything to protect him." She continued to work her hands behind her back, trying to loosen the rope. I wasn't sure what she hoped to accomplish, but I didn't want to have to fight her again.

"Sit down on the bed and stop worrying at the rope," I said. It was possible she might still attack me, and I wanted to think without having to fret about it.

She sat.

"You're right. I don't have children," I said. "I don't know what I would do to keep one safe if I did. But sacrificing yourself to protect your son is insane. Once you are dead, the Germans would have no reason to keep him alive. In fact, his very existence could be used as evidence that you were coerced by Germany into betraying France." I didn't mention her being coerced into killing me. I didn't think the French or Americans would be particularly bothered by my death. In fact, my ruminations from the night before came back to me. I was sure that the French, like the Germans, would find a silver lining in my end.

She sat on the bed, wet and dripping, hands tied behind her back, thinking about what I'd said.

"His grandparents would never let that happen," she said, but I could hear the doubt in her voice.

"German intelligence was forcing you to murder me and then commit suicide by firing squad. Do you really think they would balk at the murder of one child, no matter what his doting grandparents might think? The grandparents probably have no idea he is a hostage for your loyalty. Seven-year-olds die every day. Especially in a country that just lost a war."

Her eyes were huge as she stared at me and considered my

words. Then she started to cry. Huge shuddering gasps seized her. She tried to control them, but she must have realized that no matter what she did, her son was doomed. She folded her chest onto her knees with her head down and her wet hair covering her face as the sobs racked her body.

I cut the ties from her arms and stepped away. I didn't think she was acting, but why take a chance?

She drew her knees up onto the bed and wrapped her arms around them, rolling onto her side. Her body heaved uncontrollably.

I cursed myself. I had wondered what the war had done to her to make her a detached and dispassionate killer and whore. Now I knew. They had her son. And she would do anything, anything at all, to protect him.

I knew I would try to help her. I would try to save her son.

"You can fight them, Marie," I said softly. "You can fight them and try to take your son back. You may fail, but it won't be because you didn't try."

I waited, and slowly her grief abated.

"I will help you, but I can't do that if I'm dead."

"How?" she asked me with just the smallest splinter of hope in the question. "How will you help me?"

"We will go to Berlin and get your son. I don't know how the hell we'll get out of Germany, but we'll start by getting your son." I reconsidered. "Actually, we'll start by keeping me alive."

I didn't return her razor.

15

A Very Welcome Voice

Marie cleaned herself up after what had been a difficult morning. Even with cosmetics, there wasn't much she could do about the bruise on her chin. I escorted her to lunch in the hotel restaurant and met Dyar, Fuchs, and Krautschat.

When they saw Marie's face, Dyar shook his head and looked disappointed. Fuchs just raised an eyebrow and said nothing. Krautschat, on the other hand, gave me a hard smile, in which I thought I detected a hint of respect.

"Mrs. Griffin," Krautschat said, "I have a few questions for you." He looked at me as if for permission. I nodded briskly, playing the role of the brute, and said, "Go with him."

It appeared that Krautschat was unaware that she was a spy for Germany, and his questioning would be intense. We had agreed she would tell him that she had been searching for me. Unless she was seen meeting with her actual contact, Krautschat should accept her story. She'd told me she'd never met the man until last night. The hotel floor maid had given her a note with instructions to meet him at 10:40 p.m. at a nearby botanical garden. She'd destroyed the note as she had been trained to do.

When she arrived at the garden, her contact had been sitting on a park bench. The garden was otherwise empty. They'd spoken for less than a minute. He'd told her that if she wanted her son to live, she needed to kill me and declare herself a Bolshevik. There was no discussion. I'd asked her to describe him. She'd claimed he was unremarkable, of medium height with brown hair.

The obvious flaw in our plan was that I continued to draw breath. Her German puppet masters would be well aware of this. They could react by killing her son, but he was far away. The Germans wouldn't want to give up on her too quickly. I had convinced her that they would not kill her son until they made at least some effort to get an explanation from her for her failure to kill me. If we stayed together, they would not have the chance to question her—unless Krautschat was in on the plan of Marie's handlers. Then I'd have a problem. She'd feel forced to follow through with murdering me, and she'd find a way to stick a butter knife in my neck. We needed to get to Berlin and her son to eliminate that temptation.

I sat in the restaurant with Dyar and Fuchs, waiting for Marie's interview to finish. The wait wasn't long. Krautschat brought her to our table and declined an invitation to eat with us. Because we were not alone, I couldn't question Marie about her grilling by Krautschat. During the meal, she was lively, which I took to be positive. I confirmed with Fuchs that the airplane would be ready to return us to Berlin in the morning.

"I don't need to see any more evidence of Bolsheviks in Prussia, Karl, I assure you," I told him.

We stayed in the hotel the rest of the day and, as promised, departed for Berlin in the morning.

Once in Berlin, a car collected us at the airfield and brought us back to the Hotel Adlon. Dyar and Fuchs made plans to have dinner with us.

Marie and I were standing at the front desk, checking into the hotel again, when I heard a familiar and very welcome voice behind us.

"Why if it isn't Major Griffin and his lovely wife."

I couldn't help but smile. I turned to find William Mitchell striding confidently across the white-tiled lobby toward us. It was good to see him. He examined Marie from her shining chestnut hair to her finely turned ankles. I could tell he hadn't missed her bruised face. I could also tell that he found her to be as attractive as I did.

"William Mitchell, Mrs. Griffin," he said, introducing himself to my faux wife. Marie looked at me.

"It's good to see you, Will. My very best friend, Marie, from the service," I said by way of explanation. "You'll recall he couldn't make it to our wedding."

She offered her hand, which he kissed.

"Of course. It is a pleasure to finally meet you, and how fortunate to meet you here," she said warily.

"You seem to have been injured," he said. He knew I wouldn't beat her, but he was mischievous enough to be unwilling to let me off the hook for her battered face. He looked at me, and I shrugged.

"Clumsy of me. I walked into a door in our hotel in Königsberg," she said.

"We just flew in," I told him.

"How exciting. I love flying. Well, I'll let the two of you check in. Have you eaten? Let's have lunch once you are settled."

"You're babbling like a giddy schoolgirl, Mitchell. Come up to our room with us. We'll have a drink there and then some lunch. I'll tell you about Germany, and you'll tell me why you're here." I didn't look at Marie. I was going to tell him everything whether she agreed or not. We needed the help.

He did look at Marie, but she didn't react.

"Sure, sure. Lead the way."

———

Our room had a sitting room and a bedroom with an attached bath. It was nicer than our first stay. Marie kicked off her shoes and sat on the couch with her legs curled under her, watching Mitchell carefully.

I poured three whiskeys from the room bar.

"Marie." She looked at me. "We need his help," I said as I handed her the drink.

Mitchell didn't say a word. He studied the two of us, waiting for us to come to a decision.

She gave a curt nod.

"Mitch, you're going to wish you'd stayed in Paris. Patricia's not with you, is she?"

"She's still in France. Reynolds has disappeared, and she thinks he's up to no good on behalf of her father. But I can tell you that some other folks there are missing you." His veiled reference to Madeline gave me a pang of something: longing, regret. But not guilt. Realizing that I didn't feel guilty buoyed me. I still missed Sarah, but I realized I missed Maddy too.

I ignored his comment and asked, "And Patricia let you loose to come here?" I was surprised he was willing to leave her alone with Reynolds unaccounted for.

"She doesn't need me to protect her. You, on the other hand, do. I started planning to get here as soon as I got your telegram. Patricia, I can leave alone. You, well, you'll find trouble, or it will find you."

"True enough." I looked at Marie. She nodded once more. "You already know the French wanted me to go to Germany with Marie posing as my wife to determine if there really is any threat of the Bolsheviks taking over Germany."

"Yeah, go on."

"Well, there are Bolsheviks everywhere. We examined the body of one of the men who attacked us on the train on the way here. He was carrying a French labor union card. Probably a Red."

"John," Marie said apologetically. "I'm afraid I planted that union card on the body."

I stared at Marie for what must have been a full five seconds digesting her words. She really had done nothing but manipulate me since I'd met her. Sure, she'd told me she was a German spy, but this brought it home. She must have read my reaction on my face.

"And making me wear the uniform?"

"Both the French and the Germans wanted that. You really are more valuable to both dead."

I shook my head in disgust.

"I'm sorry," she said.

Mitchell listened to our exchange without comment. He knew he had stepped into the middle of something, and he was willing to let us tell him about it in our own way.

"Anyway," I said, putting her small betrayals behind me, "the Germans gave me some guides. Fuchs, who works for the Kraut foreign ministry, and Ditzel, who was a government translator from Königsberg. They took me to a meeting of labor union members who might have been Bolsheviks. On the way back from the meeting, we were ambushed by two men with machine pistols. Ditzel was killed, and the men disappeared."

"Well, that's terrible, but where you are concerned, commonplace. I am surprised this Fuchs fella didn't get killed too," Mitchell said unsympathetically. My reputation for mayhem meant little would shock him. I was certain that was about to change.

I ignored his phlegmatic attitude and continued. "German intelligence wanted me killed so that they could blame the

Bolsheviks. They hoped my death would confirm the reality of Reds in Germany and prompt Wilson and House to resist Germany's disarmament as required by the treaty."

"Clever," Mitchell said, "but how do you know this?"

He caught my glance at Marie. Mitchell had a sixth sense for danger. He had been leaning back on the couch with his legs crossed and his arms spread across the back. Now he leaned forward with some of the weight on the balls of his feet. I had his attention now.

"Marie, do you want to tell him or should I?"

She crossed her arms. "I will tell him," she said with conviction.

I was impressed. I would have let me do the explaining. But I'm a coward.

"I am a German spy and have been since 1915. The Germans hold my child hostage. He lives with his grandparents in Berlin, but make no mistake, he is a hostage. I have no choice in working for Germany. If I do not, German intelligence will kill him."

Mitchell waited patiently for her to continue.

"My orders were to behave as a French agent would behave, while planting evidence to influence John into believing that a Bolshevik revolution is a real possibility in Germany. My handlers changed their approach a few nights ago. John went on the late-night visit he described, and they were able to orchestrate an assassination attempt. They decided that his death at the hands of Bolshevik assassins would be more persuasive than a living John arguing that Bolshevism is a viable threat in Germany. When he left for that meeting, I got new orders."

Mitchell just cocked his head and listened. He didn't want to interrupt her story with questions.

"If he survived the attack, I was to kill him and reveal myself to the Germans to be a Bolshevik agent. This would embarrass the United States and France, and it would convince America that disarmament of Germany would be a mistake."

"Well, I'm glad you decided not to kill Griffin. I am fond of him," Mitchell said with a smile.

"Perhaps I wasn't clear. They have my son. I had no choice but to kill him."

The light bulb went on in Mitchell's head. "You did try to kill him. That's why your face is beat up." He looked at me. Now he was shocked. "John, you hit a girl!"

"You would've hit her, too, if she'd come at you with a razor in her hand."

That impressed him. "Well, I guess I might have," he said almost under his breath.

He faced Marie. "But you didn't kill Griffin. You've failed, and I'm sure the Boche won't let you get away with that. What are you going to do about your son? You'd better think of something."

Before she could answer, his jaw dropped open, and he started to shake his head. He gave me a glare that told me he knew exactly what I was going to do.

"Oh crap! Goddamn it, Griffin! You are insane."

Marie looked at me in confusion.

"He's figured it out, Marie. And yes, Mitch, we're going to save her son."

All he could do was shake his head again.

"I should have known. You do realize we're in the middle of Germany. Where is your son?"

"Here, in Berlin. With his grandparents. And we must hurry. I will be asked why I have failed, and my answer, no matter what it is, will be inadequate. Then they will kill my son, kill me, kill John, and after my death claim I was a Bolshevik. It is not as good as me alive, admitting my guilt, but it will do. And once they know you are here, they will kill you too."

Mitchell raised his eyebrows and looked at me. "So we're

gonna kidnap a little Kraut kid, no offense, Marie," he said, giving offense, "from his grandma and grandpa. We're then gonna run like hell through nearly the entire length of Germany. Running from the German cops the whole way. And assuming we actually reach France alive, we're gonna have to find a way to convince the French and Clemenceau, who ain't so inclined, to forgive a longtime traitor, who has been spying for the Germans—I repeat, the *Germans*—during the entire course of a world war that cost the French millions of lives."

"I just want to save my son. I will face my punishment," Marie insisted.

Mitchell barked out a laugh. "Lady, you really don't understand this man at all, do you? He's not gonna let you face your punishment, which is much deserved in my opinion! *He's* gonna do everything he can to save you. He can't help it. He's not very bright, but he is consistent. He'll try even if it kills him."

"Will, she had no choice," I said sincerely.

"Bullshit! But it doesn't matter now. You're an idiot, but you know that." He took a breath. "What do we do?"

I breathed a sigh of relief. Despite his anger, Mitchell was on board. Patricia might hate me for it, but I needed his help.

"I think Marie will hear from her handlers today or tonight. I think we should keep you as our ace in the hole. The Germans don't know you and don't know you're here to help us. I'll stay with Marie as much as I can. As she said, after they speak with her, they will act: to kill the boy, her, and me. So we need to delay anyone speaking with you, Marie. And we need to get the boy. As soon as possible. Tonight. To do that, we need to understand where he is. Marie, we need you to describe the neighborhood, the house, and we need a way out of Berlin. The train would be best."

"Jean-Paul's grandparents live along the Hundekehlesee, a small lake west of Berlin, near the Grunewald area. They have a large house at number 8 Gustav Freytag Strasse."

"What the hell does Hundekehlesee mean?" I asked.

"Literally, 'dog's throat lake,'" she answered, which drew a scoff from Mitchell.

"Really? Named after a dog's throat. That sounds picturesque. We're going to kidnap a boy from his granny who lives on the edge of *Dog's Throat Lake*? You couldn't make this shit up. And I suppose he's heavily guarded too?" Mitchell was making it clear to me that just because he was going to help did not mean he liked it.

"He will be watched. Well, at least the house is. His grandfather remains a high-ranking official within the foreign ministry. There will be soldiers guarding the property, and they have a large and very loyal staff."

"Dogs?" I couldn't help asking, remembering my terrifying encounter with Coco, the guard dog in Paris.

"No," she assured me.

"Marie, how will you feel if we have to kill some of the loyal staff or little Johnny P's grandparents?" Mitchell asked.

"Jean-Paul, his name is Jean-Paul." She did not find Mitchell amusing. "You may kill them all," she answered coolly.

Mitchell looked aghast. He had seen and done terrible things. He didn't expect this attractive young woman to be cut from the same cloth. Also, he hadn't seen Marie with a razor in her hand or seen her stripped naked willing to sleep with a stranger to save her son. I had no doubt she meant what she said. Of course, he didn't know that his own girlfriend was a murderer. It seemed that many young women of this postwar age were cut from fabric just as tough as ours. Sarah had been. I wondered about Madeline. She certainly didn't weep at my departure. Either tough or indifferent. Probably the latter.

"We need a map," I said. "Dyar should be able to get us one. I'm going to go by his flat and see what he can do. Mitch, stay here with Marie, and try to stay out of trouble." I stood to go and then turned back to Marie, thinking. I reached into my jacket and pulled out her straight razor. Mitchell's eyes widened when he saw it.

"Marie," I said sternly, "do not kill my friend. I'm giving this back because from here on, it's dangerous for all of us, and I think you may need it. Remember, we're here to help you. Without us, you are dead, and your son is dead. You understand."

Her eyes moved from mine to the razor and back.

"I understand, and thank you."

"Don't fall asleep, Mitch," I said over my shoulder as I left the room. I'm sure he could hear my chuckle as I started down the hallway.

16

———

Missing Linens

Dyar did have a map of Berlin and Germany as well. He'd asked me why I needed them. I told him part of the truth: the Germans were plotting to kill me as part of their scheme to convince the United States that Bolshevism was a threat to the new German republic. He nodded and didn't press me. He sensed that something else was up, and I wouldn't have been surprised if he just thought it was marital discord. A punch in your wife's kisser might make you a heel, but it sure limited questions.

"Charles, we're leaving early tomorrow morning," I explained. "There may be some interest in us after we are gone. The German security service or intelligence may want to talk to you. You tell them whatever you want, but I'd appreciate it if you didn't tell them anything about our leaving." I handed him some Papiermarks. "We're going without checking out of the hotel. Please settle our bill in a few days."

"I won't tell the fucking German intelligence folks a goddamn thing. They can't screw around with me. I'm an

American. Are you still having dinner with Richter, Dix, and Anita?" he asked.

"Yes," I said. "And don't forget Karl Fuchs will be there too."

"Well, I wouldn't talk about your plans tonight. Hans, Otto, and Anita might have no choice but to talk to the police, and let's face it, I may like him, but Karl is part of the government. He'll definitely help the German intelligence service and the police."

"None of them will know anything that could hurt us. We'll tell them tonight that we are staying for a few more days, and that's what they'll tell whoever questions them."

"Karl might be blamed for you disappearing. I'd bet he was told to keep an eye on you," Dyar said.

"I hope we don't get him in trouble. He seems like one of the good guys, if there's such a thing in this godforsaken country."

I left his flat and walked back to the hotel. As I neared the building, I saw several black motorcars parked haphazardly on the street and sidewalk in front of the Adlon. Pedestrians were craning their necks to see inside the hotel, but two uniformed German policemen were steering them past. One of them stopped me as I approached the front door.

"I'm a guest," I told him.

He shrugged.

"A guest," I said louder. "Here." I exaggerated my enunciation and pointed at the hotel.

He jabbered at me and waved me through. Goddamn Germans.

The lobby was awash with uniformed policemen and stern-looking men in long trench coats, likely left over from the war. Coppers. Almost certainly.

I took the steps two at a time up to our floor and knocked on the door to our room. Mitchell answered. He looked a little pale.

"William, are you all right?"

"Yeah, I'm fine. Jesus Christ, I'm glad to see you. Get in here."

I ducked into the room quickly. "Is Marie okay? Where is she?" I asked, alarmed.

"Yep. Happy as a dog with two tails. She's in the bathroom, *cleaning up,*" he said with curious emphasis.

"What's got you so shaken?"

"Marie's handler showed up here at the room. He knocked right after you left. We thought it might have been you coming back. I thought this whole spy thing was a joke, but there he was, knocking on the door."

"That's not good," I said.

"Well, it certainly wasn't good for him. Marie answered the door. I heard her invite him in. 'Welcome in here,' she says, almost like she's speaking English but softly and quickly, but she was speaking German. I was already reaching for my gun when he walked right in. I was standing right over there." Mitchell pointed to the middle of the sitting room. "He sees me and starts to reach under his coat. That was a mistake. 'Cause I was all ready to shoot him, but I didn't have to. As he's looking at me and reaching for his gun, Marie came right up behind him, reached around, and slit his throat from ear to ear with that goddamn razor."

"Jesus," I whispered.

"But Griff, the worst part isn't that she killed the son of a bitch. The worst part is she had the whole thing planned."

"What?" He wasn't making sense.

"I didn't know it, but as soon as you left, she'd already picked up the runner from the floor by the door and set it aside. Instead of a runner, she laid down a couple of hotel towels. He walked straight over 'em. When he fell, he landed smack-dab in the middle of the towels, and she had a whole bunch of towels just inside the door. She wrapped his neck, and he was still alive. Dying, but still alive. She stripped him of his gun, shoulder holster and all, and tossed it aside. And she tells me to grab his legs, and we drag him to the bathtub where he finishes bleeding out. We then wrapped up the whole bloody mess, body and all, in some sheets. Then, on her directions, I carry him down the hall and drop him down the laundry chute. She'd already checked to make sure a body would fit."

"How do you know that?" I was moderately horrified.

"Because I asked her!"

"Jesus," I said again.

"As he fell, she held her hand over the opening in his neck to keep the blood off the walls. I think that's why she's bathing."

"We need to get more towels and sheets. The police are downstairs. They'll start checking to see who is missing linens."

"Good luck to them," Mitchell said grimly. "While I was stuffing the poor sod down the laundry chute, she stole a bunch of sheets and towels from the floors above. Jeez, I hope she didn't steal them from my room," he said with a flash of horror.

"Better go check, Mitch."

He started for the door.

"We're going out to dinner tonight, so you're on your own," I told him. "Be back here at midnight. We'll leave for the boy then."

"John, I don't see how a person could be so coldhearted. I mean, she's just a girl. A young, pretty girl, like you'd take to a picture show. But she killed that man without a thought. How could she kill a man like that?"

"You're really asking that? Look what we've become. We're just not smart enough to do the planning she did, but that doesn't mean we couldn't do the killing."

"You're right, but it's just different. I just don't understand it. She scares the shit out of me."

I nodded sympathetically and patted him on the shoulder. "Just keep her at arm's length. That's what I do." I couldn't help but think of Patricia. The girl with whom he was infatuated. She'd shot her husband in the face from spitting distance. I was sure Patricia had been looking him in the eye at the time. That was pretty damn coldhearted too, but I didn't think I should tell my friend that.

After Mitchell left, I went to check on Marie.

I tapped on the bathroom door. The water was running, but I was sure I heard crying.

"Marie, are you okay?"

"I am fine. Why wouldn't I be? The police will be knocking on the door soon. I have flushed his identification papers, but make sure I have not missed anything."

"You're sure you're all right."

"You're wasting time," she answered. She might be in there sobbing her eyes out, but she wasn't going to show any more weakness to me. I'd seen all I'd ever see when she admitted the Germans had her son.

I left her alone. She didn't really need me to double-check her work. I was certain she hadn't missed anything. She wanted to cope with the murder of her handler alone and in her own way. The war had made her into something no woman—hell, no person—should be, but her humanity wasn't entirely gone. Her lonely struggle in the bath made me feel better. It gave me hope that, perhaps, my humanity wasn't entirely gone either.

As Marie predicted, about twenty minutes later, the police were at the door. There were two of them. When I answered, one was bending down to fit a master key to the lock. They must have been canvassing all the rooms in the hotel. Where no one answered, they checked each room anyway.

They yammered away at me, and I kept saying, "American visitor." They didn't understand me, and I didn't understand them. Marie came to the door with her hair in a towel and wrapped in a robe. She had a second towel clutched to her chest. The German coppers lost interest in investigating the moment she showed up in her bathrobe. She spoke to them for a few minutes, gestured to her towels, and pointed to the bathroom.

Their eyes noted the bruise on her jaw but then spent more time following her ankles.

"Tell them to come back later when you're dressed," I said gruffly.

I don't know what she told them, but they both gave me the evil eye as they left.

"What'd you tell them?" I asked.

"I said you were very jealous and would beat me again for coming to the door in my robe. I don't think they liked you."

I laughed. "No, I don't think they did, and I don't much blame them."

<hr>

IT HAD STARTED TO RAIN, AND THE WEATHER HAD TURNED COLDER. Dyar picked us up outside the hotel for dinner at seven sharp in a maroon Mercedes touring motorcar. Although he wasn't actually driving, he looked very proud when he pulled up, and I felt compelled to compliment the car.

"Nice motorcar, Charles. Does it belong to the mission?"

"Yes, the US commissioners to the peace conference gave me a special dispensation to buy it. The technical advisors wanted me to buy a Cadillac. Why buy German when you can buy American was their thinking. I convinced them that Berlin wasn't worth the price of a Cadillac. Really, I just wanted the car right away. Oh, and don't talk about anything you don't want reported to German intelligence. I'm sure the driver is one of theirs."

The driver was a broad-shouldered man, who was either bald or shaved the sides of his head close enough to make him look bald under his chauffeur's cap. He looked the part of a German soldier turned spy.

"The car is certainly big enough." I followed Marie into the spacious back seat, and Dyar sat in front next to the driver. I considered our plan of escape from Berlin. A motorcar would certainly be quick and quiet, but I didn't see a way to convince Dyar to give up the automobile. Also, getting rid of the driver would be awkward. Unfortunate, but we'd just have to take the train. With the Grunewald train station sitting less than a kilometer from the grandparents' house, we had no better alternative.

We drove to the east side of Berlin, and the driver deposited us directly in front of the restaurant. Karl Fuchs was waiting for us outside. To the right of the columned entryway and above two large, curtained windows, big black letters were affixed to the gray stucco building and read HORCHER.

"The Listener," Marie supplied when I looked her way. She was already reading my mind, and we'd been married less than a week. Our future was bright. I chuckled at the thought.

Marie cocked her head but refused to ask why I was laughing.

"Yes," Fuchs said as the driver pulled away. "Das Horcher Restaurant. It specializes in game. Even during the worst of the war, game meats were not rationed, and one could eat well here."

When we arrived at our table, Hans Richter and Anita Berber were laughing over their drinks. I said hello to both.

"If you walked, you'll need to take a taxicab when we leave," I told them. "It's started to rain."

"No, we came in Anita's motorcar. With her dancing shows, she is wealthy compared to the rest of us," Richter explained with a wink.

"Can we expect Otto?" I asked.

Marie was speaking with Anita.

"No. He returned to Dresden," Richter replied.

We sat. Anita was fussing over Marie. She had noticed the bruise on Marie's face. Anita caught my eye and gave me a killing look. Good for her. She thought I'd beaten my wife, and she didn't like it. I didn't fault her, but I made a point of trying to sit as far away from her as the six seats at the table would allow. Marie sat across from her at one end of the table, and I sat at the other end, kitty-corner to Marie. I managed to position Fuchs between Anita and me. A glance like the one she gave me promised action, and I didn't want a fork in the kidney.

Dyar, Fuchs, and I reviewed the events in Königsberg. Richter listened in. The ladies at the end of the table spoke in German, and I had no idea what they discussed. For dinner, I had wild boar with a spicy brown gravy, an unexpected black currant jam, and *spaetzle*. The meal was exceptional, which helped ease the fact that Anita refused to speak to me. As we worked our way through the food, she finished her wine almost as fast as it was poured.

Despite Anita's cold reception, the dinner had the odd feel of absent friends reunited, though Marie and I had only been gone a few days, and we'd only met the group once before. Perhaps it was because the chaos of that one night had bonded us together. I was surprised and pleased. Richter was funny, using his biting sense of humor to skewer the government, his fellow artists, and the German conservatives. Fuchs remained insightful, even as he pushed his government's agenda regarding the Bolshevik threat to Germany. Dyar cleverly balanced Fuchs's point of view without offending him. The six of us, with Anita pulling more than her weight, emptied a wine bottle each.

The trouble started when Fuchs excused himself to use the head. I no longer had a barrier for Anita's anger.

She smiled as she leaned over toward me to speak. Foolishly, I smiled back, believing I was forgiven.

"Men are pigs. You are a pig. You are as hideous on the inside as you are on the outside." She spoke very clearly and carefully. Then, without any warning, she swept the nearest wine bottle off the table, brandished it by the neck, spilling the dregs down her arm, and swung it at my head. Only my training from

Bullard and Carpentier and her drunkenness saved me. The bottle caught me a glancing blow on the cheek as I jerked my head to the side. Marie launched herself across the table to grab Anita's arm to keep her next swing from catching me full in the face.

As they struggled, I stood up and hid behind Dyar. I figured she wouldn't go through him to get to me.

Marie was kneeling on the middle of the table and speaking urgently into Anita's ear. Anita's hooded eyes followed me, but she didn't try to stand. In part, I think standing quickly would have been a challenge for her.

"Anita," I said sincerely, trying to placate her, "it's not what you think. I do not beat my wife." This wasn't a lie. Marie was not my wife, and even if she were, I didn't beat her as a matter of course. I'd only socked her because she tried to kill me with a straight razor.

"*Es ist war*," Marie said to Anita again and again. I didn't know what that meant, but it sounded like we were at war. Figures Marie wasn't helping.

Richter started to laugh, and Fuchs returned to the table.

"*Was ist los?*" he asked.

"Anita is convinced John is a wife-brutalizing ogre," Richter answered. He then spoke to Anita. "Even if John is telling the truth, which I doubt"—he cast me a mischievous look from the corner of his eye—"a good beating now and then is useful in a happy marriage. Yes?"

"No!" I said frantically. "Hans, this isn't funny."

He thought it was, and Fuchs was now grinning. Germans and their rotten sense of humor.

"Charles, help me out here," I begged.

Dyar raised his hands and stepped away from me. "Don't involve me in this. I'm in Berlin to observe only." His comment made both Richter and Fuchs laugh out loud.

The maître d' arrived with the waiter and barked at the six of us but Marie in particular as she was still on top of the table. Marie climbed down but kept hold of Anita's arm. Anita still held the bottle.

Fuchs responded to the maître d' and handed him some Papiermarks. "I am afraid our time here is done," he told us.

Anita spoke feverishly to Marie, and it occurred to me that with a little luck, we might get a car after all. Never let a personal humiliation go unexploited.

I turned to Dyar. "Can you get me a moment with Marie? Maybe distract Anita? I don't want to just pull Marie away. Not with Anita still wielding a bottle."

"Sure." He went over and spoke quietly to Anita in German.

I gestured to Marie and stepped away from the table.

"Marie, we need to get Anita to lend you her motorcar. We can use it to get your son away from Berlin unseen. You'd have to convince Anita you're using it to get away from me, and you'd have to convince her to lie to the German police for you."

"I can do this," she said with certainty.

"You need to find a way to get it to me so I can drive us to your son," I told her. "I think I remember where Anita lives."

"No. I can drive. I will get the car and collect you and William in the park. Wait near where you met my professor friend, Elsbeth. I will be there tonight at midnight."

I studied her and nodded. She was far more capable than I at this type of thing. Once folks needed killing, I might come in handy, but she was perfect for manipulating Anita. She was also pretty good at killing. I hoped Anita surrendered her the car without a fuss. I had no doubt Marie would kill her if she had to.

"You will have to let me go home with her," Marie said matter-of-factly.

"I know. She's crazy. Don't share an ether cocktail with her."

"I have a small bag packed at the foot of the bed in the room. Bring it. Leave the other clothes. I will see you at midnight tonight." She smiled at me and went back to the table and linked arms with Anita. "Gentlemen, Anita and I will now have a night just for the ladies. You men should do what you will, but we ladies will have some time together."

I started to protest as any red-blooded, God-fearing Christian and appropriately patriarchal husband would.

"John, please. I need some time." Excellent, now everyone at the table was convinced I beat Marie. Of course, I had beaten Marie.

"We'll speak in the morning." I relented.

* * *

DYAR DROPPED ME AT THE HOTEL. I IMMEDIATELY WENT TO Mitchell's room. I explained to him the change in our plans with the addition of a motorcar. I also borrowed a pillowcase. When I returned to our rooms, I shoved my essentials in the pillowcase and left our suitcases as instructed by Marie. I hoped there were enough clothes to convince German intelligence that we would return. Any delay in a search would help us.

I pulled on the shoulder holster with my Colt tucked safely inside. I was worried that I would need it as we fled west. Once packed, I covered the pillowcase with my overcoat, grabbed Marie's bag, and went up the steps to Mitchell's room.

He answered at the first knock. When I revealed my pillowcase sack of clothes, he laughed.

"And I thought you were kidding about using a pillowcase. You should put Marie's gear in another. Then all you need are two sticks and you and Marie can disguise yourselves as hobos carrying your bindles. The Krauts won't even notice you. You two could hop the freight cars all the way to Paris, and I won't have to worry about her killing me on a whim."

"Will, you're an ass. I'll need a new suitcase, but to get to the car, this will work." I was a little disappointed that he didn't recognize my ingenuity.

177

"And to think I thought you'd devised a clever plan for hiding in plain sight from all the German cops that are gonna be looking for us in a couple of hours."

I shook off his teasing. "There's no reason for the police to look for us. They haven't connected the dead man to us."

"Oh Johnny, you're always so optimistic. It's one of your most charming traits. As soon as the military intelligence know their man was murdered, they will use the police to find you and Marie. They'll tell the cops you two are the murderers. They might not have any evidence, but they don't need any. And once we raid granny's house, every German in the country will be looking for us."

Of course Mitchell was right. I hadn't thought it through. Surely German intelligence knew their man was dead by now. They knew he was going to see his agent, Marie, who had already disobeyed orders by failing to kill me. Even if they didn't think she'd killed him, they would want to talk to her. And to me.

17

———

Punch in the Gut

Just before midnight, Mitchell and I left the hotel. He walked out the front door, and I used the fire exit to leave from the back. I felt foolish carrying Marie's small case and my little sack. Thank God I saw no policemen. I wasn't sure I could stand the humiliation of being arrested with my skivvies in a pillowcase. I walked around the block and met Mitchell at the Brandenburg Gate. Together, we strolled into the park like we had not a care in the world. Of course, it was nearly midnight, and we must have looked suspicious as hell. Fortunately, there weren't many people out, and two men slinking about in a dark park wasn't that odd in Berlin given what I'd seen at the White Mouse.

We walked to where I had met Elsbeth Schragmüller a few days before, and we waited.

When midnight came and went, I started to worry. Anita Berber was unbalanced. While I had confidence in Marie's ability to take care of herself, I hoped she didn't have to take any drastic action to separate Anita from her motorcar.

I shouldn't have worried. A short time later, a small car

pulled up to the curb near us. Marie. We were lucky. An Opel with a bench seat in back. Ugly, but it would work. I climbed in next to Marie, and Mitchell got in back. We tossed our bags on the floorboard under Mitchell's feet.

"Do you want me to drive?" I asked.

"No, I know where we are going, and we must hurry. If they do not already know Jürgen is dead, they will very soon. They will know that I will try to get my son."

"Jürgen, is that the fella with the razor burn in your room?" Mitchell deadpanned.

Marie didn't answer, but her hands tightened on the steering wheel. I just shook my head and said nothing. They didn't like each other, which would make our job harder.

The drive west into the Grunewald neighborhood didn't take long.

Marie pulled to the side of a quiet road with large houses surrounded by ancient trees. "Do you both have guns?" she asked, as she pulled a German Luger 9mm pistol from her bag.

"Yes," we said in unison. Mitchell opened his case and handed me a box of shells and an extra clip for my Colt .45. He took the same for himself. As Marie spoke, I loaded the magazine and put a handful of rounds in my coat pocket. I handed the rest of the box back to Mitchell.

"If the guards have been warned, they will shoot us immediately. Even if they have not been warned, they will know that I should not be there alone. They will not know you, which may make them hesitate, but as soon as they know you are not German military, they will kill us. We must kill them first."

"Marie, I know you want to burst in there full of fire and brimstone, but we must be disciplined. If we can get to your son without the whole household being alerted, that increases the odds of getting him out safely," I told her.

"We must be fast," she insisted.

"Marie," Mitchell said sharply, "listen to Griffin. He is good at this stuff. He gives you the best chance to get your son and get out alive."

She looked from Mitchell to me and nodded once. "All right."

"If we face two men or fewer at any one time," I said, "you distract them, and let Mitchell and me take care of them. We'll do it quietly if we can. We're not here as murderers. You point the way, but Mitchell leads. We'll be following your directions as to where to go, but Mitchell has the greatest chance of silencing anyone we run into."

She looked at Mitchell with narrowed eyes.

"You'll have to trust me on that," I said. "And let's all agree that we don't shoot the seven-year-old."

Mitchell nodded and said, "I hope he's not tall for his age."

Marie ignored me and glared at him.

"We need something to secure anyone we find. Rope or something. I'll check the tool chest." I searched through the box on the running board and found a coil of what I took to be tow rope. It would have to do. It might be enough for three people. No more.

I got back into the auto. Marie saw the rope and shook her head.

"Marie, we're not going to kill everyone. We're not the bad guys. We're the good guys. We're here to rescue your son. Not kill people. If we turn his childhood home into an abattoir, he'll never forget it."

"I wouldn't want him to," she said vehemently.

"Marie," I said sternly as Mitchell whispered a near-silent "holy shit" under his breath, "I promise if we can't do it quietly, we'll shoot our way to your son and back out again, but we're gonna try to do it without killing a bunch of folks he probably knows."

WHEN WE ARRIVED AT THE HOUSE, MARIE STARTED TO TURN UP the gravel drive.

"Wait," I said. "Is this road the only way out of here?"

"Yes. It goes past several more houses and ends in about a kilometer."

"Drive on down and turn around before you reach the next driveway." She followed my instructions. "Now pull as far off to the side as you can, but for Christ's sake, don't get the car stuck." I was worried that the rain earlier in the evening might have made the verge muddy.

With the car past the house and off to the side of the road, I was hopeful that our escape was secure. I tossed my hat into the back seat of the car, and Mitchell followed suit. If there was any action, I didn't want to have to scramble for a hat that had flown off my head. I guessed he didn't either. We walked back to the gravel drive and up to the house. The drive circled around an empty fountain to form a horseshoe in front.

It was a three-floor stately white home with stairs leading up to a front door flanked by gas lights burning on each side. Someone was home. Mitchell and I shared a glance that confirmed we both remembered the horrible night on the rue de Babylone in Paris. Our friend, Shed Bean, had been killed in the first few seconds of our walking into that house. This time I was more careful. I examined the yard and the house. There was not a lot of cover, and no one was patrolling the yard. Behind some trees off to the right side of the house, I saw other smaller buildings of the same architecture, but whether those were for servants' quarters, yard implements, or some other purpose, I couldn't tell.

I went up the stairs and reached the door first. I turned the knob. Locked. I looked to Marie. She reached by me and tapped on the door twice.

After a few moments, I heard a bolt being drawn, and the door cracked open.

"Wer ist da?" we heard.

"Es ist Marie. Guten abend, Herr Weber." The door opened marginally wider, and an older man's head peeked out.

"Marie?" He was surprised.

Mitchell was on him in an instant. His right arm snaked around the man's throat with his left arm locked behind the man's head. It happened in an eyeblink. The man's neck was scissored between Mitchell's tightening forearms. There was a brief struggle as Mitchell brought him to the floor. Herr Weber's kicking feet caught a small table by the door, knocking it against the wall, and a small metal dish clattered to the floor. If anyone else was awake, they would have heard the noise. Marie started to raise her pistol, but I gently pushed her arm down. I looked up the stairs to the second floor and down a hallway toward the back of the house. No movement. It looked like we'd gotten lucky.

After a few seconds, the man stopped struggling.

"The night watchman," Marie explained. She pulled the front door closed.

"He's out," Mitchell said, "but he'll recover in a few seconds. We've got to tie him up quick."

I cut a long length of rope with the dead *poilu's* pocketknife acquired through Marie's skill with a razor. I wrapped the watchman's elbows and wrists and tied them to his ankles. He had a handkerchief in his jacket pocket, and I jammed it in his mouth.

Together Mitchell and I dragged him into a side room where he must have come from.

We went back in the entry hall, and I pulled both Marie and Mitchell to me.

"This isn't going to work," I said softly. "It takes too long to tie them up, and they'll only stay incapacitated for a few seconds." I could already hear the watchman stirring in the side room. "I'll be right back." I went back into the side room, cursing myself.

The watchman's eyes were already fluttering. I had that same helpless feeling you get when you've shot a deer but the shot isn't clean. The deer is dying and in pain, and you have no choice. I was going to have to kick the poor son of a bitch in the head until he stopped moving.

"Wait," I heard Marie say from the doorway. She dug through a pocket in her skirt for a moment and pulled out a small opaque, amber-colored bottle. She uncorked it. She pulled the handkerchief from the man's mouth and poured a healthy slug of a viscous fluid into a handkerchief. A sweet and medicinal smell filled the room. I recognized the combination of chloroform and ether from Anita's apartment. Marie knelt over the watchman and held the cloth to the bound man's nose and mouth. He relaxed back into unconsciousness. From across the room, I felt slightly dizzy from the vapor. I was sure I imagined this.

"How do you know what the dosage should be?" I asked.

"I don't."

We went back into the entryway.

"We go fast. Don't shoot." I tossed the coil of rope aside. "We tackle them, and Marie will knock them out." I nodded at the handkerchief she still held.

"Upstairs?" I pointed to the stairs leading up from the entry. Marie nodded. We went quickly.

We passed no one. Marie guided us to a door on the second floor. It was clear that we were at little Jean-Paul's bedroom. By silent agreement, Marie went in alone. Mitchell and I kept watch in the hallway. It seemed like Marie was in the room for hours, but it couldn't have been more than a minute. We heard talking. Mitchell gave me a look, which blamed me for our predicament. I went into the bedroom.

A middle-aged woman was standing by a single bed. She was, what my father would have called, handsome, with strong cheekbones and piercing blue eyes. She stood straight and tall.

Despite tousled silver-blond hair and being dressed in a long robe, she was the picture of a Prussian matron. She looked like the type of woman to happily give birth to a nation steeped in martial ardor and the glory of war. I disliked her immediately.

Marie was facing her, clutching the forgotten Luger to her chest. If I didn't know better, I would have thought she was pleading. Mitchell was impatiently waiting in the hallway, and I heard a clock ticking in my head. We were running out of time.

"Marie." Both women turned to look at me. "We have to cut our visit short. Where is Jean-Paul?"

"She has hidden him."

"An American. How appropriate. Arriving at the party and not smart enough to understand you are not welcome," the woman said waspishly.

"Grandma?" I asked Marie.

She nodded.

"Where's Grandpa?" I asked the woman. She ignored the question.

"I am sure he's gone for help," Marie answered. "Some of the guard staff live in outbuildings behind the house."

"That's a shame," I said. "I'd hoped we could get out of here without killing Jean-Paul's grandparents."

"Mitchell," I called out the doorway. He poked his head into the room. "Do you mind torturing Granny here to find out where the boy is?"

He gave me a hard look. Mitchell's childhood in the Philippines had taught him many things. One that I had not believed until he'd demonstrated it on me in a bunker before the attack on Soissons was the ability to deliver excruciating pain with very little effort. We'd been sharing a jug of Père Pinard[1] and arguing about some nonsense. I said something ill-judged, and he'd grabbed my arm near the elbow. Before I knew what was happening, he'd set my entire arm on fire with a quick squeeze of his fingers. It was more than just bumping my funny bone. The whole damn inside of my forearm burned. He'd used those skills on Morgan Reynolds during our search for Patricia Armistan. But he didn't want to use those skills now. He didn't like the idea of hurting a woman. Also, she was just trying to protect her grandson.

"I can do it, Mitch, but the damage I do will be more permanent." I opened the French folding knife I'd taken from my pocket. The three-and-a-half-inch blade didn't have the overt threat of a longer knife, but in the hands of French trench raiders, the sinister little drop point blade had killed plenty of German soldiers. Granny probably didn't know that, and I didn't bother to check on the woman's reaction. She wouldn't believe we would hurt her until we did. My show of the knife was for Mitchell. I was reminding him of what he already knew: with my commitment to helping Marie, I would carve up Granny if I had to.

Resigned to the need, Mitchell shrugged his shoulders. "Someone'll have to watch the hall."

I looked once more at Marie. "Search the rooms down the hallway while we work. And I'm sorry, but after this, you won't be welcome at Thanksgiving."

"How wonderfully parochial," Jean-Paul's grandmother said. "Thinking the world revolves around your home across the sea. One of the many reasons I always loathed your upstart, backward nation. That and the humidity in Washington."

"You and me both." I laughed. I shut the knife with a pull and a click. "I appreciate your bravery, lady. I do. But we need to know where the little boy is, and we're in a hurry. We've got a train to catch," I said regretfully. I tossed in the lie, hoping to misdirect the Germans when they followed. The clock in my head told me we had no more time. I stepped across the room to the woman, and she didn't even have the good sense to flinch away. With the closed knife still in my hand, I prepared myself to give her a good punch in the gut, when a call came from outside the room.

"Here, he's here!" Marie shouted. So much for staying quiet.

Out in the hallway, I found Marie hugging a child to her chest. His arms were wrapped tightly around her neck.

"Under a bed?" I asked.

Marie nodded.

"Wait out here, and I'll get him some clothes," I told her.

I went back into the bedroom. Frau Grandma was sitting on the bed with her head in her hands and crying. She wouldn't beg us not to take him. She understood there was no hope in that. I felt a sick wash of guilt. When had I become this kidnapping, woman-brutalizing animal? Blaming it on the war was just an excuse. I did not like what I was and might never have, but I had no more time to think about it.

"I'm going to get him some clothes, and then we're going," I told Mitchell. He nodded and patted the woman on her shoulder. He wouldn't meet my eyes. This was different from Reynolds in an alley. We both knew it. I'd forced him right up to the line that, in his mind, separated us from the monsters of nightmares, and I'd expected him to become a monster right along with me.

I found a little knapsack and stuffed it full of the boy's clothes and a coat. I also took a pair of child's boots from under the bed. Mitchell picked a small stuffed bear off the floor where it must have fallen, and I shoved it in the bag as well.

I looked down at the woman on the bed.

She looked up. She was done crying.

With nothing to say, I turned to leave.

"You should kill me," the woman said. "When the soldiers come, I will tell them to hunt for Marie and two Americans. With your face, you are easy to recognize. They will kill you, and I will get my grandson back."

"You realize that if they come, they will kill you too, don't you?" I said.

"Why would they kill me?" She scoffed.

"You and the boy are the link to the truth. Your knowledge and his existence spoil the story that Marie is a rogue French Bolshevik. As long as you are alive, you are witness to the fact that her son was held hostage and she was coerced to work as a spy for Germany."

"What are you talking about? You are a fool! Paul is no hostage."

It seemed *Jean-Paul* was a little too French for her Teutonic ear.

"Marie asked for him to stay with us," she continued. "She was loyal to France. We respected that. She served with the French as a nurse at the front for four years. She is no more a French Bolshevik or a spy for Germany than I am the Kaiser."

"Honestly?" I said with more than just a little bit of a sneer. "You work for German intelligence. You kept her son from her. You were willing to be beaten just to keep him as leverage over her, and you're going to pretend that you didn't know she was forced to spy for Germany—by using her son as a hostage!" I was surprised at my anger. It didn't help that I was scared because I was standing in a German aristocrat's house, waiting for the Kraut stormtroopers to arrive.

The grandmother seemed genuinely shocked by my claim.

"I'll admit I don't want her to take Paul. He is my last real connection to my son. And I admit that I have worked for German intelligence," she answered. "As has my husband. We worked for Graf Bernstorff[2] when we were stationed in Washington before and during the war. We worked to protect Germany. We are loyal to Germany and honored for our work, but we would never coerce Marie into spying for Germany. And we would never use Paul as a pawn to force her to do so. Our superiors know this."

I considered her words. "Then I have sad news for you. Your bosses have manipulated you into coercing Marie without you even knowing it, and now you would serve Germany best by dying. For with you and Paul dead and Marie dead as well, the German Foreign Office and German intelligence can tell whatever story they like. When they kill me, as you promised they will, they will claim it was Marie: a crazed French Bolshevik, who did it. All to get America and Woodrow Wilson to allow Germany to maintain its military. German officials will not even acknowledge your death or Paul's. Your deaths will be accidental, an act of God, like a fall, getting hit by a train, or the Spanish flu."

She watched me from the bed, raising her chin to show her doubt.

"Better for the boy to die with his mother than with an old woman who didn't even know she'd been tricked by her own people. How wonderfully worldly of you," I added.

18

____

The Good Guys

I left the grandmother to her fate. Marie was still by the door in the hallway. She had squatted down to examine her son.

"Marie, let's go." I handed her the boots, which she swiftly fitted on her son's feet. She tied the laces with a quick, unconscious competence. I realized that, if given the chance, Marie would be a fine mother and likely a fine wife. Watching her tie her son's shoes, although a small thing, gave me hope for her. Her brutality, amorality, and detachment were the tools she used to survive the situation she had been forced into. They were not her. They were her disguise. She was a good mother. She needed the chance to be a mother instead of the awful thing the Germans and French had made her. By forcing me into going to Germany, Raux had put me where I belonged. I was sure that I was meant to help her, but then I was always sure about such things. Recalling Sarah and her death reminded me that I could be wrong. Nevertheless, watching Marie pull Jean-Paul's laces tight gave me confidence in my purpose.

She stood, and the little sandy-haired boy peered up at me. He recoiled and curled against his mother's leg. I handed Marie the knapsack. She hooked it over her shoulder and took her son by the hand. She wouldn't look at me either. My willingness to beat and torture her mother-in-law had shown her my true colors. I might believe in my purpose, but Anita had me right. I'd been willing to brutalize a grandmother. Hideous on the outside and hideous on the inside. Consistent.

I immediately started back down the hallway to find our exit.

As I reached the top of the stairs, I heard gravel crunching under automobile tires.

"Quickly!" I went down the steps two at a time. Outside, car doors slammed.

I took a deep breath, unholstered the Colt, rechecked its magazine, and chambered a round.

"Well, shit," I heard Mitchell say behind me.

"Is there another way out?" I asked Marie. Jean-Paul's eyes were huge as he stared at the gun in my hand.

The front door opened. I guess we should have locked it.

A man in a field gray trench coat filled the doorway. A policeman, military intelligence, or a soldier. It really didn't matter. I put the front post of the Colt on his chest. He just started to register what he was seeing when my gun went off. The bullet knocked him back out the door. The pistol's report was shocking. I took a quick look outside, and I saw a motorcar and a troop truck. Men were scattering behind the vehicles they'd arrived in.

Marie scooped up the boy and, without a word, turned deeper into the house, past the stairs. Mitchell followed. I started to push the front door closed when I heard someone outside calling my name.

"John! John Griffin!"

I cracked the door again, using just one eye to peer at the speaker. He was partially shielded by the motorcar.

"John, it's Karl. Karl Fuchs."

Shit! Fuchs! I suppose it made sense even if it disappointed me. He was a German official after all. He was working for Germany, and that meant working to kill me.

"Hello, Karl. Haven't we seen enough of each other tonight? I'd have thought after dinner you'd want a quiet night at home." I hoped I could buy Mitchell and Marie enough time to find a way out of the back of the mansion.

"Unfortunately, John, my instructions are that you are not to leave Berlin alive."

"That doesn't surprise me, Karl. So, the workers at the factory. Was that all a charade?"

"No. They were workers and likely socialists. They were right to be untrusting and to send a man to make sure that troops did not surround the building. But there were no troops. At least not that night. That night the show was for you."

"Did you have instructions to kill Johann Ditzel too, or was that just German incompetence?"

"Not incompetence. An expected possibility. You were supposed to be in the front seat of the automobile. It is sad about Johann, but had you both died, it would have been a very convincing story for the Americans. With Johann dead, Charles Dyar would have had no difficulty believing that Bolsheviks had killed you. It also helps that I was a victim of the attack."

Through the crack in the door, I could see men were moving to surround the house.

"I'll bet the bullets that killed Ditzel came a little too close for comfort," I said.

He gave a small laugh. "Yes, a little too much like the war I expect. You know, John, I do like you, but this is not so different from the Weihnachtsfrieden, the Christmas truce, in 1914. We met briefly in peace in a feeling of mutual respect, but now duty requires that I kill you."

"So that's how this going to end, Karl? You kill us and the family?"

"I'm sorry, John, but we can't let you escape. You understand.

But your wife and your friend will be allowed to leave, and the little boy and his grandmother and grandfather too. But you have to come out."

He was bent over behind the car's bonnet. I could just make out his head and shoulders.

"So you're not going to kill Marie or the boy or his grandparents?" I called out through the crack in the door. I looked back into the entryway to see if there was any sign of Mitchell or Marie. Jean-Paul's grandmother was at the bottom of the staircase, watching me and listening to the conversation.

I tilted the door shut, and I asked her, "What do you think? Will he let you and Jean-Paul live?"

"Paul, we call him Paul. And the man outside is lying. You are right. He will kill us all."

I appreciated her honesty.

I opened the door just enough to bring my pistol in line with Fuchs's shadowy head. I fired twice and slammed the door and locked the bolt, closing the barn door after the horse was out.

Then I ran to the grandmother. I grabbed her hand and pulled her after Marie and Mitchell down the hallway toward the back of the house.

The loud crack of a Luger came from where Marie had gone. Several more shots followed. With Grandma in tow, I hurried down the corridor, passing a telephone call box on the wall. The earpiece swung below the box, as if it had been dropped in a hurry. We came to the kitchen. A gray-clad body lay on the floor.

Mitchell, Marie, and the boy were crouched behind a heavy wooden worktable set to the left of the doorway. A uniformed man was firing at them from a hall to the right. His shots were aimed to keep them in place, not necessarily to hit them. He was stalling them in the hope of reinforcements from outside. When he saw me, he was surprised. He shifted his aim, and Mitchell leaned out from behind the table and shot him.

Marie's boy had his hands over his ears. I thought he might

be crying, and I didn't blame him. Hell, he was only seven, and I'd brought him into a gunfight.

I let go of the grandmother and ran to the doorway on the right past the downed soldier. He was struggling to rise. I shot him once more as I passed. I must have chosen the right way out because Marie dragged Jean-Paul after me, clutching his hand tightly. I came into an eating area, which looked like it was for the staff. Two cups of coffee steamed on the table. Through a half-glass-faced door, I saw the backyard and trees beyond.

"Will, take Marie and go to the edge of the woods. I'll meet you there. Take the grandmother too."

"Why is she coming?" Marie asked. "She tried to keep us from finding Jean-Paul!"

Without hesitation, Mitchell grabbed the straps of Jean-Paul's pack on Marie's shoulder and used it as a lead to drag her out the door. Caught by the hand, poor little Jean-Paul had no choice but to follow. The grandmother gave me a hard look, but after a second, she nodded and followed.

The front door must have been broken open when we were busy in the kitchen. Feet pounded down the hallway toward me.

I fired into the hallway. A body fell, and a flurry of shots came back at me, shattering cabinetry and crockery. I turned and ran out the back door and to the woods.

Thank God the house was so damn big. Its size kept Fuchs's people from circling it quickly enough to cut us off.

I found Mitchell and the unhappy family crouched in a circle. Marie was again checking the child. I guess that's what mothers do.

"Mitch, take the ladies and the boy and go to the car. I'll be there in a bit. I want to keep the attackers from following."

"Let's go," he commanded. He stood and worked his way deeper into the trees. There was little undergrowth to hinder him. The others followed.

I fired once more into the back door and glass broke. Then I left the trees and sprinted back to the house. My plan was to work my way around to the front to disable the motorcar and the truck. I burrowed into the bushes at the back door. My lungs burned from the run.

Just as I finished hiding, six men arrived at the back door. After a hurried conversation in German, two went into the house, and three ran toward the woods. The last man started back around the house toward the vehicles. I holstered the pistol and took the *poilu's* locking knife from my pocket. I opened it as quietly as I could and followed the lone man.

I caught him when he stopped to listen to shouting coming from inside. He didn't hear me.

I didn't hesitate. I didn't think.

I wrapped an arm around his neck and pulled him backward onto the knife. He stiffened as it went into his back, into his kidney. I stabbed him once more and left him dying in the bushes.

I stood and trotted around to the front of the house as if I belonged there. No one else was nearby. The car and the truck were unattended.

I ran to the car, sliding down on the ground at its far side. Quickly I worked my way around the automobile and levered the bloody knife through each tire and tube, twisting the blade to widen the tears. I then started on the truck, but I wasn't confident I would have time to disable all four tires, and I had to satisfy myself with three.

I sprinted down the driveway, away from the mansion and toward the road like I was being chased by a farm dog. A commotion at the house drew my attention. I'd left just in time. From where I stood in the dark at the end of the drive, I could see that the front door was open and lights were on all over the house. The yard boiled like a kicked ant nest. Armed men ran to the truck and the motorcar, but they quickly realized the tires were flat.

A man ran from the house shouting. Fuchs. Too bad I hadn't killed the likable bastard. He waved to the soldiers and pointed toward one of the outbuildings. I didn't like the activity around these buildings, and shortly, it sounded disturbingly like motorcars starting. Of course they had motorcars. I'd wasted the time on the one car and truck without considering that the grandfather would have at least one or two more cars on the property.

A second man came to the front door and called to Fuchs. Fuchs turned and, raising a pistol I didn't know he carried, shot the man twice.

"*Verbrennen Sie es!*" Fuchs shouted to one of the men.

I had a bad feeling Fuchs had just killed Jean-Paul's granddad. By taking the grandmother from the house, I'd sealed the grandparents' fate. They were likely doomed anyway, but there was no way now Fuchs would consider letting the grandfather live with the grandmother gone.

From down the road, headlights approached me. Marie, I hoped. I drew the pistol and jogged toward the nearing lights. I stopped and held the gun down by my leg.

Marie leaned out of the driver's window.

"We must go!" she said.

I shook my head.

"Turn off your lights and drive past the gravel road to the house. Go down about thirty yards," I said, pointing in the direction from which we'd entered the neighborhood. "I don't want them to know we have a motorcar. It looks like they're preparing to come after us. They have more cars."

"Wait," Mitchell called from the passenger seat. He climbed out of the car with his .45 in one hand and a Luger in the other. "I'll help you discourage them."

I took some loose rounds from my coat pocket and topped off the Colt's magazine.

"I'll get them to stop. You come out and finish them," I told Mitchell.

He walked about twenty yards toward the house and knelt low just inside the trees lining the right side of the gravel drive. I moved off to the left side and took a knee as well. They wouldn't expect us to be waiting, and I could use the rest. I hoped I didn't have to run again, but I was sure I would. I was the bait. If I didn't move, I would get killed. The men in the car would focus on me while Mitchell shot them all in the back. A simple plan. I hoped they didn't have any of the Bergmann machine pistols. If they did, I wouldn't survive the action.

Someone had set the house on fire. Its glare backlit the activity in the driveway. After picking up men in front of the house, the motorcars came fast. Three in a line kicking gravel as they sped around the horseshoe and down the drive. Four men to a car. Twelve men total. I hoped my math was wrong and there were fewer. I had one spare clip for the .45. The loose bullets rattling around my pockets wouldn't be any help. There was no way I would be able to reload those fast enough. This fight was going to be over in the next minute. I could not allow it to last any longer. Fire and maneuver would have to make up for there just being two of us. Just like the damn infantry. Fire and maneuver.

When the cars were fifty feet from the end of the gravel drive, I stepped out into the middle of the road, waving my arms wildly. I had my pistol in my hand with a round in the chamber, but I didn't think that would prompt them to hit me with the motorcar.

It took just a moment for the driver to see me. He didn't accelerate into me. Instead, he hit the brakes, and the drivers behind him did the same.

Twenty feet away, the first car rocked to a stopped.

Following the advice of the great Wyatt Earp, taking my time in a hurry, I smoothly raised the Colt. The driver's door opened, and he started to climb out. His passenger must have realized who I was or at least what I planned because he lunged across the steering wheel to haul the driver back in the car.

It was a good idea, but he was too late. I fired. The driver fell. I walked forward and to the left of the car, drawing the attention away from where Mitchell hid and moving out of the headlamp light. I stopped and fired again. The windscreen of the second motorcar shattered in front of the driver's silhouette. Then things started to speed up.

As if on a signal, car doors flew open. Uniformed men leaned around the doors as they drew their weapons. Then they started to fire, and I was moving.

My heart lurched as the nearest soldier swung a Bergmann machine pistol from inside the car. He rushed to rest it on top of the car door, and he started firing before he had it aimed. Bullets ripped away to my left. I settled the Colt's sights on his torso, which was partially concealed by the car door, and fired. The window shattered, and he fell back against the car. The Bergmann spun out of his hands. When it hit the ground, it fired once more, and I felt the punch of a bullet and a burn along my side and arm.

Goddamn Kraut machine guns!

Guns were firing so fast it looked like photographer flash powder popping off all around. I hoped some of those flashes were Mitchell bettering the odds.

I scrambled forward until I was parallel with the front seat of the lead auto. I fired through the car twice. I hadn't heard Mitchell's Colt yet, which meant he was shooting the bastards with the Luger. They wouldn't notice the Luger's sound as easily as they would his .45. Smart.

I crouched by the fallen machine gunner. I put the Colt on the car seat and tugged the fallen Bergmann to me while bullets slammed into the car body. My arm began to burn with an intensity I'd felt all too recently. I'd managed to get shot again.

I tucked the weapon against my shoulder. The damn thing was unwieldy, made so by the snail magazine jutting out from the left side of the gun, but I didn't need it for long. I wondered how many of the thirty-two rounds remained. As quick as I could, I propped the barrel on the car roof and emptied the magazine into the second car. Two seconds. Less than half a magazine. I hoped Mitchell hadn't strayed into my fire.

I tossed the gun into the car and picked up the .45.

The zip of near misses filled the air around me, and I felt a tug on my jacket. Too close for comfort.

I crouched and duckwalked to the second car.

Son of a bitch! Now my side was killing me too.

I fired twice more into the car at the uniformed shadows almost within touching distance. The slide on the Colt locked back. I dropped the empty magazine and put in the fresh one. I fired twice more.

The boom of Mitchell's .45 told me that he had emptied the Luger. Eight rounds in the Luger. Seven in the Colt.

I looked for movement in the shadows. Nothing. The only sounds were moans, the labored breathing of the mortally wounded, and the ticking of the motors cooling. I found the magazine I'd dropped and carefully thumbed in new rounds. I swapped out magazines and reloaded the second magazine as well.

"Mitchell?" I called, staying on my knees behind the car. I didn't want to get shot by accident. Or on purpose for that matter.

"I'm by the last auto," he called.

One of the men inside the second car was pawing at his chest where I'd shot him. Blood frothed from his mouth. I thought of Horace Merchant, lung-shot and dying on Sarah's Paris hotel room bed. This poor bastard was dying too. Just like Merchant.

I stood. Mitchell joined me.

"We need to go," I said.

"I suppose we do. We seem to be out in the countryside, but that…" He took a deep breath. "That was damn noisy. The neighbors might come by."

"Gather the ammunition you can find. We're gonna end up using all German guns at this rate."

We quickly gathered what we could. As clumsy as the machine pistol was, I couldn't resist collecting it, along with the bag of extra magazines lying on the floorboard of the first car.

"You okay?" I asked.

Mitchell laughed cynically.

"I got a scare there. When that machine pistol started hammering, it shortened my life span for certain." He shook his head. "I'll be honest, Griff, and I'm ashamed to say it, I was glad it was shootin' at you. I was sure you were dead, but they were so busy with you they didn't even know I was killin' 'em."

I looked at the bodies around the cars. No sign of Fuchs.

Together, we walked down the gravel drive to the road.

Marie had the car reversing toward us but stayed away from the end of the drive.

I looked back at the burning house and the shattered motorcars. The car headlights were still on and outlined the bodies on the ground, some moving feebly, but most were not.

Mitchell climbed into the front seat of the motorcar with Marie, and I collapsed into the back seat by Jean-Paul, who was sitting next to his grandmother. I was in pain and barely noticed his squawk as I got in next to him.

"Go." It was all I could get out. I laid my head back on the leather seat exhausted and in increasing pain. I thought of the widowed grandmother, her dead husband, the bastard in the bushes, and the dying soldier in the car. He was almost certainly gone by now.

And we were the *good guys*? Sure we were.

19

———

Older Sister

Marie drove out of the neighborhood, and I had just enough awareness to know that she turned east.

"Why east, Marie?" I asked through gritted teeth.

"Ladoux is in Berlin. He will help us get back to France. I called him from the house. He will get the message and meet us at a prearranged location. A rendezvous."

I didn't have the strength to argue. Ladoux should have contacts in the city that could help us. We had money, but we needed food. And transportation. We sure didn't need the grandmother. I just didn't know what to do with her. Jean-Paul was curled against her as far away from me as he could get. She had one arm wrapped around him protectively. She watched me like I was a rattler.

I wanted to tell Mitchell about my wounds, but we had to get away from Berlin. I didn't know how quickly the Germans would follow.

I pressed my elbow against my side and my hand against the underside of my left arm where the bullet had hit, consoling myself with my limited first aid knowledge. If the tumbling round had hit anything important, I'd already be unconscious or dead. I looked at the offending machine pistol lying on the floor of the car as we bounced down the narrow Grunewald roads. It occurred to me that I needed to make sure the damn thing was unloaded. It almost certainly was, but I could just imagine a bump sending another round into me or into the little boy next to me.

I bent to reach for the gun, and the pain sharpened in my side.

Mitchell must have heard my involuntary hiss because he asked, "You okay, Griff?"

Marie glanced over her shoulder as Mitchell turned around to look at me. I did manage to secure the gun, removing the magazine and double-checking that the chamber was empty.

"No."

"Figures," he said. "Are you dying? I hope you're not dying. 'Cause I don't know your wife here all that well, and I'm not sure she likes me. And I'm pretty sure that Grandma doesn't either. And if you're dying, then little JP will have to see more unpleasantness."

I looked at the boy. This time he met my eyes without turning away.

"Do you speak English?"

He gave a reluctant nod.

"Are you all right?" I asked him. I knew he was not physically hurt because Marie would have been frantic if he were.

He nodded.

I turned to Mitchell. "I'm not going to die, but it hurts like I am. And Jean-Paul isn't worried about a little unpleasantness." I smiled at the boy. He didn't look away, but he did scoot sideways to put his back to his grandmother and draw up his legs between us.

"Got shot, huh?" Mitchell asked.

"Yup." Little Jean-Paul watched us both with big eyes. Marie looked back again. Was that concern I saw on her face? I shook my head. I felt light-headed. "A grazing shot, I think. Between my side and my arm. I'd be dead or cranky if it were more."

"It's always a challenge to judge your health based on your mood, Griffin. You're always cranky." He turned to Marie. "We need to stop."

"They will follow quickly," she objected.

"She's right, Will," I said.

"JP and I will switch seats. I'll climb back there and take a look, and JP can come up here. With his mom."

He looked at the boy. "You'd like that, right?"

Jean-Paul nodded.

"Two shakes of a lamb's tail, Marie, and we'll be driving again," Mitchell promised.

The switch went as planned. The grandmother now pressed herself away from Mitchell, who, while not bulky, was still big enough to take up more space than Jean-Paul had. He had my jacket and shirt off and gave a little whistle just to worry me. When he was sure he succeeded, he laughed at my fear. Jean-Paul was peering over the front seat. Although he was watching me bleed, he seemed more interested in what Mitchell was doing. Somehow Mitchell had captured the little boy's interest.

"Griffin, you baby. You don't even need stitches."

I look down at the shallow furrow just below my ribs and the messy tear along the bottom of my left arm. Luck. It all came down to luck. That accidental shot could have tumbled through my liver, lungs, or heart just as easily as my side. The trouble with luck was that it changed. I'd had an awful lot of luck. I remembered telling Sarah about the vagaries of luck. It was just a matter of time.

Mitchell dug through his bag, which we'd tossed on the floor of the car along with my make-do pillowcase luggage. He found his first aid gear and a bottle of whiskey. He cleaned and bandaged my wounds as best he could. He gave a running commentary for Jean-Paul as he did so.

"You want to make sure it's good and clean. Griffin whines a little about the pain of cleaning, but we'll just ignore that. This is for his own good. Now we're going to wrap these strips tight enough to stop the bleeding but not so tight as to be uncomfortable. Also, Griffin here tends to find trouble, and it's our job to make sure he can still run away," he explained to the little boy with a wink. "Do you understand?"

"Yes," the boy said clearly.

"Good. Next time he gets hurt," Mitchell said nodding at me, "he'll probably need to be sewn up. I'll show you how, and you can do it. Okay?"

"I'm not sure I want Jean-Paul to do that," Marie said sharply.

"I'm sure you don't," Mitchell said with certainty, "but he'll do it anyway, because it's something we may need him to know. And he's nearly a man. Yes?"

He said the last to Jean-Paul, who gravely nodded his head.

Marie saw the nod from the corner of her eye.

"Try not to get hurt again, John," she said sincerely.

"Agreed."

Mitchell had seen that the kid was afraid of me. His medical orientation had eased some of that fear, and I appreciated it.

I dozed off a short time later.

WHEN I WOKE, THE CAR WAS STOPPED ON THE ROADSIDE IN WHAT looked like a city park. It was still dark. Marie told me we were waiting for Ladoux. Mitchell, the boy, and the grandmother were nowhere to be seen. I asked Marie where they were.

"Ladoux cannot know I have a son. He cannot know who Jean-

Paul's grandmother is either. If he meets them, he will suspect that I have been spying for Germany, and he will report me to Raux. I will be dead. They are waiting in the woods just down the road."

Commandant Ladoux came not long after, driving a motorcar of his own. He arrived full of smiles shrouded in pipe smoke with not a slicked hair out of place.

"Your mission could not have gone better," he told me as we stood by the cars. He clearly didn't know I'd been shot. Or maybe he did. "My sources in Königsberg have told me of the attack on you staged by the Germans, and Madame Masson's message to me was clear that your extraction from Germany is now of paramount importance. In just a few days, you have succeeded in seeing for yourself that the Germans have fabricated the Bolshevik threat. Our task now is to get you back to France so that you can report to Colonel House."

I didn't agree with him about the threat, but I wasn't going to argue.

"How will we get out of Germany?" I asked.

"You will drive. It is the best way. Better than the train. Maybe slower, but there are many roads you can take, and the Germans cannot cover them all."

"We'll need more help before we get anywhere near the border," I said.

"Perhaps Mrs. Griffin has friends in Germany from before the war?" Commandant Ladoux asked as if he already knew the answer.

After a moment, Marie nodded. "Elsbeth Schragmüller will help us." She looked at me.

"The doctor? She's in Freiburg. That's south, isn't it? That's a long way to go without getting out of Germany," I said. "And I'm not sure why she would risk helping you."

"She is like an older sister to me. She will help. We will have to be careful what we tell her, but she will help. And Freiburg is near both France and Switzerland. Our going to Freiburg will also be unexpected," she told me.

Ladoux turned to Marie. "I will be back here in an hour. I will have gasoline and supplies. You will take my car. I will have the supplies loaded in it."

Marie nodded.

Fifty-five minutes later, Ladoux returned as promised. He brought with him several blue enamel petrol cans lashed to the platform on the back of his car and hampers of food and water inside. Like Dyar, he had a Mercedes, but his looked a little older, and it didn't come with a German driver, which I appreciated. I was surprised at Ladoux's efficiency. In Paris, I hadn't pegged him as someone we could rely on. I was wrong. He was literally a lifesaver.

He'd promised to return Anita's car. We swapped automobiles, and in less than five minutes, Ladoux was rolling away, heading for Anita's neighborhood.

We got into Ladoux's car, drove about a mile down the road, and found Mitchell, the boy, and the grandmother. All three clambered into the back of the motorcar, with Jean-Paul acting as the barrier between the two adults. Then, in the darkness, Marie drove west and south toward Freiburg and France.

As the sun rose, Marie began to tire. The car tires rumbled off the road, snapping me awake in the passenger seat. It looked like the noise had just jarred Marie awake as well. She was breathing deeply with her eyes wide open. The others in the back slumbered on.

"I can drive," I told her. I'd gotten some sleep, and despite the pain in my arm and side, I was sure I could manage the automobile.

"I will drive into Leipzig. We need to buy more gasoline and some clothing for Frau Vogt," she declared. "After that, you can drive, but I must function for a few more hours."

Frau Vogt was Frau Grandma. Nice to have her name.

Guiding the motorcar with one hand, Marie used the other to search for something in her bag. After a moment, she pulled out a vial, which looked disturbingly like the one that belonged to Anita.

"Is that what I think it is?" I asked.

One-handed, Marie twisted off the cap and inhaled some of the cocaine powder directly from the vial. She handed the vial and cap to me. She pinched her nose, sniffed sharply, and focused on her driving.

I shook my head but recapped the vial and dropped it in her bag. For Marie, the cocaine was just one more tool to be used to help save her son. She would use anything and do anything to save him.

"How did you manage to get Anita's... medicine," I asked.

"I seduced her."

She glanced over at me and smiled at my shock.

"She is besotted with me, and we needed her car," she said as if that was all the explanation needed.

"We could have found another car," I told her.

"We didn't have time. And she hates you for beating me. You are such a troll that she wanted to help me escape you. She wanted to come with me. When I refused, she insisted I take the car and the cocaine. She knew I would have to get far away and stay awake while driving. I think she felt she was doing her part for Germany too. Fighting the war that was lost, thanks to you Americans. The ether. Well, I stole that. But isn't that what unfaithful lovers do? Steal?"

I could only shake my head. I needed to remember that I was just a tool too.

By midmorning, we were entering the outskirts of Leipzig. We drove into the center of the city, and Marie found a place to park near one of the modern department stores.

"Emma," she said sternly to Frau Vogt, "you and I will go into Ury's and buy you some clothing. We will also buy food." She looked at Jean-Paul. "Jean-Paul, you must remain with John and William. They do not speak German, and I need you to keep them out of trouble."

"Yes, Mutti."

This comment prompted a raised eyebrow from Mitchell, but I said nothing. Marie didn't want Frau Vogt and the boy together in a crowded store. I didn't think she trusted the grandmother, and I couldn't blame her.

"Ury's is owned by Jews. Surely we can find somewhere more acceptable to shop," Frau Vogt said.

"Then we would have to drive back to Berlin, and all the decent stores there are owned by Jews as well! We will shop at Ury's," said a short-tempered Marie.

Frau Vogt looked shocked. I didn't know how often Marie had been allowed to visit her son at his grandmother's house, but it was clear that Frau Vogt was used to a diffident daughter-in-law and not the hellion she found herself traveling with. I was sure Granny Vogt wasn't fond of this new version of her daughter-in-law, and I knew she didn't like her friends.

"Marie, please try to find us some suitcases," I begged, embarrassed by the clothes falling from the pillowcase at my feet.

Mitchell, Jean-Paul, and I stayed in the car while the ladies shopped. We were parked on a side street between two other motorcars. When the ladies left, I moved to the driver's seat to keep Marie from reclaiming it when she returned. JP came up to sit next to me, not because he wanted to but because Mitchell kicked him out of the back.

"Kid," Mitchell said. "You don't get over your fears by

avoiding them. Go sit in the front. I want to go to sleep." The little boy had obediently moved to the front seat with me. Still, he sat crammed against the passenger door as far from me as he could get.

Mitchell lay down and went straight to sleep, or so I thought.

I slouched down in my seat and tipped my hat over my eyes. From beneath the hat, I asked, "JP, how often do you get to see your mother?"

The car was silent except for Mitchell's rhythmic breathing. I didn't turn my head to look at the kid. I waited.

"She is a nurse. She comes when she can." He sounded like he was defending her.

"Not often, huh?"

"No."

"Well, she seems like a good lady. Tough. But a good lady," I told him.

"Why did your friend call Mutti your wife?" he asked.

It took me a moment to recall when Mitchell had done so. He'd said it right after I'd told him I'd been shot. "Yeah, I'm doing a job for my country, the United States of America. You know it?"

"Yes, like France and Great Britain, America is one of the German empire's enemies," he recited. "We would have defeated all three but were betrayed by Bolsheviks and Jews, who tricked Germany into the armistice."

He'd been thoroughly indoctrinated by his grandparents. I had trouble keeping quiet under my hat, but I didn't want to scare him again. It wasn't his fault his grandparents had poisoned his little brain.

"That's certainly what some folks in Germany think, but back to your question." I wasn't going to change his mind arguing in a motorcar for an hour, and he *was* only seven. "My job is to study Germany and, now that the war is over, to make sure that there aren't a lot of bad people here. It is easier to ask questions and go places when you have a pretty wife. People trust women. They're not scared of them. They're gentler than men." I heard the lies I was telling the poor kid, and Mitchell's audible snort from the back seat confirmed he wasn't asleep.

"Anyway, your mom agreed to help me. Do you know the word *camouflage*?" I asked. I could feel him nod. "It's like that. Your mom is my camouflage. People see me, and they see an ugly, scary man. They see your mom, they see a beautiful woman. They see us together, and they see a man who is luckier than he deserves but not a scary one. See?"

"When I saw you, I thought you were scary and you were with my Mutti," he told me.

I nodded under the hat. "That's because you knew your mother and you didn't know me. If you'd never seen us before, you would have thought I was harmless. Just like your mom."

This time Mitchell groaned an "Oh my Lord" under his breath.

"Did it hurt when you were shot?" he asked, done with my relationship with his mother.

"Yup, like getting hit with a hammer and burned at the same time. I try to avoid it."

A muffled "not hard enough" came from the back seat.

"Does this mean that you have found bad people here? The ones who came to the house and shot at us?"

"Some."

"But Sebastian and Ernst weren't bad, and Mutti and your friend killed them!"

"Sebastian and Ernst?"

"In the kitchen. Our guards."

"Oh yeah. They were shooting at us. And your mother and Mr. Mitchell couldn't let them hurt you."

He thought about that for a moment. "I didn't like them shooting. I don't like shooting at all."

"Good for you. I don't much like it either," I answered.

I could feel him studying me, but he stayed quiet. I didn't know if our conversation helped, but I felt him shift away from the door just a little.

In the silence, I thought about JP and Marie and their future. I was worried about how Marie would be received in Paris. The Germans would likely find a way to notify Raux and the Deuxième Bureau that she was a German spy. They would certainly have evidence. Then the French would execute her. But I couldn't do anything about that now. One problem at a time. First I needed to get us out of Germany.

And if I made it back to Paris, what did that mean for me? Was Madeline waiting? The terror of Königsberg and Grunewald and the race from Berlin had nearly driven her from my mind. I doubted she was waiting. She didn't seem like the kind of girl who would wait. Did I want her to be? What I felt for Madeline was different from what I'd felt for Sarah. With Sarah, my emotions were visceral. All feeling and no thinking. I was too infatuated to think. Of course, given my superstitious nature and knowing what goes up must come down, I'd been worried the whole time. Worried about the Bolshevik plot, worried about Gavin, worried that Sarah was using me. And infatuated to the point of blindness about her nature.

Madeline made it easy to be with her. I didn't worry. But maybe I didn't deserve easy. Marie wouldn't be easy. She was more like Sarah. Mysterious and dangerous. I did my best to shut down that direction of thought.

I wouldn't be staying in France anyway. I needed to report to House and the president. That was what the French wanted. And I needed to get back to the States to keep my promise to Patricia to take care of her father. That promise didn't seem so important now, and I wondered if that was because my obsession with Sarah was fading. That made me sad. While the promise wasn't as important as it had seemed when I'd made it in Paris, I didn't have any qualms about killing Harry Armistan. I had strayed so far from the civilized world that I wasn't sure I could find a way back. I also wasn't sure I wanted to.

Marie and Frau Vogt returned and pulled me from my thoughts. They were successful in finding clothing and food. They had also gotten directions to a petrol filling station. I drove us there, and Marie spoke with the uniformed attendant before he could approach me.

"Einmal volltanken, bitte!" she directed him.

Without a glance at me, he proceeded to fill our petrol tank. Only one of the enamel cans had been used, and he filled that as well. Then we were on our way. Other than stopping for petrol and to piss, we kept going. Like Marie, but reluctantly, I used the cocaine in Anita's vial. Its stimulant effects remained even after the euphoria of the drug faded. It magnified my moodiness, but fortunately, I was busy driving and the noise of the car made it hard to talk.

We drove into the night. After one gasoline stop, Mitchell moved up to the front seat next to me. We had a general idea of the roads we needed to take. Mitchell pulled out the map and persisted in trying to read it in the dark with no success. He even tried to use his lighter to see the detail but quickly gave up. I think he was worried he'd run out of lighter fluid. I was sure he didn't want to stoop to using German matches to light his smokes. We traded few words as I drove into the pitch black. Even when we rolled through towns, the light was limited.

Periodically, I would uncap Anita's vial and inhale some of her cocaine. Mitchell would roll his eyes, but he couldn't argue that I wasn't alert. I did find that I had to control the urge to abuse the vial. After about twenty minutes, the euphoria would fade and the knowledge of the vial would begin to taunt me. I forced myself to limit my use to every two hours.

When the other three weren't wrapped in knee blankets sleeping, the women smoked and JP watched me and Mitchell carefully.

The drive we were making was more than five hundred miles. We passed through Stuttgart, and once the sun rose, Mitchell had enough daylight to see both the map and the road markings, and he found our position without difficulty. We realized we weren't more than sixty miles from Freiburg im Breisgau. The countryside was pretty. Low wooded hills bordered the road, promising mountains and forests to the south.

"We'll be in Freiburg in a few hours," I called over my shoulder. Despite the time of year, the car was cold, and the women were huddled together with Jean-Paul between them. "Where do we go once we hit town?" I asked Marie.

"Elsbeth lives south of the river. She has a small cottage. We can park the motorcar behind it."

Despite the fact that I was at the wheel, I had no clear memory of the last hour of the drive to the doctor's house. My thoughts were jumbled, and fatigue tugged at my brain. I was sluggish despite the cocaine. I considered using more, and the desire alone was enough to convince me to leave the vial in my shirt pocket where it had migrated when I took over the driving from Marie.

When we arrived at the cottage, I followed Marie's instructions and turned off the lane leading to Dr. Schragmüller's house down her small drive and parked where it curled behind her tidy little home.

"The university is north of the river. In the old town not far from here," Marie informed us. She was out of the car almost as soon as I stopped. She tapped on the back door as the rest of us climbed out of the car and stretched.

JP and Frau Vogt stood on one side of the car, and I stood on the other. Mitchell had walked around to the back of the car and lit a cigarette. He had one leg up on the bumper and was studying Dr. Schragmüller's house and the neighborhood.

Elsbeth Schragmüller opened the door, and a look of

surprise was replaced by one of joy. She appeared to be dressed for church or, more likely, for the classroom. A small black dog yapped at us from around her ankles.

"*Marie, willkommen!*" she said with a warm smile. After that, both women chattered away in German, and the dog barked. Marie gestured to the four of us, to me, to Frau Vogt, and finally to JP.

"*Ja, ja, natürlich,*" the doctor said firmly.

"*Vielen dank, vielen dank,*" Marie gushed.

Dr. Schragmüller turned back to us and looked us over. "You are a very welcome surprise," she said. "Please come in. I am sure you would like a bath, something to eat, and then to sleep."

We trooped into the cottage after Marie.

Although the house was small, it was packed with overstuffed furniture. It reminded me of an old lady's house with doilies and useless little pillows. I couldn't complain though. While I wasn't hungry, a bath sounded good, and I needed some shut-eye.

In short order, the doctor had organized our bath schedule and, for those interested, food.

Dr. Schragmüller gave Marie and JP her bedroom, where they rested. Frau Vogt got the small guest room, and Mitchell ended up with the overstuffed couch in the sitting room.

Despite my exhaustion, I sat in the kitchen, drinking coffee and talking with the doctor.

"Marie tells me that you work for the American commission in Paris," she said, sipping her coffee.

"Yes. My contact there is George Gordon. Charles Dyar in Berlin also works with him. I was working directly with Colonel House, but I am sure he has returned to the States by now." The lie was so automatic that I almost believed it myself. The doctor certainly did.

"Marie also tells me that you were attacked by Bolsheviks in

Königsberg." Dr. Schragmüller wasn't beautiful. In fact, she was plain, but she had a charisma about her that was undeniable.

"It certainly seems like I was."

"But you are not sure?"

She was perceptive. I supposed that's why she was a doctor.

"I do not mean to offend you," I said, "but it is certainly convenient for Germany if an American official is attacked or, better yet, killed by Reds, don't you think?"

"How so?" she asked.

"If Bolshevism is a real threat in Germany, then the allies, or at least the United States, might look more favorably at Germany keeping a credible military." I found that my fatigue and cocaine-muddled brain made me talkative. "You might not have to disarm. There is even an argument that you should keep some of the territory stripped from you."

"That is certainly one opinion."

"If I may ask, what are you a doctor of?"

"Politics and the science of politics," Elsbeth Schragmüller replied.

"What is your opinion? With a doctorate in politics, your opinion is certainly more valuable than mine."

"I think a strong Germany is a requirement for peace in Europe. I think France's passions have blinded her to this truth. I think Bolshevism is a threat not only to Germany and Europe but to the world. Based on my studies, I also think that your President Wilson's fourteen points, while well meant, cannot apply to the world as it is. In fact, they are a bit like Marxism: good in theory but, in practice, unworkable or disastrous, which is what we now see in the Bolshevism in Russia and Hungary and, however briefly, not far from here in Bavaria."

"Elsbeth, may I call you Elsbeth?" She nodded. "I don't mean to offend you, but I am very sure that a strong Germany is not what the world needs. As you likely know, I spent time fighting

Germany, and I've spent time in Berlin, and the folks in this country have lost their way."

"How very astute of you, John. We have, but we will find our path once again. I am very sure. And a strong Germany can hold Bolshevism at bay and perhaps even reverse it. You certainly know that France cannot do that."

She was probably right. Alone, France couldn't withstand Bolshevism or Germany. France needed allies. Perhaps Germany didn't.

"I agree that France alone probably can't. Not without the United States and Britain."

"But you Americans don't really want to be part of this world. That is Mr. Wilson's dream, not the American one."

"We just want it all to mean something, Elsbeth. That's all."

"We are alike in that, but we shouldn't fool ourselves. You do not seem ready for sleep. Come with me. We will meet an acquaintance of mine. He is a philosopher. Perhaps he can help you find the meaning you seek. I was to join him for coffee before my lecture."

She stood and hustled me out of the house. The others were all sleeping. I felt guilty about not keeping watch, but I wasn't thinking straight. The doctor wasn't going to take no for an answer in any event.

She started down the lane leading from her house at a brisk walk, and I had to jog to catch up. The walk to town was just that, a walk. It was not for talking. It was for walking. After about ten minutes, we came to a bridge, and I could see what had to be the center of Freiburg. A medieval clock tower rose before us as we crossed a shallow river and made our way into town.

The cocaine buzz was gone, and only a jittery discomfort remained. I wasn't sure I was fit to be strolling about a German town, but the doctor was not to be denied.

We walked under an arched gateway and passed an ornate

building with Freiburg Zeitung carved in fancy gothic script over the entryway.

Dr. Schragmüller saw my look and explained, "One of the local newspapers."

"Hell of a newspaper office."

"Indeed, but despite the grandeur of the building, the paper is historically anti-Catholic, so one doesn't complain. The coffee shop is just ahead."

As I was trying to make sense of her statement, she turned in to a café just past the newspaper office.

Only a few of the café's small round tables were occupied. A man waved at us from a table in the back. His receding hairline made it difficult to tell his age, as did his intensity, which was palpable, but he was younger than the doctor and perhaps five years older than me. He sported a mustache that went just to the edges of his mouth and gave his face a serious, almost angry cast.

When we arrived at the table, he engulfed the doctor in a hug, which I thought to be unseemly. He whispered something in her ear. I had the impression that he actually kissed her neck, but in my addled state, I wasn't certain. Were they lovers? He certainly seemed confident and comfortable around her, and his hand remained on her arm as they spoke briefly in German. Elsbeth turned to me.

"Major John Griffin, I would like to present my close friend Dr. Martin Heidegger."[1] She looked to Heidegger. "Major Griffin is touring Germany for the American Commission in Paris. He is married to one of my old students, who is traveling with him."

"A pleasure to meet you, Herr Major. Isn't Freiburg im Breisgau a bit out of the way for what you Americans might be interested in?" he asked provocatively. I wasn't sure if he was being critical of my travel choices or of Americans more broadly. I supposed it could be both.

"And what should Americans be interested in, Herr Doctor?"

"Well, as a philosopher, I am sure I don't know, but I suspect places with more military importance and perhaps less culture than Freiburg might be appropriate."

Both. He was critical of both.

"Actually, I am examining German attitudes toward the peace, the treaty, and the allies generally," I said. "So Freiburg is as good a place as any, and since you are a philosopher, perhaps you can share a German philosopher's view?"

"I am afraid that I am still struggling with my views on the war. It is difficult as a German to accept the outcome."

The waiter came and Dr. Schragmüller and I ordered coffees. Heidegger ordered a tea.

"So you are still drinking tea, Martin? Not very patriotic of you," Dr. Schragmüller teased.

"The war is over, and I find it settles my nerves. Coffee does not," Heidegger said defensively.

"Did you serve in the imperial military?" I asked Heidegger innocently.

"No. Well, yes, I was conscripted at the end of last year into a meteorological detachment. I have a heart condition and was unable to serve in a line unit."

I thought of Fuchs, who had been genuine in his joy at avoiding the fighting. I'd appreciated that in him when I'd first met him. I didn't think I'd find much about Heidegger to appreciate, but at least he wasn't trying to kill me.

"Well, you are fortunate to have avoided the fighting."

"I disagree," Heidegger exclaimed. "I saw the assault battalions march through, young pale sharp faces—resolute look in their eyes—with steel helmets and all loaded up. All silent, lost in thought, a few kilometers and they're in hell. The precious aliveness of past and future life. It was truly historical."[2]

"Resolute?" I scoffed. "If you mean determined, then I might agree. Determined to overcome the gut-watering fear they all felt. If you mean single-minded focus on victory for Germany, you're dreaming." Perhaps my reaction was a tad impolite, but I thought Heidegger was a blowhard accustomed to baffling students with disconnected words strung together to amaze and confuse. He was exactly the kind of ass who shouldn't have survived the war. Not so different from me, except smarter.

Heidegger's perpetual scowl deepened.

The drinks came.

Dr. Schragmüller interrupted our discussion.

"How are your lovely wife and little boy, Martin?" said Elsbeth, preventing Heidegger from answering me. She apparently had no interest in listening to us argue.

He didn't look like he wanted to give up the fight, but he remembered he had been flirting with Dr. Schragmüller.

"They are well. Little Jörg is just six months old."

"And Elisabeth?" Without the prompting, it seemed Heidegger might have forgotten his wife.

"She is well. Busy, but well. Enough about my family. You are looking well. I feel you may be avoiding me in favor of others."

Heidegger was a husband and a father, yet it was clear he was a philanderer. The way he welcomed Elsbeth and his cavalier attitude toward his family supported my view. I didn't like him. I didn't like him for the same reason I didn't like Germany. Besides the natural antipathy I felt toward a former, unforgiven enemy, I believed postwar Germany was fatally flawed as Heidegger was flawed. With the defeat of its military, nothing remained in Germany that warranted respect. Convention and tradition were cast aside when the Kaiser ran away. Elsbeth, an apparently sensible professor, disliked Catholics for some unknown reason. Heidegger was captivated by the historical importance of mass slaughter while being indifferent to the requirements of marriage. And Anita Berber was... unique and frightening. I thought of Fuchs. Fuchs was frightening but likely not unique.

"I brought John to meet you thinking the two of you might draw some meaning from the war." She looked at me with an arched brow as she spoke. "But I see there may be insufficient common ground for discussion."

"My apologies, Frau Doctor," I said. "I am tired, which has made me short-tempered. And my apologies to you, Herr Dr. Heidegger. Perhaps I once marched with resolution in my eyes, but I do not remember it. I will excuse myself and leave the two of you to discuss happier topics."

"Of course. No apology needed, Herr Major," Heidegger said.

"I will see you this evening, John," Elsbeth promised.

I walked alone back to the house. I wandered into Elsbeth's small study. Her desk was cluttered with books, papers, and picture postcards. I found nothing there to divert me. I sat again at the table in the kitchen. Grim thoughts of Heidegger and Germany bounced around my head. Then equally bleak memories of Sarah and the war surfaced in my sleep-deprived and cocaine-addled brain. Finally, I wrestled my mind from the darkness by thinking of Madeline. I fell asleep in the chair with a slight smile on my face.

20

———

The Last Supper

Elsbeth returned late in the afternoon. She had gone shopping and bought food and some German white wine for us to enjoy at dinner. My nap had done wonders for my mood and ability to think. I felt more rested than I had since arriving in Berlin the first time. I realized I was comfortable at Elsbeth's small cottage. It felt strange to feel safe and relaxed in a German home, but I did. I think the others did too.

Just before dinner, I found Marie and Mitchell speaking earnestly together in Elsbeth's front sitting room. Marie was pressing a small, folded bundle into Mitchell's hands that he seemed reluctant to take.

"She giving you a gift, Mitch?" I asked with a poke at them both.

They glanced up sharply, and Marie answered.

"I am. A peace offering." She showed me what she held. It was a German shoulder holster, likely the one she'd stripped from her contact in Berlin. "William has been very brave, and although I know he does not like me, he has been kind and protective of my son. And even of Emma." She said the last, reminding all three of us that I'd nearly had him torture Frau Vogt.

"Take it, Mitch. It might not hold your Colt, but it will hold one of the Lugers you have stuffed in your pants. We need every edge we can get."

He looked from me to Marie and then at the holster. He shrugged and took off his jacket. Marie handed him the shoulder harness. He put it on, adjusted the buckles, and took a Luger from behind his back. He tucked it carefully in the holster.

"Thank you, Marie," he said. He even sounded sincere.

Dinner was a hearty breaded pork dish with roasted potatoes and asparagus. It was a welcome change from the sausage, cheese, and stale bread we ate while on the road.

The six of us sat crowded around the table, laughing at Mitchell's improbable stories and Jean-Paul's painful, yet accurate imitations. I knew Mitchell could charm and entertain the ladies. Emma Vogt certainly seemed to have warmed to him. The real surprise of the meal was JP. Although still young, he was a gifted actor and mimic. He could portray the subject of his impersonation effortlessly. Oddly, I was his favorite target and, at least according to the others, his best.

When depicting me, he gritted his teeth, dropped his chin, and scowled. Once he was sure he had everyone's attention, he barked something mostly incomprehensible: "Mitchell, gograb blab blab hup tup! Quick! Marie, soflab ukgrub amit! Right now!"

All three ladies burst out laughing, and I couldn't help but smile. I was glad that he could tease me, but I wasn't fooled. Every once in a while, he would cut his eyes to me to check on my reaction. He wanted to make sure I wasn't angry. I wanted to say I wasn't like that, but I knew it was a lie.

As we were eating a dessert of berries and thick cream, there was a knock on the front door. Elsbeth went to answer. When she returned, we all looked to see who her visitor was. Karl Fuchs followed her into the kitchen.

"Mitchell, check the front," I said automatically. "Marie, stay put. Nothing silly, okay?" She nodded slowly. I had my pistol in my hand and held under the table before Fuchs was all the way in the room.

"Excuse me, ladies," Mitchell said, standing. "I just need to take a quick look outside."

"John," Fuchs said with a nod and a smile. "Please don't overreact. I have come to have a quiet chat. Nothing more. Frau Dr. Schragmüller, I am sorry to interrupt your dinner party."

Elsbeth looked confused. She could sense the tension in all of us, but she couldn't know why. She didn't know that Fuchs was a liar and murderer.

But how did she know Fuchs at all? What was he doing standing in her house?

"I was told you might be coming here. The professor, she is an old friend, yes?" He said the last to Marie.

How could he have known? Who told him? No one knew. Not Richter or Dyar. No one.

Mitchell poked his head into the room and said, "It looks clear, but that doesn't mean a damn thing. It also looks dark." He had the German Luger in his hand. He remained in the hallway behind Fuchs. If it bothered Fuchs to have Mitchell lurking behind him, he didn't show it.

"Keep an eye out in front," I told Mitchell.

JP had found a way to move his chair closer to Marie, which was a good thing. With her child hanging off her, I figured it would be harder for her to pull out her razor and slice up Fuchs.

"Frau Vogt, Jean-Paul, my heartfelt condolences for your loss," Fuchs said to the grandmother and JP. Frau Vogt, realizing Fuchs was telling her that her husband was dead, did her best to keep her composure, but I saw anger and great sadness in her eyes. Jean-Paul was just confused, but no one at the table was going to educate him. Fuchs would be wise not to turn his back on Emma Vogt.

"Things have changed," Fuchs said. "My orders in Berlin were, as I said then, to see that you didn't leave Germany. But we have learned some information that prompted us to rethink the need to..." He glanced at the little boy and then back at me. "Settle with you here in Germany."

"Well, that's mighty white of you. What brought on the change of view?" I asked sarcastically.

"The French." He watched Marie. All three of the ladies were focused on him, but Marie's face was stony. I was sure that, given the opportunity, she would kill Fuchs right there in the kitchen and find a way to explain his death to Jean-Paul.

"General Mangin,"[1] Fuchs continued, "the commander of the French colonial forces occupying the Rhineland, plans to establish an independent country there. He has support from a few German traitors in Mainz. This is not the first time he and Dorten[2] have attempted this."

"Dorten?" I asked.

"As I said, a traitor. He and his fellow conspirators want to separate the Rhineland from Germany. In June, he attempted to establish a republic there. It failed, not because France prevented it but because loyal Germans in the Rhineland refused to support it. Still, his efforts have not ceased. He continues to work for Rhinish autonomy, which will mean a Rhineland annexed by France. This is contrary to the conditions of the Treaty of Versailles, but Mangin is convinced that Clemenceau is weak, the British fickle, and the Americans skeptical of a continuing threat from Germany. But Germany will not allow the French to create a puppet regime in the Rhineland. If the German people were to learn that France intends to annex the Rhineland, they will demand war. As we discussed at our dinner in Berlin, they already feel abused by the allies and a particular sense of betrayal by you Americans."

I remembered stories of General Mangin. In a war where many generals were indifferent to massive casualties, Mangin had earned the telling sobriquet "the Butcher" for his willingness to squander the lives of his men in pointless attacks. And I thought Pershing was bad. Mangin's stubborn aggressiveness made Pershing look like a sissy.

"He may be right about the British and the Americans, but I guarantee Clemenceau's not weak," I said. "Untrustworthy, but the bastard is tough as horsemeat. And he hates Germany. How do you know Mangin isn't trying to set up this Rhinish state with Clemenceau's blessing?"

"Because Clemenceau would not risk the wrath of the *great* Woodrow Wilson," he answered with sarcasm. "He knows he needs the United States if France is to resist Germany in the future."

"It sounds like Mangin is on your side then," I said. "You Germans have been whining that you really weren't beaten. Now you've got an excuse to fight again."

"John, please don't be stupid," Fuchs said patiently. "I know that you remain angry about the attempts on your life, but that should not cause you to suspend your reason. Germany can ill afford a fight against the French even if the fight would be against the French only. That day may come again, but it is not now."

"Oh, I'm plenty angry, Karl, but not near as angry as Johann Ditzel's ma would be if she knew what you'd done to her son. But I still don't see why your plan to have me killed by your fake Bolsheviks can't work. Not that I want to encourage that. I am very much in favor of you calling off the dogs, but I'm sure you still want America to believe that the Bolshevik threat is real. Why isn't this Rhineland issue just a separate problem?"

"Perhaps it is. But our priorities have changed. You are now in a position to provide Germany a helpful service, which you could not if dead. This is your good fortune."

"Karl, I don't much want to do anything for Germany."

"It doesn't matter. You have no choice."

I waited for his demand with dread. Goddamn Germans!

"You and your warlike friend here will prevent Mangin's plot. It might be that you have to assassinate the general. We are certain that without him leading the effort, the movement will fail."

"And we would help you so you don't kill us?" I scoffed.

"Oh no, John. You and Mr. Mitchell will do what you are told not for yourselves. You will do what you arrogant, wealthy, *Christian* Americans do: you will try to save others. You will agree to do what Germany requires, or my men will come into this charming little house and kill everyone here. My apologies, professor." He gave a slight bow to Elsbeth. He looked back at me. "But please understand. We will kill Marie, little Jean-Paul, and Frau Dr. Schragmüller without hesitation. Now put away your guns."

"I don't think so, Karl. You may not have any men outside at all, and what's to keep us from blowing a hole in you where you stand?" I asked as I stood and pointed my pistol at his chest.

He smiled at the sight of the gun.

"And I thought you were listening to me attentively, John." He was unmoved by my threat.

"We could hold you as a hostage and drive right out of here."

"You could certainly try," he said with confidence.

He stretched his lips over his teeth and gave a sharp whistle. A second later, from both the front and back of the house, machine pistols fired short bursts.

Everyone in the house ducked down except Fuchs, who now wore a grin.

"They fired into the air. This time. You now have one minute," he said, looking at his watch. "At about thirty seconds I hope you don't mind if I lie down on the floor. I am sure it will be safer there when bullets start coming through the walls."

He could see the surrender in my eyes. I'd do what he wanted. I couldn't let him slaughter the ladies, and getting Mitchell killed would be poor repayment for his friendship. I put the Colt back in the shoulder holster, and Mitchell holstered his gun as well.

"No, gentlemen, put your pistols on the floor and kick them toward me."

"John, no," Marie said. "He's bluffing. They won't fire into the house while he is in here."

"I assure you, I am not. And you will recall the ambush in Königsberg, John. I knew that I would be shot at then too. I may not have been a soldier, but I am brave enough to do what I must for the fatherland."

I wouldn't want to play poker with Fuchs. If he was bluffing, I sure couldn't tell.

Still I didn't move. Mitchell was waiting for my lead.

Fuchs looked at his watch. "I'm going to lie on the floor now."

"Goddamn it!" I placed my pistol at my feet and kicked it toward him. Mitchell did the same.

Fuchs whistled twice more, and the front and back doors burst open. Marie started to stand.

"Marie, no!" I shouted. I was sure the Germans would gun her down and likely JP with her. She sagged back into her chair, and Jean-Paul held on to her tightly, as much for her security as his.

The room seemed to fill with German soldiers. Two held machine pistols. The others spread around the room. One shoved Mitchell back into his seat, and another picked up our discarded pistols.

"Sit, John," Fuchs instructed. I sat. "Now that we have come to an agreement, I face one unfortunate point. We don't need three hostages to motivate you and your associate to do our work." As his words registered, he produced a small automatic pistol. It couldn't have been more than five inches long. It was so small his fist nearly swallowed it. I didn't understand what I was seeing, and before I could even think to act or voice an objection, he shot Frau Vogt in the chest. The three loud "pops" were incongruous coming from the tiny gun. Frau Vogt slumped in her chair. She hadn't had time to raise a hand. She was dead before my mind absorbed what he had done.

Mitchell and I started to stand.

"Please sit, gentlemen," Fuchs ordered calmly. "I would prefer not to shoot the professor as well. She is a popular lecturer here at the university."

Jean-Paul stared at his dead grandmother. His mouth was open, and I was certain he was about to start shrieking. Marie grabbed him and buried his face in her shoulder, but he turned his head enough so that he could still see the dead woman. I didn't like the look in his eyes. I wondered if Fuchs had broken something inside the child.

"Again, Frau Dr. Schragmüller, my apologies, but this is for the good of Germany. Do you understand?"

The shocked doctor nodded her head slowly but didn't speak. I was sure she was wondering if she would be next.

"And my apologies about the little white lie of just wanting a chat. I mostly wanted a chat, but I knew it was the last supper for at least one of you," he said sincerely.

Before anyone else could speak, Fuchs's men clapped handcuffs on Mitchell and me. They even searched Marie. To his credit, JP tried to defend her. He was unceremoniously pushed to the ground. Lucky for Fuchs, they found her razor.

"Leave it, kid," I said sharply. I didn't want him hurt and unable to run if we got the chance to make a break. For now, we were Fuchs's prisoners.

Poor Dr. Schragmüller watched helplessly from her front door as we were taken from the house. Briefly I wondered whether Fuchs would remove Emma Vogt's body from the dining room. The question was answered as two soldiers carried her from the house and pitched her body into the canvas-covered back of a waiting German truck. The truck looked to be the equivalent of a French *camion*. Marie and JP were placed in a motorcar with Fuchs. Mitchell and I were put in the motortruck with the corpse. Our bags were piled around our legs and away from the still-leaking body. I was glad Frau Vogt's head was turned away from us. She had not liked me, but I had respected her strength. I felt a knot in my stomach at the callousness of her murder. Fuchs had achieved what he had hoped by killing her. We had no doubt he would do as he threatened. A sergeant and five armed German soldiers, wearing coal scuttle helmets, sat on the benches between us and the tailgate. The seats were no more comfortable in the German truck than in the French version.

The car started and then the truck. We motored down the lane and away from the house.

I held up my hands to Mitchell, showing him the German handcuffs, and then pulled the cuffs apart, rattling them. The soldiers watched with indifference. They thought we were trussed up good. I raised an eyebrow, and Mitchell nodded.

We were both remembering Howie Dickson. Unfortunate Howie. He'd been killed at the Meuse just before I'd been wounded, but even dead, the unlucky bastard might do us some good.

He'd been in the Forty-Ninth with me. He'd joined the unit as a replacement. We didn't much care for him, but the one good thing about Dickson was he was fascinated by the great Harry Houdini. In early 1918, Houdini had started training troops shipping out from New York. According to Dickson and the other replacements who'd arrived with him, Houdini had conducted training for them on surviving a ship torpedoing and escaping German handcuffs.[3] While not a gifted rifleman, Dickson had mastered Houdini's handcuff escape technique.

He'd even acquired a pair of cuffs, and when the company wasn't in the line, he'd practice slipping out of them in his spare time. He'd shown anyone who asked how to get free. The trick to escaping the cuffs was to carry an alternative to the key. Dickson had a piece of stiff wire that he would bend and then manipulate to unlock the cuffs. Mitchell, of course, was a natural. He learned the skill quickly when he visited the company. I could do it, but I would drop the makeshift key as often as not. We didn't have a piece of wire handy, but we had Emma Vogt's body. When we stopped in Leipzig to get her clothing, she had also bought hairpins. I could see the pins in her hair from where I sat on the wooden truck bench.

I held my cuffed hands to the nearest soldiers, pointed to myself and then pointed to Frau Vogt's body and touched the pulse in my neck. I hoped they understood I wanted to see if she was still alive. They looked to the sergeant at the end of the bench, who shrugged. They understood, but they knew she wasn't. The motortruck bumped down the road. I got to my hands and knees and crawled over to her body. I bent over her slack face as if listening for breathing. With my hands hidden by my body, I brushed them through her hair and carefully pulled out two pins. For show, I looked at Mitchell and shook my head. He shook his head as well. I stood, and the rocking of the truck allowed me to stumble into Mitchell. I passed him one of the pins.

After bending my hairpin, I spent the next hour surreptitiously trying to unlock my cuffs. I had no luck. Mitchell was slumped down as if asleep with his back half turned to our guards. I was sure he had succeeded.

After another couple of hours and more frustration with the hairpin, the truck stopped, and the soldiers jumped down from the back of the truck.

"*Raus!*" we were urged.

We didn't move until I heard Fuchs call from outside, "Climb down. You will want to urinate, if needed. We will be back on the road shortly."

Still handcuffed, I jumped out first, and Mitchell followed. He had his cuffs on, but I was confident he'd unlocked them and loosened the ratchet enough to slip free when he was ready. I needed to do my part and get the damn cuffs unlocked.

The car and truck were parked in a tidy little village next to a building with a sign above the door that said DORF APOTHEKE and carried an image of a serpent twining around a cup. An apothecary shop. Charming. I hoped Fuchs didn't feel a need to get some chloroform. I was certain Marie's drugs, ether, chloroform and all, were still in her bag at our feet. I spent a few seconds fantasizing about suffocating Fuchs with a chloroform-soaked rag.

Fuchs hammered on the door. The shop and the whole town were closed for the night, but undeterred, he pounded again. After a few minutes, a disheveled older man answered. He was angry, but after a few sharp words from Fuchs, who gestured to the soldiers, he shut up. The two spoke for a moment.

"You may use the facilities in the pharmacy if you need them. One at a time, and one of the soldiers will accompany you. We have at least another four hours to travel. I suggest you use the opportunity."

I was the last to use the pharmacy's privy. Fuchs and Mitchell were standing by the rear of the truck, not speaking. Marie and Jean-Paul were already back in the motorcar.

"Where are we going exactly?" I asked Fuchs.

"Ginsheim am Rhine. A small town near Mainz on the east side on the river. It is close enough to access the Mainz town center and the Tenth Army headquarters of the French occupiers. That is where you will find Mangin. We will wait for news of your success in Ginsheim."

"And if we fail?" Mitchell asked.

"I expect you will be dead. The French will have killed you, but I am afraid I will still keep my promise. Marie and the boy will simply disappear."

"What's the point of killing them?" I demanded.

"If you have failed, we will need to make sure there are no connections back to Germany. You are married to Marie. At least, that is your story. Thus a connection. It really is just good housekeeping. Now back into the truck. We still have a long way to go."

Mitchell looked at me, and I gave a slight shake of my head. There was no point in trying to escape now. My hands were still handcuffed, and even if we could overcome the soldiers and Fuchs, we'd still have to cross a fair chunk of Germany just to get to France. If they were going to take us to the Rhine near Mainz, my inclination was to let them. Assuming we could later escape, it was better to be escorted than chased.

Fuchs returned to the motorcar with Marie and Jean-Paul, we climbed back in the truck, and the caravan continued.

I pondered how Fuchs knew that I wasn't really married to Marie. I supposed he must know she had been a German spy. It was possible she had told him herself at some point. In any case, it didn't matter. She wasn't my wife, but I wasn't about to let her be killed if I could prevent it.

I questioned how Fuchs had found us in Freiburg. He had shot Frau Vogt without hesitation. Had she left him a trail of breadcrumbs leading him to the town on the edge of the Black Forest? She was loyal to Germany. Not that it did her any good in the end.

Knowing that I had a good four hours to work on the cuffs gave me confidence. Like Mitchell, I turned my body from the soldiers and focused on the lock. Not fifteen minutes after leaving the pharmacy, I felt the bent hairpin catch the lock bar. Carefully I turned the hairpin and pressed against the tension of the lock spring. With a roll and a little pressure of my left wrist, the ratchet came free. One hand was enough. I didn't need to loosen them both. Unfortunately, when I released the lock spring, it was too loose to remain on my hand without holding it on. My German minders needed to think I was still cuffed. I might have to climb from the truck again. The noise in the back hid the sound of the clicks as I carefully tightened the cuff around my wrist one ratchet tooth at a time until I was sure it would stay on my wrist. With the one task within my control complete, I leaned against the canvas cover of the truck bed and went to sleep.

21

______

Rusty Screwdriver

I woke when the truck tires transitioned from macadam to gravel. It was daylight, and out the back of the truck I could see the road had narrowed. We drove through a forest pressing in from both sides. I didn't think we would drive too far on an unpaved lane, and I was right. We stopped after a short ride. The soldiers hopped out of the truck bed and motioned us to follow. Mitchell and I didn't wait for Fuchs to call us out this time. We jumped down, and I caught a faint whiff of manure in the air.

The car and truck were parked at the head of a path leading to a river. What appeared to be a giant houseboat sat in the slow-moving current at the end of a narrow pontoon bridge.

Fuchs came around the back of the truck to join us. Marie and Jean-Paul followed.

"*Willkommen* to the Schiffsmühle," he said smugly.

"Shiffs mule?" I asked.

"A mill for grain. On board a boat. There used to be many in this area of the Rhine, but with the war, this is one of the last, abandoned, but still floating. It is from here that we will send you to Mainz and General Mangin."

"How exactly will you do that?" Mitchell asked.

"Simple. We have a former Kriegsmarine sailor skilled in handling small boats. He will row you across the Rhine to the French occupied side. It is only five hundred meters across. A man in a motorcar will pick you up and take you into Mainz. From there, I am afraid the success of your mission will be up to your ingenuity and good luck." He was smiling at the impossibility of our task. "Of course, we will wait until tonight to take you across. And John, please don't dillydally. I am not a patient man, and Germany needs the Mangin problem solved quickly."

"I'll keep that in mind."

"Your bags will be placed in the boat. The sergeant will remove your handcuffs when you reach the other side of the Rhine. Of course, if you flee and do not do what is required, Marie and the little boy die."

"We'll need access to Marie's bag. She's got some drugs in it that might come in handy."

"What kind of drugs?"

"Chloroform."

Fuchs laughed. "Excellent. When I was told to arrange this mission, I was skeptical. Frankly, I didn't see how two men would accomplish it, but after your murderous display in Berlin and now this, you give me hope."

"You don't really work for the foreign ministry, do you, Karl?" I asked in a friendly tone as we walked together across the pontoon bridge. I know I didn't fool him, but it couldn't hurt to learn as much as I could about the German state apparatus that had tried to kill me.

He smiled happily. "Oh, I do work at the ministry, but as you have likely now guessed, I also work for the German military intelligence. My ministry work allows me to travel and access to men like Charles Dyar. With ministry credentials and contacts, I am able to act more effectively in my intelligence capacity."

I nodded. I was almost sorry I had asked the question. Now I was sure that no matter what we did, they would kill Marie, Jean-Paul, Mitchell, and me. Fuchs wouldn't want Dyar or others to know he worked for German intelligence. The knowledge would undermine his value. He was telling me he was going to kill us, and there was nothing we could do about it. It was good to know where we stood. When there were no options, it made decisions easy.

The boat's bow pointed upriver. When we entered the long house-like structure on the back of the boat, it was clear the space hadn't been used for some time. The millhouse was open from floor to ceiling but filled with pulleys and belts used to run the two large mills installed flush with the deck. There was a raised platform toward the back and a balcony circumventing the inside walls of the millhouse. It looked like the mill workers would have hoisted the raw grain to the second level and poured it through the funnels into the grinding stones from above.

The millhouse reminded me of my grandfather's old barn in the country. It was dirty, dusty, and in need of a good sweeping. Spiderwebs were everywhere. The head was toward the back of the boat, and a ladder well went down to where the waterwheel machinery turned the millwheels from below the deck. It was not a place that promised a lot of privacy. Old tools hung from nails tacked into the framing studs, and coils of rope and chains lay abandoned on the floor. I felt a brief pang of homesickness at the look of it.

It struck me as a poor jumping-off point for a secret attack, especially when using unwilling participants as the soldiers. But then I didn't know the geography of Mainz. However, I did know old barns. There would be tools lying about that the Germans had not noticed. These tools would be useful. Nails, files, hammers, mallets. Fuchs and the other Germans must be city boys to have brought us here. I would have to be patient. There was no point in finding a weapon only to have it taken away.

The soldiers got busy setting up a cook fire in the millhouse stove, and on Fuchs's order, the German sergeant gave me access to Marie's bag. He watched me closely. I had to be careful to keep the handcuffs pulled tight. I held my wrists apart as I opened Marie's bag and searched for the gear the Germans might think we needed for the job. From the bag, I took Anita's chloroform bottle and Marie's razor in its thin holster. The sergeant had his pistol pointed at my chest. I smiled at him, but he didn't smile back. With his gun barrel, he gestured at my gear bag sitting on the floor nearby, and I put both the bottle and the razor inside. He took the bag and placed it against a wall between two of his men.

We ate potato soup made by one of the soldiers and then settled in to wait for nightfall. Fuchs would not allow us to sit together or talk. I spent most of my time outside trying to get a better sense of the river's speed. I tossed some twigs into the flow. It looked like the river was moving at two or three miles an hour. Slow, but maybe fast enough to be a problem for us. I guessed the river was about six hundred yards wide. Any boat would move downstream pretty far when covering six hundred yards.

The afternoon grew old, and I took a tour of the interior of the millhouse. The Germans watched me amble through the building. They said nothing and didn't hinder me as I poked the machines, kicked the trash on the floor, or peered out the dirty windows. Lying on one of the horizontal structural beams circling the building, I found a short, wooden-handled screwdriver. It was rusty and sat unnoticed in the grime next to a jar full of nails and a broken set of pliers.

Mitchell knew what I was doing. He was watching me surreptitiously but very closely. I turned my back on the screwdriver and looked at Mitchell.

He nodded, and in a fine tenor, broke into song.

"Johnnie get your gun, get your gun, get your gun... Take it on the run, on the run, on the run...”[1]

The Germans, Marie, and the boy all turned to stare at him as he held his cuffed hands out to the room. I slipped the screwdriver into my coat pocket.

"Every son of liberty... hurry right away, no delay, go today...”

"Enough," Fuchs called out.

"What? You're not a music lover, Karl? He does have a fine voice," I said with a laugh.

Mitchell stopped singing but continued humming the tune to the chorus of "Over There," and he winked at Fuchs.

"It is time to prepare," Fuchs ordered. It was getting dark quickly. Fuchs took us onto the boat's deck. Six of the German soldiers were with us, the sergeant, who wore his holstered Luger pistol on his hip, and four who carried rifles. The sixth was unarmed. He was the only one not wearing a helmet. I didn't have long to wonder where the seventh soldier was.

A three-bench wooden rowboat was tied below a ladder on the outside of the mill. The ribs inside the rowboat's structure were visible from where we stood looking down. It had two oars in the oarlocks over the middle seat for the oarsman and one bench in front and one in back for passengers. The missing German soldier was already sitting on the back bench armed with his Mauser rifle. The bayonets were fixed on all the rifles. I guess they didn't want to make a lot of noise if they had to kill us.

"John." Fuchs pointed at me. "Climb down into the front."

I followed his commands and sat facing the back of the rowboat.

"And you." He nodded at Mitchell. Mitchell jumped down next to me. The sergeant came down the ladder and made his way to the back bench. Finally, the unarmed soldier, who I realized was the sailor, climbed down to the center bench. The men on deck handed our bags to the sailor, and he placed them on the floor behind him, almost at my feet. They handed the sailor a rectangular metal box that had to be the German version of a trench flashlight, which he passed to the sergeant.

"*Blinken sie das Licht, zweimal,*" Fuchs said.

Even without speaking German, I figured that meant flash the light twice when we reached the far side to call the ride to get us.

Fuchs reached inside his jacket and took out an envelope, which, like the light, he passed down to the sergeant. The sergeant took the envelope and carefully tucked it inside his tunic just below the iron cross ribbon he wore in his third buttonhole.

The sailor then sat on the bench with his back to Mitchell and me and unlimbered his outboard oar. The other oar remained resting on the inboard gunwale.

Marie and Jean-Paul looked down on us from above.

"We'll see you soon," I assured them.

"Take care of your mom, JP. She's got grit, and I suspect you do too," Mitchell added.

Marie held Jean-Paul tightly by the shoulders but gave a small smile at Mitchell's compliment.

"*Jetzt,*" the sailor said.

The soldiers above us tossed the mooring line into the boat as the sergeant pushed off on the hull of the mill ship. With one short stroke of the outboard oar, the sailor pulled the prow of the rowboat toward the middle of the river. When he had sufficient clearance, he unlimbered the second oar, and in moments he had us moving smoothly across the water.

I started to hum "Over There" as I worked my left hand out of the handcuff. It was nearly time to escape. But I couldn't get my damn hand out. It just wouldn't come free. I twisted it back and forth with no success.

I could no longer see the mill ship because of the dark. I had stopped humming when I realized my hand was stuck.

"Mitch, I can't get my hand out of the cuff," I whispered. I jerked my hand again and again. It wouldn't come free no matter how hard I twisted, pulled, or yanked. I was so panicked I hardly noticed the pain. I was worried I was drawing the attention of the men at the stern of the boat.

Mitchell looked at me out of the corner of his eye and showed me that his hands were free.

"Give me the weapon," he said. He didn't know what I'd found, but he knew I'd found something. I could give him the screwdriver, but I wouldn't. I still felt like a dog for asking him to torture JP's grandmother. I wouldn't force him to kill the sailor too because of my incompetence.

"No!" I answered.

"*Ruhe!*" the sergeant barked at us.

"I don't think he likes us talking," Mitchell said.

"Fuck you, you Kraut bastard," I snarled. It was time to move. We had no choice.

Mitchell and I shifted our butts to the center of the boat until our hips were touching. I took the screwdriver from my pocket. As the sailor pulled on his oars, he leaned back toward us. I fell forward on to my knees in the center of the boat and drove the screwdriver through the back of his neck and up and into his brain.

"*Scheisse!*" The sergeant reached for his pistol. The soldier next to him started to stand and swing his bayonet in line with me and the dead sailor in front of me. Using the screwdriver handle to lift the dead oarsman, I heaved him up and shoved the body hard toward the back of the boat. Mitchell gave me a helpful push. The dead oarsman collided with the soldier, knocking him out of the boat with a splash. As he tumbled into the water, his rifle struck the sergeant's arm. The sergeant had just gotten his Luger clear of his holster, and the impact knocked it into the bottom of the boat. Without his pistol, even with my hands cuffed, he had no chance. There were two of us. He tried to fight us with his fists and then with his nails and teeth. To his credit, he even tried to overturn the boat. It didn't change the outcome. He didn't beg, and it wouldn't have mattered if he had. It was an ugly, brutal death that I hoped I'd soon forget. I pulled the envelope from his tunic, and we pushed his body into the water. The soldier who had fallen into the river had simply disappeared. The weight of his gear must have dragged him to the bottom.

Mitchell unlocked my cuffs. Ordinarily, he would have given me a smug, superior grin, but he was thinking about the damn sergeant.

"What's in the envelope?"

I looked. "Kraut money."

We pushed the sailor's body overboard, and Mitchell manned the oars. He turned us around and we headed back toward Marie. I put the envelope of marks on the bench by my side. I didn't want to put it in my pocket. It would stain my jacket.

We landed in the woods on the east side of the river a few hundred yards upstream of the mill boat. It had been a hard pull against the current, but Mitchell had managed it, although not with the same economy as the dead sailor. I wouldn't think about the sailor with a screwdriver jammed in his head, or the sergeant. At least not until one night, not too long from now, when they joined my nightmares.

In whispers, we agreed that we would use the current to float us down onto the mill boat. We had the sergeant's Luger and all our gear, including the MP-18, Mitchell's Luger, and our Colts that had been in our bags. Our plan was to board quietly, surprise the Germans, and get Marie and Jean-Paul into the rowboat. We'd row to the west side of the river, find the car that Fuchs had arranged, and flee into France. The trench light was still on the bottom boards of the boat, and we could use it to signal the car's driver. As much as I wanted to kill Fuchs, our aim was to get Marie and Jean-Paul safely off the mill boat.

I put on my shoulder holster with the pistol inside. Mitchell put on his that Marie had given him. He tucked his Colt behind his belt at the small of his back. I left the MP-18 unloaded. Once we were out of the rowboat, I would insert that magazine and cock the gun, but after getting shot by the accidental discharge in the Berlin driveway, I wasn't taking any chances. Mitchell guided us out into the flow with gentle sweeps of the oars. As we drifted down on the mill boat, he pushed us toward the bank so we would float against the pontoon bridge. We didn't want to risk the noise or the motion of boarding the boat itself. Instead, we would board from the bridge where the ship was docked. Mitchell spun us so that the back of the rowboat was downstream. With the mooring line in hand, I cushioned the impact with my feet as we came against the pontoon bridge. I tied us where we landed, and Mitchell quietly shipped the oars. The current turned the rowboat so that its side bumped gently against the bridge. We gingerly crawled onto the dock, hoping to keep our weight from shifting the mill ship and warning the Germans of our arrival.

Once up on the floating bridge, I loaded the machine pistol. Mitchell tapped my arm and pointed to where the Germans had parked when we'd arrived. Despite the darkness, it was clear that only the truck remained parked on the gravel at the end of the bridge. The motorcar was gone. I hoped that didn't mean that Fuchs had moved Marie and Jean-Paul, but the only way to find out was to go into the millhouse.

I was glad there were no neighbors.

I took the lead as we moved down the bridge, Mitchell on my left about five steps behind me.

Unless more men had arrived while we were out on the water, there should have been no more than four men in the mill. Three had died in the rowboat, and at least one had taken the car, likely Fuchs.

The millhouse door came right to the edge of the boat and opened onto the dock. On the back of the boat looking downstream, there was an open deck, like the back porch on an old wood frame house. The Germans had set no watch that I could see on the front, looking upstream. I was sure there would be a sentry, and I was sure he would be on that back deck, looking in the direction we had taken when the Germans rowed us toward Mainz. There was nothing we could do about him now. We couldn't get to him without going through the main part of the mill where Marie, the boy, and some of the Germans waited.

I put my hand on the doorknob of the millworks and looked at Mitchell. He nodded, and I opened the door.

"Wer ist da?"

I moved through the door and into the darkness beyond. Mitchell's shadow flitted after me. I pointed at the rear of the mill, hoping Mitchell understood I wanted him focused there, and I turned back to the room.

A shadow stood from the floor. Others started to stir.

"Wer ist da?" came again from the darkness.

"Marie," I said loudly, "stay flat on the floor and keep Jean-Paul there."

"Die Amerikaner!"

And then I started shooting. The fire from the machine pistol's barrel stabbed out in an almost continuous flame. Noise, flashing light, and dust filled the space. Anything that moved above waist height I shot, but it seemed only two men were in the millhouse.

Mitchell's body remained angled toward the door at the back of the boat. Although his pistol was in his hand, I didn't see him fire. He was waiting for the one on guard to come through the rear door. I had emptied the machine pistol's magazine. I drew the Colt.

"Marie?" I said softly.

"Here." Her whisper came back in the dark.

"Is Jean-Paul okay?"

"Yes. I'm going to stand. Don't shoot. There is a lamp," she said.

"Don't light the lamp yet. Is there another soldier in the back?"

"There was when we lay down."

"How many are still here?" I asked.

"Three. Fuchs left with a driver shortly after you were taken away," she answered.

"Okay, both of you, lie back down on the floor."

Marie and the boy lay back down. In the shadows, it looked like Marie covered Jean-Paul's head with her arm.

I moved behind the milling machinery and made my way toward the back deck and the door behind which the sentry waited. Mitchell worked his way down the other side of the equipment. When we reached the door, we stopped. There was no good way to go through. If I opened the door, I would be shot, but I couldn't leave a soldier out there. If I did, I knew his rifle could hit targets as distant as the far side of the river. The door was hinged on the riverside to open out onto the deck. That was the only good thing about the situation.

"Crap," I said under my breath.

We retreated from the door, and I put my lips next to Mitchell's ear.

"I'm going to go out onto the pontoon bridge. He'll be able to see me from the corner of the back deck once I'm there. As he's shooting at me, I need you to open the door and kill him. He should be on the other side of that corner." I pointed to the downstream wall nearest the riverbank.

Mitchell nodded and said quietly, "Some things never change."

I ignored him and worked my way back to Marie. I explained the plan to her. I couldn't see her face in the dark, and it didn't matter what she thought anyway.

I went to the door leading onto the pontoon bridge, still open from our earlier entrance. I needed the German to know where I was. With three deep breaths, I banged the door closed and reopened it. Then I stepped through and started down the bridge.

There is a huge difference between surprising an enemy and attacking when the enemy knows you're coming. This felt just like going over the top in an attack with my British mates. My heart was beating faster than it had when I'd first come through the door. My bladder felt full, and I felt terror again. The worst part was I needed the squarehead to know what I was doing and where I was going. I needed him to think we believed we killed them all. I needed his attention focused on his rifle sights and me. So I stood tall and started toward the rowboat. I gave him just enough time to get a good aim, a clear shot. Then I dove forward flat onto my belly, knocking the wind out of myself. My terror had made my flop violently enthusiastic.

As I dropped, he fired. With a sizzle, the round zipped by. I heard the working of a rifle bolt, then the bark of a .45. Mitchell had used his 1911 instead of the Luger to be sure of the shot. I appreciated his attention to detail.

I lay on the boards of the bridge, laboring to get air back into my lungs.

"Griff?" Mitchell called from the back deck of the boat.

I couldn't answer, but I raised an arm that he likely couldn't see in the dark.

"Shit!" I heard Mitchell say.

The lamp went on in the mill room, and Mitchell ran out

onto the pontoon bridge to check on me. I had rolled on my side. I gave him a thumbs-up.

"You okay?"

"Knocked the wind out of myself," I wheezed.

Mitchell laughed a deep, hearty, genuine laugh of relief.

"He's okay," he called to Marie and Jean-Paul.

I sat up. "We've got to go," I managed to say.

Mitchell helped me stand. We went back into the structure. I searched the three Germans while Mitchell collected Marie and Jean-Paul and hurried them to the rowboat.

Unfortunately, Karl Fuchs was not among the dead Germans. As Marie had said, only three had been on the mill boat, including the last sentry Mitchell had killed. Fuchs had left with a driver, and he could return at any moment. I wanted us to be long gone. I left the bodies where they fell. I considered trying to conceal the truck so that Fuchs would think we were still on the east bank of the river, but I didn't know where we'd hide it. The right thing to do now was run.

Mitchell had Marie and Jean-Paul in the bow of the rowboat and pointed me into the stern. He again took the oars. On his signal, I untied us from the bridge and clumsily shoved off with one arm. Mitchell took it from there and rowed us back out into the river. I picked up the trench light and tested it in the bottom of the boat.

"Marie, I'm supposed to flash it twice, right?" I didn't trust my translation of Fuchs's German instructions to the sergeant.

"Yes, the contact should be on the road along the far side of the river."

"Will, judging by the angle the squarehead sergeant was taking us across the river, I think he should be straight across."

"The contact might have seen and heard the shooting," he answered.

"He probably did. He'll either be gone, or he'll know that something is wrong, but we don't have a choice. Let's just hope

Fuchs was telling the truth, and there really is only a driver and not a whole bunch of Germans. Row upstream and drop me. I'll work my way down the bank. Marie, you'll have to operate the light and do the talking. With luck, I can sneak up on him while he's focused on you."

"With luck he won't shoot us," Mitchell said under his breath.

"You can work your way down the bank if you'd rather," I said in a flash of irritation.

"No. You went out on the bridge. The least I can do is row Marie into the sights of some Kraut gunman."

I could hear the smile in his voice, but I didn't know if Marie did, so I gave a little laugh. "Yeah, be careful with my wife and son." Jean-Paul's head jerked up at my words, and I wasn't sure he knew I was kidding.

Mitchell took the boat about five hundred yards upstream and then across to the west side. He drifted down onto the bank, and just before landing, he gave one good pull on the oars to beach the boat. I picked up the envelope of cash and clambered to the front and jumped out. Cold water filled one shoe, and the other crunched into the pebbles higher on the shoreline. The bank was heavily wooded. JP crawled past Mitchell to the back of the boat. Reluctantly I put the damp envelope in my jacket pocket.

"If he's here, he can't be far," I said optimistically. "Give me five minutes. Good luck."

I gave the boat a shove.

I heard a "good luck" echo back at me, but I couldn't tell if it was Marie or Mitchell who spoke. In no time, they were lost in the darkness.

I moved in from the river, and, after a few steps, came to a rutted dirt road. I crossed the road and stayed just inside the woods that bordered it, working my way downstream in the direction where I hoped our transportation waited. I moved quickly, gambling that whoever was there wouldn't be watching the road. I counted my steps, and at four hundred, I moved more cautiously, stopping more often, placing my feet carefully. I also kept an eye on the river.

Two flashes from out on the water confirmed that I was at least where Mitchell expected me to be. I stopped and studied the woods before me. If our ride was still waiting, he should be nearby.

From the trees not more than fifteen feet in front of me, two flashes illuminated the trees. No voices. Whoever was there was either alone or very disciplined. Undergrowth separated me from where they hid, and I couldn't pick out their silhouette.

Marie must have seen the light because I heard the steady dipping of Mitchell's oars as the rowboat drew nearer.

Carefully, oh so carefully, I crept toward where the lights had originated.

There! One man. Alone.

There was a hint of pink on the horizon, but it was still difficult to see him. He didn't move, and he looked like he had his hands in his pockets. I saw no gun. If I didn't know better, I'd have said he looked bored. I didn't know how one could be bored waiting in the dark for Germans to show up. This was not what I'd expected. Given all the soldiers Fuchs had at his disposal, I expected another soldier. Still, I drew the Colt and waited.

Only when Mitchell had grounded the rowboat did the man move. He walked forward, not trying to hide his presence.

"*Guten Morgen,*" he said softly.

From the boat, Marie said, "*Guten Morgen.*" I heard his grunt of surprise at a woman's answer.

"*Kommen, wir müssen gehen,*" the man said.

"*Sprechen sie Französisch oder Englisch?*" Marie asked.

"English is better," the man said.

Marie jumped from the boat, and Mitchell followed. Jean-

Paul was nowhere to be seen. I suspected Mitchell and Marie had worked this out while I was sightseeing.

"I was not expecting a woman. Two people, yes, but two men, who would be escorted by Germans." He stepped toward the boat. "And you are late. Does your tardiness result from the gunfire across the river, by any chance?"

"If it does, is that a problem?" Mitchell asked.

The man laughed.

"An American. I like Americans. It is no problem for me, as long as you have the money I was promised," the man said with a small shrug.

"I don't," Mitchell said.

"Then you have a problem," the man said.

"But I do," I added from behind him.

"*Mist!*" he exclaimed, jumping toward the boat and turning toward me. He shined the trench light to get a look at me.

"Be very careful, my friend. We are not here to hurt you. We just want the ride you were supposed to give to us anyway," I said.

"You say you are not here to hurt me, yet you look like the devil, you scared my heart from my chest, and you hold a giant pistol."

"The pistol's just to avoid any misunderstandings," I said with my most endearing smile.

"Please do not smile, mein Herr. It does not reassure when you do so," he said seriously.

Mitchell chuckled.

"It's almost like he knows you, Griff," he said.

"How 'bout you get the light out of my eyes?" I said less genially.

The light clicked off.

"For three of you, I should ask for more money," he said.

"That's not a good idea," I promised him. I took the envelope of money from my pocket and held it out toward the man. It was light enough now that he could see what I offered him. He seemed reluctant to come closer, but finally he did.

"It is wet. Did you drop it in the river?" he asked.

"Something like that," I said. I didn't want to tell him why it was wet. He'd figure that out soon enough.

He pocketed the envelope and said, "Come! I will take you on this tour of the town. You have already paid after all."

"What's your name?" I asked.

"Peter."

"Are you a German spy, Peter?" Mitchell asked.

"No! I am a businessman. I was a soldier but just for a short time. Now there is no more war, so it is permissible to do business. The French encourage business. Perhaps not with Prussians but with local Germans and even Americans." He said the last with a sly grin.

"So Peter, there is a change of plan. Your job just got much less complicated. Take us to the train station," I told him.

"No tour of the town to see the French troops?"

"Nope, maybe on our next visit. Just the train station for now," I said.

"Come!" He turned and started walking back to the road.

Without a sound, Jean-Paul clambered out of the boat.

The four of us followed Peter to a motortruck parked up the track.

"Where did that child come from? I do not smuggle children!"

"He is my child," Marie said reassuringly. "We are taking him home."

He looked like he was about to argue, and I decided it might be easier to shoot him and take the truck. He must have read the thought on my face.

"Of course. Climb in the back and pull the canvas flap shut."

"I'll ride up front with you, Peter," I told him. I holstered the pistol under my jacket.

I helped load the bags in the bed of the truck and handed Marie up to Mitchell. She didn't really need our help, but she seemed to appreciate it. I picked up Jean-Paul under his arms and lifted him to Mitchell, who set him down on a bench next to his mother. He seemed somewhat recovered from the terror of our trip from Berlin, the murder of his grandmother, and all the shooting, but I couldn't be sure.

I got in the cab next to Peter, and we rumbled out of the woods. He drove us away from the river and toward the lights of a town ahead. He lit a cigarette one-handed and offered me one. I shook my head and said, "Take us past General Mangin's headquarters on the way to the station."

He looked over at me.

"We will have to cross the river toward Wiesbaden. He lives at the Biebrich Palace. There are many soldiers there, as you would expect."

"Many soldiers, huh? Well, just take us to the station then."

I had wanted to see the setup around Mangin out of curiosity more than need. I found it hard to believe the Germans really thought we could have successfully persuaded Mangin to give up his plan while he sat in the middle of his army. It was more likely that they wanted us caught as a way to damage the relationship between the French and the United States.

"Do you have a shop here in Mainz?" We were in the town proper now. It was still early, and traffic wasn't a problem.

"Yes," he said proudly. "A mechanical shop for trucks and cars. It is on the way to the station. Would you like to see it?" he said eagerly. He seemed to have forgotten that I looked like the devil.

"Sure, I'd like that. Any family?"

"Yes. A wife and two boys," he said proudly. "I am glad the war is over. I would not want them to have to fight."

"I agree with that, Peter."

We took a quick turn down a side street and passed his shop.

"There, on the left. Our flat is above my shop."

The shop had a painted door and a wooden gate that could have housed a carriage. Both opened onto the street. The floors above were faced with shingles, and the building was attached to similar-looking buildings on each side. The windows on the second floor had flower boxes beneath the windows. It was charming.

"I like it. Your family must be happy here."

He looked at me out of the corner of his eye. "We are. Having the French here is not so bad. They are not Prussian. They want us to like them. They encourage business with France and within the Rhineland. We are lucky there was no fighting here. They have their colonial troops assigned here. *Schwarzen.* Some Germans complain and think this is a deliberate slight to Germany. I do not think it is so complicated. I think they are French soldiers who have longer enlistments and are easy to place here, but then I am not looking for trouble."

"Are others looking for trouble?"

"I am afraid so. I am also afraid they will find it."

I was quiet. He was probably right, judging by what I'd seen of Germany.

"The Bahnhof is just ahead," he told me.

He stopped the truck across an open square from the front of the train station. It was an impressive building likely constructed at the end of the last century. Brown stone and Greek-looking reliefs and medallions decorated the facade. A fine-looking station to get us the hell out of Germany.

We unloaded our bags, and I gave Peter an extra fifty US dollars. He beamed at his surprise windfall. "Contact me if you come back to Mainz. It would be my pleasure to transport you."

"Will do, Peter, *bonne chance.*"

"*Viel Glück,*" Marie added.

22

Dead as a Doornail

W e bought first-class tickets to Koblenz and from there to Paris via Brussels. For the first leg of the journey, we shared the compartment with a German couple. Long faces and little conversation marked their time with us. They must have been going to visit her parents in Koblenz. I said as much to Mitchell. He laughed. Marie did not.

When we changed trains from Koblenz to Brussels, we had the first-class compartment to ourselves. We needed it. We had a lot to discuss.

"The Germans will find a way to report to the Deuxième Bureau and Raux that you were a German spy," I said to Marie without preamble. "You will be arrested as soon as they know you are in Paris."

"He's right, Marie," Mitchell added. "You could be executed before the month is out."

Jean-Paul looked at me with big, scared eyes.

"But we won't let that happen, right, Mitch?" I knew Jean-Paul liked Mitchell, and I thought getting Mitch to pitch in his support would reassure the little boy. That was a big mistake.

Mitchell shook his head. "Sorry, Marie, but you're a traitorous, bloodthirsty siren, who's on her way to the firing squad. JP can stay with me and my girl when you're gone. My girl is rich and very beautiful." He said the last to Jean-Paul, as if it would make the death of his mother acceptable.

"My mother is beautiful," Jean-Paul shouted.

"She is." Mitchell nodded. "But didn't I mention that my girl is also very rich?"

"Jesus, Mitchell!" Although he had gotten along better with Marie after Freiburg, he still didn't like her. She frightened him.

"Look, the first thing we should do when we get to Paris, Marie, is clear out anything in your flat that you need," I said. "You won't be able to return there to live. You can't take much. Then we'll need a place for you to hide until we can get you out of the country."

"Where will we go?"

"The countryside, the States, Canada, it doesn't matter. You two can't stay in Paris."

She was quiet, pondering the truth of my words.

I just knew that Fuchs and the Germans would make it as painful as possible for us to extricate her from her betrayal of France even if she did it to protect her son. I also knew that Raux would never forgive her.

"I think I need to contact Raux and trade the information about Mangin's planned uprising in the Rhineland as leverage to get Marie free of France."

"It won't work. They will hunt me. Maybe Jean-Paul *should* go with you, William." She said the last sadly but with conviction. Mitchell stared at her. His mouth opened in shock.

"Marie, I just can't stomach you feeling sorry for yourself!" Mitchell said crossly. "You're gonna keep fighting for JP and yourself until you're dead. That's who you are. You may scare the shit out of me, but you ain't a quitter. And God knows you have Griffin on your side. He'll figure out something or die trying. It'll be dangerous for sure, and it might even work, so don't give up yet. Given enough time, money, and ammunition, Griffin can usually either fix things or break everything so badly nobody will be hunting you. And because he's my friend, you got me helping too, which improves your odds tremendously. It'll be okay. Just watch."

I was heartened by Mitchell's false confidence, and Marie looked like maybe she was too. She nodded and gave him a small smile.

"I will fight for Jean-Paul," she promised.

I noted that she omitted herself from her declaration.

"Hold on!" Mitchell said suddenly. "I've got it. What if Marie were dead?"

I stared at him.

"They won't hunt her if she's dead. And they sure won't bother to execute her." He was staring at Marie and Jean-Paul with an amazed look on his face. Then he looked at me. "You tell Raux she's dead. You killed her. The French don't know about JP. Marie, you go to Paris with JP, and you are just one more refugee family. Dead husband and parents and just the little boy left."

"It could work," I said excitedly.

"But the Germans know I am alive. They know about Jean-Paul. They will tell the French."

"Well, they might want to at first, but if they tell the French about you, they will be warning the French about the possibility of others like you. Your pal Ladoux will then be more careful in screening his agents, and the Germans certainly don't want that. I think they'll keep mum. And even if they don't, will the French believe some German secondhand report over Griffin telling them he killed you? The Germans remain the enemy. And they can't do anything directly," he said excitedly. "It's not like they can have a conversation with Raux over the telephone. We just need enough breathing space to get you a new identity and Jean-Paul and you a place to live. No one will ever find you. After a while, no one will even be looking. Not even that bastard Fuchs."

He was right. It could work. We wouldn't have to torture, kidnap, or kill anyone. Just tell a few lies and our problems were solved. I was getting pretty good at telling lies.

"Mitchell, you're a genius!" I said sincerely.

Even Marie had a smile on her face. Jean-Paul was smiling because his mother was, and he liked Mitchell. I'm not sure he understood the significance of Mitchell's idea, but he didn't need to. He just needed the chance to grow up with his mother by his side.

"William, when we get to Gare du Nord, go see Patricia. You've been gone a while, and I'm sure she'll want to see you. I really don't need her mad at me." *Because she's capable of murder,* I left unspoken.

"I was planning on it."

"And I'd appreciate if you could get me a room in the Vendôme and take my bag with you. Tell them I'll be in later tonight or early in the morning. In the meantime, I'll go with Marie and Jean-Paul. A happy little family. We'll find a hotel in Montparnasse near the old one you and I stayed at, but just for a couple of days. We'll need a place where a widow and her son won't stand out. There should be a lot of those in Paris, and I'll bet Eugene will have some ideas about that."

"You know he will," Mitchell said.

"I'll see you at Le Dôme tomorrow evening. I'll see Raux in the morning and get the ball rolling."

"Be careful what you say and to whom. The story you tell will require that you admit Marie worked for the Germans." Mitchell looked at Marie. "If anyone finds that out, they won't be sympathetic to you, Marie. You understand this, don't you?"

"I understand."

"We both understand!" I said, interrupting him. "She is the

victim. The damn Germans blackmailed her to save her son. She did what any mother would do."

I knew what I was saying was nonsense. In order to protect her son, Marie had betrayed her country, provided information to the enemy, and likely cost the lives of thousands of other mothers' sons. I chose not to think about that. I had hitched my wagon to her cause, and thinking wouldn't change it.

He held his hands up in surrender.

"Okay, okay, we just don't want too many folks to know you're alive. And we sure don't want those to know who you are," he said.

I nodded. He was right. Others wouldn't see her situation as clearly as I did. To me, it was black-and-white. She had no choice. I felt that way, and I didn't even have a kid. Others might not think the same. I wondered what Madeline would think. I felt sure Sarah would have fought tooth and nail for any child of hers.

———

The train arrived in Paris late. Mitchell left the station in a motorcab for the Vendôme, and Marie, JP, and I took one to Montparnasse. We found a hotel on a side street farther off the Boulevard Raspail. It wasn't fancy, but I didn't need it to be.

Once we were in the room, I asked Marie where she lived in Paris.

"The fifteenth, just east of here," she told me.

"We should go tonight."

She nodded and turned to Jean-Paul. "You will need to stay here. Just climb into the bed and sleep. We will be back shortly."

"But I'm hungry, Mutti," he said. It was the first time I'd heard anything close to a complaint from the boy.

"Maman, call me maman. We don't use Mutti anymore. We

are French." She looked at me. "And American. Do you understand?"

"Yes, Maman."

"We will eat in the morning. Everything is closed now." She helped him take off his little boots and climb into the center of the bed. She tucked him in and kissed him.

"We will be back soon. Stay in the room."

"Yes, Maman."

The kid learned fast.

We walked north from the hotel and found a horse cab to take us to her flat. She had the driver leave us in front of a nondescript building on rue de Tolbiac. As the horse cab plodded away, Marie turned back the way we had come. We stopped in front of a five-story apartment house. Unremarkable. A plain flaking stucco front accompanied by broken shutters covering the windows, and there were no balconies. The building was appropriate for a single woman on a widow's pension.

We walked up four flights, and she unlocked her apartment door.

I felt like a hammer hit me between the eyes. The smell of linseed oil and oil paints wafted from the room beyond the open door. The scents brought me back to Sarah's cottage when I first met her. A beautiful, mysterious woman who would become mine. And die. My stomach knotted. For a moment, I stood stunned in the doorway, unable to breathe.

"Come in," Marie ordered. "Shut the door."

I shambled through the door, trying to collect my scattered thoughts.

The apartment was small. Pinned to the walls were canvases of varying sizes containing painted shapes and figures. Some of the shapes were colorful, and others were dark and brooding. All were geometrical and three-dimensional. The figures were androgynous and created in the same geometric style as the shapes that dotted the walls. It was remarkable. I knew Marie was an artist because Elsbeth Schragmüller had mentioned it. But I had thought no more about it. Her apartment was full of paintings.

"Are these yours?" I asked, gesturing to the walls.

She nodded, distracted as she collected some photographs and papers. The room was full of her work.

I had not seen art like this before. I thought of Richter and Dix in Berlin and their anti-art Dada movement. While I hadn't seen their compositions, from the way they spoke their pieces, they did not sound like Marie's. Hers was art, at least to me, but it wasn't art I had seen before. It was art for the sake of color and shape. Even when she painted figures, it was about the structure and hue, weight, and tone. I was stunned.

"Who knows?" I asked her.

"What?"

"Who knows that you paint?"

"No one here. It is for me. When I am sad, I paint." She pointed to one of the darkest, bleakest of the pictures. "When I am happy, I paint." She pointed to the first picture that had caught my eye: a kaleidoscope of colors and shapes, a happy painting. "That was from before Jean-Paul was born. I had just married Albert."

"Well, your paintings are remarkable," I told her, and I meant it. Although the contrast between the light and the dark saddened me, it wasn't a surprise.

She picked up the one bag she had packed and locked the door as we left.

When we got back to the hotel, Jean-Paul was sound asleep in the middle of the big bed. His face had that angelic look children get while sleeping—innocence and beauty at rest.

"I'll head over to the Vendôme. Try not to go out too much tomorrow. I'll see Raux in the morning, and I hope by the afternoon, I'll have a more permanent place for you and Jean-Paul."

"It is late. You should stay here with us tonight and go to the Vendôme tomorrow." Somehow she was right next to me. Almost touching. I could smell her and feel the heat of her. "Please stay."

Her fingertips gently traced the scar alongside my face. "We both will feel safer if you stay. Please."

I backed away and nodded. "Sure." I knew she was manipulating me, but I couldn't help but stay. I went around to the other side of the bed, kicked off my shoes, and lay down next to Jean-Paul. He did not wake up. Marie lay down on the other side of him. Thank God we had him as a buffer between us. Yet I was not unhappy lying on the bed with the odd little family.

I thought about Sarah. If she'd had a child, she could have ended up like Marie. She would have been just as fierce, unforgiving, and pragmatic. I thought about our plan to save Marie and Jean-Paul.

I needed sleep. I was in for a busy day, but Marie had not made it easy.

I SLEPT POORLY AND WAS UP EARLY. A QUICK AND QUIET SEARCH OF Marie's bag revealed what I needed. I left them both sleeping in the room. I had a coffee standing at the bar at a nearby café and then went to the Île de la Cité to see Préfet Raux.

The same desk sergeant guarded the entry to the Préfecture. He wore the same mustache, and he still hadn't grown a new arm. Vissac. That was his name, I recalled.

"*Bonjour, Sub-Brigadier Vissac,*" I said with my best smile. "*Le Préfet Raux, s'il vous plaît.*"

"*Votre nom?*"[1] he demanded testily. My smile had no effect.

"John Griffin, *l'Américain*," I told him as I had the first time I'd come. He remembered me. I could tell because he scowled.

"*Attendez là.*"[2] He pointed to some benches against the wall. He picked up a phone and spoke into it briefly, listened, and then hung up.

I stood next to the benches and waited.

After a short time, a young police officer appeared and said, "*Suivez-moi.*"[3] So I did, up several flights of steps to a corner office.

With a sharp rap on the door, the officer ushered me inside and shut the door behind me. Préfet Raux sat behind a large, ornate, wood desk, and Commandant Ladoux stood off to the side, looking out a window and smoking his pipe.

"Where is Madame Masson?" Raux growled.

My stomach gave a little flip. I was going to jump right in with no mucking about.

"She's dead."

"How?" Ladoux asked. He didn't seem surprised. Suddenly the pieces fell into place.

"I killed her while she was trying to kill me! She was a German spy."

Neither man batted an eye. Damnation!

"You both knew!" I exclaimed. "You knew the whole time that she was working for the Germans. I was the bait to catch her. To prove she was a spy."

They shared a look.

"Please sit down," Raux said.

I sat on the edge of the overstuffed chair facing Raux's desk. "You knew that there wasn't a real Bolshevik threat in Germany. Not since May when the Bavarian Soviet collapsed in Munich. That was the last real possibility of the Bolsheviks succeeding in Germany. You knew. So you knew if *Bolsheviks* killed me, it was because Madame Masson fed me to the Germans. This whole thing was a test for her. You sent me to Germany to be killed!

Whether by that murderous slut or some starving stormtrooper didn't matter to you."

Neither man spoke. I shook my head in disgust.

"She was good at your game," I said angrily. "She pretended to work diligently for France to undermine Germany's claims of Reds in the woodwork while manufacturing evidence of a Bolshevik menace. My God! It's Machiavellian! Did you know she planted a union card on an assassin on the train to Berlin? An assassin she killed. An assassin she insisted was a German intelligence tool. It was so subtle. Clever. She insisted that the card was not evidence the dead man was a Red, but I was positive of the opposite. With that one little trick, she was well on her way to convincing me that Germany was boiling with Bolsheviks. And insisting I wear that damn uniform. You knew about the soldiers assaulted or killed by irate Germans. You did what you could to make sure I ended up dead. If I died, it was Masson's fault either way."

Realizing the illogic of what I'd just said, I stopped railing at them. They had expected me to die. They had wanted me to die. My death wasn't a test for her. My death was the cherry on top. They already knew she was a German agent! They wanted me dead in Germany, and they would tell House that the Germans had murdered me. It didn't matter if it was by a German agent or by Germans masquerading as Bolsheviks. They didn't need more than my dead body as evidence of German treachery. It was simple. I was always intended to die. The French wanted me dead in Germany and so did the Germans. Both were convinced that they would be just a little better at manipulating the evidence to sway the United States to their point of view.

I took Marie's razor from my pocket, where I'd put it after taking it from her bag, and threw it on Raux's desk in anger.

"You bastards. You sent me to Germany to be killed. Well, she did her best. She nearly killed me, you know. It was a damn close-run thing. But I broke that crazy bitch's neck!"

I recalled Raux's words to me in the hospital. He'd said something like: "You will be my agent for certain problems faced by the Republic." I supposed having a German agent in your ranks qualified as a problem.

Raux looked at me sadly and then bowed his head. "I am sorry. I tried to warn you. I did not want to believe she was a traitor. We did not want you dead."

"We are sorry for using you as a pawn, Monsieur Griffin," Ladoux said. "We did not know for certain that Madame Masson was the spy my group has been looking for. We suspected it. We thought if you traveled with her, you might discover information that incriminated her."

"Bullshit! What you thought was, if I got killed, and if she came back and told you it was Bolsheviks that killed me, it was one more nail in a coffin you'd already built for her. Hell, Raux, you probably already have the cable to House in your desk drawer that breaks the sad news of my death!"

Both men had the decency to look embarrassed.

"And Ladoux, you're counterintelligence. That's why this was your mission. When Marie introduced you as head of counterintelligence, I didn't think twice about it. But she knew you were looking for a German spy."

"She did. And she likely suspected a trap," Raux said.

"Then why didn't she run?" I asked.

"Overconfidence. Pride. Stupidity. Who knows why traitors do what they do?" Ladoux said with a sad shake of his head.

"And you allowed this? You were willing to use me, an American, who saved your damned prime minister, as your bait?" I asked Raux.

"I told Colonel House that the mission was dangerous. He assured me you were the right man, and you were."

Goddamn House! I shouldn't have been surprised that he was willing to sacrifice me after I had used him. This was the price for my lies after the attack on Clemenceau.

"Well, I suppose I was," I said callously. "She's as dead as a doornail, gentlemen, and her body is on the bottom of the Rhine."

Raux believed me, but I was not sure that Ladoux did.

"If you thought she was the German spy, why did you help us in Berlin?" I asked Ladoux to distract him.

"By then, I was starting to doubt she was the spy," he said. "We thought she would have acted against you long before your return to Berlin from Königsberg."

"You were surprised I made it to Berlin in the first place," I said with certainty.

Again, they exchanged a look. There was no guilt in their glance just acknowledgment.

"Son of a bitch," I said, shaking my head. "Well, I'm done with you and working for France. I did as I was asked." I stood and walked to the door.

"That is fair," Raux said. "We have asked much, and you have delivered. France thanks you."

I grunted. "There is one other little detail you ought to know though." I had considered ignoring Mangin's plot, but I was worried it would be disastrous for the treaty if it succeeded. "General Mangin plans on declaring Rhineland independent and securing it with French and Allied troops. I don't know how that will affect the treaty here in Europe, but I have a good idea of what it will do to the treaty in the United States. Any hope of Senate ratification will be just as dead as Marie Masson. You gentlemen might want to warn your boss."

"What is your evidence of this?" Raux asked sharply.

"Madame Masson. Before she tried to kill me, she said that her contacts in Berlin had indicated that a plot to cause an insurrection in the Rhineland, spearheaded by Mangin, was well underway."

"Dorten's[4] insurrection failed in June. Mangin did not support it then. The possibility of a second attempt at independence is a German smokescreen," Raux said with certainty.

"Perhaps," agreed Ladoux. "But a dangerous possibility if true. Monsieur Griffin is correct that such an uprising could undermine the ratification of the treaty in the United States."

"Well, I'll leave you two gentlemen to figure out what it all means and what you might want to do. Just as long as it doesn't include me."

With that, I got out of the building as fast as I could.

23

———

A New Name

The weather was good, and I decided to walk to the Hôtel de Vendôme. I hoped Mitchell had succeeded in getting me a room. After my night of crappy sleep, I could use a nap, and I couldn't risk staying in Marie's room. Even with her son there, I was worried she would try to seduce me to seal me to her cause. I already was bound to her, but she didn't seem to believe it. I knew if I slept with her, I would hate myself. And I had enough of that already.

When I got to the Vendôme, I didn't make the front desk. Mitchell came down the spiral staircase from the restaurant two steps at a time. He must have seen me on the street.

"I was hoping you'd come early," he said as he went back up the steps. He led me into the restaurant and to a window table with a coffeepot, two cups, and the remains of what looked like a croissant.

"Tricia's not here." He made the statement without alarm.

"What do you mean not here?"

"When I got in last night, the desk clerk gave me a note she had left for me. She's gone back to London with Reynolds. She says she'll be back here in a few weeks at the most."

"What? Why the hell would she do that?" Patricia's unexpected departure alarmed me.

"The message was cryptic. She said there were complications with Gavin's estate and her US citizenship. When Reynolds disappeared, he apparently went to London to arrange lawyers for her. She'll be staying at Claridge's. She asked us to meet her there once we finish our business here. If she finishes before we do, she'll come back here and meet us," he said optimistically.

"When did she leave?"

"The note is dated two days ago."

"Can I see it?"

I could tell my question worried him.

"What's the matter, Griffin?" he asked as he handed the note to me.

Patricia Kingsbury had beautiful handwriting.

"You're sure it's her writing?"

"Yes. Goddamn it, Griffin! What has you so stirred up about her going to London?"

"Maybe nothing. I just don't like it. I don't like that Reynolds went too. I don't trust him."

Mitchell smiled. "Well, we both agree on that, but she can take care of herself."

Her father and Reynolds were cooking up something to get her back under their thumbs. She knew how dangerous her father and Reynolds were, yet she was so confident in her abilities and new independence that she wouldn't wait for our return. As much as I dreaded the idea of going to England, we would have to follow her to London.

"We need to meet her," I said with certainty. "As soon as we can. I just need a couple of days to settle Marie, and then we'll go."

"Griff, you don't have to rush. Finish up what you need to. We'll catch up with Patricia either in London or back here."

"I'm sure you're right," I told him, even though I was sure of no such thing. I didn't want to worry him, and I knew that now that my work for the French was done, we could follow Patricia to London.

"How did your meeting with Raux go? You saw him this morning, right?" he asked, changing the subject.

"I saw him and Ladoux. I told them Marie was a Kraut spy who tried to kill me. I told them I'd killed her. I'm pretty sure Raux believes Marie is dead. Ladoux, I'm not sure, but it may not matter. I made it clear that I was done working for the French. I just need to get Marie set up, and we can be gone."

"Sounds good. I will be glad to see Tricia, that is for sure! For tonight, I've arranged to meet most of the gang for drinks at Le Dôme at six, and maybe we can have dinner after."

I promised I would see him that evening. I went to my room, unpacked, and slept.

I WOKE IN THE LATE AFTERNOON AND SHOWERED AND SHAVED. I was excited to catch up with the old crowd. If I was honest with myself, I was excited to see Madeline. Just the thought of seeing her undemanding smile made my heart beat a little faster.

The weather remained fair. I was the first to arrive at Le Dôme, and I sat on the terrace at the same table we had used the night we found Patricia Kingsbury.

I was still on my first beer when Eugene Bullard came onto the terrace. I couldn't keep a huge smile off my face.

"Goddamn, Griffin, your smile must be the most unwelcoming welcome I think I have ever seen," he said with a laugh and a backslap.

"Gene, earlier this week, I was just told the same thing by a German fella in Mainz."

"Did you kill him?" He said it half in jest, but just half.

"No. In fact, I think I've made a new friend."

"Was Mitchell with you?"

"He was."

"Well, then one of you might have made a new friend."

"Now you've hurt my feelings, Gene."

He laughed.

While we waited for Mitchell and the rest of our crowd, I gave him an abbreviated description of our travels in Germany. He knew that a French agent had accompanied me. A French agent who was beautiful. It helped that he knew, because he was unsurprised when I told him we were hunted across Germany. It was almost as if he expected it.

"How much of the population of the country remains alive?" was all he asked when I told him we escaped across the Rhine after a shootout with German soldiers.

I didn't tell him about the grandmother or Jean-Paul accompanying us. He was too smart. He'd figure out exactly what Marie had been doing if I had. Instead, I told him we needed a place for Marie and her son to hide. I let him assume that Jean-Paul had been in Paris all along. I felt bad for not being straight with him, but he remained a French patriot.

"Why does she need to hide now that she's back in Paris?" He *was* too damn smart.

"Gene, you know that in Paris spies are like freckles on a ginger. I'm afraid the German ones will get orders to kill her."

He nodded at that. "Okay, leave it with me. I'll find her a place where she and her son can fade into the background. The Boche will never find them."

I gave him all the money that remained of the cash Ladoux had given me for the trip to Germany. He seemed satisfied with the amount. I'd have to collect more cash from the Vendôme safe deposit box where I'd stowed the surplus of money I'd gotten from both Armistan and his daughter.

Mitchell arrived, and shortly following his arrival, Disney and Rachel came in together.

"The advantage of having a car that the Army pays for," Disney said, laughing when Mitchell teased him about having Rachel on his arm. "Pretty girls are willing to overlook my youth and awkwardness in return for a ride."

"Walt, that's a lie!" Rachel interjected. "I haven't overlooked your goofiness at all. I just find it to be charming."

"Hell, Rachel, is goofiness even a word?" Mitchell asked.

"It is now!" Walt said. "And I don't mind being goofy at all if it'll get pretty girls to ride with me."

We were all laughing, and Bullard and I were the only ones with drinks. It felt like old times. I felt like I was home.

"Is Madeline coming?" I asked innocently.

"Ohhhh, we wondered how long that question would take. Within two minutes! Pay up, Walt!"

The entire table laughed again, Mitchell hardest of all. Disney reluctantly handed a ten franc note to Rachel.

I could feel myself color at their chuckles.

"Sorry, John, but she went home."

"What? Why?" I asked more disappointed than I wanted to admit.

"Family. She said she'll come back when she can, but she was sure she'd be gone until next summer at least," Rachel answered.

"Well, that's a shame," I said as lightly as I could manage. No one at the table was fooled.

"Don't act like you don't care, John Griffin!" Rachel said reproachfully.

Her comment brought guffaws from around the table.

"Tell us about Germany," Disney demanded, saving me from more embarrassment.

And Mitchell did. Bullard didn't complain. With Mitchell's flair for storytelling, it was a much more entertaining and dramatic picture of the trip than I had provided him. I was worried that Mitchell might mention Jean-Paul and the Frau Vogt. He did mention Jean-Paul but only as part of a joyful reunion with his mother on our return to Paris. He made it sound like the little boy loved me for helping his mother, which I thought was ironic. Mitchell didn't mention the grandmother at all. I think her murder had bothered him more than he would let on. His storytelling made the trip dangerous and exciting, and when he was done, his listeners believed they knew everything they needed to know about our trip.

He had lubricated his performance with two absinthes, and he winked at me when he finished. I was sure Bullard had seen it, but he was courteous enough not to ask about it.

We split up after ten o'clock.

I went to the hotel and everyone else went with Gene to his club.

We never got dinner.

<hr>

By the next afternoon, Bullard sent me an address for Marie and Jean-Paul's new home. I collected them at their hotel, and we took a motor cab to the eleventh arrondissement, north of the river. It was a busy neighborhood and seemed as crowded as any I had seen in Paris. Eugene had done a good job in finding a place where Marie and Jean-Paul could disappear. Their new flat was on rue de Richard Lenoir on the third floor of a building not so different from Marie's original apartment in the fifteenth. It was furnished well enough though. Of course, it had none of her art on the wall, but it was comfortable.

"What will you do, Marie?" I'd asked her.

She gave me a questioning look.

"For money," I clarified.

"I have my widow's pension from Philippe's death. It is not much. One thousand francs per year. I do not get the three hundred francs for Jean-Paul because the French authorities don't know he exists. And it would not be enough to live on even if I did."

"Marie, you can't collect the pension. It is in your name. Raux and Ladoux will find you."

I took an envelope of cash from my coat that I'd brought just for this purpose. I had worried she wouldn't have enough money.

"There's about two thousand dollars here. It should tide you over until you find a job." I tried to hand her the envelope, but she wouldn't take it.

"You didn't let me finish. Working for both French and German intelligence services gave me ample opportunity to put aside some of the money that was given to me during operations. I have plenty of money in various banks. I don't need to do anything. I am sure that I will find something to do. Perhaps I'll paint, or teach like Elsbeth does," she said, referring to her mentor, Dr. Schragmüller.

"Perhaps, but you'll need to be careful, and don't contact anyone from your past. You and Jean-Paul are safe only as long as no one knows you are alive."

"Of course. I will be careful. I will need a new name. I think it shall be *Griffon*," she said with a smile.

I laughed. Manipulating me to the end. I walked to the door and turned back to look at the mother and the son.

"Jean-Paul, take care of your mother." The little boy nodded. He had tears in his eyes, which surprised me.

"Goodbye, Marie."

She followed me onto the landing in front of her apartment.

"Goodbye, John. And thank you. I owe you more than you can ever know." She kissed me on the cheek, turned back into her new flat, and shut the door. With the click of the latch, the two of them were gone from my life. I wasn't sure how I felt about it and decided not to dwell on my confusion.

I went back to the Vendôme to pack. Mitchell and I needed to be in London as quickly as we could get there.

273

24

Just the Messenger

I had planned on taking the train to Calais, a ferry to Dover, and a train on to London. Unfortunately, once Mitchell remembered my flight to Königsberg, there was no other acceptable way for us to travel but by air. He was thrilled by the possibility of flying to London.

For a fistful of francs, the concierge at the Vendôme was all too happy to arrange a plane to London. He got us tickets for the beginning of the next week. We could travel by train and get there sooner, but we both decided flying would be better. The strain of travel would be less, and it gave us a little more time in Paris.

On our last day in the city, we were sitting in La Rotonde, drinking a beer. We were saying a very conscious goodbye to one of our favorite Parisian haunts before our flight out the next day. I was glancing up to find the waiter to order another round when Bertrand walked through the café door.

Bertrand, who had sucker punched me at Le Dôme. Bertrand, who had set two killers on Marie and me on the train to Berlin. Bertrand, puppet of Morgan Reynolds.

When enduring Mitchell's persuasive talents, Reynolds had told us Bertrand worked for his father. Based on the company he was keeping on the train, whoever employed him—and I was sure it was Reynolds—wanted me dead.

Bertrand was still a poor dresser. His jacket was worn and his shoes scuffed. He wouldn't stand out in a crowd, which I supposed accounted for his sartorial indifference. He knew I had seen him, and I was surprised that he came straight to our table. I would have expected him to run. I pressed my left arm against my side to reassure myself that my pistol remained in its holster.

"*Bonsoir*, Monsieur Griffin," he said when he reached us. My stomach sank. I was sure he'd brought bad news about Patricia. I was half right.

"I never got your name," I told him as both Mitchell and I stood.

"Bertrand Rapp," he said quickly, making a calming gesture with his hands. "May I sit for a moment? I have some news for you."

I glanced at Mitchell. His eyes were narrowed. He expected bad news about Patricia as well.

"Sure," I said lightly. With unlikely Parisian waitstaff timing, the garçon arrived at the table.

"Buy us a beer," I demanded.

"*Trois pression, s'il vous plaît*,"[1] Rapp said to the waiter.

I sat, letting my jacket hang open so he could see the pistol. Mitchell and Bertrand sat as well.

"I do not want you to overreact to what I tell you," he said in very precise English. "I am just the messenger, and I have been hired in this instance as that and nothing more." He gave an apologetic smile that showed his rotten teeth.

"How's your knee?" I asked, recalling the pop the joint gave when I'd knocked him to the ground during the fight in Le Dôme.

His smile disappeared.

"You never finished the job Monsieur Fuchs required of you," he said.

I was shocked. Fuchs. How the hell did Bertrand know Fuchs?

"What are you talking about?" I said harshly. My stomach had sunk into my shoes.

From under his coat, he pulled a small stuffed bear. Jean-Paul's bear. Before I could speak, Mitchell's hand shot across the table and had him by the throat. Bertrand dropped the bear and clawed at Mitchell's hand, but Mitchell had him good. His thumb was deep under Bertrand's jaw, and Mitchell's other hand had twisted his jacket collar and tie, pulling him across the table and knocking our empty beer glasses to the floor.

The waiter was just arriving with three tall beers on his little round tray. The two men struggled across the table. Bertrand tried to feel for something in his coat pocket, and I pinned his hand to the table.

"*Un instant, s'il vous plaît,*"[2] I said, looking at the waiter.

I turned back to Rapp and leaned into his ear.

"Bertrand, you had better pray that nothing has happened to the boy or his mother," I whispered.

I let go of his arm. Mitchell released his throat, and Rapp fell back into his chair. "Keep your hands where I can see them," I said.

The waiter carefully set the beers on the table and scampered for the bar.

"As you can see from the little bear, Monsieur Fuchs has your wife and son," Rapp rasped. "Both are alive and well. I have been told to tell you that you must return to Mainz. You must do what is asked, or both the woman and the boy will die."

It was clear that he'd only been told that Marie and Jean-Paul were my family. He knew of neither her work for the Germans nor mine for the French. He really was just the messenger.

"You work for the Germans now?" I asked.

"I work for whoever pays me. I do not work for the Boche, but I have been paid by Monsieur Fuchs to give you this message, and I have done so." He started to stand, and I shook my head.

"You haven't paid for the beers." He sat.

Mitchell picked up the stuffed bear from the floor where it had fallen.

"So you're done working for Mr. Reynolds." Mitchell made it a statement, not a question.

"As I said, I work for whoever pays me," Rapp answered.

"Where do we find Fuchs?" I asked.

"Peter. I have been told you should contact a man named Peter in Mainz. He will bring you to Fuchs. You have three days. Three days to contact Peter. That is all."

I stared at him and thought about the French knife in my pocket. I could kill him now. Quieter than the pistol, but I thought better of it.

"You can go," I told him.

Rapp looked from me to Mitchell. He stood, carefully put some money on the table, and left the café in a hurry.

"Well, hell!" I said with passion.

"I guess Trish will have to wait," Mitchell said. I wasn't sure that was a good idea, but I knew I needed Mitchell to have any hope of rescuing Marie and Jean-Paul.

"How the hell did the Boche find Marie?" I was angry.

"I'm sure spies in this town are like ticks on a wild dog. Someone saw her and talked," Mitchell answered.

"I just can't believe it. This is a big goddamn city! Too big for a coincidence like that. Let's find Bullard. He might have some thoughts on how to convince General Mangin to give up on any schemes in the Rhineland."

"And he might have some thoughts on who might have betrayed Marie," Mitchell added.

We left the café, but instead of going to Bullard's club, we went to Marie's new flat first. The door was unlocked, and the latch was unbroken. Marie had done some shopping. She had bought two small canvases and some oils and brushes. On a table in the kitchen, I found some childish drawings that had to be the work of Jean-Paul and two postcards of the July Bastille Day parade, one showing US troops in front of the Arc de Triomphe and another with French tanks in the place of the Americans. Although there were postage stamps on the table, the cards had no writing and no stamps affixed.

It looked like the Krauts had knocked on the door and Marie had opened it. Their few belongings remained, but Marie and Jean-Paul were long gone.

WE FOUND BULLARD AT HIS CLUB LATER THAT NIGHT ON RUE DE Caumartin. The place seemed busier than the last time I had visited. Despite the jumping jazz music, cigarette smoke, and free-flowing drinks, the club felt refreshingly innocent when compared to the *Weisse Maus* in Berlin. We spoke to Bullard between sets.

"What do you mean the Boche kidnapped Marie?" Bullard demanded. He had a glass of champagne in one hand and a cigarette in the other, but both were forgotten. From his reaction, he didn't have any thoughts on who might have betrayed Marie.

"Somehow the Germans found her. They have her. In order for us to get her back, we have to convince General Mangin to abandon the idea of Rhineland independence."

"What? Mangin. The Butcher? What the hell do you two have to do with Mangin and the Rhineland?" Bullard demanded.

"Gene, it's a long story," I said wearily.

"Well, shorten it!" He was angry. He was angry because a place he thought was safe wasn't, but he didn't need to be angry with me.

"Goddamn it, Gene! I didn't kidnap her, so don't get sore at me!" I growled. My temper was starting to fray.

Mitchell saved us from further argument.

He laid the little bear on the table in front of Bullard. "They must have found her through the kid somehow, Gene."

Bullard looked at the incongruous stuffed animal sprawled on the table next to the bottle of champagne. He shook his head. "That makes no sense. What do you two know about the situation in the Rhineland?" he asked.

"Not much," I answered.

"Well, contact the staff for the US Commissioners. Contact House. Tell him what Mangin plans. Get some idea of what your leverage might be. We've got to plan, goddamn it!"

I liked that Bullard was including himself as part of the solution.

"Gene, you're right. Colonel House gave me the name of a captain who works at the Hôtel de Crillon, supporting the commission. I'll contact him tomorrow. Get what help I can, and then tomorrow night, we'll go to Mainz," I said.

"I'll tell Joey I need to be out. He should be able to make do. I'll go with you, and I'll bring my old uniform. It might come in handy."

I thought about the marine uniforms likely stored with left baggage somewhere in the Vendôme where I had sent them from Berlin. Those might come in handy at Mainz as well.

IN THE MORNING, I WENT DIRECTLY TO THE HÔTEL DE CRILLON. Once again, I presented myself to the soldier at the entrance, but this time, after a brief telephone call, I was admitted almost immediately. An army sergeant delivered me to an office on the third floor. I was impressed that House really had laid the groundwork for helping me. In reality, it was likely his assistant, Simms, who had done all the legwork.

A man just a few years older than me, dressed in a civilian suit, rose from behind his desk as I entered his office. He had an earnest look about him and a handlebar mustache that he would have looked better without.

"George Gordon," he said, thrusting his hand across the desk.

"John Griffin. Colonel House told me to contact you if I needed help, but he told me you were a captain in the Army."

"No longer." He smiled. "I work for the Department of State now. I'd offer coffee, but it's downstairs. Please sit." He pointed me to an armchair facing the desk. We both sat.

"Mr. Gordon, I'm in a bit of a hurry. What did the colonel tell you about my work for the French?"

"Not much. He told me you might come to me. He also said, somewhat cryptically, I must say, that you were assisting them with some of their affairs. He was clear that, if you contacted me, I was to give you any help in my power to give."

I nodded as if what he relayed was accurate.

"I've learned some important information, Mr. Gordon, and I'm afraid I may need some help in accomplishing what the colonel has asked me to do."

"Of course."

"But I must warn you that this information is sensitive, and frankly, potentially disastrous."

He nodded and leaned forward as if to better listen. He was clearly excited about the possibility of a disaster occurring on his watch. I began to suspect that Mr. Gordon was bored.

"The French used me as bait in a counterespionage plan, except they didn't bother telling me. In short, they wanted to catch a German spy inside the Deuxième Bureau. Instead, they told me my assignment was to confirm that the spread of Bolshevism was a German fabrication so the country could avoid the disarmament requirements of the treaty. I caught the spy, which pleased the French."

"Excellent!" he said.

"But I've found what I think is a bigger problem and one that the French intelligence agencies want to ignore."

He was just about to burst with anticipation.

"I stumbled onto a plot by General Mangin to stage an insurrection, a revolution, in the Rhineland. He wants to establish a republic, dependent on France and protected by the current occupying troops, including our soldiers."

He fell back into his chair. It seemed this news brought more excitement than he was ready for.

"That would be disastrous," Gordon said. "If that happened, the Senate would refuse to ratify the treaty. The Germans would refuse to pay reparations. Hell, you could have the French invade Germany proper, but this time the US wouldn't help. Far from it. France would lose all sympathy. This is exactly the type of thing we're supposed to prevent."

I wasn't sure who his "we" was intended to include, but I was sure it included me.

"I've notified both Préfet Raux with the Paris police and Commandant Ladoux of the Deuxième Bureau. They either didn't believe me or they support the idea. I don't know what Prime Minister Clemenceau would want, but..."

"I do!" Gordon interjected. "He would never want this to happen. He has worked too hard on the treaty and article 10, requiring mutual defense. The Germans might not honor the treaty at all. And France must have Germany's reparations. If the Rhineland leaves Germany, the Germans will blame France, and they won't pay what they owe under the treaty. And if Germany can't pay France, then France can't repay its loans from the United States. Clemenceau's government would fall, and the peace would fail. We need to prevent this." He looked at me.

I raised an eyebrow. "How?"

"I'll speak with House's assistant here and get a cable to the colonel immediately. I am sure he will want Ambassador Wallace[3] to warn Clemenceau. But this will take time. You've got to find a way to delay General Mangin until the French authorities can act."

"Can I kill him?" I asked sincerely.

"What? No! He's a French general for Christ's sake. But anything short of that might be acceptable."

"I leave for Mainz tomorrow." I took my French-supplied documents from my coat pocket and pushed them across his desk to him. "For the French mission, I was made a major in the Marine Corps. I need orders that get me all the assistance I ask for in the Rhineland. It would help for the orders to be as vague and as broad as possible."

"With the information you've provided, I will have orders written and signed by General Bliss. It wouldn't surprise me if he wants to send an infantry division with you."

I laughed and said, "I'd take it. Anything General Bliss can do to prevent a Rhinish insurrection would be welcome."

"As I said, getting the attention needed from the State Department and Clemenceau will take time. The orders, however, I can have ready in an hour."

Gordon was as good as his word. In an hour, I had in my hand expansive orders from General Bliss directing me to "further the interests of the United States," and my French-supplied commissioning papers back in my coat pocket. I also had a bag containing a borrowed pair of officer's boots and American captain's bars. I was starting to feel optimistic that we would gain access to Mangin, though I wasn't sure that I could successfully thwart his plans for Rhinish independence. I was even less hopeful that I would get Marie and Jean-Paul away from Fuchs alive. Still, I had to plan for success.

I could hear my mother's voice in my head.

"You must plan for success. If you plan thinking you will fail, you will," she would say in a singsong voice. I would think to my eight-year-old self, I can plan for *recess*. That's easy. She was trying to teach me that I needed plans to accomplish my goals, while I was substituting a well-understood word for one which was too abstract for my grade school mind.

Her words, however, stuck well enough that I applied them now. I had to assume that I would get Marie and Jean-Paul free. Somehow the Germans had found them, kidnapped them, and returned them to Germany. If I did get them away, I had to keep the Germans from ever finding them again.

As I contemplated the problem, an unlikely plan surfaced. It was not certain by any means, but it was all I had. And I needed to put it in place before I left for Germany. I also had to prepare as if I would not be returning from Germany. Marie had to be able to implement my scheme alone, without me. I had a lot to do before leaving for Mainz.

First I went to Marie's original apartment in the fifteenth arrondissement. The flat seemed untouched from when Marie and I first visited. The French authorities might have searched it, but I couldn't be sure. They might even be watching the building. It didn't matter. If they saw me, they wouldn't understand what I was doing. The smell of oil paints again distracted me, but I had a specific task, which required little thought. My hands could work without direction, and I could think about Sarah and Marie and conflate my experiences with them both in a way that was almost certainly unhealthy and likely dangerous.

In thirty minutes, I had gathered what I needed. I had two heavy rolled tubes of her paintings, which I tied with string. I looped both over my shoulder and returned to the Vendôme, where I left the larger of the two in my room along with the bag containing the boots and bars.

Then I went to Café de Flore. It was late morning. If I needed to, I would remain there all day. I was in luck. I was just sipping my third coffee when Eugenia Errázuriz entered and turned automatically toward where I was seated. I had placed myself in the same booth she had shared with Gavin and the other Spaniard when I had first seen her.

She was at the table before she noticed me sitting there. She stopped abruptly when she did.

"Please, Madame Errázuriz," I said quickly. I stepped out of the booth and gave a small, unconscious bow. "I would like just a moment of your time. I have something to show you."

She stood looking down her aristocratic nose with her chin raised in haughty disdain. This was difficult because I towered over her, but her manner made her seem imposing. It was clear she did not like me. I had done nothing to impress her when we spoke of Gavin before.

"Art. The work of a young war widow. I am not a good judge, but it seems to be excellent." I reached into the booth and put the tube of canvases on the table. "Compelling."

She looked at the roll of paintings and back at me. The ice in her eyes thawed just a bit.

"Please," I said again.

She sat in the booth, and I sat across from her.

"Thank you."

The waiter appeared.

"*Un café au lait, Madame Errázuriz?*" he asked. She was a regular, after all.

"*Oui,*" she answered while keeping her eyes on me.

The waiter scurried off.

When I untied the string on the canvases, they had her attention. She was no longer focused on me. Instead, she seemed almost eager to see what I had brought. I worried for a moment that she would be unimpressed or disappointed, but if so, there was nothing I could do about it.

The canvases fell open on the table. By luck, perhaps, one of Marie's more colorful paintings was on top.

"This is an irresponsible way to transport paintings. You will damage them rolling them like this," she said.

I didn't answer. If she cared about damage, I took that as a good sign.

"*Vorticisme*,"[4] she said under her breath. "She is English?"

I was surprised by the question and thought for an uncomfortable moment she was asking about Sarah.

"No. French. But she has traveled."

She moved the first painting aside to look at the second.

"Interesting. I saw this style in London before the war."

She flipped to the third picture.

"The art is certainly influenced by *vorticisme*, but this one is *cubisme*.[5] And darker. Gloomy. Using the golden ratio with *cubisme*. Daring."

I didn't understand a word she was saying.

"And she is in Paris?" Madame Errázuriz asked. I could understand that.

She was now examining the fourth painting.

She looked up when I didn't answer immediately.

"She is hiding from her husband's family. I am trying to find a place for her that is safe. Away from everyone she knows. Away from Paris."

She thought for a moment, flipping through the fifth and then sixth painting.

"And you are her lover," she said with certainty.

"No. I am not. Just her friend. She needs help. We are not lovers."

She weighed my statement, trying to judge the truth of it.

"I think I would like to meet this young widow even though she is your friend." She said that last as if she were surprised anyone would be my friend. I found myself agreeing with the sentiment.

"Perhaps I can arrange that. I will be leaving the country and might not return. Is there a way she could contact you directly?" I asked.

"What is her name?"

"Marie Dupont," I answered. It was the name we had used when we first returned to Paris.

"I stay at my nephew's house when in the city," she said. "But my home is in Biarritz. I will return there at the end of this month or perhaps next."

She waved a hand at the waiter. He hurried over, and she demanded a writing implement. He produced the stub of a pencil and an apology.

She took a square visitor card from her handbag and wrote on it briefly. She handed me the card. It was a very simple card on expensive stock, which included her name and an address in Biarritz printed on the face. She had handwritten a second address next to the printed one.

"If she returns to Paris before the end of the month, please have her leave a message for me here," she said, nodding to the card. "It is my nephew's address. If she is as interesting as her work, I am sure I can arrange a place for her to stay in Biarritz, particularly if she wishes to continue to paint."

"Thank you, madame. Could I impose upon you to hold these paintings for her? It makes no sense for me to keep them. I also have more at my hotel. My understanding of them is inadequate, and as I said, I will be traveling and may not return to Paris."

For the first time, Madame Errázuriz seemed to welcome a request from me.

"Of course. I will send for my man to take them directly to my nephew's where I will have them packaged properly."

"Thank you. I will take up no more of your time," I said and stood.

To my surprise, she offered me her hand, and I delivered the expected kiss above it.

I was pleased. I had found someone who could help Marie and was connected with neither of us. Of course, my success was a tribute to the quality of Marie's art and not my persuasive abilities.

25

Cherchez l'argent

Later that afternoon, I met Mitchell and Bullard on the terrace at Le Dôme and told them of my meeting with Gordon.

Bullard was ecstatic. "Why, this could work!"

"What could work, Gene?" Mitchell asked through the haze of his cigarette smoke.

"What are generals most afraid of?" he asked instead of answering.

"The enemy," I suggested.

"No, don't be an ass. They are all convinced they can lick the enemy if they are left alone and given what they need. And what do they need?"

"Troops?" Mitchell offered.

"No. The French can conscript those or get them from their colonies. What they're most afraid of is the lack of money. If they have no money, they can't pay the troops and they can't buy weapons. If you want to know why anything happens anywhere, but especially in France, *cherchez l'argent*, follow the money! If Mangin is convinced there's a real threat to France's military funding as a result of his scheme in the Rhineland, maybe we can get him to rethink his little *coup d'état*."

"Well, that's better than assassinating him," Mitchell said with his habitual optimism.

"It is, but I'm not sure I see how it will work," I said.

Bullard smiled as he explained the realities of funding wars to Mitchell and me.

"Guns and troops aren't free. They have to be paid for. If you don't have the money, you have to borrow it. And that's what England and France did. They borrowed millions of dollars from the United States. Hundreds of millions. And they can't repay it all at once. Hell, they might not be able to repay it at all. So one of the conditions they wrote into the peace treaty was that Germany pay reparations, hoping they'll be able to use German money to repay the Americans. How much Germany owes is still in dispute, but whatever it is, it will be in the hundreds of millions of dollars too. America demands to be repaid—even though US business benefited from all that wartime supply demands of the British, French, and US armies."

I thought of Armistan and his plot to continue the war. It was no wonder that he had conspired with Gavin and the Bolsheviks. War was good for business. Hundreds of millions of dollars in supplies used to kill and maim and perpetuate the myths I'd grown up on. Those were numbers my brain couldn't comprehend.

Despite Bullard's excitement, I was not optimistic our claims would sway Mangin. I was sure we needed better arguments to persuade him, but we didn't have them.

THE NEXT MORNING, WITH THE HELP OF AN OVERTIPPED VENDÔME bellman, we found the boxed uniforms Dyar had sent me from Berlin. Bullard had arranged for a tailor to report to the hotel at nine o'clock. We went to Mitchell's room, where the tailor adjusted one of my French-provided marine uniforms for Mitchell. The tailor made short work of the changes. Mitchell was close to my height but thinner, and the adjustments were simple. We added the captain's insignia, one of the extra officer service caps the French had thoughtfully provided, and with the borrowed boots, he looked the part of a marine officer.

Mitchell and I met Bullard, who was dressed in a French sergeant's uniform, at Gare du Nord later that morning. Bullard was to masquerade as our translator in Germany. Each of us carried a small overnight case and nothing more. We also wore sidearms with our uniforms. From Paris, as with my first trip with Marie, the train passed through Brussels, but we caught an afternoon train to Koblenz. General Allen[1] commanded the American troops stationed in Germany. He headquartered at Koblenz. Gordon had told me Allen was new to Germany and might fall prey to Mangin's influence. Part of my plan was to meet with him, make him aware of Mangin's plans, the State Department's view of them, and to secure his support, which I knew would have to be limited. It didn't help that I didn't know exactly what I wanted him to support.

We arrived in Koblenz and took rooms at a hotel near the station. The desk clerk gave Bullard a raised eyebrow. Bullard spoke to him for a time, likely telling him that he had been assigned as our translator by the French military. I could tell Bullard was getting sore. Since I didn't want the clerk beaten unconscious, I decided I needed to speed things up.

I barked at Bullard in my best impression of an impatient marine major. "What the hell is taking so long?"

The clerk studied Mitchell and me and nodded. It seemed that Americans were common and accepted, but a black French soldier was not welcome.

The clerk glared at Bullard and hurriedly gave us our keys.

"What was the problem with the Kraut desk clerk?" Mitchell asked as we thumped up the steps to the rooms.

"It seems that the Americans are fine. The Boche think they've been respectful. The French are hated. They don't like that the French are using colonial troops as occupiers. Particularly black colonial troops. He thought I was from Senegal. He said I was part of *die schwarze Schmach*. The black shame. The Boche think the French are deliberately using black troops as an insult and a threat to Germany and German womanhood. I have to say I was getting in a pet. Glad you interrupted our little discussion, Griffin. I was just about to sock that son of a bitch."

Shortly after, we were gathered in my room. Bullard suggested, and Mitchell and I agreed, that he would move on to Mainz in the morning. He would do a little scouting of the French Tenth Army headquarters and try to find a way to get us access if we couldn't work out something with Allen. We figured Mitchell and I should be fine without his translation, and a black *poilu* would have neither any influence nor place in a meeting with an American general officer. I was worried I wouldn't either.

<hr>

The next morning, after securing us a horse cab, Bullard left for the train station. The cab took us across the Rhine to see Allen at the American headquarters located in Ehrenbreitstein Fortress. The fortress sat on a promontory on the east side of the Rhine, overlooking the confluence of the Moselle and the Rhine Rivers. As the carriage wound up the cobbled road to the fortress, the turns revealed either the city below or the fortress with its gun ports above.

I was nervous. Mitchell was not. He smoked as we climbed and calmly watched the landscape pass. I didn't know if we would even get to see Allen, and I didn't know what I would say if we did.

The cab wound away from the river and behind the hill where the fortress was built. The taxi creaked between high walls with cannon loops covering the approaches. Everywhere we looked, American Army troops were marching.

We climbed down from the cab. I looked at the driver, and he pointed to an arch set between a high, prow-like wall on one side and a long fortress wall on the other.

"*Da.*" He pointed again. I patted my tunic where I had put Bliss's orders.

"It'll be fine, Griff," Mitchell assured me. "You'll say just the right words to get the general to help us if he can. Don't worry."

I nodded and marched toward the gate and the guards. Mitchell walked a half pace behind me. As we approached, the soldiers on guard came to attention and saluted.

Mitchell and I returned their salutes, and I said, "We're here to see General Allen."

"Yessir!" the corporal in charge of the guards responded. He turned to one of his privates. "Simmons, run ahead and let Colonel Bell know the general has some visitors." The soldier took off on the double.

"Please follow me, gentlemen."

He walked us down a long gravel space between two looming fortress walls into what had to be the US occupation forces' headquarters building. After just a few minutes, a lieutenant colonel appeared. Mitchell and I jumped to attention.

"As you were, marines. I'm told you're here to see General Allen."

"Yes, sir," I answered. "We're attached to the Department of State and have orders from General Bliss." I produced the orders and handed them to the colonel.

He raised an eyebrow and said, "Follow me."

The colonel walked us to a nearby sitting room that doubled

as General Allen's office. The general sat behind a large desk, glowering at us as we came to attention. He was an older man who looked like he was crafted from shoe leather. He had pale, piercing eyes, and his mouth was a stern line below a lampshade mustache. He wasn't pleased to see us.

"Are you here to create trouble with our French allies?" he asked as we stood at attention before his desk.

"I'm afraid they are creating the trouble, General," I said. "It seems General Mangin is continuing his support for an independent Rhineland, and it looks like some sort of secession from Germany could happen at any moment. General Bliss and Mr. Gordon have sent Captain Mitchell and me to entreat the general not to support any German insurrection as it will undermine the president's effort to get the Senate to ratify the peace treaty."

"And they want marines to speak to Mangin! A French general. Seems like someone in Paris didn't think this through." He said this with a straight face, but Colonel Bell smiled.

I decided to take a chance.

"Well, sir, if he gets too upset with us, who will miss a couple of leathernecks?"

Allen cracked a smile. "Too true, but let's see if we can avoid that. What do you need from me? I won't put troops in the field to support or prevent an uprising. I am sure Bliss knows that."

"He does, sir," I lied. "There is a possibility that we will be able to convince General Mangin to abandon any scheme to support the Rhineland's independence. If he does abandon it, it is also likely that he will do so only grudgingly. Captain Mitchell and I will likely be running for our lives from the German revolutionaries, and I'm sure Mangin won't go out of his way to protect us. We'd like to be able to count on your troops to keep us alive if we can get back into the American sector from Mainz."

"Well, if you're asking me to keep the Germans from killing

you, my men can certainly try. The damn French insist on using troops of lower civilization,[2] which doesn't help their relationship with the broader German population. Thank God I don't have to deal with that."

It took me a moment to realize the general was talking about black troops. I was disappointed by his attitude, and I was glad Bullard didn't have to hear it. I knew for a fact Bullard was damn well more civilized than I.

"We'd appreciate any help you can give, sir," I said instead of speaking in defense of my friend.

"If you're in the French sector, you're on your own, but my boys will look after you when you're in the American sector. Colonel Bell, I'll leave the details with you. Good luck, gentlemen. I'd hate to see the Boche or our *allies* succeed in anything that undermines our sacrifices in the damn war."

Colonel Bell took us to his office, and I explained what we needed. I hoped it was enough.

WE TOOK THE NEXT TRAIN TO MAINZ. WE HAD AGREED TO MEET Bullard at the station at five o'clock that afternoon or the afternoon of the following day if we were delayed. We arrived in plenty of time. Given nothing to do and plenty of time, Mitchell and I did what any self-respecting young men would do. We sat in a café near the *Bahnhof* I'd spotted the first time we'd come through the town. We drank beer while we waited for Bullard to appear. French soldiers were everywhere, and as predicted, they were primarily black Africans with white officers.

The Germans ignored us. Mainz was the headquarters for the French occupation, and we were just two more soldiers.

Bullard appeared just before five o'clock, marching crisply across the square from the station. He looked the part of a fierce French colonial. I think he was enjoying himself. As he arrived at the table, he stamped to attention and gave us a crisp, palm out, French salute. We were forced to jump to our feet and return his salute with ones of our own. We started to shift our chairs so he could sit down with us.

"Forget it, gentlemen. A French colonial soldier would never share a beer with his officers. I have a lot to tell you, so let's go to the hotel."

While still standing, I finished my beer and tossed a few Papiermarks on the table. Bullard insisted on taking our bags, again trying to stay in character. We followed him to a hotel not far from the station. Bullard spoke briefly to the desk clerk, who looked us over without comment and handed us our room keys.

"We are all on the second floor on the back side of the hotel. It's probably a nicer place than a French sergeant would normally stay, but I don't think we will be here long," Bullard explained as we climbed the steps. "You're here, Griffin. Mitch, next door down, and I'm at the end."

"William, toss your bag and come back here. Let's find out what our loyal *sergeant* has found." Bullard snorted at my comment.

Once we'd gathered in my room, Eugene briefed us on what he'd discovered.

"There are hundreds of French troops in the streets at any one time. Mangin lives at his headquarters on the other side of the Rhine, an old palace, with a park behind. It overlooks the river."

"Well guarded?" Mitchell asked.

"Certainly. But I am not sure it would be wise to approach General Mangin in the palace. If you walk in and accuse him of plotting a revolt in the Rhineland, which would be in direct disobedience to the orders of the French civilian government, he could have you killed, and no one would be the wiser."

"So what do you suggest?" I crossed my arms and leaned back against the peeling wallpaper.

"I don't really have a suggestion yet. Meet with Fuchs and then the General, and let's see what develops."

"Does the general speak English, Gene?" I asked.

"I have been told he speaks it fluently."

"All right. I'll see Fuchs tomorrow. I don't want you with me. Fuchs will find a way to use you both as hostages. I want you two as our reserve when we make a run for it. I've got orders from General Bliss in my pocket, and Colonel Bell promised he'd have a platoon of soldiers at the border between the French and the American sectors. If we can get to them, neither homicidal Krauts nor angry frogs will be able to touch us."

I heard the certainty in my voice. I didn't believe it, but it seemed like I fooled Mitchell and Bullard.

THE NEXT MORNING, I PUT ON A CIVILIAN SUIT WITH MY shoulder holster under the jacket and took an autocab to find Peter. I left Mitchell and Bullard to conduct additional reconnaissance. I gave them the address of Peter's garage in case I disappeared so they would have a place to search for me, and I promised I would send word to them as soon as I could. I didn't know what Fuchs and his friends had in store for me, and I could as easily end up dead as marching before General Mangin.

Other than the wooden garage door standing open, Peter's home was unchanged. I climbed from the taxi and walked through the open door into a mechanic's work bay. Peter's truck stood in the center of the space with the hood open.

"Peter," I called.

"*Guten Tag.*" He walked into the bay from a door off to the side, likely an office space. He stopped when he saw me. "Ah. I was told you might return. I must say I am sorry to see you. I had hoped you had escaped from my comrades. But we Germans are very efficient and hardworking. I cannot say I am surprised they found a way to return you."

"Hello, Peter. I can't say I'm surprised either. I hope we didn't get you in trouble for leaving in such a hurry."

"Not at all, although Herr Fuchs was intensely curious about whether any of you were injured. He also wanted to know exactly who I left at the station."

"You told him?"

"I did. He works for the government. Likely for the military. I could do nothing else."

"And he told me he worked for the foreign ministry," I said, as if disappointed at Fuchs's lie.

"Oh, he could work for both, mein Herr," Peter said, not understanding my sarcasm.

"Sure he could. Well, I guess you are my connection back to him."

"Yes, I am. Let me get my coat, and I will take you to him."

"Great," I said, unenthusiastically.

Peter not only donned his suit coat, but he'd combed his hair. I had the impression he wanted to impress Fuchs. It didn't surprise me. Despite his execution of Frau Vogt, Fuchs was the kind of man people seemed to like and the kind of man it would be good to work for. He had certainly hidden his nature well from me.

Peter closed the hood of his truck and motioned me in. He backed out into the street and drove away from the center of town. With Peter watching me out of the corner of his eye, I took the .45 from its holster and pulled back the slide, putting a round in the chamber. I clicked up the hammer lock with my thumb and reholstered the pistol. I hoped that Fuchs hadn't gone through all this trouble just to kill me, but one never knows.

We turned north toward the river.

"Where are we going?" I asked.

"Strassenbrücke. Street Bridge," Peter said by way of explanation.

I wasn't amused by his answer. "I don't care what streets we are using, Peter. Where are we going?" I asked again.

He smiled across the cab pleased with his little joke. "To the country. A small farmer's house in the *Ost feld*. The field east of the city."

"Where no one can hear gunshots or cries of pain, I'm sure," I said dryly.

In a short time, we were rumbling across the bridge and back to the German-controlled side of the Rhine. I couldn't blame Fuchs for basing himself away from the French.

The farmhouse was small, and only a single car was parked in front. Fuchs must have heard the truck because he stepped out of the house as we pulled up. I considered shooting him on the spot. We were out in the middle of nowhere, but I knew he wouldn't have Marie and Jean-Paul here. If I killed him, I'd never find them.

He had the nerve to smile when he saw me.

"Hello, John. How good to see you. And Herr Vogel, thank you for your prompt service. As always, you are reliable." He gave Peter a smile. I was waiting for him to pull out his little pistol and shoot Peter. If he did, I would do just what I did last time he'd pulled the damn thing. Nothing. I needed to find Marie more than I needed Peter alive.

Fuchs babbled at Peter in German for a moment.

"*Natürlich,*" Peter said. He then walked up the path away from the house toward the fields.

Fuchs looked at me. I stared back.

"He will be back. Come. I will make us some coffee."

Fuchs unhesitatingly led me into the little house. He was very confident, and I was sure he knew I was considering killing him.

He put a pot on top of a wood-burning stove and directed me

to a seat at a narrow table. There were only two. I took the one facing the door.

"Karl, I do find myself tempted to torture you until you tell me where Marie and the boy are," I confessed.

He smiled. "I know you are tempted, but please resist. Even if I tell you, she will be dead in an hour if I don't appear by then."

"You think you could keep from telling me anything for an hour?"

"At first I would lie. You would have to torture me some more. Then, because of the pain, I would eventually tell the truth, but time would have run out. You would still kill me, and then all you would have is a dead German patriot, a dead French traitor, and a dead little boy. Please. Let's stop the fantasy and let us talk about what you need to do. I have some distance to drive, and you don't want me to be late."

"It will be difficult to see Mangin, but I have the uniform I wore in Berlin. As an American officer, I think he will see me. I will try to convince him to stop the plan for an independent Rhineland."

"No. That will not work! You must kill him. It is the only way to be sure the plan is stopped."

"I'm not going to kill him."

"Then your wife and her son will die."

"Karl, do you want the plot prevented, or must you have Mangin dead? I have the support of Colonel House and the American Commission to the Peace. They don't want the insurrection to go forward any more than Germany does. They have empowered me to tell Mangin in the strongest possible terms that his plot must cease. It is certainly much cleaner than putting a bullet in his head. Better for Germany and better for me," I said honestly.

He looked thoughtful. I could see he hadn't considered the possibility that the US Department of State would support me. That meant that his superiors hadn't considered it either. I could feel our chances for success increase just watching the furrow appear on his forehead.

"I will need to confirm that he does not need to die, but in the interim, proceed with a meeting demanding that he cease his scheming."

I nodded. I wasn't going to argue with his ordering me around. With a little luck, I could get Marie and Jean-Paul to a safe place away from the Krauts, and Karl would find himself alone with me. I couldn't help but smile.

He took my smile as evidence of my satisfaction with his agreement and not of my murderous aspirations.

<hr>

PETER TOOK ME BACK ACROSS THE RIVER. I GAVE HIM INSTRUCTIONS to leave me at the hotel and to return at eight o'clock the next morning to take Bullard, Mitchell, and me to see General Mangin.

When I got to the hotel, I went straight to Mitchell's room and knocked, hoping he and Bullard had had a more successful morning than I had.

"Enter." Mitchell's imperious tone came through the door at my knock. He sounded exactly like every goddamn officer I'd ever served with or reported to, and he knew it.

Mitchell was sitting on his bed. Eugene had the single chair in the room reversed, and he was resting his forearms on the back. He cradled a whiskey in his hands. I noticed Mitchell's whiskey and a bottle on the nightstand next to the bed.

"Where the hell did you get a bottle of whiskey?"

"I've got a nose for whiskey," Gene said smugly.

Will smirked.

"It's not even noon," I noted, waiting for some elaboration.

"Okay, between Mitchell and me, we found an unofficial and wholly illegal market used by the French *poilus* and German civilians both. You can buy liquor, guns, girls, butter, sugar, cigarettes. You name it. If you have enough money, you can buy whatever you want."

"Did you do any reconnaissance at all?" I asked.

"We found out plenty, and maybe some of it useful. And we did find our back-alley emporium." Mitchell positively beamed, but at least he cleaned out a glass and poured me a whiskey.

"Your friend, Peter, steer you to the contact?" Bullard asked.

"Yep," I answered. "We'll go see Mangin tomorrow. In uniform. So tell me what you learned, and I can decide if any of it might help."

"The general is a hard but fair leader. His colonials love him, but they do think him too bloody-minded. They're glad the fighting is over because the general does love the attack. He works most of the day at the palace, and his family lives there with him. On Sunday, after church, he'll go to the public park behind the palace. He'll wear civvies, sit with his wife on a blanket, and watch his eight kids play football." Bullard sipped his whiskey.

"Eight kids! Did you hear that, Griff? Eight kids. Catholics and farmers breed like goddamn rabbits. Eight kids," Mitchell repeated, amazed at the number.

"That's a lot of kids but not a lot of help," I said.

"Maybe not, but wait until you hear everything," Gene said. "When I first arrived at the station while you two were in Koblenz, I ran into a couple of *poilus* being demobilized back to France. They were waiting for the train out, so I sat with them and chewed the fat for a while. They had helped guard the palace where Mangin lives. Among other things, like where the general has made the Boche set up whorehouses for gentlemen of my persuasion, they also told me about the Mangin family's Sunday outings. Yesterday happened to be a Sunday, and as it was still pretty early, I went to see for myself. I took the trolley to the park, and it dropped me at the far side, away from the palace. So I walked through the park, looking for some sign of Mangin. Sure enough, not long into my stroll, I see the whole Mangin family and half the French army marching past me. The smallest children were wheeled in prams by nannies, but any child over four years old or so followed Mangin and his wife along like little ducklings. I saluted and kept walking for a while. Then I turned around and walked back the way I came.

"With the help of some staff also in tow, Mangin's wife set up a picnic on blankets near an artificial castle ruin called the Mosberg. It's a run-down dump but looks like a great, if dangerous, place for kids to play hide-and-seek. They'd also brought a football, which the older boys were kicking around."

"How old are the boys?" I asked.

"He's got several, but only two are old enough to play football seriously. One looks to be about twelve and the other seven or eight. One or two of the girls were younger and might kick the ball around sometimes, but I didn't see that. I did see them all climbing through the old castle though."

"How long did they stay," I asked.

"I don't know," Bullard answered. "I didn't want anyone to get suspicious, so I left the park after I watched them settle in for the afternoon."

"It's not much, but it's something, Gene. We'll just have to see what develops after our meeting with Mangin."

"Assuming we even get to see Mangin," Mitchell said with a wink.

THE NEXT MORNING, PETER WAS WAITING OUTSIDE THE HOTEL. The three of us were decked out in our uniforms, looking every inch the soldiers that we weren't. He drove us to the Biebrich Palace, where Mangin had his headquarters.

The Biebrich Palace was a sprawling, white and pink Ushaped edifice that sat directly across from Mainz on the west bank of the Rhine. We were admitted to the grounds based on Bullard's lies to the French colonials guarding the gate and the orders from Bliss. Peter drove us to a horseshoe staircase in the center of the palace where a fierce-looking French sergeant stepped in front of the truck. We climbed from the vehicle.

Flanking the sergeant were two Senegalese troopers, who brought their rifles to port arms. The bayonets were fixed to the Africans' rifles. I had no doubt they could spear us in an instant if ordered.

The sergeant saluted quickly and then snapped, "*Quel est le but de votre visite?*"[3]

A French captain hurried down the steps, not to be left out.

"*Ces officiers américains sont ici pour voir—*"[4] Bullard began.

I interrupted, barking out, "*Nous avons été envoyés par la Commission américaine à Paris. Nous devons parler au général d'une question urgente concernant le traité de paix.*"[5] I took both the orders and my commission from my tunic and offered them to the captain.

The captain took the papers. He looked from me to Mitchell and back, weighing the likelihood of my claim. He examined the orders closely. He returned my commission papers but went up the stairs, still carrying my orders.

We waited just a few minutes, but the orders had the desired effect. The captain returned and nodded to the sergeant. He said to us, "*Suivez-moi,*"[6] and he started up the stairs. The three of us followed the captain, and in turn, the sergeant and one of the troopers followed us.

They took us to the back of the palace and put us in an empty yet ornate room to wait while the French decided what to do with us. We didn't speak. We stood stiffly. Between the heat of the room and my wool uniform, I started to sweat. Not the best way to impress a French general.

I wiped my forehead just as the door opened and a French colonel entered. The three of us stiffened to attention.

"Gentlemen, the general will see you, but he is busy and you are unexpected," he said in excellent English. To Bullard, he said, "*Restez ici.*"[7]

Mitchell and I followed the colonel deeper into the palace. We arrived at a heavy carved wooden door. The colonel knocked on the door with three firm raps.

"*Entrez,*" came the command from inside.

We followed the colonel into the room and braced to attention.

The general stood behind a desk. I had never seen him before, but there could be no doubt it was Mangin. His uniform was impeccable, but it could not hide his age or the weight of his responsibilities. He was not tall, and he stood with his head slightly forward. He looked tired with bags under his downward-slanting eyes. He looked like a grumpy frog, with a small chin under a thick mustache, which capped a frowning mouth. A face unaccustomed to smiling, I was sure. The word *dour* popped into my head. He was dour. Of course, with a nickname like "the Butcher," what could one expect?

"*Les Américains,*" the colonel said unnecessarily.

"At ease, gentlemen." He studied us and then looked back at my orders in his hand. "You are marines. Second American Division?"

I nodded. "We were, sir. Now we are attached to the Department of State and work for Mr. Gordon."

Inevitably, he glanced at the dog's breakfast that was the side of my face.

"Your division fought well. Magnificent dash most upsetting to the Boche. And your tenacity." He had a sparkle in his eye. "Most upsetting to the Boche,"[8] he repeated. His English was heavily accented but understandable.

"These orders are delightfully vague," he correctly noted.

"Yessir. General Bliss and Mr. Gordon thought it best that their message for you be delivered verbally."

He brought his right arm across his chest, catching his hand under his left arm. He rested his left elbow on top of the hand with his left fist perched like a small bird near his chin.

"Ahh... this is an unpleasant message you must deliver then?" He asked the question with a raised eyebrow.

I found myself liking the Butcher. God help me if I ever met Pershing and felt the same.

"Please deliver your message. It will not soften with age I expect."

"It has come to the attention of the American commissioners that the plot for Rhinish independence that failed so recently persists,[9] that Herr Dorten continues to lead the bid for autonomy for the Rhinelanders and that the French support him. As you may know, sir, France and Great Britain owe the United States a tremendous amount of money. If France were to support an insurrection in the Rhineland and the insurrection were to succeed, the United States is certain the Germans will cease paying reparations to the French. Without reparations, France will not be able to service her enormous debt to the United States. This means no additional funding will come from the United States to France. The funds supporting France's military will disappear. The United States will withdraw from Germany and from Europe, generally. In the event fighting resumes as Germany tries to retain control of the Rhineland, the United States would not support France. Obviously, the outcome of such an independence movement would be disastrous."

"What is the source of this information?" he asked.

"A confidential, reliable source, sir."

"And you believe this effort is supported by the French? Who specifically?" He was forcing me to be blunt.

"By you, sir." I obliged him.

"In this instance, your source is not an accurate one." His cheeks were flushed with anger. "I am not plotting with Dorten. Of course, I do encourage some independent thought on the part of these Rhinelanders. You would hardly believe how the iron of Prussian rule has entered into the souls of these people. Why, when we first arrived, they simply hadn't an opinion of their own.[10] But I cannot admit to working to separate them from Germany. I know you Americans would not support such a separation on your *watch*." He said the last with great bitterness.

"Would you be willing to write the same in a letter for General Bliss and Mr. Gordon, sir?" I asked.

"Oh no. I think we should follow the very wise practice of you Americans and have such sensitive tidings delivered verbally, yes?"

I had no choice but to agree. The French had been playing these games since before my damn country was born, and Mangin had been playing them since before I was born. I wasn't going to hoodwink him into doing anything that didn't fit his or France's schemes. I didn't know whether he was telling the truth or not, but it didn't matter. I was now in a tough spot. I could pull out my pistol and shoot Mangin dead. Unfortunately, that would get me killed and Will too, and probably Bullard.

"You know, Major, many Frenchmen do not believe the United States will honor its agreements in the treaty," Mangin said. "Many think America will retreat behind the Atlantic, just as many think the British will hide behind the English Channel. This will leave France to face Germany alone in the coming years. A sovereign or at least self-reliant Rhineland free from Prussian influence may be the only hope of winning a second war with Germany. And a second war is coming, Major."

"You may be right, sir, but United States policy is to remain consistent with the territorial requirements of the treaty. Any thoughts about future wars are above my pay grade, sir." I didn't tell him I wouldn't blame the Americans or the English if they left the French to fight it out with Germany. More than a hundred thousand of our soldiers had died with nothing but Clemenceau's manipulation to show for the corpses. Of course, France had lost over a million with nearly six million casualties, but there was nothing I could do for those poor sods now. Preventing the next war was worth fighting for, and fucking around with the Rhineland seemed like a good way to restart the one that just finished.

Mangin must have read my thoughts on my face. He wiped all emotion from his own, and said, "I see you do not agree. Do you have anything further to discuss, Major?"

"No, sir," I answered meekly. I'd failed. He would likely support an independent Rhineland, and Fuchs would kill Marie and Jean-Paul. Goddamn French. Goddamn Germans.

———

Peter left us in front of our hotel.

We stood on the sidewalk at a loss for what to do next. Mitchell took out his cigarette pack and knocked one free, offered it to Bullard and took one for himself. As the two of them lit up, I studied the street around us sullenly. It wasn't even noon, and Mangin had already sent us packing. Folks were strolling up and down the sidewalks in the late-summer sunshine. They avoided our eyes, but they didn't look scared or unhappy. Just cautious. I supposed that was the most I could hope for.

"Time for a beer," Mitchell said, picking a fleck of tobacco off his tongue.

"Yep. It is."

"Not sure what you're gonna tell your Kraut buddy Fuchs," Bullard noted unhelpfully.

"That's why we're having the beer," Mitchell told him. "Trust me, we'll figure it out."

Bullard shrugged, and I started down the street toward what looked like the German version of a café.

They followed, and I heard Bullard reading the name of the place where I was headed.

"*Gasthaus zur goldenen Schippe*. The golden shovel? Good choice, Griffin. Maybe this shovel will dig us out of the hole we're in."

I ignored him and led them into the café. Tables occupied by men eating lunch stood between the door and a long, nearly empty bar. The glares from the clientele made it clear that the French didn't frequent the Shovel. I didn't know if wearing a uniform was as dangerous in Mainz as it was in Berlin, but I didn't give a shit. In Mainz, I had thousands of black and North African colonials who'd keep the population from killing me. I undid the flap on the holster hanging from my Sam Browne belt just to make sure everyone behaved.

Simply by walking in the door, we captured the bartender's attention. He watched me as I worked my way between the tables, ignoring the hostile looks. When I arrived at the bar in front of him, I tried three words of my expanding German vocabulary.

"*Drei bier, bitte.*"[11]

"I'm impressed, Griff," Bullard said under his breath. I glared at him. We leaned against the bar waiting for our beers, which arrived a hell of a lot quicker than they would have in Paris, and I noted the fact to Bullard. He only shrugged and said, "German efficiency," with a grin, which frightened most of the patrons and would have frightened me if I hadn't known him.

With our drinks in hand, we took a recently vacated table, likely free because of our arrival. We were a unique sight in Mainz. Two American officers drinking with what appeared to be a Senegalese rifleman. It was clear to the three of us that our military masquerade had failed with Mangin, and there was no point in following military regulations or etiquette. We treated the Golden Shovel like it was Le Dôme in Paris.

We didn't talk much until our first beer was gone and we'd ordered another. After the publican delivered the second round, I acknowledged the obvious.

"We're not going to convince Mangin to admit he's part of a plot, and if he is involved, we're not going to get him to give it up. Even if we did, we're never going to convince Fuchs that we have."

Both Mitchell and Bullard sipped their beers and nodded.

"We do have Fuchs and his German foreign ministry and intelligence contact and probably their resources as well, and we have the Americans in Koblenz, who'll come to the sector border to rescue us if we can get there. We need to find a way to raise some doubt in Mangin's mind. At least get him to consider his future and the risks of moving forward with a plot. The problem is that we have no evidence that he is actually involved in attempting to create an independent Rhineland."

"So what if we don't have any evidence," Mitchell said. "We just make some up?"

I cocked my head as if trying to understand an imbecile, but then Bullard said, "We could do that. You just said it yourself, John. We have the resources of the German foreign ministry and German intelligence."

"Yes, but only if Fuchs will let us use them."

"Oh, I have no doubt you can convince him, Johnny." I hated when Mitchell called me Johnny. He only did it when he was trying to make a point he wasn't sure I understood. It was as if he had some sort of telepathic ability that allowed him to understand exactly how my mother had used the name.

I finished my beer, and because Mitchell annoyed me, I thumped the mug down on the table harder than necessary. The barman watched fearfully, hoping it wasn't the start of trouble.

"We'll have Fuchs create letters to and from Mangin and

Dorten. We'll even create a couple from Mangin to General Allen, asking for support of a Rhinish secession," I said. "Hell, we'll claim we got them from Allen. Mangin might want to contact Allen, but it will delay him."

"And make him pretty damn sore when he finds out we made this evidence up," Mitchell noted, indifferent to the fact that it was his idea to fabricate evidence.

"True, but we won't present the evidence at the palace," I said. "We have to catch Mangin somewhere else. And we don't leave the evidence with him. We tell him trusted agents delivered it and we are duty bound to return it to Gordon and Bliss in Paris."

Three more beers arrived unasked for. The barkeep must have interpreted the bang of my mug on the table as a demand for another round. He hurried away.

Mitchell lifted his newly arrived beer and said, "Hell, John, you speak German fluently."

Both men cackled at the remark.

I had to smile, and as I did, I found that Mitchell's prediction to Gene as we came into the bar was correct. I had figured it out. We would get Mangin to go back to Paris, and we'd save Marie and Jean-Paul too. With any luck, I might get to kill Fuchs, but first I was going to have to convince him of my plan.

Mitchell saw the gleam in my eye.

"Spill it, Griffin. What are we going to do?"

And I told him.

26

———

The Happy Family

I walked directly to Peter's shop and found him once again tinkering under the bonnet of his truck. I arranged for him to take me to Fuchs in the morning. He insisted he wouldn't know the location of the rendezvous until that evening and claimed someone delivered a note each night with a rotating location. I wasn't sure I believed him, and I considered having Bullard and Mitchell follow me to the meeting. But I decided it didn't matter. I doubted Fuchs had Marie and Jean-Paul with him, and ambushing him without knowing where they were would be a dangerous, wasted effort.

At eight o'clock the next day, Peter collected me in front of the hotel. I was anxious. I wore my pistol in its shoulder holster. I took comfort in the fact that the worst that could happen was that I would die in a bloody shootout with Fuchs. Unfortunately, this meeting would determine whether Marie and Jean-Paul lived. Any gunfight meant they died. I didn't like having their lives in my hands.

When Peter arrived, he was on foot.

"Not driving, Peter?"

"No, *mein Herr*. Herr Fuchs is at a coffeehouse near the cathedral. I will show you where and then leave you."

We walked in silence since it seemed the usually garrulous Peter could sense my disquiet. We entered a cobblestone square with the cathedral behind it. Peter pointed to a café facing us where I could see Fuchs had taken a table outside. He had a folded newspaper in front of him next to a cup and saucer and was watching us.

"I will leave you here," Peter said. *"Viel Glück."* He quickly turned away, and I crossed the square to Fuchs.

"Good morning, Karl," I said cheerily as I sat uninvited at the table. "I have good news." Despite my worry, I had decided that confidence and bravado were key to the success of the meeting.

"Oh? I am eager to hear it. There was nothing in the newspapers this morning about General Mangin's unfortunate assassination."

I laughed. The waiter arrived promptly, and I ordered a coffee using French. I figured the Germans in Mainz needed to learn the language of their occupiers.

"Karl, you know that is not a sensible approach. Also, such a move is likely to create a martyr and result in the French wholly committing to splitting the Rhineland from the Reich. Isn't that what we both want to avoid?"

His eyes narrowed with distrust.

"Please, Karl. Let me tell you what I have planned. If you don't like it, then you can give me your squinty Junker glare."

My comment caused him to relax just a bit.

"I am a Berliner and no Prussian *Landjunker*,"[1] he said proudly.

"You're all squareheads to me," I said with disdain.

"Tell me your story," he said, overlooking my insult. "It would be a shame for such a pretty woman and her son to die. The child is, after all, the only surviving heir to a wealthy *Junker* family." Fuchs was reminding me that he had murdered Jean-

Paul's grandparents and would not hesitate to do the same to the little boy.

I disregarded the vivid memory of Emma Vogt splayed dead in her chair in Elsbeth Schragmüller's cozy kitchen and told Fuchs of my meeting with Mangin. I omitted the fact that Bullard and Mitchell were with me, but I noted that I was in uniform with the orders from General Bliss in my pocket. This point particularly impressed Fuchs. He nodded as I described my plea to Mangin on behalf of the American commissioners.

"I even explained that the Rhineland's independence would cause Germany's reparations to end, and without reparations France was broke," I told him. "And if France was broke, she couldn't pay back the United States, which would make the US pretty damn sore."

"And he didn't have you thrown out at that point?" asked Fuchs with a chuckle.

"No. He gave me a fair hearing even though I said some things that made him angry."

"I wish I could have been there to see you pull on his pigtails," Fuchs said with longing.

"Well, I made my points, and he understood them. But he promised he isn't supporting any move for an independent Rhineland."

"He is lying."

"And he refused to put the promise in writing to the American Commission."

Fuchs was no longer laughing. "So you have accomplished nothing."

"*Au contraire!*" I said with a smile. I hoped Fuchs appreciated my humor in addressing him in French. "Now we present him with evidence of his lies."

"What evidence? You have no evidence." Fuchs was starting to get himself worked up.

"Karl, calm yourself. We will create the evidence. Surely, in the great German foreign ministry or in the serpentine German military intelligence apparatus, you have forgers and printers for fake letterhead. Your Teutonic artisans will create letters between Dorten and Mangin, demonstrating that the two are actively scheming exactly as you believe them to be. You get to create the evidence you want."

"This will not work. Mangin will not care about false evidence."

"He will care about what the Americans think. He believes I represent the Americans because I do represent them even if by accident. If I show him the evidence that has convinced the United States that he is plotting, he must do what he can to counter it. He will return to Paris. And in Paris, I can use the commission to persuade him to give up his support for Dorten."

"If you return to see him at his headquarters, he will refuse to see you, and if he sees you and you present him the *evidence*, he will simply confiscate it and destroy it."

"True. I have a plan that addresses this possibility, but it will require that you put a little trust in me."

He didn't respond. This would be the hardest part of the conversation.

"Every Sunday afternoon, Mangin takes his family to the park behind the palace," I told him. "While the park is open to public visitors, the Germans stay away from the French and from Mangin's family in particular. And there are certainly many soldiers around the park when Mangin and his family are there, but they are at the periphery. They give the general and his family privacy. With the right camouflage, it will be a simple thing to stroll through the park and come upon the general at his ease while he watches his children play."

"You will never get near him."

"I will. All I need is a family of my own."

It didn't take him long to understand what I meant. He

started to shake his head but then stopped as he thought about the possibilities.

"With my wife on my arm and my son kicking a football ahead, I will walk right up to him. I'll show him the documents one at a time. He will know they are not real, but it doesn't matter. He'll believe I think they are real."

"He will call for his guards."

"Perhaps, but then we run. Maybe I even drop a document or two. You have a car waiting and whisk us away. To fight what are either outrageous lies or the dangerous truths that you will have created, he will be forced to go to Paris. Once in Paris, he will rail against the claim that he is sponsoring a revolt in the Rhineland. Clemenceau and Foch, as Supreme Allied Commander, will ask him what the hell he is talking about. I will deliver the evidence to the Americans, and they will say 'I told you so' to the French. Mangin will almost certainly be removed, and he will have done it to himself."

Fuchs's mind was spinning through my tale, testing each point. He was clearly considering it. In hearing myself describe the scheme, it had sounded damn good. The key was for him to let me use Marie and Jean-Paul. Without them, the plan was useless.

He stood, threw some Papiermarks on the table, and said, "I must consider this. Be back here in two hours."

Two hours was a long time to drink coffee, especially with an efficient waiter. After the first hour and three strong espressos, I switched to beer. If Fuchs accepted the plan, I had a few days to prepare. If I got a little tight today, it wouldn't be a problem. In fact, it might help. If he didn't accept the plan, I'd be more willing to act than think. I'd follow the son of a bitch when he left, corner him, torture him for Marie's location, and then kill him. That was a backup plan worthy of my training.

The backup plan was unnecessary.

Fuchs returned with a spring to his step and a smile on his

face. He saw that I was drinking a beer and immediately ordered one for himself.

"We will do as you suggest. I have to say, John. I am impressed. My superiors and I find your suggestion to be much more subtle and imaginative then we gave you credit for. You are correct. No matter what happens at the park, Mangin must return to Paris to manage the repercussions from the *evidence*." He chuckled at the thought.

"Goddamn, Karl, you are as giddy as a maiden."

"I just find your plan to be so artful. So un-American. Please don't be offended. Your people just aren't very sophisticated in the ways of diplomacy."

"So this is diplomacy?" I asked.

"Diplomacy, espionage, manipulation. These are words that mean the same thing," Fuchs declared cynically.

"Well, I'll need to prepare with Marie and her kid for our efforts at *diplomacy*. Can you have the documents ready by this Sunday?"

"We are working on them now. In fact, when I finish my beer, I will return to assist with the wording. The letters will look very real and be very convincing."

"Make some extras in case Mangin destroys the ones I hand him," I said, realizing that Mangin might be too angry to return the documents I show him.

"Do not worry," he said, waving away my concerns with his newly lit cigarette.

"And Karl, Marie and the boy will leave with me after I deliver the message and documents to Mangin. Yes?"

He took a drag and smiled at me. "Of course. You will have accomplished what is required."

I finished my beer and stood. I didn't see any point in sitting with him any longer, and I wanted to try to follow him when he left.

"When and where should we meet for me to practice with

Marie and the boy?"

"Meet here on Saturday at nine o'clock. Surely one day of practice will be enough, yes?"

"That's fine." I left him. I walked out of the square at ninety degrees from the direction Fuchs had entered. Once out of sight of the bar, I circled toward where I'd first seen him come into the plaza. By the time I arrived back at the square and got eyes on the café, he was gone.

I RETURNED TO THE HOTEL AND FOUND MITCHELL AND BULLARD sitting in Bullard's room talking. They were in his room because that was where the whiskey was stowed. I sat on the bed next to Bullard, and the three of us talked through how we would handle the meeting with Mangin and its aftermath. The purpose of accosting Mangin and his family in the park was to find a public, and therefore safe, way to free Marie and Jean-Paul from their German captors. It was a certainty that after speaking with Mangin, we would be pursued by the Germans, the French, or both. In any case, the answer was to run like hell. Since Mangin did not expect to see me again, I was sure that the French pursuit, if any, would be half-hearted and disorganized. That would not be the case with the Germans. Fuchs would expect some treachery on my part, and he would plan for it. I hoped he didn't know I had Bullard in the wings. Peter knew of him, but I didn't think Fuchs used him for intelligence gathering, and even if he did, Peter just saw a black French translator, not an ally of mine. I did think it was too much to hope that Fuchs's spies hadn't seen Mitchell march in to see Mangin with me. It was likely they'd spotted Bullard, but he would be seen as a French colonial and part of Mangin's Tenth Army.

"We will have to get to Mangin at the park," I told them. "It's the only time when he's accessible. The three of us should go out there today and take a look around. It sounds like the best plan will be to set up our own picnic near where the Mangin family likes to go."

"And I know just what you'll put in your picnic basket," Mitchell said.

"And hope I don't need them, Mitch," I said, thinking about putting a German pistol in the basket in addition to the Colt. I had a sudden notion that I was certain was a stroke of genius. Meaning it was likely a terrible idea, but I was going to pursue it anyway.

"Gene, I need a dog."

"What?" both men exclaimed.

"A puppy. As cute as you can find, and smart, but cute is more important than smart. And some snacks for the dog. Sausage, berries. We can train it with those."

"Where the hell are we supposed to find a puppy?" Mitchell demanded.

"What the hell are you going to do with a puppy?" Bullard asked. "You know, as I recall, your history with dogs is not that rosy."

I shot Bullard a glare. It was unfair of him to remind me of my encounter with Coco, the French Rottweiler that had attacked me in Paris. "First, I'm not sure you can find a puppy anywhere, Mitchell. With your foul temper, if the damn thing is smart, it won't come near you. Second, Gene, I don't appreciate the unhappy reminder. It was an unfortunate meeting under trying circumstances. I am sure I can get along with a puppy, and I have faith in your ability to find one."

"I'll have you know dogs love me," Mitchell said with a hurt tone.

"I'll try the French barracks. They might have a pup or two. Maybe Mitchell or you can ask your Kraut friend Peter. Although, if we do that, it will get back to Fuchs."

"It's not a problem if Fuchs knows. He'll probably be dazzled by how clever we are. You would have thought he was actually impressed by my intellect if you'd heard how he gushed about the suggestion that we use forged documents to incriminate Mangin. Of course, he didn't know it was a group effort. I took all the credit myself."

"Naturally. That's what officers do," Bullard said straight-faced.

"An officer by the grace of the American Department of State and a bevy of French spy agencies only, Gene," I reminded him.

We took the trolley across the bridge and past Biebrich Palace and detrained exactly where Gene had on Sunday. The three of us spread through the park, examining the ground and the cover, looking for the best way to escape the park once the meeting with Mangin was complete.

After an hour or so of separate explorations, we gathered on the decorative drawbridge opposite the castle. A dirt path ran north and south just in front of us. Bullard had been absolutely right when he described the castle as a great place for children to play. There were nooks and crannies where they could hide, most of them in the dark and dank corners of the make-believe castle. They also smelled like urine, which meant someone was living rough near the castle and using it as a latrine or just living in the castle and indifferent to where they pissed.

"You see that break in the trees?" Mitchell pointed across the path into the darkness of trees and undergrowth.

"Not really," I said.

"Well, trust me, there's a break. Come on."

He led us across the path and into the brush. After just a few steps, we came to a shallow creek that ran south through a cobblestone-lined drain parallel to the path. It was about five feet below the level of the ground around it, and it was overgrown with trees and bushes. For its whole length that we could see, it was in shadow.

"This little stream spills down from the north side of the park. There's a neighborhood up there, and the water comes from underground. It runs south along the east side of the park for a ways. If you can reach it, you can escape out of the park without being seen."

"So we finish with Mangin and hide in the creek bed?" I asked.

"You don't hide. You run like hell south." He pointed into the shadows in the direction the little creek flowed. "Follow it two hundred paces, and it turns sharply west. You climb out there. Walk the opposite direction, that's east, in case you're confused, Griff. Bullard and I will meet you. We'll need a car, but there's a road not twenty paces from the stream. Just about the whole way is out of sight."

"But if they catch us in the creek, we're trapped. They take Marie and Jean-Paul, and I'm back under their thumb."

"You shoot your way out. If they want her or the boy as hostages, they can't shoot you. And they're not going to find you. Follow me."

He scrambled down the stone wall into the creek and started south. After five or so minutes, we came to the sharp bend west. Mitchell climbed up the stream wall, and in another minute, we were standing on an empty residential street.

"We park here."

"All right. All we need now is a puppy," I said. All of us laughed.

SATURDAY MORNING, I SAT AT THE CAFÉ IN THE MAINZ CATHEDRAL square, flipping through a copy of the *Mainzer Anzeiger*, a local daily with not nearly enough pictures to make the effort worthwhile. It was not significantly improving my ability to speak German. The puppy sat at my feet, fidgeting periodically and chewing on the lead around her neck. She had a fluffy tan body and black face. Her large expressive ears flicked in every direction as people hurried past.

"Dog." She tilted her gaze up at me. Her chocolate eyes looked alert and ready. She was still very young, but she was damn smart. "Good girl." I scratched her behind the ear.

When I looked up, I saw Marie and Jean-Paul hurrying across the square with Fuchs and three hard men in their wake.

I stood up to welcome them, and Jean-Paul broke into a run across the square. He slammed into me and hugged me fiercely. I patted him on the back. Marie saw my bewildered look and smiled. The dog had scrambled away when the boy first appeared, but she jumped up to welcome Jean-Paul after her surprise was gone.

I hugged Marie as well and gave her the requisite peck on both cheeks. She remained beautiful, but worry shadowed her eyes.

"Ahh, the happy family reunited," Fuchs said in a cheery tone. "And with a little dog. Why do you have a dog, John?" He wasn't suspicious so much as curious.

"She'll be the best way to get near Mangin," I told him. "With Jean-Paul and a puppy, I'll be able to walk right up to him. Trust me on this."

"Oh, but I do," Fuchs promised disingenuously.

"What's her name?" Jean-Paul asked about the dog frisking around his legs and twisting the lead to the point where someone, likely me, would trip.

"She's waiting for it," I told him. I picked up the puppy, untangled the leash, and set her in Jean-Paul's arms.

The boy looked at his mother and back at me in confusion.

"He is saying you should name her, Jean-Paul."

His eyes lit up with excitement.

"We should go. We have a lot to cover." I picked up the picnic basket that sat next to my chair away from the dog. "We'll take the trolley."

On a signal from Fuchs, one of the men checked the picnic basket, rifling through it to make sure there was no gun.

"Open your jacket, John."

"And you said you trusted me," I said as I opened my coat to show I had no weapon.

"About the boy and the dog, yes. About a pistol?" He shook his head.

The seven of us traveled to the park. I took them to the spot I'd chosen for our picnic and spread the blanket. I sat down and invited Marie and JP to do the same. Fuchs stood close, listening as I described the plan. The three other Germans stood farther out from us, smoking and watching.

"Can you play football, Jean-Paul?" I asked the little boy. He nodded. "Good. The four of us, your mother, you, the puppy, and I are pretending to be a family. I need to talk to an important man, but he may not want to talk to me. I will need you to play football with his children, and at some point, I will need either you or the puppy to run over to the man. I will come to get you. I will talk to him briefly. We will return here, pack up our picnic and leave." He nodded. With Fuchs listening in, I described in detail how I hoped things would go. Marie was mostly quiet, but every once in a while, she would ask me a question for the benefit of her son.

Once Marie and Jean-Paul understood what I wanted, we walked through the plan. I forced the Germans to huddle in a group as if they were Mangin's family. We rehearsed for about an hour. The boy and the puppy were naturals. We decided that the puppy would be my opening to Mangin. We practiced dropping berries near the Germans for the dog to find. She figured out quickly that if she ran to them when released, there would be a treat nearby.

As we finished our practice, I crouched down next to the boy and his dog. It was clear that the dog was his at this point.

"Jean-Paul, you did well. Understand that the plan can change at any minute. If it does, you must do what I tell you immediately. No questions. You understand?"

"Yes, Father."

I barked a laugh and looked at Marie. "You've taught him well."

"We have had time to speak," she said cryptically.

Fuchs hurried over, unwilling to give us time to talk alone.

"Mangin will likely be unhappy. Where will you collect us to get us away," I asked him, knowing I had no intention of going anywhere with Fuchs and his thugs and knowing he knew I would try to escape.

"Walk around the lake and exit on the east side." He pointed past the lake. "Peter will be waiting for you with the truck. He will drive the three of you to the station, and you will be free of me. But John, you must make sure that your friend, Mr. Mitchell, does not interfere. You must show the documents to Mangin and convince him of your seriousness."

"I'll convince him. Mitchell won't interfere, but don't get clever, Karl. Tomorrow I will be armed, and if you get clever, I'll kill you and the men with you," I told him matter-of-factly.

Fuchs turned away with Marie and Jean-Paul herded after him by his men.

"And tell Peter he'll be taking the dog to the station too," I said, as if that was the most important thing on my mind.

"Her name is Anneli," Jean-Paul called to me with a wave. "Anneli, like in the storybook."[2]

I didn't know what story he meant, but I called back, "Anneli, she is." Then they were out of sight.

That night, I put a call through to the US headquarters in Koblenz. I left a message for Colonel Bell with the duty officer alerting the colonel that the next afternoon we would be arriving at the American sector.

27

———

Deluge and Double-Cross

Sunday was overcast. I was nervous. The whole thing could go wrong in so many ways. Just like the war. I thought of the Robert Burns poem Evelyn had introduced to me. Glorious, bright Evelyn. The font and rock of all my dreams. It was before the war, before the reality of the horror of failed plans revealed itself to me. We would lean our heads together and chuckle over the nearly incomprehensible Scots, our fingers tracking together down the page.

> *The best laid schemes o' Mice an' Men*
> *Gang aft agley,*
> *An' lea'e us nought but grief an' pain...*[1]

Since 1915, these lines would force their way into my head as I crouched in the mud at the bottom of the trench waiting. Waiting for the attack, the shell, the gas, the splinter, the bullet. Waiting for death.

I wondered if the Mangin family would go to the park in the rain. Sunday afternoon at the park. That had been my scheme.

They had to show up for me to get Marie and Jean-Paul free. With the weather, I wasn't sure the Mangins would go to the park. Anxiety gripped me. If we missed this Sunday, we would have to wait another week. The knot in my stomach told me Fuchs wouldn't allow us another week.

Trapped on my path, I followed the practice of the past four years. I ignored the knot and the shivers. I dressed meticulously as if such care at the moment would make a difference. I took a Luger from my new suitcase and an extra magazine. I put the magazine in my left jacket pocket and the pistol behind my belt at the small of my back. I pulled on a slicker, hoping that if I wore it, the rain would refuse to come because I was prepared.

I went downstairs to breakfast to meet Mitchell and Bullard. They weren't there yet. I drank coffee, my mood as dark as the forbidding sky.

We would go to the park even if it were sheeting down rain. I would insist. Once there, anything was possible. Maybe the plan could still work.

Bullard and Mitchell arrived. Their moods matched mine. We felt the same gravity as the night we raided rue de Babylone and lost Shed Bean and the evening we ambushed the Bolsheviks and Gavin was killed.

At the appointed hour, we wished each other luck. I left for the café where I was again to meet Fuchs, and they left to collect the motorcar and then drive to the park. I found myself wishing Disney were with us. I had never seen Gene drive. He said he could, and I had no reason to doubt him. But I knew Disney's skills, and we would need a good driver today.

I was early to the café. More coffee wouldn't help my nerves, and despite the habits I'd learned from the British army, I had no desire for a drink before the coming action.

I walked around the square, which was emptying as people went into the cathedral for the Sunday service. I sat down and watched them until they were gone. Then I observed anyone who entered the square, eager for Fuchs to arrive and get started. It started to mist down rain. Fuck! I hoped Jean-Paul had spent time training the puppy. I hoped the Mangins were a hardy family. I hoped the goddamn creek didn't flood. My thoughts raced along finding all possible disasters. My superstition convinced me that by thinking of every eventuality, I prevented them from happening. It was the possibility you didn't think of that killed you. I took no comfort in the lie.

Fuchs saw me on the bench and started across the square to meet me. The mist had turned to rain.

"John, I am sorry to say I am not sure the general and his family will go to the park today."

"Perhaps not, but the only way to know if he will be there is to go ourselves. Let's hope the rain passes. Lead the way."

I wasn't going to discuss calling off the plan. We were going to the park. I was going to get Marie and Jean-Paul free.

Without another word, he turned back the way he had come. In twenty minutes, we were closer to the river in a residential district with buildings crowded against each other. A trolley ran down the center of the street, and Fuchs took us to one of the houses, which was indistinguishable from the rest.

Marie and Jean-Paul were sitting at a table in the kitchen crowded with men. Six obvious former soldiers leaned against the walls and cupboards, smoking cigarettes and pipes. The puppy was curled at JP's feet. She barely lifted her head when I entered. A large picnic basket and an oiled canvas tarp sat on the table. I sat down and pulled the basket to me. Inside the basket, I found a bottle of Riesling wine, an opener, a block of cheese wrapped in paper, a length of sausage, a loaf of heavy bread, and some green apples. There were some serviettes, two cheap glasses, and a pocketknife on the bottom. I noted there was nothing for the boy to drink. Well, he was half French, so he could drink the wine. I kept the Luger at my back. I didn't want to rub Fuchs's nose in the fact that I was armed. He expected me to be, but I didn't want to argue about it now. With six toughs in the room, it was an argument I was sure to lose. I closed the basket.

"The letters?"

Fuchs made a great show of removing a waxed packet from his coat. He handed it to me reverently, as if passing a holy relic. I opened it and found inside letter after letter in French and German. Some of the missives were from Mangin, and others were to him. In some, he was not named at all. They all appeared to address the urgency of the independence of the Rhineland. Dorten's name was on many, and there were some names I didn't recognize: Adenauer, Mathes, Deckers. The letters looked real enough to me. I didn't bother to do more than skim them hastily. I was impressed, and I let Fuchs see it.

"He may know these are fakes, Karl, but he will have to act," I said as sincerely as I could. I knew I was convincing because he smiled and nodded vigorously.

"Indeed. He will at least need to address their existence."

"Good work. These should do the trick," I said tucking the bundle into the basket. I stood. "Ready?" I asked the room.

"One slight modification of the plan, John." He nodded, and before I could move, two of his men seized me, and a third searched me. They took the Luger, but I had nothing else. I had given a second Luger and the Colt to Mitchell. I was confident he had done with them what was needed.

"Nothing else, John. I am surprised."

"You aren't going to double-cross me, are you, Karl?"

"No, I am just looking out for the safety of my men. You will take the *Straßenbahn* to the park," Fuchs declared.

There was nothing I could do about being stripped of my weapon.

"The streetcar? Sure. We'll look just like an honest-to-god family," I said.

For one glorious moment, I thought he intended to allow the

three of us to travel without an escort, but as I gathered the basket, four men pushed erect to accompany us. Our chaperones. So much for skipping the park entirely.

"Do your men speak English?" I asked.

"No, but they are very alert. The rest of us will travel by car to the park to observe from afar."

"Fine, but tell your boys not to crowd us. I'd like us to look like a family, not a circus act."

He gave me a small polite laugh. None of the men looked particularly offended, so perhaps they really didn't speak English.

"Of course." He rattled some instructions in German.

We left the house and crossed to the trolley stop. Marie took my arm and, with her other hand, held Jean-Paul's. He, in turn, held the dog's leash. The puppy followed calmly at his knee. The picture of a family out for a rainy afternoon in the park.

"You have been training her," I said to Jean-Paul.

"Yes," he said with happiness. "She is very smart. She will do exactly as we need."

I nodded. I hoped she didn't mind loud noises. There was something about the way the men held themselves and Fuchs's nonchalance that made my anxiety worse.

The ride to the park was uneventful. It remained overcast, but the rain had stopped. That wouldn't last. I could tell. I'd spent enough time in the field to know when it was going to rain. I didn't bother praying for the weather to clear. That was a fool's game. Whatever happened, I would deal with.

The park was nearly empty. We walked slowly along the path to our agreed-upon spot, where Jean-Paul let Anneli off her leash, and she leaped and gamboled around us as we all laughed. Jean-Paul chased after the dog as she ran toward the ruined castle.

I knelt down and pretended to unfold our picnic tarp. Instead, I removed the square plug of grass that Mitchell had cut out the night before. He had marked the spot with a rock. Under it was a waxed paper packet. I took the packet and replaced the plug. I threw the rock toward the creek.

I unwrapped the paper and revealed a Luger, my .45, and Marie's razor. I put the Luger in the nearly empty basket.

"Marie, in case you need it. Fuchs is up to something. He didn't want me armed. And, if you're not near the pistol and they try to take you again, don't let them. This time they will kill us if they can." I handed her the razor. She nodded and secreted it in her blouse.

A thin rain started again, and Jean-Paul and the puppy returned from the ruins. The boy was bubbling with excitement. It occurred to me that he had been locked up for days. His life before with his grandmother and grandfather at an estate guarded by soldiers couldn't have been much fun either.

"There are many rooms, and it is dark, like an old castle in a storybook. There should be a witch or a dragon. What a wonderful place," he told us, his eyes shining. We laughed, and I tried to relax and share the boy's joy. With Fuchs's men in the shadows and the miserable weather, it was hard.

"General Mangin and his family may not come, John," Marie said. She was having no problem staying focused on the job at hand. She would protect her son to the exclusion of all else.

"I won't let Fuchs take you," I told Marie.

"I won't let Fuchs take us," she answered. I believed her promise more than mine.

I'd just opened the wine when the Mangin family marched into view through the mist.

The puppy noticed them first. She stood from where she had curled on the tarp. Her whole body wagged with her tail. I followed her look and saw the family tromping toward the location where Bullard had seen them. The servants laid out a tarp, not so different from ours, but larger. The children scattered. Some went to the castle. Two boys made a desultory effort to kick a soccer ball in the wet grass.

I looked at Jean-Paul. He quivered with excitement almost like the puppy. I nodded. He put the lead on Anneli and handed the end to his mother. I used the knife from the basket and cut off two small pieces of sausage and gave them to the boy. He took them, bent to the puppy, and held them to her nose. Then he stood and put the slivers in his pocket. The dog stood on her hind legs to reach him, but he ran toward the boys playing with the ball. Marie held firm to the lead while I took the bundle of letters from the basket.

I heard Jean-Paul speaking French to the boys, but I couldn't make out what he said. I was sure he was asking if he could play. They shrugged and the younger boy kicked the ball to him. Jean-Paul was skilled for his age. He controlled the ball well and hit it to the older Mangin boy. Consistent with our plan, Jean-Paul navigated himself between the boys and where their parents and a few of the youngest children sat.

He called to the older boy, who had the ball at his feet, and pointed up. Jean-Paul made clear he wanted the ball in the air. The older boy laughed and struck the ball high. Jean-Paul slipped, or pretended to, and the ball sailed past him and rolled toward the Mangins' picnic. Jean-Paul sprinted after it. It rolled almost directly to the general. Marie let Anneli off the lead. The dog played her part by racing across the grass to the Mangin family. Unseen, Jean-Paul took the sausage from his pocket and dropped it at the edge of their seating. I thought he had only dropped one piece, and I hope it was enough. He scooped the ball up and ran back toward the boys. I stood and pulled my hat low. I hurried quickly to the Mangins' picnic as an embarrassed father might and called, "*Je suis vraiment désolé!*"[2]

The shadows of Mangin's guards at the edges of the field and in the woods didn't move to intercept me. I was a harmless father and puppy owner.

Anneli snared the treat from the grass but then was captured by the Mangin children. When I arrived, she was rolling on her back as the little girls scrambled to pat her squirming body. Even their mother reached over to rub her head. Mangin was smiling at the antics of the dog and the children. Then he looked up to greet me, and he stopped smiling.

"General," I said in English, "I am sorry to interrupt your afternoon. But I have some documents you must see. I know you insisted there is no French plot to assist the Rhineland in pursuing its independence, but these documents are most compelling."

I took the packet from my jacket and handed him the first of the letters. His eyes skimmed it quickly. I handed him the second. "I have no choice but to deliver these to my superiors in Paris. I wanted to do you the courtesy of showing them to you first, but I knew I would not get in to see you at the palace. Forgive my impertinence. As you can see, I have a folio full of such letters. General Bliss and Mr. Gordon will take a very dim view of such plotting."

His wife had stopped patting the dog. She was dividing her attention between me and the colonial soldiers fifty yards away. She could sense something was amiss.

"These are forged. They are good forgeries, but they are not real," Mangin said coldly.

"Perhaps, General, but I have no choice. I must deliver them to Paris," I said.

"I could take them from you here," he said with certainty.

"You could, sir, but I would still report what I have found."

"I could kill you."

"You could, but I do not believe you will. And my son and wife are here. I do not believe you would kill them either."

At that moment, our standoff was rendered moot. The pop of a handgun changed everything. I whipped my head around in time to see one of the colonial soldiers crumple to the ground.

"General, there are Boche assassins in the park." I tucked the packet of letters back in my jacket. I did not bother collecting the two letters I had given Mangin. "They could be here for me or for you, but most likely, they are here for us both."

I knew the answer. The Germans had decided my plan was too subtle. They were going to kill all of us.

Three Germans stepped from the tree line near where the colonial had stood guard.

I looked for Jean-Paul. He had strayed in his play toward the ruins.

"Jean-Paul," I shouted. "Hide in the castle! We'll come for you there."

From the corner of my eye, I caught movement at the site of our picnic. I turned to see Marie, with her skirts hiked up in one hand and the Luger in the other, running as fast as her ungainly clothes allowed toward her son. He would be hidden in the castle long before she crossed the grass to the castle bridge.

The rain started to come down harder. In the space of a few seconds, a cold wind whipped across the park. I turned to Mangin.

"General, collect your family and run. Hurry to the palace."

It seemed as if my words opened the heavens. Sheets of water poured down. At first the rain hid the attackers, but they knew very well where we were. In just a few moments, three gray shadows emerged from the weather. I drew the Colt, pulled back the slide, and fired. Whether because I'd hit my target or he had decided to take cover, my target went to the ground. I shifted my aim and fired at the second man. It was a rushed shot, and I knew I missed, but he dropped to the ground as well. Both men started firing back. That answered the question about whether I'd hit anything. Unfortunately, the entire Mangin family seemed to jump to their feet all at once, with the mother closest to me.

The shadow of the third attacker resolved into one of the

men who'd ridden the tram with us. I fired at him and knocked him back.

I grabbed Madame Mangin's arm.

"*Mon dieu!*" she wailed. I didn't know whether her cry was from my assault on her person or the gunshots.

"*Pardon, madame,*" I said in hope of calming her. I pushed her toward her husband and scooped up the dog.

The men had come from the direction of our escape. The two prone men continued to fire their pistols at us. Judging by the results, they were worse shots than I was.

"We will not reach our men or the palace before we are killed," Mangin declared with one arm around his wife and the other holding his smallest child.

"Shit!" I swore. "Go to the castle. We will hide you in the ruins." I shooed the Mangins toward the broken walls. I fired once more to hold our attackers in place. They, of course, fired back.

The Mangins gathered their children around them. For a moment, it seemed as if Madame Mangin was counting heads to make sure she had all her children. Then, together, we hurried, stumbling through the deluge. I couldn't see Marie. She must have reached the castle.

More pops and now rifle shots rang behind us. It was unclear where they were aimed. I would hide Mangin and his family in the ruined castle and escape with Marie and Jean-Paul from the park.

We ran across the drawbridge and through a gate with a pointed archway. Marie stood in the center of the castle courtyard, calling Jean-Paul's name. She was soaked but seemed not to notice. The din of the downpour and the thickness of the walls must have kept her calls from reaching him. He could have taken any one of the doorways that led off into the darkness of the ruins. Smart kid.

I set the puppy on the ground.

"Find Jean-Paul. Find him." The little dog's eyes sparkled in readiness, but her ears flopped over, belying her determined gaze. I gave her a rub on the head and a little push, and she was off like a shot. She ran past Marie into the blackness of one of the passages. We followed slowly because of the darkness and called out for the boy. We lost sight of the puppy, but our cries must have reached Jean-Paul. His pale face appeared in the shadow from a darkened and previously unseen doorway. Anneli was in his arms.

Marie ran to him and hugged him. I took the forgotten Luger from her hand and held it out to Mangin butt first.

He considered me and then the pistol.

Barely heard shots and pops came from outside the walls. He took the pistol.

"Your men will drive off the Germans," I told him. "Stay here. Your soldiers will find you. Your family should be safe."

"You should stay as well," he said.

"I am sorry, sir, but I don't want to tempt you to take the documents I carry."

"You will force me to go to Paris to answer the lies in your pocket?" he asked coldly.

"General, I have my duty and can do nothing else."

He was offended and used to others following his orders in all things, but he had been a soldier all his life. He believed in duty and honor and all that drivel. He believed me when I told him I was obligated to report what I had found. It was what he would have done.

"Very well," he said grimly. "I will not stop you." He held out his hand. "And Major, thank you."

I didn't understand at first, and then Madame Mangin put her hand on my arm and said, "*Merci, monsieur, merci.*" They were thinking of their children. They were thinking I had saved them because I was a good and honorable man.

"*De rien, madame,*"[3] I answered, feeling like the scoundrel I was. I had drawn the murderers to the Mangins, and they thought I had rescued them.

I shook Mangin's hand. Without another word, Marie, Jean-Paul, and I fled the ruins for the creek. The dog was curled in the crook of my elbow like a football, and not the European kind. She smelled like wet dog, but that was no surprise.

We skidded down the rock wall of the streambed into a torrent of water, twigs, and trash. The sound of gunfire crackled behind us. I hoped that Mangin and his family escaped. I felt like a cur for leaving them, but I had promised Marie I would help her, not Mangin, his wife, or their eight children. I was beginning to understand how Marie had betrayed thousands of her countrymen just to protect one little boy.

As we worked our way down the watercourse, we had trouble keeping our balance. The water pushed us, branches tripped us, and despite the stones paving the bottom, the footing was uneven. The three of us clung to each other as we shuffled along the creek bed toward our exit. As we walked, the rain began to ease, and after a short time, it stopped altogether. Trees on both sides of the stream curved overhead, and the undergrowth came right to where the stone-lined bank dropped into the water. Unless the Germans had scouted the park as diligently as we had, they would have no idea where we had vanished.

It seemed to take hours, but it couldn't have been more than ten minutes before we reached the turn where we were to exit the sunken waterway. I boosted Marie up the stone bank first and gave her Anneli. Then I shoved Jean-Paul up the cobbled wall, but he barely needed my push. He scrambled up like a monkey and took the puppy from his mother. I climbed less gracefully. I slipped, tore a hole in the knee of my pants, and nearly slid into the stream.

We quietly worked our way through the undergrowth to the

road parallel to the park. There we found Mitchell and Bullard, with pistols in their hands, standing under umbrellas by a car.

"Well, lookie here, Gene. Three less reputable-looking tramps would be hard to find. As grumpy as wet cats with the littlest of dogs," Mitchell said, chuckling at his own humor. He had us labeled right. We were soaked through, and the storm had brought a chill with it.

"We heard shooting," Bullard said.

"Thank God you left the pistols. Fuchs and his boys decided that leaving the general and the three of us alive was not straightforward enough. They came to kill us and Mangin. Probably planning on making it look like Reds were to blame. We left Mangin in the fake castle with a Luger and his family. His troops will comb the park and either kill all of Fuchs's men or drive them from the park."

"Let's hope the general and his family aren't dead by the time they do," Gene declared.

I heard criticism in his statement and was about to snarl back at him. But I didn't. He was right. I had abandoned Mangin and his family. Getting sore at Bullard wouldn't change the truth.

Instead of answering, I bundled Marie and the boy into the back of the car. Gene climbed into the driver's seat, Mitchell gave the car a crank, and we were away.

Unfortunately, the general's colonial troops were so successful at driving the Germans from the park that we passed Fuchs and his men climbing into their truck as we drove south toward the river. I didn't see them at first, but Mitchell did.

Bullard roared by them, and Mitchell squawked, "Christ! That was Fuchs! His face flashed by so close I swear he made goo-goo eyes at me!"

I twisted my head around in time to see Fuchs shouting and pointing as his men swarmed into their motortruck.

"You *are* a good-looking devil, Mitchell," Bullard cracked. He wasn't smiling though. He was concentrating on driving as fast as the conditions allowed.

"Gene, cross the river and turn west toward the American sector. We'll see if General Allen is as good as his word," I said. "I don't know if Fuchs will chase us, but I don't want to take any chances."

Our car was faster than the German truck. Unfortunately, it made no difference as we drove across the Kaiser Bridge and through the crowded Sunday afternoon streets of Mainz. The rain had stopped, and the sun appeared. It seemed like everyone was celebrating by promenading along the river and through the center of town. Also, although Gene had a map and Mitchell was navigating, the Germans chasing us knew shortcuts we didn't. We'd lose sight of them behind us, and then we'd see them again sometimes in the distance and, once, frighteningly close. We reached the road that ran along the south side of the Rhine, and they hadn't caught us. Bullard opened up the motorcar as much as the road would allow. I was sure we were leaving the Germans behind, but Fuchs would not stop chasing.

We followed the Rhine for the most part, but after about an hour of driving, we came to a fork in the road. The sign for Koblenz pointed left, away from the river, and a smaller country road continued along the bank of the Rhine.

"As the crow flies, it's shorter down that little road," Mitchell told me, lifting his head from the map. "I don't know what we might run into though."

I was torn but didn't want any delay. The shorter distance had to be better.

"Take the little road along the river, Gene."

He looked back at me to confirm the choice and just shrugged when I stared back at him. He put the car in gear, and we were off again, slower than before but heading more directly to our rendezvous with the Americans.

My choice seemed to be a good one. Across the river,

vineyards covered a low ridge. A monument of some kind sat on the crest overlooking the river. It was far away and very large. God only knew what the memorial was celebrating. It felt like we were in the middle of nowhere. We drove through a small village, over a creek running toward the Rhine, and were back out in the countryside in moments. A broken castle loomed above the river on our right, and a small tower sat on an island in the middle of the flow. The knot in my stomach that I hadn't realized was there started to loosen. We couldn't be more than a few minutes from the American sector.

That was when we came upon the cows. Ten or twelve red Holsteins stood placidly in the road between us and safety. Their tails swished and ears flicked at the buzzing flies around their eyes. A calf looked at us curiously. Anneli gave small barks of excitement.

The farmer herding the cattle was standing in the middle of the road with his cloth cap low on his forehead. He was a wizened, bent old goat. He studied us for a time and then seemed to recall his business. He made a clicking sound and waved his walking stick to interest the cows in moving along the road.

The manure smell outside the mill ship should have warned me. I hadn't thought of cows. Goddamn it! If I'd thought cows might be a problem, there wouldn't be any cows.

Bullard gave the bulb on the horn a squeeze.

Neither the farmer nor his charges bothered to turn a head to acknowledge the thin tooting.

Bullard leaned his head out of the window and called out something in German. It sounded to my ear like he was telling the man we had eyelids, but the farmer wasn't impressed.

The farmer shook his head and said, "*Schwarzer.*" He then clucked a few more times, and the cows moved a few feet.

The knot was back in my stomach.

I jumped out of the car and waved my arms, shouting, "Hey, goddamn it! Move your cows!"

I had the man's attention, but he didn't move any faster.

I pulled the pistol from under my arm and pointed it at the ground.

His eyes grew round. He clicked more energetically and waved his stick, but the cows just didn't believe he was serious.

I fired once into the air, and the farmer and his cows froze. Then the whole group, cows, calf, and man, streamed off the road and onto the verge.

I was back in the car in a flash, and Bullard had us rolling past as soon as the cattle cleared the road.

Unfortunately, the delay cost us. As we merged back with the main road, we could see Fuchs's truck had caught up. They weren't more than a half a klick behind us.

Ahead I could see what I hoped was the castle where we were to meet Colonel Bell's men, assuming he had sent them. Rheinstein Castle. If it was the right one, it was certainly picturesque. The stone walls ran down to the road and rose nearly vertically up the steep, rocky slope above. As we drew closer, I saw two trucks parked along the road. Soldiers in US Army khaki stood around them. They'd set up a roadblock. They were stopping all traffic going in and out of the American sector. I could have kissed Colonel Bell. The soldiers were where he'd promised they'd be and when he'd promised. Fuchs could not drive up to the checkpoint because the whole west side of the Rhine was a demilitarized sector. They were not allowed weapons here. They'd be arrested and their weapons taken. They also wouldn't risk a gunfight. On both sides of the road, the soldiers had set up Hotchkiss heavy machine guns. Fuchs would not be running this blockade.

After the soldiers manning the roadblock performed preliminary checks on our vehicle, they pointed us down the road to a mobile headquarters, a civilian car confiscated for the purpose. An officer stood over a map spread on the bonnet, but he looked up to watch me hurry toward him.

"Major Griffin?"

"I am," I said, nodding. My civilian clothes didn't help identify me.

"I'm Major Dwyer. The colonel asked that I have you escorted back to Koblenz." He offered his hand, which I took.

"That would be excellent, Major."

I looked over my shoulder at the truck carrying Fuchs and his men. It had pulled off to the side of the road two hundred yards from the roadblock. Fuchs remained inside the cab. I was tempted to grab a Hotchkiss and spray all twenty-four rounds from the feed strip into the truck, but I restrained myself. I didn't want to alienate the major or his troops, but I also didn't want Fuchs to find a way to follow.

"And Major, if that truck tries to come through your checkpoint, please tell your men to machine gun everyone inside it. They've been chasing us since Mainz. They shot up a park and tried to kill us and General Mangin and his family."

"I wish my orders were flexible enough for me to blow them to hell from here, but Colonel Bell was very clear that, for this job, I had to keep my boys in our sector. Even the loosest interpretation of my orders requires our bullets stay here with us. Assuming they don't fire on us."

He gave me a raised eyebrow, as if inviting me to walk down the road toward Fuchs and his men to draw their fire. I shook my head.

"No reason to give them cause to shoot at us," I said. With Marie and Jean-Paul finally safe, I didn't want to risk any gunfire just to satisfy my desire to kill Fuchs.

The major waved over a very young-looking captain.

"This is Captain Casey.[4] He'll escort you to Koblenz. We've got a motorcar," he said, thumping the hood with his knuckle. "But if he'll fit in yours, you'll save me the need to send it.

Perhaps we can send your driver back to Mainz with one of the motorbuses that pass through, and Pat could ride with you." Dwyer gestured to Bullard, who had stepped from the car and was leaning against the hood, smoking with Mitchell. Marie and Jean-Paul remained in the car.

"Mr. Bullard is part of my team, and he'll be returning to Koblenz with us. I am sorry to inconvenience you, but the captain will have to take your motorcar."

Dwyer studied Bullard with surprise but nodded.

"Okay. Captain, you heard the man. Mount up. Take them to the colonel, and good luck to you, Major Griffin." We shook hands once more, and Dwyer turned back to watch Fuchs's truck.

I decided to ride with Casey. My hope was to pick his brain for any information that might be helpful. Unfortunately, he was a wet behind the ears recent graduate of West Point. His entire class of 1918 had graduated early because of the war. He told me he spoke some German and was getting better at it. He also said he was an engineer. I found him to be sharp and thoughtful. I liked him. He was eager and ambitious but not to a fault. And he was young. I couldn't have been more than two or three years older than him, but I felt like an ancient as we talked. He was full of hope and belief in America's importance in the world. I felt sorry for him, or maybe I felt sorry for myself.

He asked about my reason for being in Mainz. I told him it was confidential but I was doing some work for the Department of State. Not a lie, really. Gordon had sent me to Mainz after all. Casey nodded, as if he encountered spies every day.

"How do the Germans accept occupation?" I asked.

"They accept it, resent the fact of occupation, but don't hate Americans. I'm not sure how long we'll be here, and I'm not sure we're accomplishing much beyond populating the world with half German, half American babies."

I laughed.

"I'm serious," he said. "The Krauts are forced to billet our soldiers. They have daughters. It's the birds and the bees in the Rhineland."

"That's going to complicate things if we have to fight them again," I said.

"I doubt it. Our boys will either marry the girls or shun them. If the first, everybody becomes an American. If the latter, the kid is a fatherless Kraut bastard." He said the last with a twinkle in his eye.

"Literally."

"Yup, literally."

We were silent for a time, but eventually I asked him where he was from. He told me Brooklyn. New York Irish. I learned that his grandfather died at Antietam fighting in the Irish Brigade, and we were off to the races. I told him mine had survived Antietam only to die from wounds suffered at Gettysburg. We spent the rest of the two-hour drive jawing about the Civil War. As we rolled up the hill to Ehrenbreitstein Fortress, he did tell me that Colonel Bell would be happy to see our backs.

"I suppose that means the General will be happy to see us gone as well?" I asked.

"Yup," he confirmed. "He doesn't want any shooting if he can avoid it."

"I don't blame him. I don't either."

"Hah! And the brass was a little worried you looked like a fellow who might enjoy shooting up the Rhineland."

"Me? They should know you can't judge a book by its cover," I said.

We were back in Paris the next afternoon.

28

Ordered Priorities

Mitchell and I had held our rooms at the Vendôme, and the concierge knew us well enough to find a room for Marie and Jean-Paul. Really, he knew Mitchell well enough. He wasn't pleased by the puppy, but two hundred francs won him over.

While on the train back to France, I had ordered my priorities. I had to have Marie and Jean-Paul disappear. This needed to happen before I did anything else. For this, I needed the goodwill of Madame Errázuriz.

Early the next morning, I took a motorcab to the address on the card Madame Errázuriz had given me earlier in the month. The day was overcast and promised rain. The driver took me to a neighborhood at the edge of the Monceau Park in the eighth arrondissement and left me in front of a grand stone-and-brick home with a low wrought iron gate. A short path led to the heavy wooden front door. When I knocked on the door, no one answered. I had written a short note on Vendôme stationery just in case. I dropped the letter through the brass slot in the door and hoped it would reach Errázuriz.

Since I had nothing to do until the meeting time proposed in the note, I went to the Café de Flore for breakfast. My note suggested a meeting there in the late afternoon, but it was always possible Madame Errázuriz might be at the café enjoying a morning coffee. She was not. I went back to the hotel, found Marie and Jean-Paul in their room, and instructed them to lie low. It wouldn't do for Raux or Ladoux to see Marie, who they believed was dead, lunching in a café or dog-walking in a park. Both the woman and the boy were peevish upon learning that they needed to stay in their room. The dog wasn't too happy either.

"Marie," I reminded her, and the boy indirectly, "the Germans found you somehow. You had an apartment no one could trace you to, which means they must have seen you. Stay put. I know Anneli is restless, Jean-Paul." I could see him gathering the courage to interrupt me. "I'll take her for a walk."

Jean-Paul dutifully gave me her leash and a few berries left over from their room service breakfast to serve as treats. Together Anneli and I left their room. The dog was indecent in her joy, which made neither mother nor son any happier. I decided we'd go for an extremely long walk, and we did.

Despite the off-and-on rain, I remained out with the puppy until just an hour before I was due at the Café de Flore. I enjoyed the time with the dog and found that, for any child, family, or young woman, the puppy was a magnet. Footsore, I returned a very happy and tired pup to Marie's room. They received the dog more graciously than they received me. I left quickly for de Flore.

I had just ordered a beer when a small, tidy, dark-complexioned man entered the café. He spun his head about, exaggerating the act of looking for someone inside the café. He was my age or perhaps a bit older, but he had a devil-may-care air about him. His comical searching ended when his eyes settled on me.

He glided gracefully to my table, held up the letter I had left at the house near Monceau Park, and raised an eyebrow. He didn't say a word.

"Please." I pointed to the chair across from me.

"I am Tony Gandarillas.[1] Eugenia Errázuriz is my aunt, and she told me you might come by my house. My apologies for not answering when you knocked. I was smoking."

I must have looked confused. I'd never heard of someone failing to answer the door because they were smoking.

"Opium," he clarified. He clearly wanted to scandalize me. He spoke English with only a slight accent. Spanish perhaps? I wasn't sure.

"Ah. Well, I can understand not wanting to interrupt a pipe. I have a friend who has smoked a time or two. Never more than ten pipes a day, of course. He believes it is important to meter one's entertainments." I almost laughed out loud at the fact that I was using Mitchell's lies about smoking opium in Asia to ingratiate myself to Errázuriz's nephew.

"Just so, I should meet this friend," he said, impressed.

"Your aunt told you she was interested in sponsoring a young artist of my acquaintance?" I asked, ignoring his comment.

"Yes, she did. She wanted me to give this to you or your young friend in the event it was she who arrived at my door." He took an envelope from his inner jacket pocket and handed it to me. The letter was addressed simply: Care of Mr. John Griffin. "It contains information about what is offered, what she can expect, where she should go, and how she may contact my aunt. There is also some money inside. My aunt insisted that I make clear this is not for you. It is for your friend."

"I can't blame your aunt for that," I said. "Would you like a drink?" I felt I owed him something. He had done me a favor by just coming to the café.

"I would like that." He summoned the waiter. As we waited, Gandarillas took out a blue pack of Gauloises, which he offered to me. I shook my head, and he lit his with a flashy gold lighter. When he exhaled, the strong-smelling smoke of the unfiltered cigarette swirled across the table.

The waiter appeared.

"*Un Pépa s'il vous plaît*," Gandarillas ordered.

"*Vermouth, cognac, et vodka?*" the waiter clarified.

"*Oui.*"

Gandarillas turned to me.

"A Pépa?" I asked.

"It is new, named for Pépa Bonafé, the film star."

"Never heard of her," I said with a shake of my head.

"Americans," he said with mock disgust.

"What can you expect?" I said, laughing. I liked Gandarillas despite his effeminate airs, but after my trip to Berlin, I was an old hand at handling that.

"Is she your lover?" I knew exactly who he meant, but he was fishing. He took a drag on his cigarette with exaggerated care.

"Who? Your aunt? She's an attractive woman, older, but attractive. But no, we are not lovers."

The inhaled smoke exploded from his lungs with his shock.

"No, no! Oh my God, no! The young artist. Is she your lover?"

"We are very close." I was being indirect because I knew what he was asking.

"I see." Gandarillas was flirting with me. The old me would have missed it. The new, worldly me couldn't possibly. Madeline would be impressed.

His drink arrived.

"Are you an artist as well?" I asked. I didn't want to discuss Marie, and I knew he really didn't want to either.

"No, no. A diplomat. And a patron of the arts and artists."

"So, not so different from your aunt." That made him laugh.

"I am entirely different from my aunt, but we love each other and share the love of art."

"It's nice to have family." At my words, I found myself

missing my sisters. I made a silent promise to myself to visit when I got back to the States.

I finished my beer.

"Tony, thank you." I offered my hand, which he took. "I very much appreciate what you've done."

"My aunt may not have time for you, Mr. Griffin, but I do. Please feel free to drop by if you are ever in the eighth."

"Of course."

I put some money on the table and waved a hand over my shoulder as I left.

I went back to the hotel to inform Marie that she and Jean-Paul had an escape from her German masters. Jean-Paul answered the door, and Anneli met me with great enthusiasm. She didn't jump, for Jean-Paul wouldn't allow that. His mother didn't like it. The puppy did wriggle around my legs in an effort to trip me. I was relieved that she wasn't one of those dogs that pissed itself upon greeting people.

"Your mother?"

"Napping," the boy said with a roll of his eyes. "We went for a walk, and I think it tired her."

"I will wake her. We have much to discuss. The first thing being that she shouldn't have gone out for a walk. She could be recognized. You, on the other hand, can't be. You're a kid. Do you think you can take Anneli for a walk without being snatched by the Kr— Germans?" I didn't want the kid to feel bad about his heritage, and I thought I'd caught the slur in time.

"Of course, with Anneli, they wouldn't come near me. She is very fierce." I watched the little dog worrying at one of Marie's shoes, and for the dog's sake, I prayed that it wasn't one Marie liked.

"Okay, off you go. Keep your eyes peeled, and don't hesitate to run if you see something suspicious. And take this." I handed him the French pocketknife. His eyes lit up. He dropped it in his pocket, leashed the puppy, and both literally skipped from the room.

I remembered my first pocketknife. It had been my eighth birthday, and my father had given me the knife with a penny taped to the box. He'd made me give him the penny before I opened the box. It was my first exposure to the power of superstition. A power I had come to worship far more than any imaginary god in a mythical heaven. The knife had been small with two blades, one longer and one short. It didn't lock. My father wouldn't let me carry it until I could close it with one hand. He sat me down in our kitchen and watched me struggle to close it for what seemed like hours but couldn't have been more than ten minutes. When I failed, he took it from me. He told me to think about it and to come back when I was sure I would succeed. I spent a couple of days thinking and finally asked my sisters for help.

"Close it against your leg, dope," the oldest had said kindly.

I went to my father and showed him I could manage the little knife. I was so proud with it in my pocket. I felt responsible, like an adult.

I'd already shown Jean-Paul how to operate the French knife since he had no sisters to help him. He was very proficient, but the locking knife couldn't be closed with one hand.

I went into the bedroom. Marie was dressed, facing away from me, and lying on top of the bedclothes. I shook her.

She rolled toward me and gave me an evil eye.

"You and Jean-Paul are very noisy."

"And you are very lazy to be napping."

"I am bored, and sleeping makes the time go faster."

"And yet you two went out for a walk. That's not what I call lying low, Marie."

"It was a short walk to a newspaper kiosk just down the street. The dog needed to go out. I needed to go out. I had no cigarettes left, and I wanted some postcards. We weren't out long."

"Well, I have good news for you. I have a letter. It should describe how you and Jean-Paul will disappear. At least, I think that's what it will tell you."

She threw her legs over the side of the bed and sat up. I saw a flash of ankles and calves, and part of me regretted that she had stopped trying to seduce me.

"Where is Jean-Paul?"

"I sent him out with the dog."

"What!" She jumped to her feet.

"Stop! He'll be fine. He is a boy. No one will recognize him. Raux and Ladoux don't know he exists. Let him have a little independence," I said. Even though I had told them to lie low, I was sure the boy would not be noticed.

She glared at me, and I worried that I had made a mistake in giving her a new razor.

"Fine. Where is this letter?"

I handed her Madame Errázuriz's letter. She sat on the bed, opened it, and began to read. She read it once and then again. She took her time. When she finished, she stared at me with glistening golden eyes.

"This is remarkable. How did you manage this?" she asked.

"I showed Madame Errázuriz some of your paintings, and she was impressed enough to be willing to help you. But, Marie, I don't want to know what the arrangements are or where you're going. No one from your past life can know. Do you understand?"

"You don't want to know what becomes of us?" She was teasing, but there was still hurt in the question. She really was a master of her art.

"Somehow they found you before. No mistakes this time," I insisted.

"All right. According to this letter, we are expected. We can leave whenever we want."

"Then you should go. The sooner the better. And no contact with anyone."

She followed me into the sitting room.

I saw the postcards she had purchased on the coffee table. I picked them up.

"You won't need these, Marie."

She nodded her understanding. "We will miss you, John."

"Oddly, Marie, I'll miss you as well. Say goodbye to Jean-Paul for me."

I gave her a farewell kiss on a cheek wet with tears. Crocodile tears, I was sure. It was sad that even at the very end her manipulation continued.

<hr>

NEXT, I NEEDED TO MEET WITH RAUX AND THEN GORDON. I WAS sure it was too late in the day to see either one, but I didn't want to waste any time. I dispatched notes to both using the Vendôme concierge and some francs. I advised them I would seek them out in the morning. The urgency to find Patricia was nagging me now that I'd taken care of Marie and Jean-Paul. I felt maudlin, depressed, out of sorts, and I was sure it was because the delay in following Patricia was wearing on me.

With my messages sent, I sought out Mitchell. I hoped a few drinks and dinner with him might ease my angst, but he wasn't in his hotel room. It was still drizzling, but I walked across the river to Le Dôme anyway. There wasn't much of a crowd, and I sat in a booth near the bar. I sat alone for a time and drank beer, feeling sorry for myself and not understanding why. Sarah was gone, Madeline home, but my work for the French was done. I was free to help Mitchell and Patricia, free to pursue Armistan. But I felt blue, so damn blue.

I was just about ready to drown myself in beer when Rachel Eisen breezed into the bar. She didn't see me, and I waved at her like a schoolgirl.

When she did notice me, she came right over.

"John! I heard you were back." She gave me a peck on both cheeks as she sat down. She was very much adapting to her Parisian life.

"I arrived last night. How'd you hear?" I asked, already grateful to her for diverting me from my miserable mood.

"Walt. He saw William here last night, and they went on to Zelli's."

I was surprised. I hadn't known Mitchell was going out. He hadn't asked me to go. It was as if I had become a family man in his mind. That thought made my stomach sink, and I felt blue again.

"Have you written Maddy?" she asked pointedly.

"Not yet. I need to, but we just got back."

"And you don't have her address," she said, finishing my excuse for me. She raised an eyebrow and took a pen and a crumpled restaurant trade card from her purse.

"At least a postcard to let her know you're alive," she said, jotting Madeline's address on the back of the card.

"I know. I will, Rachel. Really. I miss her."

"Well, you should. She's too good for you. But then we're all too good for you. Of course, that doesn't mean you can't buy me a drink." She smiled at the last.

I waved the waiter over. For better or worse, the waitstaff at Le Dôme knew me by now. I spent enough money that they didn't keep me waiting too long.

"*Un soixante-quinze, s'il vous plaît,*"[2] she ordered.

I ordered another beer.

"You look as down as when your girlfriend died, John. What's the matter?" she asked bluntly.

I wanted to take offense. I wanted to ask her how she could

be so unfeeling, but I wasn't down because of Sarah.

"You a Sigmund Freud, Rachel?"

"Doesn't take Freud to see you're down. Come on. Spill!" she demanded.

"I think I am chafing at the delay in helping Mitchell find Patricia. She left and went to London. We're not exactly sure where she is."

"Patricia Kingsbury missing again. My God, I wish I'd figured out that men would chase me if I just got lost."

"Men chase you when you're right in front of them, Rachel."

She smiled at the compliment.

"It's not Patricia, John. I'm not positive, but I'm not even sure you like her."

"Hell, I'm not either, but Mitchell does, and I think she needs help."

"Could it be anything else?" she asked, probing.

"Not that I can think of. I was working for the French, but that's done now."

"Maybe it's related to the work you did for them. Related to the lady spy Mitchell told us about." She watched me closely to see how I reacted.

"I don't think so. That had a happy ending. She got out of Germany and reunited with her son. The mission was accomplished, at least as far as the French are concerned."

"But what did you do? What did you see? Maybe that's why you're blue? You're just a man, John. Things affect you, too, you know."

I nodded.

"Germany is a mess," I told her. "No rules. Violent. Perverted. Dangerous. I saw school-age prostitutes, ether used for fun, a grandmother shot at a kitchen table. But on the bright side, I helped a mother and her son. And I even got them a puppy." I had a smile on my face, but it didn't feel genuine. I didn't think I was telling Rachel too much. I hoped she would assume that I'd gotten the dog in Paris.

She sat back and sipped her drink with a thoughtful look in her eye.

"How long did you spend with them?"

"Who? The family? Oh, I don't know." Now I was going to have to lie. "Probably just a couple of days."

She shook her head. "The family? Jesus, John. If you're not finding people who want to kill you, you're finding ones who pull at your heartstrings."

"What are you talking about?"

"You're down because you've left the little family you saved. In your screwy head, you've probably adopted them, you simp!" she said with very little sympathy.

"They're not my family," I protested.

"I know they're not, your head knows they're not, but your heart is telling you they are."

"And you think that's why I'm so low?" I asked, but in asking, I acknowledged there was some possibility she was right. "Well shit!"

She sat back with a satisfied gleam in her eye.

"Thank you, Mademoiselle Freud."

She laughed. "You'll feel better now that you know what the problem is," she promised me. Perhaps she was right. I wasn't sure that was the problem, and maybe I would feel better with time, but not today. Today I felt like I'd abandoned John-Paul and Marie.

"Here, have another beer," she said, waving at the waiter. "Disney and Kiki should be here later. Kiki's got a new man. An artist. Hungarian, I think. You won't like him at all. He'll give you plenty to think about."

As she had promised, my friends did arrive later. I mostly ignored the new boyfriend but enjoyed speaking with Kiki again. She lived in the present much better than I, and I pretended a lightness of heart I didn't feel.

She and her man ordered French Seventy-Fives, but Disney ordered a Greyhound.

"What the hell is that, Walt?" I demanded.

He laughed. "I've met some Brits who hang about with Pershing's staff. They served in Egypt during the war and discovered the drink there. They told me it was originally called a 'Suffering Bastard' but now it's a 'Greyhound.' Gin and grapefruit juice. I love 'em."

I nodded and found the name reminded me of Anneli, the puppy. I missed that damn dog. She was a well-behaved, cute little gal. That's why I felt so low. I missed Anneli. I felt a little better once I understood what was really bothering me.

<hr>

The next day, I presented myself at the Hôtel de Crillon and asked to see Gordon. After a short wait, a corporal escorted me up the stairs, and Gordon greeted me enthusiastically.

"So glad you made it back in one piece," he said as he shook my hand. "General Bliss should be here shortly. We've learned that General Mangin is returning to Paris. The diplomatic grapevine seems to think he's been recalled for plotting in the Rhineland. Your visit to the general did all we could have hoped."

When Bliss arrived, his welcome was nearly as warm as Gordon's.

"You impressed General Allen, Mr.—or should I say Major—Griffin. I have heard of no revolt in the Rhineland, and Mangin is returning to Paris to consult with Clemenceau. It appears your trip was a success."

"Honestly, sir. I am not sure. Mangin denies any participation in a plot to establish Rhineland independence, but

I have no doubt that he would welcome it. Also, sir, the Germans attacked him. I was there, and we drove them off," I said. Since it sounded like Mangin was still alive, I thought it was fair to claim that I helped drive off Fuchs and his boys. "But I came across some documents that showed Mangin was in cahoots with a Rhineland politician named Dorten. I showed them to Mangin, but he claimed they were forgeries. And maybe they are, but I told him I'd have to show them to you both. He was angry, and I am sure he's returning to Paris dispute their authenticity."

"Where did you get the documents?" Gordon asked.

"Honestly, sir, the Germans gave them to me." I decided there was no harm in telling him the truth. "The German foreign ministry is trying to prevent any insurrection and hope we'll help." Claiming Fuchs was operating as part of the foreign ministry might have been stretching the truth, but it was close enough for my conscience. "You have these documents?" Gordon asked.

"I do." I handed Fuchs's packet to Gordon.

"They look pretty damn real to me. We need to show these to the French," he said, handing them to Bliss.

Bliss scanned the letters quickly. "They look real to me too. We need to get these to Clemenceau. This evidence should certainly force the French to withdraw any support, whether overt or covert, for independence."

"Mangin claims these are false," I reminded both men.

"Perhaps they are. But the French need to know that we have seen them. It will be enough," Gordon assured me.

"I plan on seeing Préfet Raux of the Paris Préfecture later today," I told them. "He was my liaison with the French. I can share these with him. I cannot promise he will forward them to Clemenceau."

"I will set up a meeting with Prime Minister Clemenceau to let him know what we have discovered and that you are forwarding the information through proper channels." Gordon handed me back the letters. "Give them all to the French. We'll get credit for trusting them to do what is right."

I wasn't so sure, but I wasn't going to argue. I'd done my part in preserving the peace. I took the envelope bundle, returned it to my pocket, and stood.

"Once we find out, I'll send you word about when Mangin will be arriving in Paris," Gordon promised. "Where are you staying?"

"The Vendôme and when I'm not there, Le Dôme is a good bet. I'll go see Raux immediately," I told them.

Their words of encouragement followed me from the office.

THE PRÉFECTURE WAS NOT SO WELCOMING AS THE CRILLON HAD been. I was left waiting on a hard bench in the entry hall for nearly an hour. Two stone-faced men in civilian suits collected me and escorted me up the stairs to Raux's office. I felt very much like a suspect on his way to an interrogation.

Raux sat behind his desk, puffing on a cigar, his head wreathed in smoke, frowning. He was alone.

"I did not expect to see you again after our last meeting," he said brusquely.

Uninvited, I sat down across from him.

"I did not expect it either," I said. "But I have acquired information from the Germans that I feel compelled to share with you."

"The Boche lie. Anything they have told you is a lie."

"Perhaps, but from their lies you might learn something." I laid the package of letters on Raux's desk. I didn't need them. I didn't want them. Raux was right. They were lies, but I wanted him to know what the Germans were about. I wouldn't tell him I was part of their scheme because that would beg the question: Why?

Raux flipped through the letters quickly. He frowned a few times but gave nothing else away. When he finished, he pushed the letters back into the envelope and flipped it across the desk toward me.

"As I said: lies."

I made no move to retrieve the packet. "I showed the letters to General Mangin. He said the same. He knew I was going to share these with my people and with you. It would not surprise me if he returned to Paris."

"You are lucky he did not just kill you."

"I am sure he considered it. Will you share these documents with the prime minister?" I asked.

"I will not. As I said, lies, forgeries. Mangin may not support all the policies of the current government, but he would not actively seek to undermine them."

"I am sure you know best." I stood. "I trust this really is the last time we see each other, Préfet Raux."

"As do I," he said in dismissal.

As I stepped from the Préfecture, I breathed a sigh of relief. My work in France really was done. I thought of Marie and Jean-Paul. And the puppy, and I felt a brief pang of... something.

Time to find Patricia. Time for a reckoning with Armistan. It was time to go home. I went straight back to the hotel. When I arrived, I was tempted to ask the concierge if Madame Dupont and her son had checked out. We'd used the pseudonym when we'd arrived with Marie and Jean-Paul in case Raux or Ladoux were searching for her. I resisted the urge. The less interest shown in them, the less memorable they would be. It was bad enough that they'd arrived with a damn puppy.

I went to Mitchell's room, but he was out. I left a note for him at the hotel front desk in which I promised to meet him at Le Dôme at five p.m. Then I went to find Eugene. Mitchell and I needed to prepare for our return to the States.

I had no luck finding Bullard and eventually settled for going to Le Dôme to wait.

I didn't wait long. Mitchell's clairvoyance led him to the café shortly after I sat down.

"I left you a note," I told him.

"Didn't get it. I figured I'd find you here once you finished your business. Have you?"

"Finished my business? Yes. I saw Gordon and Bliss this morning and Raux afterward. The Americans are happy that we appear to have prevented a revolt in the Rhineland, and the French, or Raux at least, thinks the Krauts are lying shits and we are their dupes."

"Seems like both are right," Mitchell concluded. "But enough about world peace. We need to go collect Tricia from London and get her back to Paris."

"We do. Find Patricia, push Reynolds in front of a train, and then I'll head back to the States to have a chat with her father," I said.

Mitchell laughed. "I'm serious. We need to find Patricia. I'm worried about her being with Reynolds."

"I don't know why, Griff. She can handle herself."

Mitchell didn't know the history of Patricia and her father. If Mitchell ever learned of her father's abuse, there would be hell to pay, and I didn't know what part, if any, Reynolds had played in her subjugation. But Mitchell was confident in Patricia's ability to take care of herself. He was certain she was managing Reynolds and didn't understand the risk her father posed. I needed to keep Mitchell in Paris with Patricia when I went back to see her father.

"I just don't trust Reynolds," I said. "I'm pretty sure he hired men to kill me and Marie on the train to Berlin. If he's willing to do that, who knows what he's willing to do to keep Patricia under his control."

"Okay, okay. I'm prepared to go back to London, but are

you?" he asked. "My recollection is that you were pretty nervous about being there."

He was being kind. He knew that I feared discovery in England. He didn't know why. If he did, he would likely laugh at me, and he would probably be right to do so. An American volunteer, who returned home after being blinded, wouldn't be considered a deserter. Even by the most particular, severe judge of such things, my return to the United States would be understandable. Unfortunately, I was a much more scrupulous and unforgiving judge. And I knew what was in my heart. I had left because I was afraid. No. I was terrified. I couldn't face the front anymore. It was cowardice. I knew it even if no one else would believe it. The thought of an old regimental mate calling my name in recognition drove an icy bolt through my heart.

Still, I needed to return to London. I needed Patricia safe in the same way I needed Marie safe. I had promised. I might be a coward, but I kept my promises.

"Do you think Eugene is coming tonight?" I asked. "I have a laundry list of things I need that will be easier to find here than in the States, and it starts and ends with weapons."

"What? Do you expect a war?"

If Reynolds delivered Patricia to her father in New York City, that was exactly what I expected, which was why I wanted Gene to gather an arsenal for me.

"Humor me, Mitch."

"Sure. Gene will show, but I don't know why you think we need more than our pistols in London. It's not like we're going to have to shoot our way to Patricia."

"You're right. We don't need machine pistols in England, but I want to have every advantage when I go back to the States." My plan was to resolve the Armistan problem without involving Mitchell at all. I wanted him safely in Paris in Patricia's arms, but her disappearance with Reynolds might have frustrated that hope.

"Okay. This could be fun. Gene will be happy to help," he said, deciding to jump in with both feet. "And we've certainly got the money."

Mitchell had told me that Patricia had given him access to the hotel safe on her behalf. Out of curiosity, once the concierge had told him, Mitchell had reviewed the contents of her lockbox. He'd wanted to know if she'd left her jewelry, which would confirm that she intended to return to Paris. Most of her jewelry was in the box and stacks of one-hundred-dollar bills as well. Mitchell also confirmed that only Patricia and he had access to the box. Reynolds did not.

Of course, Mitchell thought my insistence on warlike preparations was dramatic and alarmist, but he was happy to indulge me because he enjoyed the cloak and dagger of arranging access to surplus military weapons. I thought it ironic that, in preparing to leave France, I had stumbled into Gavin Kingsbury's shoes of acquiring weapons for my own private war.

We drank beer and added to my list, arguing about what should be included. It felt like we were writing Vladimir Lenin's Christmas list, and we took great joy in creating it.

Eugene arrived just after seven with an attractive French woman on his arm. Her dark hair was bobbed short, and she wore a sheath dress. Both her short hair and the low-waisted dress with a flattened bust line were in the modern fashion. She was a white woman. On the arm of a black man. A man who, I quickly reminded myself, was my friend.

I stood with a smile, and I hoped my deplorable, regrettable dismay hadn't shown on my face. I could tell from Bullard's eyes that it had, and I was sorry.

"Mademoiselle Camille Proulx, please meet Mr. John Griffin and William Mitchell, friends of mine who are visiting from America." He said this looking me directly in the eye, and I nodded.

"Thank you, Gene. Mademoiselle, it is a pleasure to meet you."

"It is indeed," Mitchell added. "I don't suppose you have a sister or two who are coming later. They'd be most welcome."

She laughed sweetly. "No. I am sorry. Just me." Her accent was charming.

"Well, you and Gene are more than enough," I said. I waved an arm for the waiter, knowing that Gene's arrival was much more likely to draw him than any signal from me. They ordered their drinks, and Gene asked, "Are you done with the French yet?"

"I am. And now Patricia has gone missing again."

"Well, not really missing," Mitchell chimed in optimistically. "She went to England with Reynolds. We're not sure why and we're not sure when they'll be back, so Griff and I are going to head over there to hurry them along."

"And then I'm going back to the States to have a heart-to-heart with her father, who was up to his eyeteeth in the Bolshevik plot to restart the war," I said.

"And he thinks he needs weapons," Mitchell added. He pushed our list across to Bullard.

"That surprises me not at all," Bullard said, and he winked at Camille. "Give me a week. I'll get you what you need."

29

———

Cunning Snares

Early the next afternoon, I had a surprise visitor. A call from the desk brought me to the lobby of the hotel where Commandant Ladoux waited. He remained unctuous, sporting his slicked-back hair and earnest manner. I would never like Ladoux, but I did appreciate his help in Berlin.

"Major Griffin, thank you for seeing me. May I have a few moments of your time?"

"I am very busy with preparations to leave Paris, Monsieur, but I can take a moment."

He pulled the envelope I'd left on Raux's desk from his coat pocket.

"You showed these letters to Préfet Raux yesterday, and he showed them to me."

I nodded.

"I disagree with his assessment," Ladoux continued. "These show a great danger to our relationship with the United States and to the ratification of the treaty in your country."

"Perhaps, Monsieur, but Préfet Raux believed those letters to be forgeries."

"I do not. These represent a monumental danger to France and her alliance with America."

"I'm not sure what that has to do with me." I shrugged.

"I have a favor to ask of you, Monsieur," Ladoux said seriously. "It will not take more than an hour, but it may mean the difference between war and peace in the future."

Frustration and anger bubbled under my heart. It seemed Ladoux had been given the map to manipulating me. Next he'd mention there was a pretty girl who needed help.

Reluctantly I nodded. "All right, Commandant. Just an hour."

He took my arm and led me out of the lobby. A motorcar waited at the curb, and he climbed in immediately. I followed more slowly and got in the car.

We pulled away from the hotel in a hurry.

"Where are we going?" I asked again.

"To Clemenceau."

"Oh shit!" I said vehemently.

It was too late. I was in the automobile, and we were speeding through the streets toward rue Franklin, a neighborhood I knew too well.

A policeman still guarded the door to number 8. He didn't appear to be any more vigilant than the poor bastard that Merchant and the Reds had killed.

Ladoux jumped from the car, and I followed. The policeman let us pass, and Ladoux entered without knocking. He was intercepted by a man who had to be an aide to Clemenceau.

"Nous avons besoin de voir le premier ministre! Tout de suite!"[1]

"Bien sûr, Commandant Ladoux,"[2] the underling answered. He ushered us down the entry hall to the very room where I'd first met Préfet Raux. It was the same room where the French had held me while they decided Germans and not Bolsheviks had attacked Clemenceau on the rue Franklin.

The room was unchanged. The rectangular table still stood

in the center of the wood-paneled walls waiting for important men to make weighty decisions around it. I doubted any meaningful decisions would be made today. I certainly didn't want any part of such work.

Ladoux took the cursed packet from his coat, extracted the letters, and laid them neatly on the table in front of the chair facing the windows. Clemenceau's chair. It had to be.

He gestured for me to sit but propped himself near the window and lit his pipe, looking calm and unconcerned. Now that he had me in Clemenceau's apartments, he was transformed from the anxious man who had rushed me to this room.

Unfortunately, we were kept waiting, and the agitated version of Ladoux reappeared as the delay lengthened. He began to pace and then fuss with his pipe.

The door opened, and the great man entered.

In just the few months since I had last seen him, Prime Minister Clemenceau had aged. He had already been an old man. Now he was a tired old man. I would have thought the war would have been enough to break his strength. The war was not, but it looked like the peace might be.

"Georges." He nodded at Ladoux, who gave a short bow and relaxed back against the window.

"Mr. Griffin, or is it Major Griffin now?" Clemenceau said this with a smile, knowing full well what France had required of me. I appreciated that smile. It reminded me that I hated the man. A hate I'd inherited from Sarah. Curious that Ladoux had not required that I leave my pistol with one of the policemen in the hall. If he'd known what was in my heart, he'd call for help as he tried to wrestle me to the ground.

If Clemenceau read my feelings on my face, he gave no sign of it.

"Once again, France appears to be in your debt." He glanced down at the papers on the table. "Where did you get these?"

"As I told Commandant Ladoux, the Germans. They don't want an independent Rhineland, and they thought the best way to stop that was to give evidence of the plot to an American..." I looked for the word to describe my role but had to settle on "...representative."

"Ah. They do not trust the French to address this information in a manner consistent with the treaty."

It was not a question, but I answered anyway.

"They do not, but the Americans do. My superiors asked that these be delivered to the French for appropriate action."

"And these papers are genuine?"

I shrugged. "I am no judge. I gave the information to Préfet Raux. He thought them forgeries."

"Yesss." Clemenceau dragged the word out. "Did you know, Major, that France is plagued with traitors? Traitors who spy on France for the Boche for money!"

He didn't want an answer.

"It is necessary to find such traitors. To do so, we must create the most cunning snares. Yes, Georges?"

Ladoux nodded. He was, after all, the head of French counterintelligence.

There was a knock on the door.

"*Entrer!*" Clemenceau called.

Préfet Raux came into the room. His dark eyes passed over me and came to rest on Ladoux. Ladoux pushed himself off the windowsill. Was the delay to allow Raux time to travel to Clemenceau's house?

"We were sure we had another traitor, but we were not sure who the traitor was," Clemenceau said. "The préfet left the papers you gave him on his desk. Unsecured. He was curious who would find them and, when found, what they would do with them." He looked at Ladoux. "And it was you, Georges, you who brought them to me. Even though they are fake. Even though they lie about a hero of France. You brought them to me because your paymaster required that you do so!" He no longer looked tired. He looked deadly with anger.

Ladoux? Ladoux was a traitor. As soon as my brain made sense of the fact, I surged out of my chair and had Ladoux by the lapels in a heartbeat. I hadn't planned it, but poor Frau Vogt sprawled dead in the chair compelled it.

"You son of a bitch," I hissed. "You son of a bitch!" I spun him from the window and slammed him down on the polished wood of the table. His pipe flew from his hand. When it bounced on the floor, the dottle came free of the bowl. The unburnt tobacco smoked for a moment before Raux calmly crushed it under his toe.

"*Mes excuses pour le gâchis*,"[3] Raux said to the prime minister.

Clemenceau shrugged his shoulders.

Ladoux struggled under me, but I had a good grip. His face was turning a satisfying shade of red. It all made sense now. Ladoux. Our helpful French contact. The French commander of counterintelligence, who worked for the Deuxième Bureau and, along with Raux, sent us on this damn mission in the first place. Raux's trusted man. Ladoux's unexpected, eager efficiency in getting us out of Berlin now made sense. It was a sham. Helping us was part of the German plan. He knew Fuchs. He worked for Fuchs and the Germans. He had told Fuchs exactly where we were going when we left Berlin. He had suggested to Marie that she should seek her friends in Germany, and she had picked up his suggestion, which brought us to Freiburg. Exactly where Ladoux wanted us.

"When I was trying to escape Berlin, he got me a car," I said with a snarl. "He suggested my path out of Germany. He had the Krauts waiting for me." My left hand held his squirming body tight to the table and my right forearm was crushing down on his windpipe.

"Please, Monsieur Griffin, could you release the

commandant?" Clemenceau asked. "He seems to need some air."

It appeared Clemenceau didn't want me to murder Ladoux.

I pulled Ladoux off the table and thrust him in a chair.

"He was such a pompous shit in Paris when I got my orders. But in Berlin, he bent over backward to help."

"This is outrageous," Ladoux said, coughing. "I am no spy for Germany—and to be manhandled by this primitive!"

"Quiet!" Clemenceau said. "We will ask questions. You will answer, or I will let this barbarian do as he pleases, and perhaps add a few suggestions."

Clemenceau nodded at Raux. It would be the préfet's show.

"Who is your contact with the Germans?" Raux asked.

"I have no contact. I am not a spy. There is no reason to believe I am a spy," he said in a rush.

"Why did you take the fake letters then, Georges?" Raux asked softly.

"I don't know if they are fakes. You think they are fakes, but how do you know? The prime minister needed to know of the threat Mangin poses to the peace. You may think they are fakes, but what if you are wrong and Mangin succeeds in rousing the Rhineland and it becomes independent of Germany?"

Clemenceau smiled.

"Why then, Georges, we would have the buffer state the Americans would not allow in the treaty. A friend on our border instead of an enemy. And I am sure that we could convince the Americans that we had nothing to do with it," he said. "Isn't that right, Major Griffin?" He turned to me.

"The major's friends would certainly agree," Raux volunteered. He was staring a warning at me. He knew Kiki and Eugene had helped me thwart the original plot against Clemenceau. In doing so, Gene had certainly broken French law. This was the same leverage Raux had used to get me to take the goddamn job for the French in the first place.

I had stepped away from Ladoux, thinking that some distance made it less likely that I would kill him out of hand.

I looked at Clemenceau and pursed my lips in indifference and gave my best imitation of a Gallic shrug.

"Perhaps," I answered.

If Ladoux was a German spy, he would know I hadn't killed Marie, but I wasn't worried he would betray that fact. If he told them Marie was alive, he would doom himself, for only the Germans could know that.

"*Les lettres ne sont pas des preuves réelles. Monsieur le Premier Ministre, s'il vous plaît. Fernand.*"[4] In his distress, Ladoux had reverted to French. He gave Raux a pleading look, but Raux was unmoved.

"We will find more evidence," Raux told him. "Perhaps Major Griffin would be willing to help?"

"Don't push it, *Monsieur le Préfet*," I said sharply. "You sent me to Germany with one spy, who nearly killed me, and you sent another to help me, who tracked me for the Boche. And you knew you had a spy unaccounted for! Who's to say there aren't more?"

"Sad, but too true," Clemenceau said.

Raux summoned two policemen from the hallway, who took Ladoux out in handcuffs. His arrogance was greatly diminished by his new jewelry.

"But if you happen to come across evidence of commandant's perfidy," Raux said, optimistically continuing the previous discussion, "please do not hesitate to share it."

"If I come across any information, I'll be happy to share it even if I know it's fake," I promised.

With that, I left the room, and as I closed the door behind me, I heard the sound of both men chuckling in appreciation of my wit. Of course, I wasn't kidding.

T_{HE} weather was clear enough for me to chance walking to Le Dôme. I took my time, musing as I strolled. Thirty-five minutes later I turned in to the café, looking forward to a drink. Dealing with the French tested my patience. It was still early afternoon, but I found Mitchell and Rachel sitting at a table near the back, eating pastries and drinking coffee. They clearly hadn't been dealing with the French.

It was just the two of them. Perhaps Rachel would manage to steal Mitchell away from Patricia, but I doubted it. Rachel was a pretty, witty girl, but Patricia was a dream. Still dreams could turn to nightmares, as I knew too well.

Without hesitation and uninvited, I walked right up and pulled out a chair. Sadly, neither looked offended at the interruption. They acted like two friends who'd just had a third join them. Patricia still had her hooks in Mitchell.

"Hello, John," Rachel said warmly. "You look like you want to kill someone."

"He always looks like that," Mitchell said sweetly.

"The goddamn French found another spy."

Mitchell raised an eyebrow.

"Ladoux," I told him.

He whistled. "Well, son of a gun."

"Yeah, exactly. He knew everything we were doing, but Raux and that wily bastard Clemenceau trapped him with the very letters the Germans had given us."

"You got letters from the Germans?" Rachel asked.

"Yup, long story, but the Krauts blackmailed us into confronting General Mangin, the chief French general in the Rhineland, with forged documents," I said.

"The general told Griff to get lost," Mitchell chipped in.

"True, but I brought the letters back to Raux, and he used them as bait for the spy." I told them of the meeting at Clemenceau's apartment.

"That isn't very strong evidence this Ladoux fellow is a

traitor," Rachel said. "Maybe he just didn't want to take the chance with a revolt. Like he said."

"He's the only way the Krauts could have known we were going to Freiburg. No one else knew. He's the traitor."

"Well, it's good you're done with the French," Rachel said earnestly. "What will you do next?"

"To England and then back to the States, Rachel," I said.

"Well, I'll sure miss you both." she said as she waved at the waiter. "Better have a drink to remember you by."

But I was wrong. I was not going to England or the States.

Two hours later, George Gordon found us sitting at the same table laughing.

"Griffin, there you are!" he said as he arrived.

I'd had a few beers, and I didn't react to his urgency.

"George! George, please meet Rachel Eisen and William Mitchell. Both great friends of mine. George works for the peas commission," I said, laughing at my mistake. "Pull up a chair."

"I like to think of it as the Peace Commission, and I am pleased to meet you both," Gordon said, shaking Mitchell's hand. "I decided to try here instead of your hotel. Looks like I made the right choice."

"What's the matter, George?" I asked, finally sensing his gravity.

"I got an urgent message for you. Dyar in Berlin forwarded it to me. It's from a Kraut professor. Schragmüller. He needs to see you. Pronto."

"She. Schragmüller is a woman," Mitchell volunteered.

I had sobered up.

"Do you have the message, George?" He handed me the cable. It was as he described.

"Urgent Stop Must see you immediately Stop KF knows location of mutual friends Stop Basel train station Stop Sept 4 Stop 1900 Stop Professor Schragmüller Stop."

"KF." Karl Fuchs. How could Fuchs know where Marie and

Jean-Paul were? I didn't even know where they were. But how had Bertrand and Fuchs known where they were the first time? Did the Germans already have them?

There was only one way to find out. I would go to Basel and meet Elsbeth. I was confident she would help me if she could.

<hr>

I HAD A FULL DAY TO GET TO BASEL. MITCHELL HAD WANTED TO come, but I pressed him to finish collecting the weapons and ammunition I'd need for the trip to the States. He would arrange for a flight to England later in the week. I promised I would return as quickly as I could.

There were two trains a day to Basel, and I would have to take the first in order to be sure that I arrived on time. In addition to my .45, I also brought one of the Lugers we'd acquired in our travels.

In the morning, Disney drove, and William accompanied me into the train station. He looked grim.

"I'll see you in a couple of days," he said. "I wish I was going. Since I'm not, you're going to have to make good choices all on your own, Griffin." We shook hands. I climbed the steps into the passenger car and turned to see Mitchell's brief wave and then his back. He wasn't one for long goodbyes.

30

Reality Broke

As the train steamed across France through Strasbourg and then south, I considered the information I had. Elsbeth thought Fuchs knew where Marie was. It could be that she was unsuspecting bait. Fuchs was using her. He could have fed Elsbeth just enough information to stoke her worry for her friend. Naturally, she would turn to the only person she thought might be able to help. Heidegger certainly couldn't. No one in Germany could or would. I had mentioned both Gordon's and Dyar's names to her in Freiburg. She would seize on those links and use them to find me. That was why she wanted to meet in Basel. She didn't want to risk meeting in Germany. She was smart not to trust anyone, and Basel couldn't be more than an hour's train ride across the border from Freiburg.

Of course, it could also be that the Germans really had found Marie. I didn't know how they'd found her the first time, which meant they could have found her again. In the end, it didn't matter. I couldn't risk leaving France to pursue Patricia and, ultimately, Armistan while the possibility existed that Marie and Jean-Paul were exposed. For the Germans and for me, they were loose ends. Fuchs and his masters would want Marie dead for what she knew and who she could tell, and little Jean-Paul, as the leverage used to force her to act for Germany, would have to disappear as well. I knew I couldn't leave for London until I was sure my two charges weren't at risk.

The train arrived in Basel a few minutes late, but since I was already at the station, there was no chance I would be tardy for my meeting with Elsbeth. With my small but heavy bag, I left the train and walked down the platform to the stairs leading to the crosswalk over the tracks to the main hall.

An iron-framed, wood ceiling stretched in a long curve over the arrival-and-departure hall. Light streamed in from large, many-framed windows under each side of the arching roof. I was shocked by the number of troops standing about eyeing the travelers. The soldiers weren't going anywhere. They looked like they were guarding the station.

Elsbeth's message had not said where exactly to meet. I found the nearest bench, which had a good view of the two entrances to the station, and sat with my bag at my feet. The sun wouldn't set until after the meeting time, and the light from the huge windows meant I didn't have to worry about missing Dr. Schragmüller.

Just before seven, Elsbeth entered through the street entrance farthest from me. She walked into the hall, her head swiveling to find me. I waited to see if anyone suspicious followed her. She continued toward the middle of the hall, and I saw nothing that warned me off, so I gathered my bag and stood. The motion caught her attention.

"John, I am so glad you got my message. I have been so worried." She grabbed my free hand with both of hers. "Come, I have a car and a place we can talk. It is not far. I am not sure what to make of what I have learned."

"Why so many soldiers?" I asked.

"Strikes and riots by Bolsheviks in the last month. The

government is keeping the troops in place to prevent any reoccurrence or spread of the unrest. Although the strikes did spread to Zurich."

I was surprised that Bolshevism had reached so far as tiny, quiet Switzerland. Perhaps the Germans were right to worry about its spread, but that was no longer my problem.

I followed Elsbeth out of the hall to the street. An expensive dark blue four-door automobile waited at the curb.

"The driver?" I asked.

"Hired. We will have to wait to speak until we are at the house."

"A house?"

"Yes, you will see. It belongs to a doctor friend of mine. He is not home now. With the war over, he does research at my university part of the year and teaches here the rest."

"The same kind of doctor as you?"

"No," she said. "He is what you would call a "medical" doctor. Psychiatry and neurology. He is very talented."

I nodded, not thinking about her doctor buddy but instead thinking about Fuchs and Marie. It was hard to sit quietly in the back of the car, receiving meaningful glances from Elsbeth without really knowing what they meant.

As we drove, we ran parallel to a river.

"The Rhine?" I asked.

"*Ja*. You know Basel?"

"Lucky guess. I can't seem to get away from that damned river."

She had the courtesy to share a slight smile.

Although the ride was short, I saw at least two armored cars patrolling the streets we used. The house was large with three floors, a cream stucco over stone with apple-green shutters, and a faded red door. The small, metal-shuttered windows of the basement showed along the sidewalk. Blocky and conservative. It was a house from the previous century surrounded by adjoining houses very much like it.

"We are across from the university. The house is very convenient," she explained, climbing from the auto.

We walked up the three steps with Elsbeth in the lead. She pushed the door open to a narrow foyer with rooms off each side. My stomach clenched at the layout, which was so similar to the house on rue de Babylone.

"Coffee or tea?"

"Coffee, please."

She showed me into a sitting room.

"Please be comfortable. I will be back with the coffee, and then we can talk."

I sat down on an overstuffed couch with my bag resting against my right leg. After a few minutes alone, I began to pace. Fortunately, not long after my first tour of the room, the doctor returned with a silver coffee and tea service tray. She set it down on the table before us and poured me a cup.

"Milk?"

"No, thank you."

I watched as she poured herself a cup of tea.

"You're not drinking coffee today. Didn't you tease Dr. Heidegger about drinking tea?" I chuckled at the memory.

She smiled too, and said, "I did, but if I have a cup now, it will keep me awake tonight."

I nodded and sipped my coffee. It was absurdly strong and bitter.

"I think I will have a dash of milk," I said, helping myself to the creamer. I poured a generous splash in to cut the strength of the god-awful coffee she had brewed. She might be a good friend and a good professor, but she made terrible coffee.

She followed me in adding a dash of milk to her cup in the English fashion.

"You take your tea like the Brits," I noted.

"Yes," she said, sipping from her cup. "I picked up the habit in Belgium."

She was in Belgium? During the war? Curious. But I didn't have the time to dwell on her past.

"So Elsbeth, tell me what you have learned. Your message very much worried me."

She stirred her tea longer than seemed necessary as if the motion helped her think.

"Herr Fuchs recently came to me at the university," she said. "I was afraid, as you can imagine. He told me that he was continuing to hunt for Marie. I was worried for her and worried for me, but I didn't want to show it."

I nodded, sipping the coffee. I gestured with my cup for her to continue.

"At first I wasn't sure why he came to me. He asked about our relationship. How long we had known each other. Who else we had known. I was frightened."

I wanted to hurry her, but instead, I took a deep breath and tried to project calm. I leaned back in my chair with my cup and saucer in my lap, having an afternoon coffee with a friend.

"But then he asked me if I had received any postcards from Marie."

It was hard to act calm now. I leaned forward in my seat. She thought I wanted more coffee, and she poured me some as she considered her next words. Again, I added milk to cut the bitterness.

"In fact, I had received a postcard. She had sent it to me from her new address," she said, smiling at the memory. "A picture of the Eiffel Tower, I believe."

"When was this?" I asked. Something wasn't right. The postcard. I remembered the postcards in Marie's abandoned apartment.

"The middle of August, maybe a little after. Perhaps a week

after Herr Fuchs took you from my home and killed that poor woman in my kitchen."

"Did you tell Fuchs Marie's new address?" I asked with urgency. That must have been how Fuchs had found Marie the first time. A postcard to her friend. How could she have been so stupid?

I drank the remainder of my cup, thinking to stand and pace away my anxiety. But when I went to set the cup in its saucer, I missed. It took me two tries to finally settle the cup safely.

"No. No, of course not," she answered.

I needed to stand and walk, but I felt like I was sliding sideways in my chair. I gripped the arm of the seat with both hands and found I wasn't slipping at all. I considered standing, but I wasn't sure I could. Why was that? Something was wrong. With me.

She had answered my question, but I couldn't remember the question.

The professor smiled at me. She had a nice smile....

***

I woke sluggishly. Cold. I was on my back, looking at a plaster ceiling. So cold. I couldn't move my arms or my legs. Or my head. Only my eyes. I was on a table. The table was cold. Metal. I realized I was naked. Straps crossed my forehead, torso, hips, thighs, and ankles. My wrists were held in separate cuffs. I was bound to the table.

I was having trouble remembering.

Why was I naked? Where was I? Why?

The room was dim and too large for me to see completely. Looking up and back revealed the top of a stucco wall with small windows set high. Boards sealed the windows, but some thin light snuck through. Those windows and the stucco walls were trying to tell me something, but I was too dazed to piece it together.

I was freezing and dizzy. Nausea gripped me, and I took a deep breath to keep from vomiting.

A slight angle of the table allowed me to see past my toes. Stairs. I tried counting them, but the bottom ones were hidden from my view. It took a long time to count the stairs I could see. I kept losing focus. Eleven stairs. At the top, there was a door. A cellar. Where was the goddamn furnace? It was downright arctic in this place. My thoughts wouldn't connect. I closed my eyes to help me focus.

Dr. Schragmüller! Elsbeth! I had been speaking with Elsbeth. Drinking coffee.

The horror I felt helped clear my head. There was something in my coffee? A drug. Fuchs. Fuchs had found me. He'd found a way to drug me. Had he killed Elsbeth?

The woozy, addled feeling in my brain diminished as my fear increased. Fucking Fuchs drugged me and bound me to a table in a basement.

Elsbeth was drinking tea. The irrational thought popped into my head. Who cared what she was drinking?

But it mattered. She drank coffee with me in Freiburg. She mocked Heidegger for drinking tea.

I was strapped to a table. A steel dissection table? Please, no. A surgical table. That was better. I'd think of it as a surgical table. Why was *that* better?

I remembered the postcard. Marie had sent Elsbeth a postcard.

Why were there postcards in Elsbeth's cottage in Freiburg? The question intruded on my building terror. Marie had postcards in her new flat. Of Bastille Day. She'd gone to buy more when she was at the Vendôme.

I pulled against the thick bands holding me to the table. No loosening at all. Every muscle must have been slack when they'd lashed me down.

Marie was sending postcards. Despite my nakedness, the cold, and being trapped on the table, my mind began connecting the dots that had been bouncing around my befuddled mind.

Marie was sending postcards to her friend. Her German friend, who was like a sister to her. Marie had included her return address so they could stay in touch. Keeping in contact with Elsbeth Schragmüller.

Schragmüller wasn't Marie's friend. She was keeping tabs on Marie. Unknown to Marie, Schragmüller was a spy. For Germany. She'd been in Belgium. Drank her tea, when she drank it at all, with milk. She must have been exposed to the British. British prisoners? British spies working with her? For her?

That was how Bertrand and the Germans located Marie and Jean-Paul. Through Elsbeth. That must be how Fuchs knew we were going to Freiburg. Maybe Ladoux wasn't a traitor at all. Maybe it was just Elsbeth Schragmüller all along with Fuchs working with her.

A wave of nausea seized me, and I couldn't help but vomit. Only the slight angle of the table kept me from inhaling my own spew.

Despite the smell and the cold wetness on my chin and chest, I felt better.

I realized there wasn't time for Schragmüller to have contacted Fuchs and for Fuchs to travel to Freiburg. Ladoux had to have told him. Both Schragmüller and Ladoux were German agents.

The basement was icy. A small wave of trembling ran up my spine.

I was strapped to the table because I was a fool. I liked Schragmüller. She was intelligent. I thought her straightforward, honest about her thoughts on the world and Germany's place in it.

Why not kill me? Did they think I would lead them to Marie?

The door at the top of the stairs opened. Electric lights came on.

Two sets of feet. A man and a woman.

My heart told me who they would be before I saw their faces.

Karl Fuchs and Elsbeth Schragmüller.

They came down the steps and stood before me. Examining me like they were at the butcher shop trying to judge a cut of beef.

"Good. He is cold. He will be ready when Dr. Plöchner returns," Fuchs said.

"Hello, K-k-karl," I said. The shivering made it difficult to speak. "Elsbeth, I'd stand, but I... I seem to be strapped to a bed." I started to chuckle weakly. Bed sounded better in my head than dissection table.

"John, thank you for coming," Elsbeth said. "I am sorry for the discomfort, but I must follow the judgment of the expert when it comes to readying you for what will come next."

"Why, Elsbeth? What can you possibly want with me?" Now I was sure they would torture me for the information I had about Marie's disappearance, assuming they didn't already have her.

"We have a job for you, John, but you must be prepared for it," Elsbeth told me.

"Then why drug me? Why not just hire me? It's what the French did?"

Fuchs laughed, and Elsbeth smiled sadly.

"The addition of scopolamine and morphine in your coffee was to get you down here without any ugliness," Elsbeth said. "But to do the job we have in mind, you must be in the proper mental state. You have the physical skills, but the right *frame of mind* will come only with the mental training that Dr. Plöchner will provide."

"Training?" I asked with dread.

"Yes, John. I am sorry. From what I understand, it won't be particularly pleasant," Elsbeth said.

"I must be honest, John. It will be quite dreadful," Fuchs elaborated. He seemed genuinely sorry for the misery that was about to befall me.

"And to think the French thought Ladoux was a German spy," I said as I tried tucking my chin into my chest for warmth. Unfortunately, I couldn't move my head enough. I squeezed my arms against my sides. That helped. I couldn't unstick my tongue from the roof of my mouth. I was too cold. I told myself I wasn't cold at all. It was a lie my body refused to believe.

"Oh, he is a German spy," Elsbeth explained. "But to divert the French and you from what we are doing, he was a necessary sacrifice. The French are now satisfied they have discovered all plots and named all spies, even if those spies are not convicted and executed. All is right with their world."

"As Marie was to be a sacrifice in Königsberg," I concluded from her words.

"Yes. But that was a simple plan. It would have been effective but very simple. And when she failed to kill you and you succeeded in escaping Berlin, I found a more interesting use for you and for her," she said.

"Yet you had tried to kill us both on the train to Berlin," I said, recalling Bertrand and his thugs.

"No, we did not. We needed you to reach Berlin. The train would have been too soon for you to die, and we certainly wouldn't have squandered Marie in a premature double murder on a train," Elsbeth said, taking offense.

I had managed to learn something of value. Bertrand and his boys were working for Reynolds. That was the only explanation for why they were on the train to Berlin. Not that having the information would do me any good now.

"But you did try to kill us in Berlin and then in Mainz," I said accusingly.

Elsbeth gave Fuchs a perturbed look. Fuchs looked down at his feet like a schoolboy caught in a prank.

"Marie did kill her handler, so I reacted," Fuchs said. "In Berlin, I was still operating under the earlier orders, John. My apologies. Mainz. Mainz was a mistake. I thought the opportunity too good to pass up with the blinding rain and the general unguarded," he said, not meeting Elsbeth's eyes.

"It was definitely a mistake," she said.

"No hard feelings, Karl. Just unstrap me, and we'll call it quits."

"I do like you, John, but I am sorry, that is not to be," Fuchs answered.

"As I said, we have a job for you," Elsbeth Schragmüller repeated. "You are a killer, and we need you to kill."

"Who now?" I asked with dread.

"Why, Woodrow Wilson, of course," she answered.

They left me alone with a jumble of thoughts that were disconnected by the cold. I was tired. So tired. The cold was draining the life from me.

President Wilson. They wanted me to kill the president. His death would bring an abrupt end to any dream of America leading a League of Nations. Without him, the treaty would fizzle in the Senate, talked to death by the grasping old men who cared nothing for a war to end all wars.

But I wouldn't kill Wilson.

The light coming through the cracks in the boards dimmed. Night was coming. Darkness. How long would they make me wait? I needed to piss. I didn't think they'd let me up to use the head.

I shivered on the table. What the hell were they going to do to me?

Later. The lights came on again. How much later, I didn't know. My sense of time was still warped from the drugs Schragmüller had given me. Judging by the pressure in my bladder, it couldn't have been more than an hour.

Again two sets of feet, but this time both men. Big men. Dressed like medical orderlies. My stomach twisted at the sight of them.

They made several trips up and down the steps, carrying equipment. Bottles of solution. Tubing. A motion picture projector and reels of movies. I was sure I saw a phonograph, but that was just crazy. Moving day in this creepy basement. A basement where I would be tortured.

"I need to piss," I said.

They ignored me. It was so damn cold.

"*J'ai besoin de pisser,*"[1] I tried in French. That got a glance and a shrug from one of the men. He backed away from the table.

"Fine," I said. I let my bladder loose and proceeded to urinate as the other man worked near the table.

"*Verdammt Ami!*" He jumped back. He walked past the steps. I couldn't lift my head far enough to see where he was going. I heard a valve turn and water splashing.

The spray from the hose hit me in the groin and splashed down my legs. He also rinsed my chest and face. Then he sprayed the floor. Cold water ran under my back but didn't pool there. It drained. There was a hole in the center of the table at the small of my back. A dissection table after all. There had to be a drain in the floor as well. Now I was very cold but my bladder was empty.

Once everything was hosed off, they set up the equipment around me. They ran electric cables to the top of the stairs and through the door. Whatever they were doing, they wanted electricity. They loosened the restraints across my chest and hips to attach some sort of harness around my waist. Then they left. When I relaxed back on the table, I felt some sort of box or disk attached to my back. God only knew what they'd stuck to me.

I had been prepared for sacrifice. I just didn't know for whom.

THE DOOR AT THE TOP OF THE STEPS REOPENED. DREAD WASHED over me. Now the real torture would begin. My limbs began to tremble. I told myself it was the cold, but it wasn't the cold. Two men. Fuchs and another. Older. He had a beard and looked disturbing like the pictures I'd seen of Sigmund Freud. The doctor. He had an air of excitement.

He spoke to me in German.

"How do you feel? Fuchs translated.

"Fuck you, Karl." I was tired and cold. Shaky inside and out.

"I am sorry for the cold. But we need you to be unresisting. Malleable. And I am afraid you will only feel worse."

"You have a shitty bedside manner."

He wasn't bothered by my bluster. He knew he had me as weak as a woman's handshake.

The doctor prepared a bottle with an intravenous tube and needle attached. He grabbed my arm. I tried to jerk away, but my arm hardly moved. He was very handy with a needle. He found the big vein at my elbow and taped the needle in place.

"What is he doing, Karl?"

The doctor spoke to Fuchs. He had an earnest, thoughtful manner now. As he talked, he made expansive motions with his hands to emphasize certain points. I caught an unwelcome glow in his eyes that made my heart race. I tried to calm myself, but my body and mind were having none of it.

"Dr. Plöchner asks that I explain to you what he will be doing," Fuchs said. "He is as much a teacher as a doctor. He feels that, as the subject, you have the right to know what will happen."

The doctor spoke again, and Fuchs continued.

"He is administering a drug called mescaline. It is used by various red Indian tribes in South America for religious purposes. They generally drink a tea made from the cactus that contains the drug. Herr Dr. Plöchner has taken the ingredients and improved both the concentration and the administration. The drug will cause hallucinations. Violent hallucinations."

The doctor rattled off some more German.

"We will couple this with other stimuli to prepare you for your mission. Specifically, we will need to keep you awake. That is the purpose of the switch on your back. If you sleep, you will relax against the table and close an electrical circuit. The shock will wake you."

The doctor turned from the table for a moment.

"The switch is now live. Depriving you of sleep will add to the hallucinogenic effect and make the mind that remains more accepting of suggestion."

"What the fuck does that mean?" The two of them had succeeded in terrifying me. This was no charge into machine guns or enduring an artillery barrage. This was premeditated horror, which made it feel so much worse.

Plöchner spoke again.

"During the war, the doctor did some experimentation but not enough. He believes that, in high enough dosages, this drug will start to fray your connection with reality. It will take some time, but he assures me that as he builds on the initial doses, you will no longer know what is real and what is not. He will start with two hundred milligrams, and over the coming hours you will reach a dose of eight hundred milligrams. He apologizes that this is an imprecise science."

Fuchs looked at Plöchner, who said a few short sentences and nodded.

"To succeed, he must remove your conscious overlay, your sense of self. Once that is gone, he will work to provide a new pliable consciousness for your mission. But that effort must wait. First things first, yes?"

The anger, fear, and darkness that lived under my heart erupted. All rational control gone. I jerked against the straps like a feral animal in a trap. Spittle flew from my mouth, my muscles strained, my body arched and bucked. A scream ripped from my lungs. I raged.

"Goddamn it, Karl, just put a bullet in my brain!"

He was unmoved.

I sagged back against the table and an electric charge coursed through me. I'd connected the switch on my back.

"If you don't kill me, Karl," I said softly, "I'll find you. And I'll kill you. I swear to God. I'll kill you. I'll find a way to kill you all." I was past panicking. I'd never thought it would come to this. Kill me. Cripple me. Maim me. I had lived with those possibilities and realities for so long that they were endurable now, but the thought of more ghosts swirling around my brain was too much.

"The doctor tells me you will have some time before you'll feel the effects," Fuchs said.

"Karl, please, just kill me."

"John, I am afraid that is exactly what the doctor is doing."

Plöchner tidied his gear, nodded to Fuchs, and went up the steps.

"The doctor will return once the drug takes hold. Goodbye, John."

The doctor was right. It took a while before reality broke.

The first warning of the impending wave that engulfed me was a vibration of the room. All lines and planes of the walls and ceiling hummed. I studied this effect only to realize that I had been so absorbed in the waves rippling across the ceiling that I didn't register that the doctor was standing over me.

He shined a light into my eyes. I fell into it. For a few seconds or minutes. I didn't know. When I came out, the table was rotated upright. My feet rested on a platform on the bottom. I was standing. I moved off the table without leaving it. I ran my hand across the stucco wall before me. Images of Woodrow Wilson flickered across my hand. Not my hand. Plöchner's.

In a brief moment of lucidity, I realized that I was still strapped to the table. It was nearly upright, and the wall before me displayed newsreel footage of Woodrow Wilson. Wilson walking, speaking, smiling artificially. The tinny sound of his voice reverberated from behind my head. The pictures took on a sound and feel and the words a taste and smell.

Invisible fingers trail across the back of my neck. Armistan's fingers on Reynolds's hands.

Wilson with Clemenceau and Lloyd George. Holding hands. Then pointing. Smiling. They are pointing at bodies. Bodies hanging on wire. In shell holes.

Gas floats toward me.

My heart races.

Wilson speaking again.

"The day of conquest and aggrandizement is gone by..."

Lights flash. Artillery. Gas. There's gas! I jerk away and a jolt shoots through me. Shot. I've been shot.

"...the day of secret covenants entered into in the interest of particular governments..."

I can't understand Wilson's words.

A fog of gas. Slightly yellow. I can't see through it. It smells of newly mown grass. Phosgene! Phosgene and chlorine! My lungs lock. I panic. Shuddering and jerking. A jolt from the table jars my mind loose of the choking gas.

And I am buried. Covered by mud and dirt and stone. I cannot claw my way free. For years, I try. My muscles cramp.

Wilson drones on "...and likely at some unlooked-for moment to upset the peace of the world."

Plöchner and Fuchs stand next to me. "...und jetzt vierhundert Milligramm," Plöchner says as he adjusts the tube that runs into my arm.

Sweat drips into my eyes. No longer shivering, I thrash, yet I do not move.

The walls press down upon me. Crushing me against the table. The weight traps me.

A shock rips through me, and my body arches against the walls but remains frozen in place.

I can't breathe. I don't need to. I am vapor. I am gas.

Disconnected images flicker through my scrambled brain: Wilson grinning, Sarah dying, Schragmüller sipping tea, Reynolds peering at me through the smoke of his cigarette, Armistan crushing Patricia's throat in his hands.

My mother shakes her head and my father nods. What have I become?

I shrink back and electricity jolts through me.

Tippy Frederickson, my old English mate, looks on sadly.

"Can you hear me?" Fuchs asks.

"He's daft," Frederickson answers. "He's in the darkness."

The known and unknown cavorting. Dancing. Fornicating. Laughing... with me. At me.

Plöchner's face elongates into a canine jaw. When did he return? Did he ever leave? His hands stretch into clawed paws. His smile shows the canines in his muzzle.

"Sehr gut." I don't understand how he can speak. "Sechshundert Milligramm."

His paws grope at the table and my arm. Horror rises in my chest. I try to curl in on myself. Electricity flashes through me.

"Hello, John. How are you feeling?" Elsbeth. Good. Not Plöchner. Not Fuchs.

"Poorly, Elsbeth. Poorly." I am not sure if I spoke. The air glows around her. I want to speak. I want her to hear me. I want it to stop.

"The president misled you, John."

Wilson lopes past me in a top hat. Improbably walking upright on his hind legs. He shakes his head at her claim.

I want to answer, but my jaw is deformed. A whine escapes me.

Wilson preaching.

"We have no jealousy of German greatness..."

Dogmen charging. I can't escape. Lizard men slashing. Burning surges through me.

Blown apart by artillery and hanging dead on wire.

"He lies," Elsbeth tells me.

"Who?" I want to ask.

"We grudge her no achievement or distinction of learning or of pacific enterprise such as have made her record very bright and very enviable."

I smell death. Rotten meat, rent bowels.

"Wilson lies," Marie says again.

"He lies," Sarah agrees.

It all loops together.

Seamlessly.

For minutes or hours or days.

And Wilson is always there.

"What we demand in this war, therefore, is nothing peculiar to ourselves. It is that the world be made fit and safe to live in; and particularly that it be made safe..."

Reality shifts, and I begin to slide off. Shaking, gibbering, crying.

Another shock.

And Wilson promises me...

"...the program of the world's peace, therefore, is our program; and that program, the only possible program..."

"*Er ist fast katatonische*," Plöchner said.

Fuchs, Elsbeth, and Plöchner stood before me, wearing canine features with tongues lolling. I stared straight ahead. I was not sure I could do anything else. The doctor removed the needle from my arm. It seemed impossible to accomplish with paws, but he managed.

"Can you hear us?" Schragmüller asked me.

I nodded my head dumbly.

"*Das Skript vom Arzt. Ich habe es ins Englische übersetzt,*" Fuchs said, handing Schragmüller a sheet of paper.

Elsbeth looked at it briefly and looked back up at me. Her big brown eyes seemed sad somehow.

"Hello, do you remember me?" she asked.

"Yes, but you weren't a dog before," I answered.

She looked at Fuchs and then Plöchner, who made a sign with his paw for her to continue.

"Your name is John Griffin. Do you remember that?" she said.

"Yes."

"You are an American hero. You love America," she read from the paper.

I made no comment, but part of me wondered if those statements were true.

She looked down at the sheet. "Woodrow Wilson has betrayed America. Wilson is a traitor to America. Do you understand my words?"

"Yes."

"Wilson should not be allowed to betray America," she finished reading.

All three of them studied me. They seemed to be waiting for me to comment.

So I did.

"No, he shouldn't."

They smiled at my answer.

"We will speak again later," Elsbeth said as she draped a blanket over me with her paws.

MARIE WAS STANDING BEFORE ME. A BEAUTIFUL AFGHAN HOUND with her long chestnut locks framing her aristocratic muzzle. How gracefully she balanced on her hind legs. The straps across my legs and hips were gone, but her paws struggled with the strap across my chest. Mitchell stood behind her. He looked worried, his ears twitching in distress.

"He's out of his head," he said.

The strap came free, and my body poured to the floor.

"Let's get him up. Come on, Griff. Help me," Mitchell said.

Strong hands pulled me up. Who?

I had no bones to support me. My claws scrabbled at the stone floor. I tried to tell Mitchell this, but I couldn't recall the words.

I was outside. In an automobile. The wind pulled at my hair and my cheeks. At my clothes. I wore clothes.

The vibrations in the sky distracted me. Trees glowed against the darkness as they flashed past the automobile. Thank God Wilson was gone and the artillery. Reynolds still leered at me from the running board.

"Will," I croaked. He looked back at me from the front seat of the car.

"Yes, Griff. Walt's here too. We stole Pershing's car."

"Walt?" I didn't understand.

Marie sat next to me. Just Marie. Not an Afghan hound at all.

"Hello, Marie." I collected myself. I had to warn them. "Be careful. Elsbeth can hear us. She knows where you are." I wasn't sure the words left my mouth. Shimmering trees flashed by in the darkness. I was glad Wilson was gone. I hated the sound of his voice. Reynolds was gone too. The car was so peaceful with just the sound of the wind and the tires on the road.

"We will be quiet, John. She will not hear us. You should try to sleep," Marie said.

That was a fine idea. But I was afraid.

"The button in my back?" I asked. I didn't want to fall asleep only to be shocked awake.

"It's gone, John. It's gone," Marie promised.

I needed sleep. I hadn't slept for a while. Canine Wilson and explosions rattled through my brain, but they were distant, less threatening now.

"Ten hours to Paris, Will," I heard Disney say.

"And straight to Military Hospital No. 1," Mitchell said.

———

My memory of the drive was like a dream. What was real and what was not, I couldn't tell. I sobbed a confession to Billy Jones, my closest friend in the British army, begged Sarah not to leave with her dead husband, James. I'm pretty sure I collapsed into Marie's lap when Sarah left with Billy instead of James. I shouted obscenities at Elsbeth Schragmüller as she held me in the car, and I laughed maniacally with my head outside the car window and my tongue lolling like a dog's.

"You will need to leave me in Montrouge," Marie told Disney.

"Sure, just tell me where."

And then Marie was gone, a figment of my imagination, and I was back in the hospital I wasn't sure I'd ever left.

I was tucked in a bed.

A ghostly Alma Clarke sat at my bedside. She would protect me.

I felt the coil inside my chest release, and I slept.

31

————————

Effectively Insane

When I woke, I found I really was in the hospital.
Military Hospital No. 1.

I was in the same room I'd been in after I'd been shot. Light streamed through the windows. I watched for vibrations but didn't see any. As before, the other beds were empty.

Alma Clarke was indeed in a chair drawn up next to my bed. She saw that I was awake and poured me a glass of water.

"Drink," she ordered. "The doctor was clear. You need to drink as much water as you can hold."

I took the water. "Hello, Alma. I'm sorry to bother you again."

"I'd say it's good to see you, John, but when you came in, you gave us all a scare."

"Not as much of a scare as I was having." I felt the light fingers of hallucination feather across the back of my neck. I ignored them. "Who's my doctor this time? Doc Ryan was good with holes, but I suspect he's not the man for cracked heads, is he?" I asked.

"Dr. Richardson. He's the man for cracked heads. He worked

with shell shock cases during the war. He's a talented doctor. He doesn't have Dr. Ryan's gallows sense of humor, which is probably good. I'll let him know that you're awake."

"Thanks, Alma."

She stood, gave me a peck on the cheek, and went to find the doctor.

When the doctor arrived, he checked my pulse and shined a light in my eyes. I managed to keep from falling into it, but I was tempted.

"Tell me what happened to you. You were drugged, but I'll be damned if I know what it was."

"Mescaline. Eight hundred milligrams through an IV line for I don't know how long."

The doctor whistled.

"What day is today?" I asked.

"September 10," he answered.

"Five days. The Boche had me drugged for five days." I didn't tell him about the Woodrow Wilson footage, the canine and reptile transformations, or the smell of death that still hung about me.

"Did they tell you what they hoped to achieve?"

"No, they didn't," I lied. "I'd had some run-ins with these particular Krauts in the past. Spoiled some of their plans while I worked for the State Department. I guess they were trying to get even."

"Why not just kill you?" he asked.

"Great question, Doc. I can tell you, I'd rather they had."

"Well, son, with what they pumped into you, you're lucky to have your sanity."

I tried not to flinch when he patted my leg with his paw.

THE DOCTOR SAID THEY'D KEEP ME A FEW DAYS FOR "OBSERVATION" and then release me. He seemed to think I was hale and whole.

It was important to lie to my doctor. If I didn't, he would keep me in the hospital and take pains to heal what cannot be healed. I knew there was no way Dr. Richardson was going to pull the images from my head that overlaid my reality. He wouldn't change my skin crawling at any thought of Wilson. He couldn't erase the terror that bubbled just under my heart when I recalled Armistan or Reynolds. I had no idea how they had snuck their way into my hallucinations, but they had.

There was only one medicine for what ailed me. I would kill them all. Make sure of it. Stick my fingers in the holes I made in them.

But I wouldn't kill Wilson. Unless he was still a dog. We needed a man as president. Not a dog.

SOMEHOW PRÉFET RAUX LEARNED THAT I WAS BACK IN THE hospital. One morning, I heard him in the hallway, warring with Miss Clarke. Rather than have American-French relations deteriorate to the point of breaking, I called out, "Alma, it's okay. I'll see him."

She led him into the room, turned to the préfet, and said, "If you upset him, you will be out on your ear before you can say 'Clemenceau.' Do you understand?"

The expression on Raux's face was perfect. His dark eyebrows were arched into his white hair. He looked shell-shocked. I couldn't resist winking at Alma, which got me a smile despite her worry for me. She turned, glared at Raux once more, and was gone.

"Préfet Raux. I am glad you came. I needed to speak with you, but I am here for a little longer."

"I am sorry for your return to the hospital, Major."

"Please, just mister. I sat up in the bed and put my feet on the floor. Feet. No paws. Progress. "Perhaps we could walk. I could use the exercise." I pushed my feet into the cheap slippers at the side of the bed and tugged on the thin striped robe I'd been given. I walked slowly, and Raux kept pace, not trying to hurry. He had the courtesy not to offer any help.

"What have you been told, Préfet Raux?"

"Nothing really."

I gave him a look that told him I knew he was lying.

"Well, just that you had gone to Switzerland and been captured by German agents, and"—he looked for the word—"abused."

I gave a soft laugh and repeated, "Abused. Yes. But that is not why I wanted to speak with you. I have learned more information. There may be nothing you can do about it, but you should know."

I could feel his nod of encouragement as I continued shuffling down the corridor.

"The Germans trapped me and drugged me. They wanted information about American and French knowledge of their operations. Once they had it, they were going to drug me so heavily that I was effectively insane." The lie was close enough to the truth for my purposes.

"Yes," he said to let me know he was following along.

"I was confronted by the head of their operations. In person. Her name is Professor Dr. Elsbeth Schragmüller. She is part of the teaching staff at the University of Freiburg im Breisgau. She trained and, I think, managed French and British citizens as spies for Germany during the war. She is still involved in German intelligence. She was supported by a German foreign ministry official, Karl Fuchs. If you ever have the opportunity to speak with her, you could learn a great deal about their operations during the war and now."

"A woman and a university professor. Truly?" he asked.

"Believe me, I wish I had seen the possibility sooner. She was the one who recruited and ran Marie Masson. She did the same with Commandant Ladoux."

"You have proof?" Raux asked eagerly.

"Only what she told me. Hearsay. She explained that she was responsible for Marie Masson's attack on me. Whether she succeeded or not, it would appear to America that Masson was a Bolshevik. Even if the French believed she was a German spy, I was to believe she was a Bolshevik. She was a sacrifice. Through me, the United States would believe a Bolshevik revolution in Germany was a real possibility and a strong, well-armed Germany necessary to resist it. One spy is a small sacrifice for that result."

"And Ladoux."

I couldn't tell Raux the truth of the German plans because that would cast doubt on my sanity and endanger my freedom. So I lied.

"She prized Ladoux. As you know, he was able to reach the prime minister directly in an attempt to discredit Mangin. But I have no proof other than my word."

"A shame," he said. "But I do not understand why you were in Switzerland."

Clever Raux was now probing my story for flaws. His lips peeled back from his extended jaw to reveal his canines.

I turned away.

"I had met Schragmüller in Berlin. She was Madame Masson's professor," I told him. "They were friends. Or so I thought. Schragmüller contacted me and told me she had proof that Marie Masson had been coerced to spy for Germany. I went to Basel because I wanted to see this information. I feel guilty about killing Marie. I liked her. Just as you did. I didn't want to believe I'd killed a woman who had been forced to spy against her will. I went to examine the information for myself." Perhaps not the best deception, but I believed it would be good enough for Raux. I knew he liked Marie.

"And what did you find?" he asked.

"The Boche had Marie's son. A hostage to her service. Marie Masson was a victim."

Raux didn't speak. We walked for a few moments.

"That is truly terrible. A great tragedy," he finally said, shaking his head. "But it is good to know. Your information about the Germans and Ladoux is very useful information, Mr. Griffin. Once again, France is in your debt, but I think, for your own good, you should go home. If you don't, I fear my country will be the death of you."

But I wouldn't go home. I would go to England.

By the next day, I was physically recovered enough to be propped up in bed. I needed to be out of the hospital and in pursuit of Reynolds and Armistan. The thought of them both made my stomach clench. I would kill them.

Miss Clarke did her best to distract me, but the most welcome diversion came when Mitchell visited. He didn't come alone. Miss Clarke came to the room first to warn me of my guests.

"Your friend, Mr. Mitchell, is here to see you," she said, flushing. William Mitchell had that effect on women. "He's brought your sister and her son."

"Really? Well, this will be an interesting visit," I told her.

Mitchell escorted Marie and Jean-Paul into my room.

"I'll leave them with you, John," Alma said as she left with one last look at Mitchell and my very attractive sister.

"How did you find me?" I asked. They knew what I meant.

"It bothered me that the Germans found us in Paris," Marie said. She clearly felt guilty about my situation. "I racked my brain to think of how it was possible. I worried that someone had seen me, but it was just too coincidental. Then when you sent me to Eugenia Errázuriz, the first thing I wanted to do was send Elsbeth a postcard telling her where to contact me. She really was my only friend left from before the war. But I recalled you telling me not to send any postcards. And then I got a sick feeling in my stomach, and I knew. I knew it was Elsbeth. I went to William and told him."

"Then it was just a matter of trying to figure out where you were," Mitchell added. "Once Marie knew it was Basel, she remembered that Schragmüller had a doctor friend there."

"With a house on Petersgraben, across from the university. When I lived in Basel, I had met Elsbeth at the house. She was staying there, and we went for a coffee," Marie said.

My stomach cramped at the thought of Elsbeth and coffee.

Jean-Paul had climbed up on the end of my bed.

"It was a long shot that you were there, but we had nowhere else to look," Mitchell said.

"And you two came to get me." I was a little choked up but tried not to show it.

"And Walter," Marie added. It took me a second to realize she was talking about Disney. "He did all the driving. Through the night."

"Like a bat outta hell," Mitchell added. "Some of your hallucinations must have been doozies, Griffin. We were all scared listening to the shit you were babbling. Numbers, names, threats."

"I thought I'd dreamed all that," I said.

"You were pretty crazy, Griff."

I nodded. "I think I still am, but don't tell Miss Clarke or the doc. Other than tranquilize me, there's not a damn thing they can do about the visions I've got swirling around in my head. And I refuse to be drugged into tranquility."

They both looked worried at my admission of visions.

"You didn't happen to kill Fuchs and everyone else in the house, did you?" I asked hopefully.

"No. Only two men were in the house, and we took care of them in short order." I could tell from the look Mitchell shot at Marie that she'd used the new razor I'd given her. "Maybe you should talk to the doc about your visions, Griff."

"I'll be fine, and neither of you are covered in fur or sporting paws or claws. Speaking of which, Jean-Paul, how is the dog?"

They didn't know what to make of my comment, and Jean-Paul didn't give them time.

"Anneli is growing so fast!" he declared. "And she is very smart. She is with Madame Eugenia right now. I stayed with Madame Eugenia when Maman went with Mr. William to find you. She likes me but worries about Anneli. Are you okay, Mr. Jack?" His words all came out in a rush, and I had to laugh. I tried to imagine Madame Errázuriz watching a seven-year-old and a puppy, and I laughed some more. It sounded a little hysterical to my ears, but I knew I couldn't trust them.

"I am about as okay as I'll ever be, Jean-Paul, and both you and your mother must have impressed Madame Eugenia for her to let you and Anneli stay with her while Mitchell and your mom went off to rescue me."

"She likes it when Maman paints," the little boy said.

Marie nodded. She was more beautiful now than I remembered her being. She had a glow I did not recall. I was sure it was the result of having her son with her and being free of both French and German intelligence services.

Miss Clarke poked her head in the door. "Visiting hours are just about up. I am sorry to cut short your stay. He should be getting out any day now," she said optimistically.

Jean-Paul hopped off the bed.

Mitch patted my knee.

"Get well, Griff. As soon as you're out and up to it, we'll head over to England to get Patricia."

The boy patted my knee in a mimicry of Mitchell.

"Get well, Mr. Griff," he said seriously.

I was relieved to note that they both possessed human hands.

"I will," I said, hoping it was true but knowing it probably wasn't.

Marie leaned over and kissed me on the cheek. "We will be in Biarritz if you ever get a chance to visit. And John, thank you. Thank you so much. *Au revoir.*"

I felt an odd tug under my heart as I watched JP and Marie leave. Mitchell waved and followed them out. I was alone with my thoughts and the memory of Marie's scent. Musky yet fragrant. With just a hint of dog.

I needed to get out of the hospital. A soft bed and kind words weren't going to heal me. Woodrow Wilson's face hovered before me. Worms in my head squirmed at the sight of him. I didn't know what I would do about the president, but I knew what I would do about Reynolds and Armistan: cold-blooded murder.

AFTERWORD

The endnotes are intended to help the reader understand which characters in the story are actual historical figures. I include in the notes some limited information about each character. Nearly all deserve more study than a few lines that the endnotes provide.

In researching the story, I have read too many books to list. All contributed to the atmosphere and accuracy of Griffin's world. In particular, the *New York Times* archive was invaluable in finding exactly what people were told or believed in 1919. *Voluptuous Panic, the Erotic World of the Weimar Berlin* by Mel Gordon provided a wealth of information about the clubs, habits, and extremes of Berliners and Anita Berber in particular. *French Secret Services* by Douglas Porch was particularly helpful in building my understanding of the French intelligence services. *My Rhineland Journal*, by Henry T. Allen, gave me insights into the American occupation of the Rhineland and General Allen himself, and *Peter and Anneli's Journey to the Moon*, Marianne H. Luedeking's translation of Gerdt von Bassewitz's story *Peterchens Mondfarht,* is a children's book that I wish I had discovered when my children were young enough to appreciate it. Hans Richter's book *Dada: Art and Anti-Art* was very helpful in building the circle of Germans Griffin met in Berlin. Otto Dix and Hans Richter were almost certainly acquainted if not friendly, but I have found no firm connection between Richter and Anita Berber. The evidence that Dix knew Berber is his 1925 painting of her.

I have tried to honor the actual timeline of events discussed in the book, but the attempt by German intelligence to assassinate General Mangin because he was sponsoring an independent Rhineland is a product of my imagination. That said, I don't doubt for a minute that the general would have welcomed a successful succession of the Rhineland from Germany. He was ultimately recalled to Paris in October 1919 and replaced.

The Ury Department Store was first established in Leipzig in 1896 by two Jewish brothers, Moritz and Julius Ury. In 1937, as a result of the "Aryanization" program of the Nazi regime, the brothers lost the business and left Germany. This forced transfer of ownership was common to the Jewish-owned businesses in Germany at the time.

I might have done Georges Ladoux a disservice by making him a traitor to France, and it is worth noting that, although he was tried for treason in 1929 as a result of his activities during the war, he was acquitted. Two others similarly accused were not. One man was sentenced to five years in prison and another executed. Ladoux was famous enough that his death in 1933 was reported in the *New York Times*.

Dr. Kurt Plöcher in the story is modeled after Kurt Plötner (October 19, 1905–February 26, 1984). Plötner was too young to have participated in Griffin's torture, but just a few years later, he conducted mind-control experiments using mescaline on Russian and Jewish prisoners at Dachau concentration camp during World War II.

Elsbeth Schragmüller did teach at the University of Freiburg and worked for German intelligence during the world war. Her continued work for German intelligence after the war is, as far as I know, fictional. She was awarded the Iron Cross First Class for her work during World War I.

Joseph Heidegger also taught at Freiburg during this period. I found no evidence that he knew or was friendly with Elsbeth Schragmüller, but given the size of the university, it is not entirely unlikely.

On September 2, 1919, President Wilson began a train tour of the United States, traveling nearly eight thousand miles in twenty-two days, giving as many as three speeches per day in support of treaty ratification. The words attributed to Wilson regarding his position on the Treaty of Versailles are a slightly modified rendering of his various speeches but particularly his speech given at Pueblo, Colorado, on September 25, 1919. The quotes attributed to Wilson during Griffin's torture in Basel are his actual words.

NOTES

Chapter 2

1. Alma A. Clarke. June 10, 1890–March 16, 1963. Appears to have returned to the US on July 28, 1919.
2. Eugene "Jacques" Bullard. October 9, 1895–October 12, 1961. Boxer, musician, club owner, war hero.
3. Alice Prin aka Kiki of Montparnasse. October 2, 1901–April 29, 1953. Entertainer and entrepreneur.
4. April 23, 1919.
5. Walter Elias Disney. December 5, 1901–December 15, 1966. Cartoonist and entrepreneur. Disney came to France with the Red Cross after the armistice and returned to the United States in November 1919.
6. Martinis, for three, quick.
7. June 16, 1919, the allies gave Germany an ultimatum to accept the draft treaty or face resumption of hostilities. The treaty was signed June 28, 1919, exactly five years after the assassination of Archduke Ferdinand.

Chapter 3

1. A paraphrasing of Wilson's speech given at Pueblo, Colorado, on September 25, 1919.
2. Georges Clemenceau, Prime Minister of France.
3. The Fourteen Points were presented by President Wilson to Congress in his speech of January 8, 1918.
4. George A. Gordon. November 19, 1885–May 11, 1959. Attorney, soldier, diplomat, ambassador.

Chapter 4

1. A bakery.
2. Prefect Raux, please.
3. Who are you?
4. Your name?
5. Okay. Tell Prefect Raux that I asked to see him.
6. Wait over there.
7. For Prefect Raux.

8. Mr. Griffin, you have visitors in the lobby. Would you like me to send them up?
9. Who are they?
10. Prefect Raux and a young woman.
11. I'll come down.
12. Fernand Raux. May 25, 1863–February 23, 1955. Civil Servant and Prefect of Police.
13. Close the restaurant. Now. State security. And bring coffee.
14. Understood?

Chapter 5

1. "A Piece of Steak." Jack London, 1909.
2. Henry Johnson. July 15, 1892–July 1, 1927. Croix de Guerre and Posthumous Congressional Medal of Honor Winner (awarded June 2, 2015).
3. Until tomorrow, gentlemen.
4. Bullard established a gymnasium at 15 rue Mansart around this time.
5. May I join you for a moment?
6. Eugenia Errázuriz. September 15, 1860–November 26, 1949. Art collector and benefactor.
7. Georges Carpentier, January 12, 1894–October 28, 1975. World champion boxer, pilot, French war hero (Croix de Guerre). American boxing promoters created the "White Heavyweight Championship" in search of a white boxer who could successfully challenge Jack Johnson, a black man, who was the heavyweight champion of the world. Carpentier won this title from "Gunboat" Smith in 1914.

Chapter 6

1. Irrelevant.
2. Good luck.

Chapter 7

1. Georges Ladoux, March 21, 1875–April 20, 1933. Major and Commandant of the Deuxième Bureau from 1914.
2. The Silver Tower.

Chapter 8

1. Tickets, please.
2. The Battle of Sedan was a pivotal battle fought in Northern France during the Franco-Prussian war. It resulted in the defeat of the encircled French army and the capture of Napoleon III.
3. Special to the *New York Times*. "Tells of Horrors Seen in Belgium." *New York Times*, January 16, 1919, p. 5.
4. Coffee, please.
5. And a beer.
6. Battle of Belleau Wood, June 1–June 26, 1918.

Chapter 9

1. The Danzig Corridor promoted by Wilson in his Fourteen Points.
2. Come in. Shut the door.
3. Now!
4. For the money.
5. Bitch!
6. Poilu, a French soldier, especially during World War I.

Chapter 10

1. A diplomat stationed in Berlin sometime after May 1919.
2. Tasker Howard Bliss. December 31, 1853–November 9, 1930. US Army Chief of Staff until May 1918, the American Permanent Military Representative to Supreme War Council, and American representative to the Paris Peace Conference.
3. Walter Gheradi, Vice Admiral US Navy. August 8, 1875–July 24, 1939. First US officer to visit Berlin after the armistice.
4. "France Demands Reparation of $220,000 from Germany for Killing of a Soldier," *New York Times*, July 17, 1919.
5. "Documents Prove Lenine (sic) and Trotzky Hired by Germans," supplied by the Committee on Public Information, *New York Times*, September 15, 1918.

Chapter 11

1. Elsbeth Schragmüller. August 7, 1887–February 24, 1940. University lecturer and Assistant Chair at the University of Freiburg im Breisgau.

Chapter 12

1. Otto Dix. Artist. December 2, 1891–July 25, 1969.
2. Anita Berber. Actress and dancer. June 10, 1899–November 10, 1928.
3. *Reflections of a Nonpolitical Man*, Thomas Mann, first published in 1918.
4. Teenage girls.
5. Match seller, 1920. Otto Dix. Oil on canvas and collage.
6. Black Cat.

Chapter 17

1. Cheap red wine.
2. Johann Heinrich von Bernstorff, January 12, 1894–October 28, 1975. Ambassador to the United States from 1911–1917. Coordinated espionage activity in the United States until he returned to Germany in 1917.

Chapter 19

1. Martin Heidegger. September 26, 1889–May 26, 1976. Philosopher.
2. William H. F. Altman, *Martin Heidegger and the First World War: Being and Time as Funeral Oration*, pp. 109–110. Paraphrased letter from Heidegger letter to his wife September 13, 1918.

Chapter 20

1. Charles Mangin (Moe-jah). July 6, 1866–May 12, 1925. General of France and the primary advocate of using black colonial troops in the French army. He was responsible for the selection of Senegalese Infantry to occupy the Rhineland.
2. Hans Dorten. February 10, 1880–April 1, 1963. German Lawyer. Iron Cross, First and Second class. Rhineland nationalist.
3. "Houdini to Do His Bit," *The Evening World*, Feb. 27, 1918, p. 20.

Chapter 21

1. Cohan, George M. 1917. "Over There."

Chapter 22

1. Your name?
2. Wait there.
3. Follow me.
4. Hans Dorten. February 10, 1880–April 1, 1963. Lawyer, war hero, Rhineland political activist.

Chapter 24

1. Three draft beers please.
2. One moment please.
3. Hugh Campbell Wallace. February 10, 1864–January 1, 1931. Politician and businessman. Ambassador to France from April 22, 1919, to July 5, 1921.
4. Vorticism.
5. Cubism.

Chapter 25

1. Henry T. Allen. April 13, 1859–August 29, 1930. Soldier. Explorer. Commanding general of American forces in Germany.
2. *New York Times.* June 17, 1922. Page 4. Associated Press.
3. What is the purpose of your visit?
4. These American officers are here to see...
5. We were sent by the American Commission in Paris. We need to speak to the General on an urgent matter concerning the peace treaty.
6. Follow me.
7. Remain here.
8. Paraphrased quote Mangin's August 7, 1918, order of the day. "Mangin's High Praise of American Troops," *New York Times.* August 8, 1918, p.9. Associated Press.
9. In early June 1919, Hans Dorten named himself president and declared Rhineland's independence from Germany. The declaration of independence failed because it was unsupported by the general population.
10. "French Fostering Rhineland Spirit," *New York Times.* June 26, 1919, p. 2. Walter Duranty.
11. Three beers, please.

Chapter 26

1. Country squire. In 1919 and before, a politically powerful class from Prussia and eastern Germany.
2. *Peterchens Mondfahrt,* 1912. Gert von Bassewitz.

Chapter 27

1. "To the Mouse." Robert Burns, 1876.
2. I am very sorry!
3. You're welcome, Madame.
4. Hugh John "Pat" Casey. July 24, 1898–August 30, 1981. Major General US Army.

Chapter 28

1. Jose Antonio Gandarillas Huici. July 23, 1885–1970. Diplomat, playboy, opium addict.
2. A seventy-five, please.

Chapter 29

1. We need to see the prime minister! Right away!
2. Of course, Commandant Ladoux.
3. My apology for the mess.
4. The letters are no real evidence. Prime Minister, please. Fernand!

Chapter 30

1. I need to piss.

ACKNOWLEDGMENTS

Before acknowledging the gracious support I've had in writing this story, I must make clear that all the mistakes in language, grammar, and historical accuracy are mine and mine alone.

My family has had to live with Griffin and Mitchell for two years now, and they have been instrumental in the development and change of these two fictional friends. My wife, Michelle, remains my editor-in-chief and big-picture questioner. My three children, through their own dialogue with each other and their friends, have contributed to the voice of Griffin and his friends. They have also been helpful in providing thoughts on the cover, book description, and for *Crossing Darkness*, the ending. My youngest son thought it would be a good idea to brainwash Griffin. Brainwashing was a very new concept in 1919, but I gave it a go anyway.

I remain indebted to my editors and mentors, my sister Elizabeth Christy, and her friend and author Debbie Garner (DeborahGarner.com). Their comments have tremendously improved the quality of the book. Without Annie Sarac of TheEditingPen.com, I would have embarrassed myself many times over. She helped the story flow and was unafraid to ask hard questions.

Also my thanks to Julie Witmer of Julie Witmer Custom Map Design (maps@juliewitmermaps.com) for the very clear easy-to-read map that gives the reader a sense of the geography through which Griffin, Marie, and Mitchell travel. My wife wisely suggested including a map, and Julie made it happen.

For review of the French language and the book generally, I

must thank my friend Catherine Poupeau. Who knew what a wonderfully versatile word *salope* was?

I have strived to keep the language and attitudes in the book consistent with the times. Sadly, some language and attitudes were unattractive then and now.

ABOUT THE AUTHOR

Alex Juden is the author of one previous Griffin Post Great War mystery, *Red Tiger Hunting*. He lives with his wife in Houston, Texas. Two of his three children remain in Texas while the third has moved to California (for college anyway). Prior to writing, he enjoyed a variety of jobs, including naval aviator, trial lawyer, and public company general counsel. Alex now has a small farm in Texas where he is struggling with a stubborn vineyard and other fruiting greenery.

He studied history and political science at Rice University.

ALSO BY ALEXANDER C. JUDEN

Red Tiger Hunting

www.ingramcontent.com/pod-product-compliance
Lightning Source LLC
Chambersburg PA
CBHW062109290726
48975CB00001B/166